Born in 1861, Rabindranath Tagore was one of the key figures of the Bengal Renaissance. He started writing at an early age, and by the turn of the century had become a household name in Bengal as a poet, a songwriter, a playwright, an essayist, a short story writer and a novelist. In 1913 he was awarded the Nobel Prize for Literature for his verse collection *Gitanjali*. At about the same time he founded Visva Bharati, a university located in Shantiniketan near Kolkata. Called the 'Great Sentinel' of modern India by Mahatma Gandhi, Tagore steered clear of active politics, but is famous for returning the knighthood conferred on him as a gesture of protest against the Jallianwala Bagh massacre in 1919.

Tagore was a pioneering literary figure, renowned for his ceaseless innovations in poetry, prose, drama, music and painting, which he took up late in life. His works include some sixty collections of verse, novels like *Gora*, *Chokher Bali* (A Grain of Sand) and *Ghare Baire* (Home and the World), plays like *Rakta Karabi* (Red Oleanders) and *Post Office*, over a hundred short stories, essays on religious, social and literary topics, and over 2,000 songs, including the national anthems of India and Bangladesh.

Rabindranath Tagore died in 1941. His eminence as India's greatest modern poet remains unchallenged to this day.

*

Radha Chakravarty teaches English in Gargi College, University of Delhi. She has translated several of Tagore's works, including *Boyhood Days*, *Chokher Bali* and *Farewell Song: Shesher Kabita*. Other works in translation include Bankimchandra Chatterjee's *Kapalkundala*, *In the Name of the Mother* by Mahasweta Devi, and *Crossings: Stories from Bangladesh and India*. She has edited *Bodymaps: Stories by South Asian Women* and co-edited *Writing Feminism: South Asian Voices* and *Writing Freedom: South Asian Voices*. Her latest book is *Feminism and Contemporary Women Writers*. She is currently translating a collection of Tagore's writings for children and co-editing *The New Tagore Reader* for Visva-Bharati.

GORA

Rabindranath Tagore

Translated by
Radha Chakravarty

PENGUIN BOOKS

PENGUIN BOOKS

Published by the Penguin Group

Penguin Books India Pvt. Ltd, 7th Floor, Infinity Tower C, DLF Cyber City, Gurgaon 122 002, Haryana, India

Penguin Group (USA) Inc., 375 Hudson Street, New York, New York 10014, USA

Penguin Group (Canada), 90 Eglinton Avenue East, Suite 700, Toronto, Ontario, M4P 2Y3, Canada

Penguin Books Ltd, 80 Strand, London WC2R 0RL, England

Penguin Ireland, 25 St Stephen's Green, Dublin 2, Ireland (a division of Penguin Books Ltd)

Penguin Group (Australia), 707 Collins Street, Melbourne, Victoria 3008, Australia

Penguin Group (NZ), 67 Apollo Drive, Rosedale, Auckland 0632, New Zealand

Penguin Books (South Africa) (Pty) Ltd, Block D, Rosebank Office Park, 181 Jan Smuts Avenue, Parktown North, Johannesburg 2193, South Africa

Penguin Books Ltd, Registered Offices: 80 Strand, London WC2R 0RL, England

First published by Penguin Books India 2009

Translation copyright © Radha Chakravarty 2009

All rights reserved

12 11 10 9 8 7 6

Reprinted in 2014

ISBN   9780143065838

Typeset in Perpetua by SÜRYA, New Delhi
Printed at Repro India Ltd., Navi Mumbai

A PENGUIN RANDOM HOUSE COMPANY

INTRODUCTION

Gora was serialized in *Prabashi* from Bhadra 1314 to Phalgun 1316 in the Bengali calendar (August 1907 to February 1910), and appeared as a book in the Bengali year 1316 (February 1910). Several portions of the serialized original were omitted from this book version. Some of the deleted passages were restored in the Visva-Bharati edition of 1928. The *Rabindra Rachanabali* of 1941 restored some more of the excised passages, and is now regarded as the standard edition, upon which the present translation is based.

This monumental, dynamic novel, so vibrant with ideas, passions and conflicts, has lost none of its immediacy and relevance today. The idea for the book probably occurred to Tagore in 1904, when he narrated the story at the request of a visitor to Shilaidaha, the Irishwoman Margaret Noble who took the name of Sister Nivedita when she became the disciple of Swami Vivekananda (Dutta and Robinson 154). In a letter to W.W. Pearson (July 1922) Tagore says: 'You ask me what connection had the writing of *Gora* with Sister Nivedita. She was our guest in Shilida and in . . . improvising a story according to her request I gave her something which came very near to the plot of *Gora*' (Pal 1990, 215). The basic plot concerns the extraordinarily fair-skinned young man Gora, an orthodox Hindu nationalist who spurns the Brahmo Samaj but falls in love with a Brahmo girl Sucharita. Gora ultimately discovers that he is not a Hindu, but the orphaned child of an Irishman killed during the 1857 uprising. In the published novel, Gora and Sucharita are united in the end, but in the story that Tagore narrated in 1904, the Brahmo girl rejects Gora upon discovering his European origins. Tagore says he wanted to demonstrate to Nivedita the strength of orthodox prejudice against Europeans, but his story made her angry, and she accused him of being unfair to Hindu women. 'No, it can't be so. It will be a great tragedy not to unite the two. Why won't you let things happen in literature that do not happen in real life? . . . Unite them. United they must be.'[1] This might explain why Tagore changed the ending in the published version, but it is equally likely that the change of storyline was triggered by his disillusionment with the Swadeshi movement in 1905 and his awareness that women were now coming out of purdah to claim greater autonomy in their lives.

Since Gora was born in 1857, the narrative is probably set in the 1880s, when he would have finished his studies at the University. The action of the novel thus takes place about three decades before the date of its composition. In the last quarter of the nineteenth century, the initial euphoria about the benefits of exposure to western culture had begun to give way to a certain disenchantment, for it had become clear that access to western education and culture did not grant Indian intellectuals equality with their British rulers. Bengali society at that time was divided into two wings, the liberals and the conservatives, who were engaged in a lively debate about

---

[1]Banaphul, *Rabindra-Smriti* 72-4, cited in Majumdar 298, translated by Anisuzzaman (personal interview). See also Tagore's letter. '[genesis of] *Gora*' to W.W. Pearson, 1922, 'Letters to W.W. Pearson', *Visva-Bharati Quarterly* (Aug.-Oct. 1943), 179, cited in Dutta and Robinson 1995, 154 and E. P. Thompson, *Alen Homage* 147.

every aspect of Bengali life. The social reform movement in
Bengal was being countered by a new revivalism, a nationalism
based on Hindu values (Mukherjee ix). The liberal movement
was led by the new monotheistic Brahmo sect, but it also had
other followers, educated Bengalis who had not joined the
sect formally (Chaudhuri 608-9). The conservative school was
led by Bankimchandra Chatterjee and Swami Vivekananda,
who created a revised version of Hinduism that Nirad C.
Chaudhuri calls Bengali Neo-Hinduism, which had a larger
following at the turn of the century (Chaudhuri 609). Its
power was reinforced by Bengali nationalism, and during the
agitation of 1905, conservatism dominated Bengali thinking.
The popular Hindu conservatism was a 'mixture of chauvinism
with crude and often superstitious religious beliefs and cultural
obscurantism. Hindu megalomania and xenophobia were their
strongest passions. They were wholly impervious to any ideas
not in agreement with the nationalist myths, and were also
fiercely intolerant' (Chaudhuri 609).

Nationalism forms an important aspect of the historical
context of *Gora*, but instead of focusing solely on Indo-British
relations, the text lends greater prominence to Hindu-Brahmo
tensions. The novel dramatizes these internal conflicts within
Bengal society, but without resorting to simple polarizations.
Instead, the text presents a spectrum of possible positions
within Hindu and Brahmo systems of thought. The elite
Hindu group is not homogenized: from the rigid, unworldly
orthodoxy of Krishnadayal to Abinash's naïve celebration of
ritual and Harimohini's growing inflexibility about Sucharita's
habits, the narrative represents varying facets of religious
conservatism. Within the domain of Brahmoism, too, the
characters chart a range of attitudes, from Poreshbabu's tolerant
liberalism to Baradasundari's shallow adherence to convention,
Haranbabu's extreme rejection of Gora and Binoy, and
Sucharita's spirit of intelligent enquiry. Poised between these

two factions, unable to find a place in either party, is the figure of Anandamoyi, who in a single gesture of defiance gives up all claim to social acceptability when she adopts the orphaned Gora as her foster son. In a parallel gesture, Lalita too breaks away from societal straitjackets when she leaves on the steamer with Binoy. Through these acts of rebellion, the text gestures at the need to seek alternatives beyond the prevailing tensions of factionalism. Gora's Irish birth is also no accident, for the context of Irish nationalism locates him beyond the simple opposition of British and Indian, colonizer and colonized.

Though ostensibly set in the 1880s, *Gora* is in many ways charged with the political consciousness of the Swadeshi movement of the early twentieth century. This movement, part of the Indian struggle for Independence, involved boycotting British goods in support of indigenous products, in an effort to promote economic self-sufficiency. Gora's confrontation with the British magistrate, which results in his imprisonment on a flimsy pretext, reveals a spirit more in tune with the period in which the novel was actually written (Malini Bhattacharya 130). There are thus two contexts to the anti-colonialism of Gora and Lalita. As Michael Sprinker says: 'the titular hero's strict observance of traditional Hindu customs throughout the novel is directly linked to his patriotism. Extremism is not yet on the horizon in the novel itself, which is set in the late 1870s or early 1880s, but Tagore composed it after the demise of swadeshi during the moderate-extremist Congress split. Interpreting the narrative in the light of its contemporary context is surely justified' (125n). Through the figure of Gora, the text expresses Tagore's interrogation of the more extreme forms of nationalism.

The tensions in *Gora* are also the product of Tagore's own inner conflicts, dramatized through the extensive use of dialogue, argument, discussion and disagreement. Despite his liberal leanings, Tagore also sympathized with certain conservative principles. The school at Shantiniketan for instance was based on ancient Hindu ideals of education such as the Guru-Griha described in Hindu sacred law. According to Nirad C. Chaudhuri, 'Tagore also gave the most competent description of the nationalistic Neo-Hinduism in his novel *Gora*. Although in it he made Liberalism win, he also showed how strong the Hindu case was' (Chaudhuri 609). *Gora* is a powerful dialogic novel. The text seeks to tackle its own creative tensions through its use of doubles or paired characters such as Gora and Binoy, Sucharita and Lalita. This technique anticipates, for instance, Joyce's use of Bloom and Stephen in *Ulysses* (Ray 30-31). It expresses a modern awareness of the fragmentary, incomplete quality of the human self, which can seek completeness only outside itself, in its opposite or 'other' (Ray 28). *Gora* in this sense is a novel that is ahead of its time, though some readers have compared the text with nineteenth century European novels such as George Eliot's *Felix Holt* and Ivan Turgenev's *Fathers and Sons* (Priyaranjan Sen 224-5; Mazumdar 87-93). Contradictions and paradoxes haunt the narrative of *Gora*, culminating in the ultimate paradox at the end, when Gora's cry of pain upon discovering the truth about his birth becomes simultaneously a cry of liberation. Ironically, it is in losing everything that had previously marked his sense of identity—nation, caste, religion, parentage—that Gora becomes free to claim his identity as a true Indian, Bharatvarshiya. Irony is central to the narrative mode, for the reader is privy to the secret of Gora's parentage, which he discovers only at the end. The reader's perception of Gora's words and actions is constantly coloured by this secret knowledge, and the disclosure of Gora's identity at the end comes as no surprise. The revelation is also not entirely devastating for Gora himself. He is able to recognize the positive potential of his dispossession, because he has already undergone a process of mental development, and the preceding events have conditioned him for a transformation of perspective.

Tagore's *Gora*, *Ghare Baire* and *Char Adhyay* ushered in a new kind of novel in Bengal, the political novel. Between 1910 and 1934, there were only two other significant novels in this genre: Sarat Chandra Chattopadhyay's *Pather Dabi* (1926) and Tarasankar Bandopadhyay's *Chaitali Ghurni* (R. Bhattacharya 143). But from the late 1930s onwards came a spate of political novels in Bengali, of which Tagore must be acknowledged the forerunner. In his analysis of *Gora*, *Ghare Baire* and *Char Adhyay*, Ashis Nandy takes an ahistorical view of Tagore as a political novelist: 'Tagore's political concerns in the three novels were roughly the same; they did not change over the twenty-five years of his life that the writing of the three novels spanned' (Nandy 10). This is not an accurate observation, for Tagore's views on nationalism actually remained complex and mutable. At first, he participated actively in the Swadeshi movement. He composed songs and even led demonstrations. But gradually, he became disenchanted with the growing signs of communalism, extremism and factionalism within the movement. Eventually, he left the National Council of Education and turned away from political activities. It was not through any overt public statement, though, but through his fiction, in novels such as *Gora* and *Ghare Baire*, that he expressed his disillusionment with the Swadeshi movement. *Gora* thus marks a particular phase in Tagore's evolving attitude towards the discourse of the nation (Sumit Sarkar 2003, 154).

Gora is today widely recognized as an important postcolonial text. There is a strong anti-colonial vein in the narrative, underscored especially in two episodes where Indians oppress other Indians, but in the context of colonial influence (Malini Bhattacharya 130). One occurs on the steamer where an Englishman and a 'babu' mock the plight of less privileged passengers. In the second incident, a poor Muslim is almost run over by an affluent 'babu' as he walks down the street carrying a load of household provisions for his English 'master'. The novel is also frequently compared to Kipling's *Kim*, because the shared motif of the Irish foundling makes it easy to read *Gora* as Tagore's subversive reworking of Kipling's colonial text (Spivak 143, Nandy 43, Mehta 199). As Meenakshi Mukherjee argues, however, this deflects attention from the central issue in *Gora* (xxiv). Rather than a literary source in Kipling's *Kim*, some readers trace the origins of Gora's character to historical figures, such as Swami Vivekananda and Brahmobandhav Upadhyay (Mukherjee xiii, Pandit 213).

Despite Tagore's growing reservations about Swadeshi, '*Gora* is more about inclusion than rejection' (Anisuzzaman). The real strength of the novel lies in its critique of both colonial and nationalist extremism in favour of a more inclusive vision. Edward Said insists that the postcolonial intellectual must use his critical sense in all public matters, giving priority to 'critiques of the leadership, to presenting alternatives that are often marginalized, or pushed aside as irrelevant to the main battle at hand' (41). He praises Tagore as a model intellectual of this type, a nationalist who never allowed his patriotic sentiments to cloud his critical sense (41). As a political novel, *Gora* wrestles with the challenge of defining the 'real India,' an issue that remains alive even today (Ray 26). The narrative charts the quest for a resolution to the tension between the integrative impulse and the divisive forces that make it so difficult to construct a collective idea of the nation (Nair 57-8). The image of 'Bharatvarsha' is crucial to this project. At first Gora identifies country with religion, but his vision of Bharatvarsha slowly evolves 'from the abstract to the concrete, from the symbolic towards the actual' (Mukherjee xviii). In this evolution, his dialogues with Sucharita play a dynamic role. The vision of Bharatvarsha that emerges in the course of the novel suggests the need to think beyond the limiting, opposed ideologies of colonialism and nationalism: 'Tagore uses Bharatvarsha as a heuristic concept, an ongoing and unfinished experiment: it serves as an open gestalt, an inclusiveness that accommodates disparities and differences in its hunger for wholeness, free from the totalizing and homogenizing impulse implicit in colonialism/imperialism as well as nationalism on the imperial model' (Chakrabarti 70). Bharatvarsha in Tagore's novel is not a fixed, immutable idea but a fluid, changing concept.

The text also destabilizes the notion of identity in order to demonstrate its mutable, multiple and contingent nature. The presence of many orphaned characters in the text— Sucharita, Binoy, Gora—constitutes a questioning of the myth of fixed origins (Nair 59). Gora for instance has three father-figures: Krishnadayal, Poreshbabu, and his biological father (Nair 57). Colour does not matter, the rhetoric of the text would suggest, but culture and character do (Nair 60). 'Character' too is not an unchanging essence, but a process of development, both individual and a matter of locating the characteristics of Bharatvarsha. Seen in this way, the recurring motif of the foster-parent's love for the foster-child may be taken to represent the 'inexhaustible generosity and hospitality' of Bharatvarsha (Chakrabarti 70). Nowhere is the idea of identity subjected to more intense scrutiny than in the figure of Gora, whose entire sense of self is premised upon a lie. It is this spirit of constant questioning and self-criticism, this rejection of dogmatic certitudes, that Said admires in Tagore.

This same spirit pervades the way Tagore's text challenges caste hierarchies. Through Gora's mistaken pride in his caste and his eventual disillusionment, the novel makes a powerful statement against caste discrimination. In the essay 'Brahman' (1902), Tagore had supported the varna system, but by 1910, his perspective had begun to alter (Sumit Sarkar 2003, 154). In the *Gitanjali* he wrote:

> *My wretched country, those whom you have crushed and trampled, deprived of their rights, made them stand and wait and never drew them close,*
>
> *Share you must their indignities and sufferings*
>
> . . .
>
> *Can you not see Death's messenger at the door Stamping his curse on the arrogance of your superiority;*
>
> *If you still do not beckon them, and remain coldly distant and still immured in pride, then equal must you be in death and ashes of pyre.*[2]

The textual rhetoric of *Gora* evinces a similar sentiment. 'If caste discrimination causes men to treat other men with such humiliation and contempt, how can I call it anything but antireligion?' Poresh says to Sucharita (165).

Gora's attempts to connect with the masses, and his travels in the countryside, especially his visit to Chor Ghoshpur, underscore the related issue of class discrimination and the rural-urban divide. Readers point out an autobiographical element in Tagore's portrayal of Gora's exposure to the common people of the land. It is only by stepping out of Kolkata that Gora is able to expand his sense of the vastness of Bharatvarsha. Tagore, too, had attained a sense of another India beyond the city, after observing rural life in his role as member of a zamindar family. Here he saw poverty, and also, from visiting Muslim localities, realized that Bharatvarsha did not belong to Hindus alone (Murshid 66). Tagore at this stage

---

[2]Tagore, *Gitanjali*, verse 108, *Rabindra Rachanabali* 2 (Santiniketan: Govt. of West Bengal, 1961), trans. Sisir Kumar Das (Das 151).

blamed village poverty on 'an educational system which alienated English-educated urban elites from the rural population; and absentee landlords who had abandoned their responsibility for the welfare and cultural life of their tenants . . . He also blamed superstition, credit procedures and oppressive social customs' (O'Connell 192). In a similar vein, Gora too observes 'that in these rural areas, social restrictions were far more powerful than in educated, cultured society . . . The practices that only drew boundaries, divided people and tormented them, that would even deny the intellect and keep love at arm's length, were the ones that constantly hindered everyone in every respect' (261-2). Patrick Colm Hogan cites two historical prototypes for Gora's defiance of the magistrate and his subsequent imprisonment: Ram Gopal Ghose, who traveled across the indigo plantations and described in a book the injustices he had witnessed; and the Irishman, Reverend James Long, who was imprisoned for a month after he arranged the translation and publication in 1861 of Dinabandhu Mitra's play *Nil-darpan* (1860), depicting the brutality of the indigo planters and the magistrates (Hogan 194). *Gora* thus provides an example of postcolonial historiography, which tries to recover unwritten histories, especially of the masses (Nair 52). Rukmini Bhaya Nair calls it '*the* Indian novel of high bourgeois nationalist aspiration,' citing Gora's rejection of Marshman's textbook as Tagore's bid for rights over history (Nair 53-55).

The altruistic impulse behind this attempt to reclaim history illustrates what Dipesh Chakrabarty describes as the emergence of a modern and collective Bengali subject marked by the will to witness and document oppression and injury, capable of a compassion that is as much the product of reason (a western ideal) as of the Bengali 'hriday' or qualities of the heart (Chakrabarty 51). The gender divide provides another significant instance of social discrimination addressed in *Gora*.

Early in the novel, Binoy criticizes Gora's version of nationalism for its exclusion of women:

> 'I think there is a serious lack in our patriotism. We see only half of Bharatvarsha.'
>
> 'Why do you say that?'
>
> 'We see Bharatvarsha only as a land of men; we don't notice women at all.' (p.110)

When Gora protests, Binoy insists: 'You know the nation as a place without women. Such knowledge can never be true.' By the end of the narrative, Gora learns to accept Binoy's point of view. Through Binoy's victory over Gora in this debate, the text underscores the need to rethink women's place in the discourse of the nation. Elsewhere, Tagore expresses the same idea: 'Especially since women have no place in our outer society, our social life itself is seriously incomplete' (Chatterjee 38). In *Gora*, despite the presence of the strong male protagonist in his self-fashioned role of the revolutionary, it is the women who emerge as the true figures of revolution. Sucharita and Lalita challenge the conservative Hindu idea that a woman's place is in the home. Both Anandamoyi and Lalita make private choices with public consequences, which they are strong enough to face (Malini Bhattacharya 133). In boarding the steamer with Binoy, Lalita simultaneously defies orthodoxy and colonialism, flouting the Hindu-Brahmo divide while also refusing to take part in the performance at the British official's house. Anandamoyi, Sucharita and Lalita serve as signposts in Gora's journey to self-discovery and enlightenment. For Gora's humanization also involves an element of feminization, a softening of the aggressive, dominating stance he assumes in challenging the colonial stereotype of the effete, servile Bengali babu (Mukherjee xviii).

Nationalism and the liberal/conservative debate provide

the contextual frames for the exploration of female autonomy in *Gora*. The ritual practices of nationalism created a mingling of male and female spaces, enabling a reordering of gender relations (Tanika Sarkar 263-4). The text demonstrates the controversies that surrounded the changing perception of marriage in Bengali society in the late nineteenth century, and reflects Tagore's ambivalence about the idea of companionate marriage. According to Sutapa Bhattacharyya, *Gora* reveals these inner tensions, for the text sometimes seems to endorse the traditional idea that a woman's place is in the home, while at other moments it seems to make a strong case for female choice, autonomy, and the importance of love and compatibility in marriage (Bhattacharyya 46). At one point, Sucharita accepts Gora's decree that domesticity is a woman's dharma irrespective of conjugal bliss, although it is Harimohini who forces Gora to write these words in a letter: *'Marriage is a woman's path to religious pursuits, domesticity her main dharma . . . Whether the home is a happy one or not, to welcome that home, to remain virtuous, devoted and pure, to preserve the image of dharma within the house—that is the holy pledge of womanhood'* (495). Yet Gora's entire spirit rebels against the idea of Sucharita being married off to a man like Kailash, suggesting that compatibility and marital happiness are important foundations for marriage.

A similar double perspective underlies the representation of motherhood in *Gora*. Unlike Bankimchandra Chatterjee, Tagore was critical of the tendency to deify woman as motherland. Instead of the rhetoric of deification, which apparently idealized the woman while actually marginalizing her, he sought, in novels like *Gora* and *Ghare Baire*, to inscribe women centrally in the narrative of the nation (Mukherjee xviii). Anandamoyi for instance expresses Tagore's disagreement with Hindu orthodoxy, for Tagore's representation of motherhood eschewed the Hindu revivalist tones of the mother goddess. (Bagchi WS-70). Women's special place in Indic civilization, according to Ashis Nandy, is to be located in maternity, rather than conjugality. 'Of the women who resist the contesting ideologies of conventionality, collaboration and defensive neo-conservatism, it is Anandamoyi whose resistance is the deepest and most 'natural' . . . In Tagore's world motherliness questions the dominant consciousness and resists it more radically and effectively than does conjugality' (Nandy 41). This notion of a 'naturally' radical mother-figure is questioned by Sumit Sarkar, who reminds us that the widow Harimohini, once a victim of domestic oppression, begins to reproduce the patterns of that oppression by trying to dominate Sucharita as soon as she assumes charge of a household of her own. Baradasundari is another maternal figure without any radical overtones. Though she belongs to the progressive Brahmo sect, she adopts the outer forms of Brahmolism without comprehending its spirit, presenting an inverted mirror-image of orthodox conformity. Both Harimohini and Baradasundari reproduce the conservative ideas that they have internalized, and the rhetoric of the text presents their limited perspectives in a negative light. For Sarkar, this illustrates Tagore's 'emphasis on the need of women's self-development for genuine women's freedom, and the insufficiency of even the best-intentioned male reformist benevolence' (Sumit Sarkar 2003, 166).

Such is the self-development that Sucharita and Lalita seek. 'I don't understand why I must bear everything in silence just because I'm born a woman,' Lalita protests. 'Even women are capable of distinguishing between just and unjust, possible and impossible' (203). But the text also makes it apparent that any freedom these women achieve is extremely constricted. There is no public space where their resistance might be articulated in the shape of a counter-discourse; the only space available to them is outside the community: they must join the marginalized (Malini Bhattacharya 133). The interrogation of gender roles in *Gora* thus raises questions that are not fully resolved within the text.

This is largely true of all the broad social issues raised so powerfully in the novel. While transformation is possible for Gora as an individual, the world he inhabits remains unchanged, and the divisive forces continue to be at work. Those who regard *Gora* as a thesis novel, one that sets out a problem and then proceeds to solve it, have surely missed the point. For the novel's immense rhetorical power lies in its cogent articulation of questions, uncertainties and contradictions, rather than in any attempt to provide facile solutions to prevailing social problems. Buddhadev Basu insists that despite its concern with ideological conflicts, *Gora* is not a novel that articulates a problem and then sets about solving it. The characters, he says, are not pawns in an intellectual chess game, but flesh and blood figures, for Tagore wrote *Gora* not to preach an idea but to create a work of art that also becomes a vehicle for the history of its times (Basu 66). Amartya Sen appreciates this 'celebration of the unresolved and the incomplete' as one of the strengths of Tagore's writings (xx). In the 'domain of unfinished accounts', he says, 'Rabindranath saw not a defeat but a humble—and also beautiful—recognition of our limited understanding of a vast world, even an incomprehensibly large, possibly infinite, universe' (ix).

It is this visionary dimension, gesturing at future goals beyond the narrative time-frame, that accounts perhaps for the continued appeal of *Gora*. The novel gestures not towards a 'hybridity' that hovers in-between two worlds, but a 'syncretism', a community of interests among the oppressed, to overcome discriminatory practices (Malini Bhattacharya 131). This is the significance of the indigenous syncretism of the baul whose song occurs like a refrain in the first few pages of the novel. In the end, Gora finds his natural place with outsiders, a modernity outside the contours of revivalist nationalism (Malini Bhattacharya 129). Sumit Sarkar cites the final pages of *Gora* to highlight Tagore's 'vision of an India united on a modern basis transcending all barriers of caste, religion and race' (85). Humayun Kabir argues, in his essay 'Tagore was No Obscurantist,' that it was Tagore who first promoted non-alignment and federalism, based on a recognition of multiplicity and difference: '. . . if God had so wished, he would have made all Indians speak with one language . . . the unity of India has been and shall always be a unity in diversity' (Kabir 122-5). 'If there is an ideal in the novel,' says Shirshendu Chakravarti, 'it is perhaps to be found in the infinite capacity of average humanity for tolerant, caring and transforming love across barriers and divisions, for a continuous giving away of oneself in defiance of the emerging ideology of possessive individualism' (70). *Gora*'s Irishness is significant here, for it marks Tagore's move away from a narrow neo-Hindu patriotism towards a broader, more inclusive perspective. In the novel's quest for a non-sectarian, tolerant humanism lies a clue to its relevance in our present day world.

When *Gora* was published, it was favourably received by most readers, including Tagore's stringent critics, such as Dwijendralal Roy.[3] It has since been canonized as the quintessential postcolonial novel, widely read and taught at universities. In 1938, it was made into a feature film by Naresh Mitra, with music by Kazi Nazrul Islam. Western readers, however, often found *Gora* a difficult text, because its setting and subject matter struck them as alien and unfamiliar. Tagore was aware of the problem. He had apparently tried without success to persuade Edward Thompson to translate the novel, and years later, urged him to revise the text for a western readership (Trivedi 117).

---

[3]See Pal 1993, 149.

The first English translation of *Gora* was published in 1924. The title page of this book does not bear the name of any translator. On the following page is a note saying: 'My thanks are due to Mr. Surendranath Tagore, who very kindly made the final corrections and revisions for this translation. Any merits it possesses are due to his painstaking efforts to rectify my mistakes—TRANSLATOR.' The translator was actually W.W Pearson, who took many liberties with the original. In a letter to Thomas Sturge Moore dated 20 May 1924, Tagore expressed his dissatisfaction with this translation: 'If you could read the Bengali book you would at once know how extremely unsatisfactory the translation is' (Dutta and Robinson 2005, 311). He explains: 'Pearson did not know enough Bengali to be able to give a correct rendering of the story in English. My nephew Suren revised it comparing it with the original. Macmillan in their haste only had half of the corrected version and the latter half remains untouched with its ludicrous mistakes and crudities' (Dutta and Robinson 2005, 311).

Tagore's anxieties were not unfounded, for when the 1924 translation first appeared, most readers in the west dismissed the novel as dull and tedious. Leonard Woolf was enthused by the novel though: 'The subject of *Gora* is intensely interesting to me, and Mr. Tagore's handling of it kept me absorbed throughout the book. His thesis is the social, political, and psychological problems which confront the educated Bengali in Calcutta today' (Woolf 669). Woolf read *Gora* as a thesis novel, but was mistaken in assuming that the action of the novel is contemporaneous with the time of its publication.

Sceptical about how his western readers might respond to the localized, Bengali elements in his writings, Tagore had urged Pearson to abridge his translation before it was published. In 1922, he wrote: 'I find that English readers have very little patience for scenes and sentiments which are foreign to them; they feel a sort of grievance for what they do not understand—and they care not to understand whatever is different from their familiar world . . . This makes me think that after you have done with your translation it will have to be carefully abridged.'[4]

Pearson did not accept Tagore's suggestion, but in 1964, Macmillan published an abridged edition, translated by E.F. Dodd. Although this edition went through numerous reprints and was widely circulated as a textbook, the Macmillan translation left much to be desired, as it was an incomplete version, stilted in style, and full of errors and inconsistencies.

In 1997 came Sujit Mukherjee's translation, published by the Sahitya Akademi. The first academic translation of *Gora*, and a major improvement on its predecessors, this book proved a valuable resource for scholars. Not all readers were satisfied though with all aspects of Mukherjee's painstaking effort. In his perceptive review of Mukherjee's translation for instance, Shirshendu Chakrabarti finds the translation 'flat, uninspired, occasionally pedantic' (70). Though appreciative of Mukherjee's attempt to translate a difficult Bengali text, he points out several discrepancies, distortions of meaning and omissions, as minor 'blemishes' that have the cumulative effect of diluting the quality of the original: 'In general, the passionate intensity and polemical brilliance have been consistently blunted into a kind of academic blandness bordering on the insipid' (71).

The present translation attempts to redress some of these lapses and omissions, seeking to offer a lucid, readable version of this massive, complex novel to twenty-first century readers who do not read Bengali. This is no easy task, for the language

---

[4]Tagore to Pearson, 1922, *Visva-Bharati Quarterly* 9:2 [Aug.-Oct. 1943] 178-9, cited in Dutta and Robinson 2005, 310.

of *Gora* poses an immense challenge for the translator. Tagore's elastic prose accommodates a wide range of registers, from the sharply colloquial to the abstractly intellectual, from the passionately polemical to the tenderly lyrical. It is difficult indeed to capture such versatility in the English translation, harder still to avoid the risk of opacity when negotiating the passages of dense rhetorical argument. Cultural nuances are often diluted or flattened out in translation. Where facile, literal translation can only produce bathos, it is imperative for the translator to devise strategies for a less superficial, more sensitive rendering. In this translation, the word 'Khristani' for instance has been retained wherever the term carries pejorative, prejudicial overtones in the original; in all other instances, the more neutral term 'Christian' has been used. Bengali kinship terms, names of months, days and seasons, have also been retained. Some displacements of meaning are of course inevitable, for a translation is not just a linguistic but also a cultural transfer, and in a text such as *Gora* there are many elements that resist such a move. Yet it is through such displacements that the original remains alive, albeit in a new and transformed guise. For that is the nature of translation: in seeking to bridge linguistic and cultural divides, it also highlights the persistence of differences and the provisionality of meanings. In a very important way, *Gora* is about words and their power over us. Translating this major Tagore text has brought home to me the extraordinary ways in which that power may work.

New Delhi   Radha Chakravarty
September 2008

REFERENCES

Anisuzzaman. Personal interview. Dhaka: August 23, 2008.

Bagchi, Jashodhara. 'Representing Nationalism: Ideology of Motherhood in Colonial Bengal'. *Economic and Political Weekly* 25.42-43 (Oct. 20-27, 1990): WS 65-71.

Basu, Buddhadev. *Rabindranath: Kathasahitya* (Bengali). Kolkata: New Age Publishers, 1955.

Bhattacharya, Malini. '*Gora* and *The Home and the World*: The Long Quest for Modernity'. Datta, ed. 127-142.

Bhattacharya, Ramkrishna. 'Rabindranath Tagore and the Politicization of the Bangla novel'. *Tagore and Modernity*. Ed. Krishna Sen and Tapati Gupta. Kolkata: Dasgupta and Co., 2006. 136-148.

Bhattacharyya, Sutapa. *Shey Nahi Nahi: Rabindra-Sahitye Narimukti Bhavana* (Bengali). Kolkata: Subarnarekha, 2004.

Chakrabarti, Shirshendu. 'Universalist Paradigms of Nation and Narration.' *The Book Review* XXII. 1-2 (Jan.-Feb. 1998). 70-71.

Chakrabarty, Dipesh. 'Witness to Suffering: Domestic Cruelty and the Birth of the Modern Subject in Bengal.' *Questions of Modernity*, ed. Timothy Mitchell. 49-86.

Chatterjee, Partha. 'Two Poets and Death: On Civil and Political Society in the Non-Christian World.' *Questions of Modernity*, ed. Timothy Mitchell. 35-48.

Chaudhuri, Nirad C. *Thy Hand, Great Anarch!*. London: Chatto and Windus, 1987.

Das, Sisir Kumar. 'The Narratives of Suffering: Caste and the Underprivileged.' *Translating Caste*. Edited by Tapan Basu. New Delhi: Katha, 2002. 150-180.

Datta, P.K., ed. *Rabindranath Tagore's* The Home and the World: A Critical Companion. Delhi: Permanent Black, 2003.

Dutta, Krishna and Andrew Robinson, eds. *Rabindranath Tagore: The Myriad-Minded Man*. 1995. New Delhi: Rupa, 2000.

_____. *Selected Letters of Rabindranath Tagore*. New Delhi: Cambridge University Press, 2005.

Hogan, Patrick Colm. '*Gora*, Jane Austen and the Slaves of Indigo.' *Rabindranath Tagore: Universality and Tradition*. Edited by Patrick Colm Hogan and Lalita Pandit. Cranbury: Fairleigh Dickinson University Press, 2003. 175-198.

Kabir, Humayun. 'Tagore was No Obscurantist'. *Calcutta Municipal Gazette*, 1961. Tagore Birth Centenary Number. 122-5.

Majumdar, Archana. *Rabindra-Upanyas-Parikrama* (Bengali). Kolkata: Orient Book Company, 1970.

Mehta, Jaya. 'Some Imaginary 'Real' Thing: Racial Purity, the Mutiny, and the Nation in Tagore's *Gora* and Kipling's *Kim*.' *Rabindranath Tagore: Universality and Tradition*. Edited by Patrick Colm Hogan and Lalita Pandit. Cranbury: Fairleigh Dickinson University Press, 2003. 199-212.

Mitchell, Timothy, ed. *Questions of Modernity*. Minneapolis: University of Minnesota Press, 2000.

Mukherjee, Meenakshi. 'Introduction'. *Gora*. Translated by Sujit Mukherjee. New Delhi: Sahitya Akademi, 1997. Rpt. 2001. ix-xxiv.

Murshid, Ghulam. *Rabindrabishwe Purbabanga: Purbabange Rabindracharcha* (Bengali). Dhaka: Bangla Academy, 1981.

Nandy, Ashis. *The Illegitimacy of Nationalism: Rabindranath Tagore and the Politics of the Self*. Delhi: Oxford University Press, 1994.

Nair, Rukmini Bhaya. *Lying on the Postcolonial Couch: The Idea of Indifference*. New Delhi: Oxford University Press, 2002 .

O'Connell, Kathleen M. *Rabindranath Tagore: The Poet as Educator*. Kolkata: Visva-Bharati, 2002.

Pal, Prasantakumar. *Rabijibani* (Bengali). Vols. 5 & 6. Kolkata: Ananda Publishers, 1990, 1993.

Pandit, Lalita. 'Caste, Race, and Nation: History and Dialectic in Rabindranath Tagore's *Gora*.' In *Literary India: Comparative Studies in Aesthetics, Colonialism and Culture*. Ed. Patrick Colm Hogan and Lalita Pandit. Albany: State University of New York Press, 1995. 207-33.

Ray, Debes. '*Gora*: Chirakaler Samakal' (Bengali). *Desh* Year 66: 6 (23 Jan. 1999). 25-31.

Said, Edward. *Representations of the Intellectual: The 1993 Reith Lectures*. New York: Pantheon Books, 1994.

Sarkar, Sumit. *The Swadeshi Movement in Bengal 1903-1908*. New Delhi: People's Publishing House, 1973.

_____. '*Ghare Baire* in its Times'. 2003. Datta, ed. 143-173.

Sarkar, Tanika. *Hindu Wife, Hindu Nation: Community, Religion and Cultural Nationalism*. New Delhi: Permanent Black, 2001.

Sen, Amartya. 'Introduction'. *Boyhood Days* by Rabindranath Tagore. Translated by Radha Chakravarty. Penguin India/Puffin Classics, New Delhi: 2007. ix-xxiii.

Sen, Priyaranjan. *Western Influence in Bengali Literature*. 1947.

Spivak, Gayatri Chakravorty. 'The Burden of English.' *Orientalism and the Postcolonial Predicament: Perspectives on South Asia*. Edited by Carol A. Breckenridge and Peter van der Vier. Philadelphia: University of Philadelphia Press, 1993. 135-57.

Sprinker, Michael. 'Homeboys: Nationalism, Colonialism, and Gender in *The Home and the World*.' *Reading the Shape of the World: Towards an International Cultural Studies*. Ed. Henry Schwartz and Richard Dienst. *Politics and Culture 4* (1996). Rept. in Datta, ed. 107-126.

Thompson, E.P. *Alien Homage: Edward Thompson and Rabindranath Tagore*. Delhi: Oxford University Press, 1993.

Trivedi, Harish. *Colonial Transactions: English Literature and India*. Manchester: Manchester University Press, 1993.

Woolf, Leonard. '*Uncle Tom's Cabin*'. *Nation and Athenaeum* (9 Feb. 1924). 669.

~1~

The clouds had cleared this Sravan morning, leaving the Kolkata sky filled with pure sunshine. On the streets, traffic moved ceaselessly; hawkers called their wares without pause; baskets of fish and vegetables had been delivered to the homes of those about to leave for office, college or courthouse; and smoke arose from their kitchens as stoves were lit. But still, the golden light streamed through the myriad streets and alleys of this vast, ruthless, workaday city of Kolkata, in a flood of exquisite youthfulness.

On such a morning, at an idle moment, Binoybhushan stood alone on his first-floor balcony, gazing at the movement of people in the street. Having completed his college education long ago, he had not yet entered the world of domesticity. He had immersed himself in organizational and journalistic activities, but they did not entirely satisfy his heart. This morning, at least, a lack of purpose made him restless. On the adjacent rooftop, some crows were cawing raucously over something, and in a corner of his balcony, a pair of nesting sparrows were chirping encouragement to each other. All these incoherent bird-sounds stirred up a vague emotion in Binoy's heart.

Outside a nearby shop, a long-robed baul burst into song:

> *In and out the cage, how the unknown bird doth flit;*
> *I'd chain it with my heart, if I could but capture it.*

Binoy longed to send for the baul, to write down the lyrics about this unknown bird. But out of languor—just as we shiver at dawn yet lack the energy to reach for the coverlet—the baul was not summoned, and the lyrics remained uninscribed. Only the melody of that unknown bird continued to hum within his heart.

Just then, directly in front of his house, an enormous coach-and-pair rammed into a hackney carriage, smashing one of its wheels, then speeding away heedlessly. The hackney did not overturn, but tilted crookedly. Rushing out into the street Binoy found that a girl of about seventeen or eighteen had descended from the carriage. Within was an elderly-looking gentleman, preparing to alight. Binoy helped him down.

'You are not hurt, I hope?' he inquired, observing his pallor.

'No, there's nothing the matter with me,' the gentleman replied, forcing a smile; but the smile faded instantly, and he seemed about to faint. Binoy caught him in his arms.

'This is my house,' he said to the agitated girl. 'Let's go inside.'

Once they had helped the elderly man to bed, the girl looked about and noticed a kunjo in a corner of the room. Pouring a tumbler of water from the pitcher, she sprinkled some of it on the old man's face and began to fan him.

'Shouldn't we send for a doctor?' she suggested to Binoy. He sent a bearer to fetch a doctor who lived nearby.

On a table at one end of the room were a mirror, a bottle of hair oil, and some combs and brushes. Standing behind the girl, Binoy gazed at the mirror in silence. Since childhood, Binoy had lived and studied in Kolkata. All he knew about the world had been gleaned entirely from books. Never before had he encountered an unattached woman from a respectable family. Looking in the mirror, he marveled at the beauty of the face reflected in it. His eye was not experienced enough to analyze the individual features of her countenance. But the tender glow that the anxious affection had awakened in that young face appeared to Binoy like a newfound wonder of the world.

Shortly after, the old man slowly opened his eyes and sighed, 'Ma!' The girl's eyes glistened with tears.

'Baba, where are you hurt?' she asked agitatedly, bending her face close to his.

'Where am I?' The old man tried to sit up.

'Don't get up, please!' cried Binoy, coming before him. 'Please take some rest, the doctor is on his way.'

The old man now recalled the entire incident. 'It hurts a little here, on my head,' he said, 'but it is nothing serious.'

At that moment the doctor arrived, his shoes squeaking on the floor. 'It's nothing serious,' he also confirmed. He departed, having prescribed warm milk laced with brandy. At once the old man grew very embarrassed and agitated.

'Baba, why are you so anxious?' said his daughter, sensing his feelings. 'We shall send across the money for the doctor's visit and the medicine.' She glanced at Binoy.

What extraordinary eyes! Whether they were large or small, dark or amber, one did not notice at all. At the very first glance, one felt the unquestionable power of that gaze. There was no coyness in it, no hesitation: it was full of calm strength.

'The doctor's charges are trifling,' Binoy tried to insist. 'So . . . you need not . . . I will . . .' With the girl's eyes fixed on his face, he could not complete his sentence. But there remained no doubt that he must accept the money for the doctor's fee.

'Look, I don't require any brandy . . .' the old man began.

'Why Baba, didn't the doctor prescribe it?' his daughter interrupted.

'Doctors often prescribe such things; it is one of their vices,' the old man replied. 'A little warm milk is enough to dispel any weakness I feel.'

'We'll take your leave now,' he said to Binoy, after the milk had revived him. 'We have caused you a lot of trouble.'

'A carriage . . .' requested the girl, looking at Binoy.

'Why trouble him any further?' protested the old man, embarrassed. 'Our house is quite close after all, we'll walk this little distance.'

'No, Baba, that can't be allowed,' his daughter insisted. The old man did not contradict her. Binoy went personally to summon a cab.

'What is your name?' the old man asked, before mounting it.

'My name is Binoybhushan Chattopadhyay.'

'I am Poreshchandra Bhattacharya,' the old man said. 'I live close by, at number 78. If you ever find the time to drop by, I shall be delighted.'

Raising her eyes to look at Binoy, the girl silently reinforced this request. Binoy was ready to mount the carriage instantly to visit their house, but unsure if such conduct would be proper, he remained standing there. As the cab drove away, the girl joined her hands in a brief namaskar. Utterly unprepared for this gesture, Binoy remained frozen, unable to respond. Back home, he repeatedly cursed himself for this minor lapse. Scrutinizing his own conduct in their company from their first encounter to the moment of parting, he felt his manner throughout had been rather uncivil. He tormented himself with futile thoughts of what he could have said or done at specific moments. Returning to his room, he found on the bed the handkerchief which the girl had used to wipe her father's face. Quickly, he picked it up. The baul's song rang in his ears:

In and out the cage, how the unknown bird doth flit.

As the day advanced, the monsoon sun grew harsher, and a stream of office-bound carriages sped through the streets. Binoy could not concentrate on any of his daily tasks. In his whole life, he had never experienced such exquisite joy, mingled with such intense anguish. His tiny apartment and the hideous city of Kolkata that surrounded it now appeared to him like a fantasy kingdom. He seemed adrift in a lawless realm, where the impossible becomes possible, the unthinkable can be accomplished, and transcendent beauty assumes visible form. At this early hour the radiance of the monsoon sun penetrated his mind, coursed through his blood, and descended like a curtain of light, screening his inner being from the paltriness of everyday life. Binoy yearned to express his fulfillment in some extraordinary form, but failing to find the means, his heart began to chafe. He had presented himself to the visitors in an utterly ordinary light. His home was extremely humble, its interior disorderly, the bed none too clean. Some days, he would adorn his room with a bunch of flowers, but as luck would have it, there was not a flower-petal in his room that day! Everyone said it was evident from Binoy's gift for spontaneous public speaking that he would one day become a great orator; but that day he had not uttered a single word that demonstrated his intelligence. 'When that giant carriage was about to crash into their cab,' he repeated to himself, 'if only I had rushed into the street at lightning speed, and effortlessly reined in those wayward horses!' When this heroic fantasy arose in his mind, he could not refrain from glancing at himself in the mirror once.

Just then he noticed a boy of about seven or eight, scanning the number on his building from the street.

'Here, this is the very house you want!' he called from above. He never doubted that his house was indeed the one the boy was trying to locate. Binoy rushed downstairs, sandals flapping noisily. Eagerly leading the boy indoors, he gazed at his face.

'Didi has sent me to you,' the boy said, handing a letter to Binoybhushan.

Taking the letter, Binoy first saw his name inscribed in English on the envelope, in a clear, feminine hand. There was no letter inside, only a few rupee-notes. When the boy prepared to leave, Binoy would not let him go. His arm round the lad's shoulders, he led him to the room upstairs. The boy's complexion was darker than his sister's, but his features resembled hers somewhat. Looking at him, Binoy's heart filled with affection and joy.

The boy was quite quick-witted. Entering the room, he noticed a picture on the wall. 'Who is this?' he enquired.

'A friend of mine.'

'A friend? Who is he?'

'You wouldn't know him,' Binoy smiled. 'He's my friend Gourmohan. We call him Gora. We have been fellow-students since childhood.'

'Are you still a student?'

'No, not anymore.'

'Have you finished studying e-v-e-r-y-thing?'

'Yes, I have,' answered Binoy, unable to resist bragging, even to this young boy. The boy gave a small sigh of surprise. He probably wondered when he too would be done with all this learning.

'What's your name?' Binoy asked him.

'Sri Satishchandra Mukhopadhyay is my name.'

'Mukhopadhyay?' repeated Binoy, in surprise.

Gradually, in bits and pieces, details of the boy's identity emerged. Poreshbabu was not the father of this brother-sister duo, but had reared them from infancy. The boy's didi was formerly called Radharani, but Poreshbabu's wife had changed her name to 'Sucharita.' In no time, Binoy and Satish had become fast friends.

'Can you get home on your own?' Binoy asked when Satish prepared to leave.

'I go about alone,' was his proud reply.

'Let me see you home.'

'Why, I can go by myself!' protested Satish, offended at Binoy's lack of faith in his abilities. By way of example, he began to recount several amazing anecdotes about his solitary wanderings. Why Binoy still accompanied him to his doorstep, the lad could not quite fathom.

'Won't you come in?' Satish asked him.

'Another day,' replied Binoy, quelling all his inner urges.

Back home, Binoy extracted from his pocket the envelope with his name on it, and gazed at it for a long time. He memorized the shape and form of every character inscribed on it. Then he lovingly placed the envelope, money and all, inside a box. There remained no possibility of his ever spending that money in some hour of need.

~2~

That rainy evening, the darkness of the sky seemed damp and heavy. Beneath the oppressive silence of those colourless, monotonous clouds, the city of Kolkata lay motionless like a giant despondent dog, curled up with its face tucked under its tail. It had drizzled incessantly since the previous night. The drizzle had turned the streets to mud, but lacked the force to wash away the slime. It had not rained since four this afternoon, but the clouds did not augur well. Fear of an impending downpour made it difficult to stay in alone after dark, but there was no comfort outdoors, either. At such a time, occupying cane moras on the damp terrace of a three-storied building, sat two men.

As children, the two friends would run about on this terrace after returning from school; before their examinations, they would pace like maniacs up and down this terrace, reciting their lessons aloud; in summer, back from college, they would dine on this same terrace, then argue sometimes until two in the night; when the sun touched their faces at dawn, they would awaken with a start to discover that they had fallen asleep on the floor-mat at that very place. When there were no further college degrees to be pursued, one friend would preside over the Hindu welfare society's monthly meetings on this terrace, with the other as secretary.

The president's name was Gourmohan; friends and relatives called him Gora. He seemed to have surpassed everyone else, to a disproportionate extent. His college professor had named him the Silver Mountain. His complexion was rather blatantly fair, not softened by the slightest hint of yellow. Almost six feet tall, he was heavy boned, with fists like tiger-paws. His voice was startlingly deep and resonant, enough to give one a fright if heard suddenly. His facial contours were also unduly large and excessively firm, the chin and jawbone resembling strong bolts on a fortress gate. He had virtually no eyebrows, and his brow was wide at the temples. The lips were thin and compressed, his nose suspended above them like a scimitar. The eyes were small but sharp, their arrowlike gaze seemingly fixed on a remote, invisible target, yet capable of turning instantaneously, like lightning, to strike an object close at hand. Though not exactly handsome, Gour was impossible to ignore. He would stand out in a crowd.

And his friend Binoy, like the average educated Bengali bhadralok, was gentle but bright. His gracious nature, combined with his sharpness of intellect, had lent his countenance a distinctive air. In college he had always earned high marks and scholarships; Gora could never keep up with him. Gora felt little attraction for academic subjects; he lacked Binoy's quick comprehension and powers of retention. It was Binoy who had borne him like a vehicle through the sequence of college examinations.

'Listen,' Gora was saying, 'Abinash's denigration of the Brahmos is a sign of the man's good health. Why did it suddenly infuriate you?'

'How extraordinary! I could not have imagined that such things were open to question.'

'Then you have lost your reason. It's not natural for members of a society to adopt a calm, rational stance towards a group of people who violate social restrictions to act in a contrary fashion in all matters. Society is bound to misunderstand them, ascribing perverse motives to their straightforward actions, viewing as evil whatever they regard as good. So it should be. It is one of the penalties to be paid for deliberately breaking social laws.'

'I can't say that the natural alone is good.'

'I have no use for goodness!' exclaimed Gora, heatedly. 'If there are a few good people in the world, let them be, but may all others remain natural. Otherwise, work can't go on, nor can the soul survive. Those who fancy the heroism of becoming Brahmo must endure the minor pain of having all their actions misunderstood and denounced by non-Brahmos. That they should strut about puffed up with pride, while their opponents trail behind applauding them, is not the way of the world; and if it were so, the world would not benefit.'

'I'm not referring to criticism of the group. It is personal . . .'

'Criticism of the group is no criticism at all! It is a weighing of opinions. It's personal criticism we want. Tell me, O saintly one, did you never criticize anybody?'

'I did. Excessively. But I am ashamed of it.'

'No, Binoy, that won't do!' cried Gora, clenching his right fist. 'Not at all.'

'Why, what is the matter?' Binoy asked, after a short pause. 'What are you afraid of?'

'I see clearly that you are weakening.'

'Weak!' exclaimed Binoy, in some agitation. 'Do you know, I can visit their house this very moment if I wish? They had even invited me, but I did not go!'

'But you are unable to forget that you didn't go there. Day and night, you remind yourself: I didn't go, didn't go, didn't go to their house. Better to have gone there, indeed!'

'So you insist that I go?'

'No, I don't insist!' cried Gora, slapping his thigh. 'I can give it to you in writing that the day you go there, you will be well and truly gone. From the very next day, you will start dining at their house, and having enrolled with the Brahmo Samaj, you'll become a world-famous preacher.'

'What do you say! And then?'

'And then? Curse you! Son of a Brahman, you will end up in the dumping ground for dead cattle, with no way to preserve your purity, lost like a sailor with a broken compass. You will imagine then that docking your ship at port is a narrow-minded malpractice, that merely to drift without purpose is true navigation. But I have no patience with such prattle. I say you should go. Why keep us in suspense too, with one foot over the precipice?'

'When doctors give up, patients don't always die,' laughed Binoy. 'I see no signs that my end is near.'

'You don't?'

'No.'

'Don't you feel your pulse grow faint?'

'No, it feels as strong as ever.'

'Don't you feel that, if served by those gracious hands, even the outcaste's food can become a feast for the gods?'

'Enough, Gora!' cried Binoy, highly embarrassed. 'Stop now.'

'Why, there is nothing improper in what I say. It's not as if those gracious hands are screened from public view. If you can't tolerate even the bare mention of those pure, petal-like hands, hands that often exchange handshakes with men, that means you are as good as dead!'

'Look, Gora, I honour the female sex. Even in our holy texts the shastras . . .'

'Don't quote the shastras to defend your way of honouring the female sex! That is not honour; if I called it by the right name, you'd assault me.'

'You say this with brute force.'

'*Pujarha grihadiptayah*: so our shastras describe women. Women should be worshipped, for they light up our homes. It is best not to use the word 'worship' for the kind of respect English culture accords to women when they light up the hearts of men.'

'Should you so despise a noble emotion, just because it sometimes assumes a distorted form?'

'Binu,' urged Gora impatiently, 'Now you have lost your reason, you may as well accept my advice. In the English scriptures, all that hyperbole about women conceals one inner motive, sexual desire. We should worship the female sex at the mother's chamber and the virtuous housewife's holy shrine; when women are worshipped elsewhere, such adoration conceals an element of degradation. "Love" is the English word for what makes your heart circle Pareshbabu's house like a moth around a flame. But may you not ape the English in becoming obsessed with the frivolous notion that this "love" must be revered as life's ultimate goal!'

'Oh, Gora!' Binoy winced like a restive horse under the lash. 'Let it be, that's enough!'

'Enough? By no means. It is because we have not learned to regard men and women normally, in their own proper places, that we have conjured up a cluster of poetic notions about them.'

'Very well, granted that our passions impel us to and falsify the ideal situation where man-woman relationships could be normalized; but is the foreign culture entirely to blame? If the claims of English poetry are false, so is our excessive insistence on renouncing the lure of women and gold. To protect human nature from easy distractions some people poeticize the beautiful aspects of love, ignoring its darker side, while others exaggerate the evils of love, prescribing renunciation. These are merely two different modes adopted by two kinds of people. If you blame one, you cannot absolve the other.'

'No, I must admit I had misunderstood you. You are not in such bad shape, after all. Since your mind still has room for philosophy, you can fearlessly indulge in "love". But pull yourself back in time. That's a well-meant, friendly request.'

'Are you crazy?' exclaimed Binoy, in agitation. 'Me, and "love"? But I must admit, from whatever I've seen of Poreshbabu and the rest, and whatever I've heard about them, I've developed considerable respect for them. Perhaps that explains my urge to see their lifestyle at home.'

'Excellent! That's the very attraction you must resist. Let their life-cycle remain an undiscovered chapter, especially since they are predatory creatures. In your attempt to explore their private lives, you might ultimately delve so deep as to disappear altogether.'

'Look, this is one of your faults. You imagine that you alone are empowered by Ishwar our Lord, while the rest of us are weaklings.'

Gora seemed to be struck by the novelty of this. 'Right you are!' he cried, slapping Binoy on the back. 'That is indeed my fault. A grave fault it is.'

'Oh, you have another major fault. You are utterly incapable of gauging the severity of the heaviest blow a person's spine can bear.'

At this point, Gora's elder step-brother Mahim came upstairs, his heaviness making him pant. 'Gora!' he called.

'Yes, sir!' responded Gora, rising quickly.

'I've come to see if the rumbling rain-clouds have descended upon our terrace. What's the matter tonight? Have you dispatched the English halfway across the Indian Ocean, by now? No loss to the English it seems, but all this roaring might inconvenience Boro Bou, who's nursing a headache in bed downstairs.'

Mahim went back downstairs. Gora stood there, overcome by shame. Along with shame, a degree of rage also began to smoulder within him, whether directed at himself or others, it was hard to say. 'In every matter, I end up applying more force than necessary,' he said slowly after a while, as if to himself. 'I fail to remember how intolerable that must be for others.'

Coming close, Binoy grasped Gour's hand affectionately.

~3~

As Gora and Binoy were preparing to leave the terrace, Gora's mother arrived there. Binoy touched her feet respectfully.

From her appearance, it would not seem that Anandamoyi was Gora's mother. She was very slim, with a compact figure; if she had any grey hair, it could not be seen; at first glance she appeared to be under forty. Her lineaments were extremely graceful, as if someone had painstakingly used a lathe to carve the lines of her lips, chin and forehead. Her body was shorn of all excess; her face always bore an expression of clear, alert intelligence. Her complexion was dark, in no way comparable with Gora's. There was one thing about her that everyone immediately noticed: she wore a chemise with her sari. At that time, though women of the modern set had begun to adopt the blouse or chemise, elderly housewives continued to dismiss the trend as a flagrant Khristani custom, a Christian practice. Anandamoyi's husband, Krishnadayal Babu, worked at the Commissariat. Since childhood, Anandamoyi had lived with him in the western parts of the country. Hence she did not harbour the superstitious notion that it was shameful or ludicrous to cover one's body properly. Even after scrubbing the house, polishing, washing and mopping, cooking and serving, sewing, counting, keeping accounts, dusting, airing, enquiring after neighbours and relatives, time still hung heavy on her hands. If she fell ill, she would never want to take it seriously, saying, 'Falling ill can do me no harm. Without work, how will I stay alive?'

'Whenever Gora's voice can be heard from downstairs, we know that Binu must have come,' said Gora's mother. 'The house was absolutely quiet these last few days. Tell me, son, what's the matter? Why haven't you been coming? You haven't been ill, have you?'

'No, Ma, not ill,' replied Binoy, diffidently. 'It's been raining so.'

'Indeed!' cried Gora. 'When the rains end, Binoy will say it's too sunny. After all, when you blame the gods, they don't answer back. Only the omniscient One knows what's really on his mind.'

'What nonsense, Gora!' Binoy expostulated.

'Truly son, you shouldn't say such things,' Anandamoyi agreed. 'Men's minds are sometimes cheerful, sometimes sad; moods don't always stay the same! To make an issue of it amounts to harassment. So Binu, come along to my room. I have arranged some refreshments for you.'

'No, Ma, that's not allowed!' Gora intervened, vehemently shaking his head. 'I shan't let Binoy eat in your room.'

'Is that so indeed!' said Anandamoyi. 'Why bapu, I never ask you to eat with me, after all. Meanwhile your father's grown so fanatical about purity, he refuses to eat anything but self-cooked food. This Binu of mine is a good boy, not a fanatic like you. You always try to keep him away by force.'

'You're right, I will force him to stay away,' Gora asserted. 'We can't have meals in your room until you dismiss Lachhmia, that Khristani maid of yours.'

'Oh Gora, don't say such things!' protested Anadamoyi. 'She has always fed you by hand, reared you since you were a child. Until just the other day, you wouldn't relish your food without her chutney. I'll never forget the way Lachhmia nursed you back to health when you contracted smallpox as a child.'

'Give her a pension, buy her land, build her a house, whatever you please. But she can't continue here, Ma'

'Gora, do you think money can settle all debts!' Anandamoyi expostulated. 'She wants neither land nor a house. She'll die if she can't see you.'

'Then keep her on if you please,' said Gora, 'but Binu can't dine in your room. We must follow restrictions, there is no getting away from them. Ma, you belong to such a distinguished professor's family: for you not to follow traditional restrictions . . .'

'Oh your mother used to follow traditional custom, once,' Anandamoyi assured him. 'I had to shed many a tear on that account. And where were you then? Everyday, I would set up a clay Shiva and prepare to pray, but your father would come and fling it away. Those days, I'd even shrink from tasting rice cooked by any Brahman I didn't know. The railway network was not extensive then; how many days I spent fasting, on bullock carts, postal carriages, palkis or camelback! Was it easy for your father to break my orthodoxy? His saheb-masters would applaud him for having his wife accompany him everywhere. He even got a pay-rise. For that very reason, they'd keep him in the same post for extended periods, often reluctant to let him move. Now in old age, having relinquished his job and acuired heaps of money, he has suddenly done an about-face, becoming very fastidious about purity. But I can't do that. The superstitious ideas I had inherited from my ancestors have been uprooted, one by one. Can they now be retrieved at anyone's bidding?'

'Achchha, forget your ancestors,' urged Gora. 'They won't raise any objections, after all. But for our sake, there are a few rules you must observe. You may not honour the shastras, but your son's honour must surely be preserved?'

'O, why reason with me at such length! I alone know what goes on in my mind. If I hindered my husband and my son at every step, wherein would my happiness lie? But do you know that I threw orthodoxy to the winds when you were still a babe in arms? The moment you clasp an infant to your heart, you realize that nobody is born into a caste. Ever since I realized that, I knew for sure that if I despised someone for being a Christian or a lowcaste person, Ishwar would snatch you away from me as well. May you continue to occupy my lap, light up my home, and I'll accept drinking water from every caste in the world!'

Anandamoyi's words suddenly roused a hint of doubt in Binoy's mind. He glanced at Anandamoyi, then at Gora, but at once dismissed any wish to argue.

'Ma, your logic is not clear,' Gora protested. 'Boys survive even in the homes of those who are discriminating enough to obey the shastras. What gave you the idea that Ishwar might apply special rules in your case?'

'He who gave me a son like you also gave me such ideas. So, what am I to do? I have no hand in this. O you crazy boy, I don't know whether to laugh or cry at your lunacy. Anyway, let such things be. So, can't Binoy dine in my room?'

'He's so greedy he'd rush there at once, given the opportunity,' said Gora. 'But, Ma, I shan't let him. With a mere handful of sweetmeats, we can't delude him into forgetting he is a Brahman's son. He must sacrifice a lot, control his passions, only then can he preserve the glory of his high birth. But please don't be angry, Ma. I bow at your feet.'

'Me, angry? How can you say that!' Anandamoyi exclaimed. 'You are acting in ignorance, I tell you. I must privately bear the pain of knowing that although I brought you up, you still . . . Anyway, I can't practice the dharma you preach. Never mind if you don't let me feed you in my room, but at least I get to see you in the evenings, and for me that's enough. Binoy, don't look so miserable, baap. You have a soft heart and feel I must be hurt, but it's nothing really, baap. I shall invite you some other time, and serve you food prepared by an expert Brahman cook, not to worry! But as for me, bachha, I shall accept water from Lachhmia: let me make that clear to everyone.' Gora's mother went downstairs.

'Gora, things have gone too far!' said Binoy slowly, after a brief silence.

'On whose part?'

'Yours.'

'Not in the least. I want to protect each person's boundaries. Once you begin to yield the slightest ground on some pretext, you're ultimately left with nothing.'

'But she's your mother!'

'I know what it means to have a mother. As if you need to remind me of it! How many people have a mother like mine? But if I don't begin to obey orthodox restrictions, I may one day cease to obey my mother as well. Look Binoy, let me tell you something: remember that the heart is a wonderful thing, but not above all else.'

'Listen Gora, Ma's words have created strange stirrings in my heart today,' Binoy ventured hesitantly, after a while. 'I feel Ma has something on her mind that she can't explain to us, and that is tormenting her.'

'Oh, Binoy, don't let your imagination run wild!' cried Gora impatiently. 'It's a mere waste of time, and quite futile.'

'Because you never look closely at anything in this world, you dismiss as fanciful whatever escapes your notice. But I tell you I've often observed that Ma seems to nurse a certain anxiety about something, as if there is something amiss that she can't put right, which causes some hidden pain in her domestic life. Gora, listen closely to what she says.'

'I listen as closely as possible. If I try any harder, I'm likely to misconstrue her words, so I don't even try.'

~4~

An idea that sounds definite when aired as an opinion may not always appear so certain when applied to human beings. At least, not to Binoy, who had very strong sensibilities. During an argument he might vociferously defend an opinion, but in practice, he could not help respecting human beings more than opinions. In fact it was doubtful whether Binoy had accepted Gora's public views out of conviction, or his deep love for Gora. Emerging from Gora's house, as he slowly picked his way through the slush that wet evening, his mind wrestled with the dual claims of ideas and human beings.

Binoy had readily embraced Gora's stated conviction that to protect itself from various direct and indirect attacks, society must now remain especially alert about purity of touch and taste. He had engaged in sharp debates with those who opposed this view, arguing that when a fortress is besieged from all sides, there is nothing narrow-minded about guarding it with one's life, sealing every pathway, every door and window, even the tiniest aperture. But when Gora forbade him to dine in Anandamoyi's room, he was now inwardly tormented with pain.

Binoy was fatherless, and had also lost his mother at an early age. His khuro, his father's younger brother, lived in the countryside. Since childhood, for the sake of his education, Binoy had grown up alone in the Kolkata house. Ever since he got to know Anandamoyi through his friendship with Gora, he had regarded her as his mother. How often had he visited her room to harass her for food, eagerly snatching at the morsels! How often had he feigned envy, accusing Anandamoyi of partiality to Gora in serving their portions of food! How anxious Anandamoyi became if she did not see Binoy for a few days, how often she would eagerly wait for their society-meetings to end so she could personally supervise his meal, Binoy was well aware. Could Anandamoyi bear it if that very same Binoy, out of communal hostility, refused to dine in her room tonight? Could Binoy bear it?

'From now on, Ma will offer me food prepared by a good Brahman cook. She'll never cook for me again. She said it cheerfully, but what a heart-rending thought!' Binoy made way his home, turning this thought over and over in his mind.

The room was dark and empty. Books and papers lay scattered everywhere. Striking a match, Binoy lit the sej. The oil lamp's glass chimney was smudged with the bearer's fingerprints. The white cloth on the writing table was stained in places with ink and grease. The room felt stifling. The absence of human company and affection seemed to choke his heart. Saving the nation, protecting the community—try as he might, he could not see these duties as real or true. Truer by far was that unknown bird, which had approached the cage one bright, beautiful Sravan morning, then flown away again. But Binoy must not dwell on memories of that unknown bird. Certainly not. So his mind sought refuge in drawing a mental picture of Anandamoyi's room, from which Gora had banished him.

The bright parquet floor, sparkling clean; at one end, a spotless, soft bed resembling white swan-wings; beside it, on a small stool, a castor-oil lamp would have been lit by now;

leaning towards the light, Ma would be embroidering a
kantha using skeins of many-coloured thread, with Lachhmia
on the floor, prattling away in her broken Bengali; Ma would
ignore most of what she said. Whenever Ma felt hurt, she
would take up her embroidery. Binoy fixed his mind's eye on
the image of her quiet, work-absorbed countenance. 'May the
glow of affection on this face save me from all perplexity,'
wished Binoy. 'Let this very face become my image of the
motherland; may it inspire me and keep me steadfast in my
devotion to duty.' In his heart, he invoked her once as 'Ma!'
and declared: 'No shastra can convince me that your rice is
not my heavenly nectar, my amrita!'

In the silent chamber, the large clock ticked away. Binoy
could not bear to remain in the room. After gazing for a while
at a lizard hunting an insect near the light on the wall, he rose
and went out, carrying an umbrella. He was not sure why.
Perhaps it was his inner purpose to return to Anandamoyi.
But it occurred to him presently that as it was Sunday, he
could attend Keshabbabu's lecture at the Brahmo gathering.
Immediately discarding all his hesitation, Binoy strode ahead.
He knew there was not much time left for the lecture to end,
but that did not deter him.

Arriving at the venue, he saw the devotees emerging.
Umbrella aloft, he stood at the corner of the street. That very
moment, Poresh Babu came out of the temple, his face calm
and serene. He was accompanied by a few relatives. For an
instant, in the light of the gas streetlamps, Binoy glimpsed a
youthful face among them. Then, to the sound of rolling
carriage-wheels, the scene vanished like a bubble in the ocean
of darkness.

Binoy had read many English novels, but how could he
relinquish the beliefs of a genteel Bengali family? That it was
dishonourable for the woman and degrading for him to seek
her out so eagerly, was a notion that no argument could drive

from his mind. So a terrible sense of shame mingled with the joy that filled Binoy's heart. 'I seem to be heading for a moral downfall!' he thought. Although he had argued with Gora about this, his lifelong inhibitions would not let him regard a woman in a romantic light if society did not sanction it.

Binoy did not make it to Gora's house. He went home, his mind in turmoil about many things. The following afternoon, when he arrived at Gora's place after leaving his house and wandering here and there, the shadows were deepening at the end of a long, rainy day. Gora had lit the lamp and settled down to write.

'So Binoy, which way does the wind blow now?' he enquired, without raising his head.

'Gora, let me ask you something,' said Binoy, ignoring his words. 'Does Bharatvarsha, the idea of India, appear very real to you? Very clear? You think of it day and night, but in what form?'

Gora stopped writing and fixed his penetrating gaze briefly on Binoy's face. Then, laying down his pen, he leaned back on the chowki and said: 'I think of Bharatvarsha, like the ship's captain who constantly bears in mind the port at the other end of the sea, whether he is feasting or reveling, at work or at rest.'

'Where is this Bharatvarsha of yours?'

'Where the compass here points, day and night,' replied Gora, touching his heart, 'not in your Marshman saheb's *History of India*.'

'Where your compass points, does something exist?'

'Indeed it does!' cried Gora, indignantly. 'I may lose my way, or even drown, but my treasured port remains. It is my Bharatvarsha in all its glory, replete with wealth, knowledge, spiritual faith. To say that this Bharatvarsha does not exist! That only the falsehood around us is real! This Kolkata of yours, with its offices, its courthouses and its few brick-and-wood bubbles! How disgusting!' Gora gazed intently at Binoy for a while. Lost in thought, Binoy made no reply.

'Here, reading and writing, running after jobs, slaving away from ten to five without any sense of purpose, this false, illusory Bharatvarsha is what we have taken for the truth,' declared Gora. 'That is why we rush about dementedly day and night, all twenty-five crores of us, mistaking false prestige for honour, futile labour for accomplishment. Caught in this delusion, can we ever find the impulse to strive for a new life! That is why, day by day, we are fading away. There is a real Bharatvarsha—a complete India. Unless we establish ourselves there, we can't absorb its true living essence into our minds and hearts. Therefore I say, forgetting all else, discarding book-learning, the lure of prestige, and the temptation of odd profits, we must set sail for that very port, whether we drown or perish. No wonder I can never forget the true, complete image of Bharatvarsha!'

'Aren't these merely words spoken in the heat of emotion? Do you mean what you say?'

'Indeed I do!' thundered Gora.

'What about those who don't see your point?'

'We must show them the way!' cried Gora, clenching his fists. 'That is our duty. If they cannot clearly discern the image of truth, will the people not surrender to some false idea? Hold up Bharatvarsha's complete image to the public, and they will go berserk. Must we then go from door to door, seeking subscriptions? People would vie with each other to lay down their lives!'

'Either show me that image, or let me remain all at sea, like everyone else.'

'Strive for it. If you are a believer, you will find happiness in sincere effort. Because they have no real convictions, all our fine patriots cannot place any strong demands either on themselves or on anyone else. Even if the god of wealth,

Kuber himself, were to offer them a boon, they probably wouldn't dare ask for anything beyond the gilt badge sported by a governor's peon. They have no belief, and therefore, no self-assurance.'

'Gora, everyone's nature is not alike. Because you have found your convictions within yourself and can take refuge in your own strength, you fail to realize the predicament of others. Assign me any task you please, I tell you; let me labour day and night. Otherwise, though I have a sense of achievement while I am in your company, I have nothing to cling to when I move away.'

'Do you speak of tasks? Our sole task now is to express unhesitating, undoubted, complete respect for everything swadeshi, to generate the same respect in the hearts of the unpatriotic. Ashamed of our country for so long, we have weakened ourselves with the poison of slavery. If each of us opposes this by personal example, we can claim a space for future work. Anything we attempt now proves to be a mere imitation, learnt from the schoolbooks of history. Can we ever truly devote ourselves wholeheartedly to such false pursuits? They would only degrade us.'

Just then Mahim sauntered in, hookah in hand. Back home from office, after his evening snack, this was Mahim's hour for smoking tobacco by the roadside with a paan in his mouth and a few more in his betel-box. Soon his neighbourhood friends would arrive, one by one. In the room beside the entrance, they would assemble for a game of primero. As soon as Mahim entered, Gora rose from the chowki.

'You are busy saving your nation Bharat, but meanwhile, please come to your own brother's rescue!' observed Mahim, puffing upon his hookah. Gora stared at him.

'Our new boss at the office has a face like a greyhound. He's a very nasty man,' Mahim declared. 'He calls the clerks

baboons. If someone's mother dies, he doesn't want to grant
them leave of absence, dismissing it as a lie. Bengalis can
never draw their full month's salary, because he riddles their
claim with a hundred fines. A newspaper carried a letter
about him, and the bastard has concluded it was my doing.
He's not entirely wrong either. So unless I publish a rejoinder
in my own name, he won't let me survive. As twin gems cast
up by churning the ocean of the university, you two must
compose this letter properly. It must be littered with phrases
such as *even handed justice, never failing generosity* and *kind
courteousness.*'

Gora remained silent.

'So many lies in one breath, Dada?' Binoy smiled.

'Let the rogues have a dose of their own medicine,' said
Mahim. 'I have associated with them for a long time, and
there is nothing I don't know about them. Their knack for
supporting falsehoods is admirable. They stop at nothing, if
need be. If one of them lies, the rest sing the same tune, like
a pack of howling jackals. Unlike us, they don't seek applause
by exposing each other. Know this for sure: there's no sin in
deceiving them, as long as we don't get caught.' Mahim burst
into loud laughter, puffing away at his hookah. Binoy couldn't
help laughing, either.

'You wish to embarrass them by confronting them with
the truth!' Mahim scoffed. 'If Ishwar hadn't given you such
ideas, would the nation be in such a plight? We must realize
indeed that those who possess brute force will not bow their
heads in shame when we heroically expose their deceit.
Instead, they turn their weapons of crime upon us, threatening
us like the purest of saints. Tell me if I am wrong.'

'True, indeed,' remarked Binoy.

'Instead, let us grease their feet with drops of free oil
wrung from the mill of falsehood, and say: "O saint, Baba
Paramhansa, please shake out your holy bag, for even the dust

from it will save us!" Then you may retrieve at least a portion of what's rightfully yours, without any fear of disrupting the peace. That's true partriotism, if you like. But my brother here is getting annoyed. Ever since he became a devout Hindu, he has shown me great deference as his elder brother, but I haven't quite spoken as an elder brother in his presence, today. What's to be done bhai, we must be truthful, even about untruths. Binoy, I want that piece of writing from you though. Wait, let me fetch you my notes.' Mahim left the room, puffing on his hookah.

'Binu, please deal with Dada in his own room,' Gora requested. 'Let me complete what I was writing.'

~5~

'Ogo shunchho, do you hear me? I shan't enter your prayer-chamber, don't worry. When you're through with your ahnik ritual, please come to the other room once. I need to talk to you. Now that two new sanyasis have arrived, I know I won't see you for some time; that's why I've come here to speak to you. Don't forget to come there.' With these words, Anandamoyi returned to her household chores.

Krishnadayalbabu was dark and well-built, not very tall. His large eyes were the most prominent feature in a face otherwise largely obscured by a salt-and-pepper moustache and beard. He was always draped in saffron silk, with a brass kamandulu close at hand and wooden kharams on his feet. His hairline was receding; the rest of his long hair was tied in a knot on top of his head.

Formerly, during his soujourn in the west, he had indulged excessively in meat and liquor in the company of white army-men. Those days he thought it manly to deliberately humiliate the priests, holy men, vaishnavas and sanyasis of the land. But now, there was no orthodox rule he would not follow. He would seek training in new devotional modes from every new sanyasi he encountered. There was no limit to his fascination for obscure routes to salvation, and esoteric yogic practices. For some time, Krishnadayal had been receiving guidance in tantrik ways, but of late, news of a Buddhist priest had stirred his mind.

He was twenty-three when his first wife died after giving birth to a son. Blaming her death upon the son, he left the boy with his in-laws, and in a fit of detachment, traveled far west. Within six months, he married the fatherless granddaughter of Shri Sarbabhouma, a resident of Varanasi. In the west, Krishnadayal found himself a job and by various means, gained his employers' esteem. Meanwhile, Sarbabhouma passed away. As she was left with no guardian, Krishnadayal was forced to bring his wife to live with him.

When the sepoy Mutiny broke out, he gained glory as well as property by strategically saving the lives of a few highly-placed Englishmen. Soon after the Mutiny he gave up his job, and spent some time in Varanasi with the newborn Gora. When Gora was about five, Krishnadayal moved to Kolkata, brought his elder son Mahim back from his maternal uncle's house, and raised the boy himself. Now, by the grace of his father's patrons, Mahim was making great headway in the government accounts department.

From his childhood days, Gora would dominate the boys in his neighbourhood and at school. It was his chief aim and source of entertainment to make life hell for the teachers and pundits. When he was a little older, he became the leader of a band of young revolutionaries, by reciting 'Who would wish to live sans freedom' and 'The abode of twenty crore humans' at the students' club, and delivering lectures in English. Eventually, when Gora broke out of the students'-club eggshell to spread his wings in adult gatherings, Krishnadayalbabu was greatly amused at his chirping.

In no time at all, Gora had gained great popularity with people outside his family; but at home, he received scant support from anyone. Mahim was by then a working man. He tried in various ways to dampen Gora's spirit, taunting him as 'Uncle Patriot' or 'Harish Mukhujje the Second.' Often, those days, Gora and his dada would almost come to blows. Privately, Anandamoyi felt very anxious about Gora's hostility towards the British. She would try to pacify him in many ways, but to no avail. Gora thought it glorious to engage in public combat with the British at the slightest opportunity.

Meanwhile, overwhelmed by Keshabbabu's speeches, Gora felt intensely attracted to the Brahmo Samaj. Simultaneously, Krishnadayal became so rigidly orthodox in his ways, he would grow flustered if Gora so much as set foot in his room. He set up his own independent living quarters, occupying two or three rooms in the house. With great pomp, he hung a wooden sign at the door, bearing the incscription *Sadhanashram*, 'Hermitage of Holy Pursuits'.

Gora's heart rebelled at his father's antics. 'I can't stand such idiocy!' he declared. 'It is unbearable.' He was now ready to leave home, severing all ties with his father, but Anandamoyi managed, somehow, to prevent him.

Gora would seize every opportunity to argue with the holy men who visited his father. The encounters were more like fisticuffs than verbal debates. Many of them had limited knowledge and unlimited greed for money. They were no match for Gora, and feared him as if he were a tiger. Only one of them, Harachandra Vidyabagish, earned Gora's respect. Krishnadayal had employed Vidyabagish to discuss the Vedanta. Trying at first to fight him aggressively, Gora found it impossible to provoke him. The man was not only learned, but also extraordinarily large-hearted. That mere knowledge of Sanskrit could produce such sharpness and breadth of intellect, was beyond Gora's imagination. Vidyabagish's nature

was so calm and patient, so forgiving and serene, that Gora
could not but behave with restraint in his presence. Under
Harachandra's guidance, he began to study the Vedanta
philosophy. For Gora there were no half-measures; he
immersed himself completely in philosophical discussions.

At this time, an English missionary happened to publish a
newspaper article attacking Hindu religion and society, and
challenging the people of the country to a public debate. Gora
was incensed. Although he himself denounced the shastras and
popular superstitions at the slightest opportunity, harassing his
opponents in every possible way, a foreigner's contempt for
the Hindu community seemed to wound him like a goad.
Gora began his battle through the columns of the newspaper.
All his opponent's arguments against Hindu society, he rejected
outright. After both parties had exchanged many rejoinders,
the editor decreed: 'Henceforth we shall not publish too
many letters.' But Gora's blood was up. He began to write an
English book titled *Hindooism*.

Sifting all the ideas and scriptural sources at his command,
he set about compiling evidence of the unblemished supremacy
of the Hindu religion and society. Thus, in his attempt to fight
the missionary, Gora was gradually outwitted by his own
judicial arguments.

'We shall not allow our own country to be placed in the
dock in a foreign court and judged like a criminal by a foreign
law!' he declared. 'We shall earn neither shame nor glory in
judging ourselves minutely by British ideals. We shall not feel
ashamed in the least, either inwardly or before others, of the
rituals, beliefs, scriptures and customs of our birthplace. We
shall shield our country and ourselves from humiliation,
boldly and proudly accepting all that our nation has to offer.'

Gora now took to bathing in the Ganga and performing
the sandhya-ahnik rituals at dusk and dawn. He grew an uncut
tuft of hair as a tiki on his crown, and began to observe the

rules of purity in touch and taste. Every morning, he would respectfully touch his parents' feet. Upon seeing Mahim, whom he formerly addressed unsparingly as 'cad' or 'snob' in English, he would now stand up respectfully or greet him with a pranam. Mahim swore at him for this sudden display of deference, but Gora would not answer back.

By precept and practice, Gora inspired a group of people in the area. 'Whether we are good or bad, civilized or barbaric, we refuse to be answerable to anyone about such things!' they proclaimed in relief, as if rescued from a dilemma. 'We are what we are. We want to fully experience our own selfhood.'

But Krishnadayal did not appear pleased at this new change in Gora. In fact, one day, he summoned Gora and said: 'Look baba, the Hindu shastras are extremely profound. No ordinary person can plumb the depths of the religion our sages had established. In my opinion, it is best not to dabble in such things without understanding them. You are young, educated in English throughout. You were within your rights to develop leanings for the Brahmo Samaj, hence it did not anger me at all; on the contrary, I was rather pleased. But the path you have now adopted does not seem appropriate. It is not the right path for you, at all.'

'How can you say that, Baba!' Gora protested. 'I am a Hindu, after all. If I can't grasp the profound concepts of the Hindu dharma today, I shall master them tomorrow. Even if I never comprehend them, I must still follow this path. Because I could not shed the Hindu connections of my past life, I was born into a Brahman family in my present life. In this way, through a succession of births, it is via the Hindu religion and community that I shall ultimately arrive at the highest stage. If I ever forget myself and tend to follow some other direction, I must return to my faith with redoubled conviction.'

'But, baba, you can't become a Hindu simply by calling yourself one,' said Krishnadayal, shaking his head. 'It is easy to become a Muslim, and anyone can become a Christian, but to become a Hindu? Bas re! That would be difficult, indeed!'

'True,' conceded Gora. 'But being born a Hindu I have already entered the main gate. Now, if I sustain my efforts, I can gradually move ahead.'

'Baba, I can't explain properly by way of argument. But what you say is also correct. One day, by whatever circuitous route, one must return to the fruits of one's karma, one's assigned faith; no one can prevent that. It is the Almighty's will. Is anything within our power? We merely serve His purpose.'

Fruits of karma and divine will, the soul's identity with god and the devotional path of bhakti—Krishandayal accepted all these beliefs in equal measure, without feeling any need for compatibility between them.

~6~

Today, having completed his ahnik, bath and morning repast, Krishnadayal, after many days, placed his woollen mat on the floor of Anandamoyi's room and sat stiffly upright, as if carefully detaching himself from all contact with his surroundings.

'Ogo shunchho, listen to me, you remain lost in meditation without sparing a thought for the household, but I'm constantly anxious about Gora,' Anandamoyi told him.

'Why, what are you anxious about?'

'I can't quite say. But it seems to me that Gora can never adapt to these Hindu ways he has taken up of late. If he tries to follow this path, it will ultimately lead to some calamity. I had advised you at the time against initiating him into

Brahmanism with the poité ceremony. But those days, you didn't believe in anything. It makes no difference if we string a thread round his neck, you said. But it's not just a thread, after all! Now there's no stopping him.'

'So! Am I entirely to blame! What about the mistake you made at the very beginning? You refused to give him up under any circumstances. I too was rather headstrong then, quite ignorant about religion and the like. Could I ever take such a step today?'

'Whatever you might say, I can never accept that I broke my faith in any way. You remember don't you, the lengths to which I went, just to have a son! I followed any advice I received, accepted any number of amulets and mantras. One night I dreamt I was at my prayers, a basketful of togor blossoms beside me, when I suddenly opened my eyes to find that the saji contained no flowers, but a little boy, fair as a blossom. Ah, how can I describe what my eyes beheld! Eyes streaming with tears, I reached forward to take him in my arms when all at once, I awoke. It was barely ten days later that I received Gora as a gift from my deity. Was he a gift from someone else that I should return him to anyone? In some other birth, I must have suffered greatly when I bore him in my womb; that is why he has come to me now, to call me "Ma". Think of the circumstances in which he came to us. With people fighting, killing each other, all around us, and all of us fearing for our own lives. At such a time, when that white mem sought refuge in our house in the wee hours, you were afraid to even let her in. I hoodwinked you and hid her in the cowshed. That very night she died after giving birth to this boy. Would that orphaned boy have lived if I had not saved him? Not that you cared! You wanted to hand him over to the priest, after all. Why! Why should I give him away to the priest? Was the priest his father or mother? Had he saved the boy's life? To acquire a son in this way—is that any less than carrying him in the womb? Whatever you may say, unless this boy is claimed by the One who gave him to me, I'll die rather than let anyone else take him away!'

'I know that! Well, you can keep your Gora. I have never tried to prevent you in any way. But our community wouldn't accept it if we identified him as our son without performing the poité ceremony. So the sacred thread was obligatory. Now, there are only two concerns. By law, all my property should go to Mahim. Therefore . . .'

'Who wants a share of your property!' Anandamoyi protested. 'Leave all your earnings to Mahim, Gora won't touch a paisa of it. He's a man, and educated; he'll work for his livelihood. Why would he seek a share of someone else's wealth! Let him live, that is all I ask. I have no need for any other property.'

'No, I shall not disown him completely. I'll leave the estate to him. In time, it may yield a thousand rupees a year. Now it's his marriage that poses a problem. Whatever I may have done earlier, I can't let him marry according to Hindu rites into a Brahman family now. Too bad if that makes you unhappy.'

'Alas!' cried Anandamoyi, 'you seem to think, because I don't go about scattering cowdung and spraying holy Ganga-water everywhere, that I have no religious sense whatever. Why would I marry him into a Brahman family, and why should I be unhappy?'

'How can you say that! You, a Brahman's daughter!'

'So what if I'm a Brahman's daughter? I have given up Brahman practices, haven't I? Just recently, at Mahim's wedding, the bride's family had threatened to create trouble about my Khristani ways. So I had deliberately remained aloof, not said a word. The entire world calls me a Christian, and many other things besides, but I accept everything, saying: Aren't Christians human beings, after all! If you are of such high caste and so dear to the Almighty, why does He let you suffer defeat at the hands of Pathans, Mughals and Christians, in turn?'

'That's a long story. You're a woman. Such things are beyond your comprehension. But you do understand don't you, that there is something called a community, which you should respect?'

'I have no need to understand such things. I only understand that having reared Gora as my son, if I now pretend to be orthodox, my faith will certainly be lost, whether the community remains or not. It is out of respect for religion that I have never concealed anything. I let everyone know that I don't follow any restrictions, and suffer everyone's contempt in silence. There's only one thing I've concealed, and for that I live in constant fear of what Thakur might do to me someday. Look, I think we should tell Gora everything. After that, let destiny take its course.'

'No, no, not as long as I live!' cried Krishandayal in agitation. 'You know Gora. There is no saying what he might do if he gets to know. And it will throw our community into a turmoil. And that's not all. There's no saying what the government might do, either. Gora's father died fighting, and I know his mother's dead as well, but we should have informed the magistrate after all that turbulence had subsided. Now, if trouble breaks out over all this, it will put an end to all my prayers and rituals, and who knows what other problems may arise.'

Anandamoyi remained silent, offering no reply. 'As for Gora's marriage, I have thought of a plan,' resumed Krishandayal after a while. 'Poresh Bhattacharya, my former classmate, has recently settled in Kolkata after retiring from his position as school inspector. He is a dedicated Brahmo. And he has several daughters, I'm told. If we can introduce Gora to his family, he might even take a fancy to one of

Poresh's daughters in the course of his visits to their house. Then it's up to Prajapati, the god of marriage.'

'How can you suggest that! Gora visit a Brahmo household? He's past all that now.'

As Anandamoyi spoke, Gora entered the room. 'Ma!' he called, in his deep, thundering voice. He was rather surprised to see Krishnadayal there.

'Yes baba, what is it you want?' Anadamoyi asked, quickly rising to go up close to Gora, her eyes shining with affection.

'No, it's nothing important. Let it be for now,' Gora answered, preparing to leave.

'Stay awhile,' said Krishandayal, 'there's something I want to say. A Brahmo friend of mine has recently arrived in Kolkata. He stays at Hedotola.'

'It isn't Poreshbabu is it?'

'How do you know him?'

'Binoy lives close to his house. He has told me about them.'

'I would like you to go and enquire after their well-being.'

'Very well, I'll go there tomorrow itself,' said Gora suddenly, after some consideration. Anandamoyi was rather surprised. Gora paused again to think, then said: 'No, I can't go tomorrow, after all.'

'Why?' asked Krishnadayal.

'I must travel to Triveni tomorrow.'

'Triveni!' exclaimed Krishandayal, in astonishment.

'Tomorrow's solar eclipse calls for a holy bath,' Gora informed him.

'You amaze me, Gora!' said Anandamoyi. 'If you want a holy bath, there's the Ganga in Kolkata. No bath except at Triveni! I must say you have outdone all your countrymen!'

Gora left the room without offering any reply. He had decided to bathe at Triveni because many pilgrims would gather there. Merging with that mass of humanity, he wanted to surrender to the vast current of national life, and to feel the nation's turbulent pulse within his own heart. At the slightest opportunity, Gora wanted to forcefully cast aside all constraints and prejudices, to come down to the level the general public, and declare with all his heart: 'I am yours, and you are mine!'

~7~

Awakening at dawn, Binoy found that the sky had cleared overnight. The morning light had dawned, pure as the smile of a suckling infant. A few white clouds floated aimlessly in the sky. As he stood on the balcony, rapt in the memory of another pure dawn, he saw Poresh walking slowly down the road, grasping a stick in one hand and Satish's hand in the other. Spotting Binoy on the balcony, Satish at once clapped his hands. 'Binoybabu!' he called. Raising his head, Poresh also saw Binoy. As Binoy hurried downstairs, Poresh entered his house, accompanied by Satish.

'Binoybabu, you promised to visit us the other day, but you didn't come!' complained Satish, grasping Binoy's hand. Binoy smiled, patting Satish affectionately on the back.

Carefully propping his stick against the table, Poresh took a chowki. 'Without you, we would have been in deep trouble that day,' he said. 'You did us a great favour.'

'How can you say that! I hardly did anything at all!' said Binoy, flustered. 'Tell me, Binoybabu, don't you have a dog?' Satish suddenly inquired.

'A dog?' laughed Binoy. 'No, I don't have a dog.'

'Why?' asked Satish. 'Why haven't you kept a dog?'

'I never thought of keeping a dog.'

'Satish visited you the other day, I'm told,' said Poresh.

'He must have really pestered you. He talks so much, his didi has named him Bakhtiar Khiliji, the Orator.'

'I too have the gift of the gab,' replied Binoy. 'So we've become great friends, the two of us. What do you say, Satishbabu!'

Satish did not reply. But he became anxious not to let his new name lower his dignity in Binoy's eyes. 'Well, why not?' he said. 'Bakhtiar Khiliji is a fine name. Tell me, Binoybabu, Bakhtiar Khiliji was a warrior, wasn't he? Didn't he conquer Bengal?'

'He used to be a warrior once,' answered Binoy with a smile. 'But now he has no need to engage in combat. Now he only delivers speeches. And he still manages to conquer Bengal.'

Thus they conversed for a long time. Poresh spoke least of all, smiling occasionally with a cheerful serenity, and making only a couple of remarks. When it was time to leave, he rose from the chowki and said:

'To get to our House, number 78, you need to keep to the right . . .'

'He knows our house,' Satish interrupted. 'He escorted me all the way to our own doorstep, the other day.'

There was nothing embarrassing about this, yet Binoy felt secretly ashamed, as if he had been caught red-handed somehow.

'You know our house then,' said the old man. 'So, if you ever . . .'

'Of course. Whenever . . .'

'We belong to the same neighbourhood, after all,' Poresh said. 'It's only because this is Kolkata that we haven't yet become acquainted.'

Binoy escorted Poresh down to the street. He lingered at the door for a while. Poresh walked slowly, leaning on his stick, with Satish prattling away by his side. 'I have never seen an old man like Poreshbabu,' Binoy said to himself. 'I feel like bowing at his feet in reverence. And what a wonderful lad Satish is! If he lives, he will be a special person, as bright as he is simple!' However worthy the old man and the boy might have been, such an effusion of admiration and affection could not have occurred under normal circumstances, after so short an acquaintance. But such was Binoy's mental state, he did not wait to get better acquainted.

After this, Binoy began to think: 'For civility's sake, I must visit Poreshbabu's house.' But he seemed to hear Gora's voice warn him on behalf of their own group's version of Bharatvarsha: 'It's not acceptable for you to frequent their house. Watch out!' At every step, Binoy had followed many restrictions imposed by their group's image of Bharatvarsha. He had often hesitated, but had obeyed, all the same. Today, his heart rose in rebellion. He began to feel that Bharatvarsha was only a figure of negation.

The servant came to announce the midday meal, but Binoy had not even bathed yet. It was already noon. Suddenly, Binoy shook his head vehemently and declared, 'I shall not eat. Leave me alone, all of you.' So saying he picked up an umbrella and emerged into the street, without even a chador on his shoulder.

He went straight to Gora's house. Binoy knew that an office of the Hindu welfare society had been set up in rented premises on Amherst Street. Gora would go there everyday at noon, and write letters to inspire his party members everywhere in Bengal. This was where his devotees came to hear his words of wisdom, and to seek glory in supporting him. That day as well, Gora had gone to the office for some work. Binoy rushed to Anandamoyi's chamber in the private antahpur of Gora's house. Anandamoyi was at her meal. Lachamiya sat by her side, fanning her.

'Why, Binoy! What's the matter with you?' Anandamoyi exclaimed.

Binoy sat down facing her. 'Ma, I am very hungry,' he said. 'Please give me something to eat.'

'Now you've put me in a fix!' said Anandamoyi, flustered. 'Bamun-thakur, the Brahman cook, has left. Because all of you . . .'

'As if I've come to taste Bamun-thakur's cooking! Then the Bamun in my own home would have done as well. I want prasad from your own platter—food sanctified by your touch, Ma. Go Lachhmia, fetch me a glass of water!'

Binoy gulped down the water Lachhmia brought him. With loving care, Anandamoyi mashed the rice on her own thala and served portions of it to Binoy on another thala. He began to devour the morsels as if he had been famished for days.

A source of anguish was removed from Anandamoyi's heart. The sight of her cheerful face also made Binoy's heart feel lighter. She settled down to sew a pillowcase. From the adjacent room came the fragrance of keya blossoms, collected to prepare the screwpine-flavoured catechu called keyakhoyer. Binoy reclined at Anandamoyi's feet, head propped on his arm, and prattled on joyfully just as in previous times, forgetting everything else.

~8~

When this dam burst, the new flood in Binoy's heart seemed to grow even more turbulent. Emerging from Anandamoyi's room, he flew down the street as if on winged feet. He wanted to proudly proclaim to everyone the secret feelings that had been making him feel so awkward these last few days. At the very moment when Binoy reached the door of House 78, Poresh also arrived there from the opposite direction.

'Welcome, welcome, Binoybabu! What a pleasure!' With these words, Poresh ushered Binoy into the sitting-room facing the street. On one side of a small table was a bench with a back-rest, and on the other, a chair made of wood and cane. On one wall hung a painting of Jesus Christ, and on the wall opposite, a photograph of Keshabbabu. On the table, under a glass paperweight, lay the folded newspapers of the past few days. Books by Theodore Parker were arranged in rows on the upper shelves of a small almira in the corner. On top of the almira was a globe, covered with cloth. Binoy sat down, his heart racing. What if someone entered the room through the door behind him?

'On Mondays, Sucharita goes to tutor my friend's daughter,' Poresh informed him. 'Satish has also accompanied her, because a boy of his own age lives there. I have just returned after dropping them there. A little more delay, and I would have missed you.'

At this news, Binoy's heart simultaneously felt a pang of disappointment and a sense of relief. He could now chat with Poresh at ease. Poresh learnt all about Binoy in the course of their conversation. Binoy was an orphan. His khuro and khurima lived in the ancestral village and supervised property matters. Their two sons, Binoy's paternal cousins, used to stay with him while they pursued their studies. The elder one became a lawyer and practised in the local district court. The younger brother had died of cholera while still in Kolkata. The khuro wanted his nephew to aim for the district magistrate's post, but Binoy made no effort in that direction, busy instead with all sorts of trivial pursuits.

Almost an hour passed by in this fashion. It would seem uncivil to linger there needlessly any longer.

'It's a pity I didn't get to meet my friend Satish,' said Binoy, rising to his feet. 'Please tell him that I had come.'

'If you had stayed on a little longer you could have met

them,' responded Poreshbabu. 'It won't be long before they return.'

Binoy found it embarrassing to change his mind merely at this assurance. A little more persuasion, and he might have stayed on. But Poresh was a man of few words, not given to pressuring anyone, so Binoy had to leave.

'It would be nice if you dropped by now and then,' said Poresh.

Out in the street, Binoy felt no need to go back home. He had nothing to do there. He wrote for the papers. People praised his writings in English, but these last few days, when he sat down to write, no words would come to mind. He felt so restless, it was hard to spend much time at his desk. So he now headed in the opposite direction, for no reason at all.

He had barely walked a few steps when he heard a boyish voice cry: 'Binoybabu, Binoybabu!' Looking up, he saw Satish calling out to him, leaning out of the door of a hired cab. The glimpse of a sari corner and a white blouse-sleeve left him in no doubt about the identity of the passenger within. Constraints of Bengali respectability made it difficult for Binoy to stare at the cab. Meanwhile, Satish dismounted at that very spot, and grasped his hand.

'Come, let's go to our house,' he urged.

'But I've just left your house,' Binoy protested.

'Bah, we weren't there after all, so you must come again.' Binoy could not ignore Satish's importunations.

'Baba, I've brought Binoybabu!' announced Satish loudly, as soon as he had led his prisoner into the house.

'You are in the clutches of a harsh captor,' smiled the old man, emerging from his room. 'You won't escape in a hurry. Satish, send for your didi.'

His heart pounding, Binoy entered the room and took a seat.

'Out of breath, aren't you!' Poresh observed. 'Satish is a very mischievous boy.'

When Satish entered the room with his elder sister, Binoy first felt the whiff of a sweet fragrance. Then he heard Poreshbabu say:

'Radhé, Binoybabu is here. You know him, of course!'

Binoy looked up with a start, to see Sucharita greet him with a namaskar before occupying the chowki opposite his. This time, he did not forget to return her greeting.

'He was walking down the street,' Sucharita explained. 'There was no stopping Satish once he caught sight of him. He got off the cab and dragged him here. Perhaps you were out on some business. I hope this hasn't inconvenienced you?'

Binoy had not even dared to hope that Sucharita would address him directly. Flustered, he quickly blurted out: 'No, I was not out on any business. It was not inconvenient at all.'

'Come on Didi, give me the keys,' begged Satish, tugging at Sucharita's sari. 'Let me fetch our organ for Binoybabu to see.'

'Here we go!' laughed Sucharita. 'For anyone Bakhtiar befriends, there is no respite. He must not only listen to the organ, but suffer much worse besides. Binoybabu, this friend of yours is tiny, but his friendship is a heavy burden. I wonder if you can bear it!'

Binoy could not summon up any easy response to Sucharita's unselfconscious conversation. 'No, not at all,' he stammered somehow, despite his firm resolve not to be shy. 'You, he—me—I rather like it!'

Extracting the keys from his didi, Satish fetched the organ and presented it before the company. Inside a square glass cover, on a bed of blue fabric meant to represent ocean waves, rested a toy ship. As soon as Satish wound it up, the ship began to sway to the organ's musical rhythm. Glancing now at the ship, now at Binoy's face, Satish could not contain his excitement. In this way, little by little, Satish's mediation broke down Binoy's restraint. Gradually, Binoy even discovered it was not impossible to meet Sucharita's gaze and exchange a few remarks with her.

'Won't you bring your friend here one day?' asked Satish suddenly, out of the blue.

This led to questions about Binoy's friend. Poreshbabu and his family were new to Kolkata, and knew nothing about Gora. Speaking of his friend, Binoy grew animated. Describing Gora's rare genius, his largeness of heart and unswerving courage, he did not seem to know when to stop. Gora would one day shine above Bharatvarsha's crest like the glory of the midday sun. 'I have no doubt of that,' Binoy declared. As he spoke, his face grew radiant, and all his diffidence seemed to evaporate. In fact, he even exchanged a few arguments with Poreshbabu regarding Gora's opinions.

'If Gora can unhesitatingly accept Hindu culture in its entirety, it's because he regards Bharatvarsha from a very broad perspective,' argued Binoy. 'To him, Bharatvarsha appears in its entirety, all its features, major and minor, merged into a great unity, a vast harmony. Because all of us are not capable of such a vision, we constantly misjudge Bharatvarsha, seeing it in fragments and comparing it with foreign ideals.'

'Do you say caste discrimination is a good thing?' Sucharita asked. She spoke as if there was no scope for argument.

'Caste discrimination is neither good, nor bad,' Binoy declared. 'In other words, it is good in some situations, bad in others. If you asked me whether the hand is a good thing, I would reply that it's best judged in relation to the rest of the body. If you asked, is the hand good for flying?——I would reply in the negative; likewise, wings are not good for grasping things, either.'

'I understand nothing of all this!' exclaimed Sucharita, getting agitated. 'My question is, do you believe in caste distinctions?'

'Yes, I do!' Binoy would have emphatically asserted, had he been arguing with someone else. But now he found it hard to insist, whether from timidity, or whether his heart on this occasion was unwilling to go so far as to declare categorically: 'I believe in caste distinctions', it cannot be said for certain. Lest the argument go too far, Poresh intervened at this point.

'Radhé, send for your mother and all the others,' he said. 'Let me introduce him to them.'

Sucharita left the room, with Satish prancing along by her side as he chattered away. After a while, she returned to say: 'Baba, Ma wants you to come to the terrace upstairs.'

~*9*~

Upstairs, on the terrace above the portico, chowkis were arranged around a table covered with a white cloth. On the cornice beyond the railing, crotons and flowering plants grew in tiny flowerpots. From the terrace, one could see the rain-washed, glossy foliage of the acacia and gulmohar trees that lined the edges of the street. The sun had not yet vanished; from the western sky, the fading sunshine slanted down upon one end of the balcony.

The terrace was deserted at that hour. Soon, Satish arrived there, accompanied by a small black-and-white dog named Khudé, the tiny one. Satish had the dog display all its tricks for Binoy's benefit. It saluted with one paw, bowed its head to the ground in a pranam, knelt on its hind legs to beg for a biscuit. Satish basked in reflected glory, taking all the credit for Khudé's accomplishments. Khudé had no interest in earning such glory. In fact, the biscuit meant much more to him than fame.

From a room somewhere wafted occasional bursts of female laughter and merriment, accompanied by a single male voice. The sound of such unchecked mirth filled Binoy's heart with exquisite tenderness, mingled with aching envy. Never before in all his life had he heard such joyous female gaiety emanate from a room. The source of this sweet exuberance was so close to him, and yet he was so far removed from it! Binoy found it impossible to focus on what Satish was babbling, close to his ear.

Poreshbabu's wife now appeared on the terrace, accompanied by her three daughters. With them was a young man, a distant relative.

Poreshbabu's wife was called Borodasundari. She was not young, but had clearly dressed with special care. Having followed the provincial mode until she grew up, she had suddenly, at one point, become desperate to keep abreast of modern trends. So her silk sari rustled too much, and her high heeled shoes clattered too loudly. She was always extremely alert about the distinctions between what was Brahmo, and what was not. That was why she had changed Radharani's name to Sucharita. One of the elders in her in-laws' family, having returned after a long stint of work abroad, had sent them presents for the Jamaisashthi ritual in honour of sons-in-law. Poreshababu was away on business at the time. Borodasundari had returned all the Jamaisashthi gifts. She regarded such things as social evils, forms of idol-worship. She considered it a part of the Brahmo worldview for women to sport socks or hats when going outdoors. But seeing people use asanas on the floor at a Brahmo family meal, she had voiced the fear that the Brahmo Samaj was now lapsing back into idol-worship.

Labanya was her eldest daughter. She was chubby and jovial, fond of company and conversation. Round of face, with large eyes and a dark, glowing complexion, she was by nature careless about her dress and appearance, but had to follow her mother's dictates in such matters. Though uncomfortable in high-heeled shoes, she had no choice but to wear them. When it was time for the evening toilette, her mother personally powdered her face and patted colour on her cheeks. Because she was somewhat plump, Borodasundari had her blouses stitched so tight that Labanya emerged looking like a trussed-up machine-stuffed jute sack.

The second daughter was named Lalita. Taller than her didi, thinner and darker, she could be described as the very opposite of the elder daughter. She said little and followed her own whims, and could be sharp-tongued if she chose. Borodasundari was secretly scared of her, and usually did not dare to provoke her.

The youngest, Leela, was about ten years of age, a tomboy, always engaged in physical tussles with Satish. In particular, the two of them had not yet agreed upon the true ownership of Khudé the dog. Had the dog been consulted, he would probably not have chosen either; but still, between the two, he probably had a slight preference for Satish. For it was not easy for this tiny creature to withstand the force of Leela's caresses. It was relatively easier for him to tolerate the boy's authority rather than the girl's affection.

As soon as Borodasundari appeared, Binoy arose and bent to greet her with a pranam.

'It was at his house, the other day, that we . . .' Poreshbabu explained.

'Oh!' said Boroda. 'You were a great help. Many thanks.'

Binoy was too embarrassed to reply. He was also introduced to the young man named Sudhir who had accompanied the girls. He was in college, studying for his B.A. degree. His appearance was pleasant, his complexion fair; he wore glasses, and had a thin moustache on his upper lip. He seemed extremely restless, unable to sit still for long, always rearing to go. He would constantly joke with the girls and tease them, never allowing them a moment's peace. The girls, too, would keep reprimanding him, yet they could not

manage without Sudhir. He was always ready to take them to
the circus or the Zoological Gardens, or to buy them something
they fancied. Sudhir's easy familiarity with women struck
Binoy as a complete novelty, quite amazing. At first he
metally condemned such behaviour, but a tinge of envy began
to colour this critical attitude.

'I think I have seen you at the Samaj, once or twice,'
Borodasundari remarked.

Binoy felt as if he had been caught out in some crime.
'Yes, I go there sometimes, to listen to Keshabbabu's lectures,'
he admitted, with unwarranted embarrassment.

'You're a college student I suppose?' Borodasundari
inquired.

'No, I am not in college anymore.'

'What is the extent of your college education?'

'I have received my M.A. degree.'

Borodasundari felt a certain respect for this boyish-looking
young man. 'If my Monu had been here today, he too would
have acquired an M.A. degree by now,' she sighed, glancing
at Poresh.

Boroda's first child Monoranjan had died at nine.
Whenever she heard of any young man obtaining a major
degree, attaining a high professional position, writing a good
book, or doing something worthwhile, Boroda would
immediately assume that if Monu had lived, he would have
accomplished exactly the same things. But since he was no
more, it was now one of Borodasundari's special duties to
publicize the talents of her three daughters. She made a point
of informing Binoy that her daughters were studying very
hard. Nor was he left in the dark as to how their white
governess, the mem, had praised the daughters' intelligence
and accomplishments on various occasions. Binoy was also
told of the time when Labanya had been specially selected
from among all the girls in her school, to present flowers to
the Lieutenant Governor and his wife when they visited the

girls' school on prize-distribution day; and of the sweet words of encouragement that the Governor's wife had spoken to Labanya.

'Ma, my little one, fetch your prize-winning piece of embroidery!' Boroda urged Labanya, finally. A parrot, embroidered in silk, had gained considerable fame among relatives and friends of the family. Labanya had created this piece long ago with the mem's assistance; nor did Labanya herself deserve much of the credit for this work of art; but it was taken for granted that every new acquaintance must be shown this creation. Poresh would object at first, but now he no longer resisted, realizing the futility of such protests. As Binoy gazed in wide-eyed amazement at the artistry that had produced the silken parrot, the bearer brought a letter for Poresh.

'Bring Babu upstairs,' Poreshbabu instructed, cheering up as he read the letter.

'Who is it?' Boroda wanted to know.

'My childhood friend Krishnadayal has sent his son to meet us,' Poresh informed her.

Binoy's heart suddenly skipped a beat, and his face grew pale. The next moment, he clenched his fists and stiffened his body, as if bracing himself for a confrontation with some adversary. He seemed already flustered, anticipating that Gora would view this family with disrespect, and pass judgement on them.

~10~

Having arranged tea and snacks on a khunche, Sucharita handed the small tray to the attendant and came up to the terrace. At that moment, Gora also arrived on the scene, escorted by the bearer.

Everyone was wonderstruck at Gora's tall, fair figure and his attire. His forehead was marked with a tilak of sacred Ganga soil. He wore a coarse dhoti, a knotted upper garment and a wrap made of rough fabric. His feet were shod in Cuttack shoes with pointed, curling toes. He was the living image of rebellion against the modern age. Even Binoy had never seen him in such garb.

Gora's heart was indeed aflame with revolt today. He had reason to feel rebellious. The previous day, a steamer-company had set out at dawn with a group of passengers going to Triveni for their ritual holy bath during the eclipse. On the way, hordes of female passengers boarded at each station, accompanied by a few male guardians. The urgency of finding a place caused a great deal of pushing and shoving. With their muddy feet, some lost their balance during the tussle and fell off the boarding plank into the water in an unguarded moment; some were pushed off by the seamen; some managed to clamber on board, but were desperate because their companions had been left behind; sometimes, a shower of rain would drench their bodies; their seating area on board was soiled with mud. Their expression was anxious, agitated and pathetic. They were feeble, but knew they were so insignificant that nobody, from oarsmen to captain, would offer them the slightest assistance in response to their pleas; hence there was a terrified pathos in their struggles. In this situation, Gora was trying to help the passengers as much as possible. On the first class deck above, an Englishman and a Bengali of the modern breed were leaning on the railing, engaged in good-humoured conversation, watching the entertaining spectacle as they smoked their cigars. From time to time, seeing a passenger suffer some sudden mishap, the Englishman would burst out laughing, and the Bengali would also join in his mirth. Having crossed two or three stations in this fashion, Gora could bear it no longer. He ascended to the upper deck.

'Shame on you! Aren't you ashamed of yourselves?' he roared in his thunderous voice.

The Englishman glared at Gora, surveying him from head to toe.

'Ashamed?' the Bengali replied. 'One is ashamed of all the idiots in this country, no better than animals!'

'There can be people even more bestial than idiots; they are the ones with no heart!' retorted Gora, his colour high.

'You don't belong here!' cried the Bengali, enraged. 'This place is reserved for first class passengers!'

'No, you and I don't belong together,' replied Gora. 'My place is with those passengers over there. But let me warn you in parting, don't compel me to enter this class of yours again.'

With these words, Gora marched down to the lower level. The Englishman immersed himself in a novel, lounging on the armchair with his legs on the armrests. His Bengali co-passenger made a couple of attempts to revive their conversation, but failed to generate much warmth. To prove that he did not belong to the ordinary masses, he sent for the khansama and enquired if any chicken dish was available.

'No, only bread-and-butter with tea,' replied the attendant.

'Their arrangements for our creature comforts are appalling!' complained the Bengali in English, for the Englishman's benefit. The Englishman did not reply. A gust of wind blew his newspaper off the table. The Bengali babu rose to pick it up, but received no thanks. While disembarking at Chandannagar, the saheb suddenly went up to Gora and raised his hat.

'I'm sorry about the way I behaved,' he apologized. 'I hope you will forgive me.' He hurried away.

But Gora seethed with indignation at the arrogance of an educated Bengali who could invite a foreigner to join him in mocking at the plight of the masses. Gora's heart seemed to burst with anguish at the deep-seated, nationwide ignorance at the root of his countrymen's submission to all sorts of humiliation and ill-treatment, for even when abused like animals, all of them would accept it as natural and appropriate. But what galled him most was the educated class's indifference towards the nation's constant degradation and misery. Such people could heartlessly remain aloof and bask in glory without any qualms. When he came and stood proudly before the Brahmo family, it was to show his complete disregard for the bookish and imitative ways of the educated class that Gora had applied Ganga-soil to his forehead and bought an odd pair of Cuttack sandals to wear. Binoy privately sensed that Gora had come armed for battle. Uncertain of what Gora might do, Binoy felt a sense of apprehension, mingled with embarrassment and a will to resist.

While Borodasundari was conversing with Binoy, Satish had been obliged to amuse himself, spinning a tin top in a corner of the terrace. When he saw Gora, his top-spinning came to a halt; he crept close to Binoy and stared at Gora. 'Is this your friend?' he whispered to Binoy.

'Yes.'

When Gora arrived on the terrace, he glanced at Binoy's face for a fraction of a second, but after that, seemed not to notice him at all. Greeting Poresh with a namaskar, he dragged a chowki away from the table and seated himself without any embarrassment. He deemed it uncivil to notice the presence of women anywhere on the scene. Borodasundari had almost decided to take her daughters away from this uncouth person's company, when Poresh informed her:

'This is Gourmohan, my friend Krishnadayal's son.'

Gora now turned to greet her with a namaskar. Although Sucharita had already heard about Gora from Binoy, she had not realized that this visitor was indeed Binoy's friend. At very first sight, she resented Gora. It was not in her upbringing or temperament to tolerate such extreme Hindu fanaticism in a person with an English education.

Poresh asked Gora for news of his childhood friend Krishnadayal. Then, speaking of his own student days, he mused: 'We were quite a twosome those days. Great iconoclasts, we believed in nothing. We only considered dining at restaurants a worthwhile duty. How many evenings we'd spend at Goldighi, devouring kababs from a Muslim shop, arguing into the wee hours about ways to reform Hindu society!'

'What does he do now?' Borodasundari wanted to know.

'Now he follows the Hindu code,' Gora informed her.

'Isn't he ashamed of himself?' asked Boroda, aflame with rage.

'Shame is a sign of weakness,' smiled Gora. 'Some people are ashamed of acknowledging their own fathers.'

'Wasn't he a Brahmo earlier?' Boroda inquired.

'Even I was a Brahmo once,' Gora retorted.

'Do you believe in image worship now?'

'I am not superstitious enough to disrespect the concept of embodied form without any reason. Does form diminish if abused? Has anyone penetrated the mystery of form?'

'But form is finite,' Poreshbabu gently pointed out.

'Without finitude, there can be no expression,' Gora argued. 'The infinite takes refuge in the finite only to manifest itself, else how would it find expression? That which remains unexpressed cannot be complete. The formless finds completion in form, just as the idea is fulfilled in words.'

'Would you say that form is more complete than the formless?' exclaimed Boroda, shaking her head.

'Even if I didn't say so, it would make no difference. The status of form in this world does not depend upon what I say. If the formless were truly complete, there would be no place for form at all.'

Sucharita longed for someone to utterly vanquish this high-handed young man in argument, leaving him humiliated. She was secretly angry with Binoy for listening to Gora in silence. Gora spoke so forcefully that Sucharita also felt a powerful inward urge to subdue him.

Just then, the bearer arrived with a kettle of hot water for tea. Sucharita got up and busied herself making tea. Every now and then Binoy shot a quick glance at her face. Although Gora and Binoy did not differ much in their views about forms of worship, Binoy was troubled at the way Gora was unhesitatingly flaunting his contrary views before this Brahmo family, after joining them uninvited. In contrast to Gora's militant behaviour, the elderly Poresh's manner displayed a self-contained calm, a profound grace transcending all argument, which filled Binoy's heart with devotion. 'Opinions don't matter,' he told himself. 'For the mind and soul, wholeness, stability and self-satisfaction are the rarest values of all. Much as we may argue about the truth or falsehood of words, when it comes to attainment, only the truth is real.' In the midst of the conversation, Poresh habitually closed his eyes from time to time, to sound the depths of his own heart. At such moments, Binoy closely observed his self-absorbed, tranquil expression. He was extremely disturbed at Gora's failure to restrain his words in deference to this old man.

Sucharita poured a few cups of tea, and glanced at Poresh, unsure who should receive their hospitality.

'You won't accept anything to eat, will you?' Borodasundari blurted out pointedly, looking at Gora.

'No.'

'Why?' asked Borodasundari. 'Will you lose your caste purity?'

'Yes,' Gora replied.

'Do you believe in caste?' Boroda inquired.

'Is caste of my own making, that I should reject it?' Gora

demanded. 'If I believe in my community, I must believe in caste as well.'

'Must you believe in everything the community prescribes?'

'To disbelieve would be to destroy the community.'

'What harm in that?'

'What harm in sawing off the very branch we occupy?'

'Ma, why argue in vain?' protested Sucharita, inwardly disgusted. 'He will not accept any food that we have touched.'

For a moment, Gora rested his sharp gaze upon Sucharita's face.

'Will you . . .?' faltered Sucharita, looking at Binoy.

Binoy never drank tea. Long back, he had also given up bread and biscuits prepared by Muslims. But today he had no choice. 'Yes, indeed, I'll have some,' he forced himself to say, raising his head. He glanced at Gora. A faint sneer appeared on Gora's lips. The tea tasted bitter upon Binoy's tongue, but he swallowed it nevertheless.

'Aha, this Binoy is such a nice boy!' said Borodasundari to herself. She turned her back on Gora and devoted all her attention to Binoy. Noticing this, Poresh drew his chowki close to Gora and began to converse with him in a low voice.

Presently, a hawker came down the street, selling warm, roasted peanuts. Hearing his call, Leela clapped her hands in delight. 'Sudhirda, please send for the peanut-seller!' she pleaded. Satish at once began calling out to the peanut-seller from the terrace.

Meanwhile, another gentleman joined them. Everyone greeted him as Panubabu, but his real name was Haranchandra Nag. Within their circle, he was known for his learning and intellect. Neither side had said anything definite, but the likelihood of his marrying Sucharita was in the air. That Panubabu was attracted to Sucharita was something no one doubted, and the girls never spared a chance to tease Sucharita about it. Panubabu taught at a school. Because he was a mere schoolmaster, Borodasundari did not respect him much. Her manner indicated it was just as well Panubabu had not dared to express a preference for one of *her* daughters. Her future sons-in-law must vow to attain a deputyship, a feat of marksmanship as challenging as the legendary lakshyabheda.

When Sucharita pushed a teacup towards Haran, Labanya smirked at her from afar. That smirk did not escape Binoy's notice. Very quickly, his eye had grown quite sharp and alert in certain matters, though he had not been known earlier for his acuity of vision. Haran and Sudhir had known the girls in this house for so long and were so closely involved in their family history, they had become the subject of secret signals between the sisters. This now struck Binoy as a painful instance of divine injustice.

Meanwhile, Sucharita felt more hopeful, now that Haran had arrived. She could overcome her indignation only if someone curbed Gora's arrogance somehow. Previously, she had often been irritated by Haran's argumentativeness, but now, upon seeing this champion debater, she delightedly plied him with tea and bread.

'Panubabu, meet our . . .' Poresh began.

'I know him very well,' Haran interrupted. 'He was once a very enthusiastic member of our Brahmo Samaj.' With these words, he turned to his cup of tea, making no attempt at conversation with Gora.

At that time, only a couple of Bengalis had come to these parts after entering the civil services. Sudhir spoke of the welcome that one of them had received.

'However successful they may be at passing examinations, Bengalis are incapable of doing any work,' Haran declared. To prove that no Bengali magistrate or judge would be able to discharge his duties after assuming charge of a district, he began to analyze the faults and weaknesses of the Bengali nature.

In no time, Gora's face reddened in fury. 'If that is indeed your opinion, aren't you ashamed to sit at this table, chewing bread?' he demanded, restraining his lion-like roar as far as possible.

'What do you suggest I should do?' asked Haran, raising his eyebrows in surprise.

'Either erase the blot on the Bengali character, or go hang yourself. Is it so easy to declare that our race will forever remain good for nothing? Didn't you choke on your bread, saying such things?'

'Should I not speak the truth?' Haran retorted.

'No offence meant, but if you really took it to be true, you could never have stated it so casually, with such arrogance. It's because you know them to be false that such words could pass your lips. Haranbabu, uttering falsehoods is a sin, making false accusations is a greater sin, and there are few sins to match that of falsely condemning one's own community.'

Haran was beside himself with fury.

'Are you, alone, superior to your entire community?' Gora asked. 'You, alone, have the right to be angry, whilst all of us must tolerate all your remarks on our ancestors' behalf?'

Now it became even harder for Haran to admit defeat. His condemnation of Bengalis grew even more shrill. Referring to sundry Bengali social customs, he declared: 'As long as such things prevail, there is no hope for Bengalis.'

'Your account of social evils is merely learned by rote from English books,' Gora asserted. 'You yourself know nothing of such practices. You should voice your opinions on this subject only when you are capable of expressing a similar contempt for all English malpractices.'

Poresh tried to change the subject, but there was no restraining the incensed Haran. The sun went down. From within the clouds, an exquisite rosy glow lit up the sky. Overriding the babble of argument, a certain melody stirred

Binoy's soul. To attend to his evening prayers, Poresh left the terrace for a paved platform beneath the large champa tree at one end of the garden.

While Borodasundari had developed an aversion to Gora, she was also not particularly fond of Haran. When she could no longer bear the argument between them, she called out:

'Come, Binoybabu, let us go indoors.'

Borodasundari's affectionate partiality compelled Binoy to leave the terrace and go indoors. Boroda called the girls to join her. Sensing which way the argument was going, Satish had already vanished with Khudé, on the pretext of getting a small serving of peanuts.

Borodasundari began to sing her daughters' praises to Binoy. 'Why don't you fetch that notebook of yours, for Binoybabu to see?' she proposed to Labanya.

Labanya had grown used to displaying this notebook to all new acquaintances who visited them. In fact, she now looked forward to such occasions. This evening, she had been upset at the argument that had developed. Opening the notebook, Binoy found inscribed in it the poems of Moore and Longfellow. The handwriting was neat and laborious. The titles of the poems and the first letter of every line were etched in Roman characters. The sight of these writings filled Binoy's heart with unfeigned wonder. In those days, it was no mean feat for girls to copy Moore's poems into their notebooks.

Observing that Binoy was suitably impressed, Borodasundari addressed her second daughter: 'Lalita, my angel, that poem of yours . . .'

'No, Ma, I can't,' protested Lalita firmly. 'I don't remember it properly.' She moved to a window at a distance, and gazed at the street.

Borodasundari explained to Binoy that Lalita remembered everything, but was too reserved to display her erudition. Recounting a few anecdotes as proof of Lalita's extraordinary learning and wit, she said Lalita had been like this since infancy, unable to shed tears even when she wanted to weep. She commented on the girl's similarity to her father in this respect.

Now it was Leela's turn. As soon as she was asked, she burst into a peal of laughter. Then like a clockwork organ, she rattled off the nursery rhyme *Twinkle twinkle little star*, all in one breath, without understanding a word of it. Realizing it was now time to display their musical talent, Lalita left the room.

Out on the terrace, the argument had gone out of hand. In a fit of rage, Haran was on the verge of abandoning argument for abuse. Embarrassed and annoyed at his lack of restraint, Sucharita had taken Gora' side. Haran did not find this comforting or soothing at all. The sky grew heavy with darkness and rain-clouds. From the street came the call of a hawker selling jasmine garlands. Fireflies twinkled in the clustered foliage of the roadside krishnachura tree opposite the house. A deep blackness descended upon the pond next door. Done with his evening prayers, Poresh appeared on the terrace. Seeing him, both Gora and Haran subsided, feeling embarrassed.

'It's late. I'll take your leave now,' said Gora, rising to his feet.

Binoy, too, made his exit from the room and appeared on the terrace.

'Listen, you must come here whenever you like,' Poresh invited Gora. 'Krishnadayal was like a brother to me. We don't see eye to eye now, nor do we meet or correspond, but childhood friendships remain in the blood. My relationship with Krishnadayal makes me feel very close to you. May the Almighty bring you good fortune.'

At the sound of Poresh's calm, affectionate voice, Gora's heated, argumentative mood seemed to soften. When he first came there, Gora had shown scant respect for Poresh. But while taking leave, he touched Poresh's feet with genuine deference. Gora made no gesture of farewell to Sucharita. He thought it uncivil to make any move acknowledging her presence. Binoy bowed at Poresh's feet, and turning to Sucharita, offered a namaskar before quickly stepping out after Gora.

Avoiding these farewell greetings, Haran went indoors, picked up a book of Brahmosangeet from the table, and began to leaf through the musical score. As soon as Binoy and Gora had left, he hastened to the terrace. 'Sir, I don't like the idea of your introducing the girls to all and sundry,' he told Poresh.

Sucharita was seething inwardly. 'If Baba had followed that rule, we couldn't have met you, either,' she protested, unable to restrain herself.

'It is best to confine introductions to our own circle,' Haran declared.

'You wish to extend the inner quarters of the home, to create an antahpur within society,' smiled Poresh. 'But I believe the girls should mingle with gentlemen of various persuasions, or we'd be deliberately curbing their intellect. I see no cause for anxiety or shame in this.'

'I don't say girls shouldn't mingle with people of diverse views, but these people lack the civility to know how to conduct themselves with girls,' Haran expostulated.

'No, no, how can you say that!' cried Poresh. 'What you call lack of civility is merely an awkwardness that cannot be overcome unless one mingles with the female sex.'

'Listen, Panubabu, during today's argument I felt ashamed at the way members of our own community behaved!' declared Sucharia indignantly.

At this moment, Leela came running to her. 'Didi! Didi!' she cried, and dragged Sucharita indoors by the hand.

~11~

Haran had been particularly keen that day to humiliate Gora, to flaunt his own victory before Sucharita. At first, that was also what Sucharita had wanted. But by a quirk of fate, quite the opposite happened. In religious faith and social perspective, Sucharita differed from Gora. But affinity with her nation and sympathy for her countrymen came naturally to her. Although she did not always involve herself in political issues, Gora's sudden, thundering outburst against criticism of his own people had struck an answering chord in her heart. Never before had she heard anyone speak of the nation so forcefully and with such conviction. Generally, our countrymen like to wax eloquent about our nation and its people, but they don't have a deep, sincere belief in such ideas. However lyrical their patriotic utterances, they have no faith in the nation. But Gora could look beyond all the sorrows, travails and weaknesses of our land to perceive the manifestation of a great truth. That was why, without ignoring its impoverished state, he still cherished such strong reverence for the country. He was so firmly convinced of the nation's intrinsic power, that in his company, listening to the unquestioning patriotism of his utterances, skeptics were compelled to admit defeat. Confronted with Gora's unqualified faith, Haran's contemptuous arguments struck Sucharita as painfully insulting. Throwing decorum to the winds, she could not refrain from protesting indignantly at certain moments. Later in Gora and Binoy's absence, when Haran, in a fit of petty jealousy, accused them of being uncivil, Sucharita felt compelled to take Gora's side against such unfair meanness.

Not that Sucharita's heart had completely ceased to rebel against Gora. Even now, she felt inwardly offended by Gora's rather overstated, flagrant display of Hindu orthodoxy. She could somehow sense that this Hindu fanaticism had a perverse quality; neither natural and peaceful, nor replete with personal devotion, but constantly and aggressively militating against others.

That evening, in all her words and actions, at dinnertime, and during Leela's storytime, Sucharita was constantly tormented by some unknown pain in the recesses of her heart. It was a pain she could not dismiss by any means. One can remove a thorn if one knows where it is lodged. That night Sucharita lingered alone on the terrace above the porch, trying to locate the thorn in her heart. With the night's gentle darkness, she tried to wipe away the unwarranted burning sensation within, but to no avail. The indeterminate heaviness in her heart made her want to weep, but no tears came.

That Sucharita should be tormented all this while merely because a young stranger had arrived with a tilak on his forehead, or because he could not be humbled in argument! Nothing could be more ridiculous! She dismissed this reason as utterly impossible. Then she remembered the real reason, and felt very ashamed. For three or four hours that day, Sucharita had sat opposite the young man, and had even supported his arguments from time to time, yet he appeared not to have noticed her at all, seemingly oblivious of her presence even at parting. Doubtless, it was this complete disregard that had stung Sucharita deeply. There was a shy diffidence in the behaviour of someone unaccustomed to mingling with women of other families, an awkwardness apparent in Binoy's conduct. But there was no trace of it in Gora's manner. Why did Sucharita find it impossible now, to either tolerate or dismiss his tremendous, heartless indifference? She wanted to die of shame at her own garrulity for having joined the argument with such lack of restraint, despite this great indifference. Once, when Sucharita reacted strongly to

Haran's unfair arguments, Gora had glanced at her face; there was no diffidence in that gaze, but it was also hard to gauge its meaning. Was he saying to himself, 'What a brazen girl!' or 'How arrogant of her, to join a male argument uninvited'? But if that was how he felt, what did it matter? It did not matter at all, yet Sucharita was deeply disturbed. She struggled to forget it all, to erase it from her mind, but without any success. She began to resent Gora. She longed fervently to dismiss him as a prejudiced, arrogant young man. But the memory of the self-assured gaze of that towering male figure with his thundering voice made her feel very small. Try as she would, she could not sustain her pride. Sucharita had grown accustomed to being the apple of everyone's eye. Not that she craved such affection, but why then did Gora's indifference feel so intolerable? After much thought, Sucharita concluded it was her keen desire to outwit Gora that made his unshakable indifference so painful to bear.

Thus she wrestled with her own thoughts, until it grew quite late. Everyone at home had gone to bed, putting out the lights. The door at the entrance clanged shut, indicating that the bearer was preparing to retire, having completed his chores. At this moment, Lalita appeared on the terrace, dressed for bed. She walked past Sucharita without a word and leaned on the railing in a corner of the terrace. Sucharita smiled to herself, aware that Lalita was sulking. She had completely forgotten that she was to sleep in Lalita's room that night. But Lalita was not willing to forgive a lapse of memory, for forgetting was the greatest crime of all. She was not a girl to remind one in time about one's promises. Until now, she had remained stiffly in her bed, her petulance increasing as time went by. Ultimately, when it became intolerable, she left her bed and came only to signal silently that she was still awake. Leaving her chowki, Sucharita went slowly up to Lalita and hugged her.

'Bhai Lalita, don't be angry!' she pleaded.

'No, why should I be angry?' protested Lalita, pulling herself away. 'You can stay on here if you like.'

'Come bhai, let's go to bed,' said Sucharita, tugging at her hand.

Lalita remained standing there, making no reply. Finally, Sucharita dragged her to the bedroom by force.

'Why did you take so long?' cried Lalita, in a choking voice. 'It's eleven, do you know? I've been listening to the chiming of the clock. Now you'll doze off at once, of course.'

'Bhai, I have acted wrongly tonight,' said Sucharita, drawing Lalita close.

As soon as she had acknowledged her guilt, Lalita's anger evaporated. 'Who were you thinking of all this while, all by yourself, didi?' she asked, her heart melting. 'Was it Panubabu?'

'What nonsense!' Sucharita rapped her with her forefinger.

Lalita could not stand Panubabu. Unlike her other sisters, she found it impossible to even tease Sucharita about him. It angered her to think that Panubabu wanted to marry Sucharita.

'Tell me, didi, Binoybabu is quite nice, isn't he?' she proposed, after a short silence. It would be hard to say definitely that her question was not intended to probe Sucharita's feelings.

'Yes,' replied Sucharita. 'Binoybabu is nice indeed, quite a decent person . . .' Her words did not strike the expected note.

'But whatever you might say didi,' Lalita persisted, 'I didn't like Gourmohanbabu at all. What a strange, pale colouring, and such a rigid air, as if he doesn't care for anybody in the world. What did you think of him?'

'His Hindu fanaticism is quite excessive,' observed Sucharita.

'No, no,' said Lalita, 'Meshomoshai—our maternal uncle—is a staunch Hindu after all, but in a different way. But this seems—rather strange.'

'Strange, indeed!' laughed Sucharita. The memory of Gora's image, with the tilak on his broad white forehead, made her angry. What angered her was that Gora had inscribed the tilak on his forehead as if to proclaim: 'I am different from all of you'. Only by demolishing his tremendous pride in that difference could Sucharita have overcome her indignation.

Discussion over, the two of them eventually fell asleep. At two o'clock, Sucharita woke up to find it raining heavily outside. Flashes of lightning lit up their mosquito net intermittently; the lamp in the corner had gone out. In the dark stillness of the night, listening to the sound of incessant rain, Sucharita began to feel an aching sensation in her heart. Envying Lalita who slept soundly by her side, she tossed and turned, struggling for sleep, but to no avail. Frustrated, she left her bed and stepped out. Standing at the open door, she gazed at the terrace before her. Occasional gusts of wind sprayed her body with rain. Over and over again the evening's events surfaced in her mind, recalled in minutest detail. Clear as a picture, she remembered Gora's animated face as it had appeared in the rosy sunset glow on that terrace above the portico. She recapitulated, from beginning to end, all the arguments that evening, resonant with the timbre of Gora's deep, powerful voice.

'I belong with those you call uneducated!' his voice rang in her ears. 'I believe in the ideas you denounce as superstition. Until you can love your country and join your own countrymen on an equal footing, I shan't tolerate the slightest criticism of the nation from your lips.'

'But in that case how will our nation be reformed?' retorted Panubabu.

'Reform!' thundered Gora. 'Reform must come much later. Love and respect are more important by far. We must unite first; then reform will follow automatically, from within.

Remaining separate, you all want to fragment the nation; alleging that the nation is full of social evils, you wish to keep aloof as a band of do-gooders. I tell you, it's my greatest desire not to separate myself from anyone else on the pretext of superiority. Afterwards, when we are one, the nation, and the Maker of its destiny, will decide which customs to retain, and which ones to discard.'

'There are customs and beliefs that prevent the unity of the nation,' countered Panubabu.

'Expecting to uproot those customs and beliefs one by one before uniting the country, is like dredging the ocean before attempting to cross it,' Gora declared. 'With humility and love, banishing contempt and arrogance, surrender yourself wholeheartedly to all, and such love will easily overcome a thousand faults and shortcomings. Every country, every society, has its faults and shortcomings, but as long as the people of a nation are bound together by love for their countrymen, they can deal with the poison. The germs of decay exist in the air. As long as we stay alive, we manage to survive them, but once dead, we succumb to decay. I tell you, we shan't brook any attempts at reform, whether from you or from the missionaries!'

'Why not?' demanded Panubabu.

'There are reasons. One can tolerate reforms imposed by one's own parents, but those imposed by watchguards are humiliating rather than corrective. It is dehumanizing to tolerate such reforms. First join the family, then assume the reformer's role. Otherwise even your well-meant observations will do us harm.'

So, one by one, Sucharita's mind recalled all the things that were said. She was also inwardly tormented by some indeterminate anguish. Exhausted, she returned to bed, and pressing her palms over her eyes, she tried to sleep, pushing her thoughts away. But her face and ears were burning, and fragments of the conversation kept haunting her mind.

~12~

As they emerged from Poresh's house and stepped into the
street, Binoy pleaded: 'Gora, please slow down bhai. Your
legs are much longer than ours; unless you shorten your
stride, we'll get exhausted trying to keep pace.'

'I want to proceed on my own,' Gora replied. 'I have
many things on my mind today.' He hurried away at his usual
rapid pace.

Binoy was hurt. He had broken his own rule and rebelled
against Gora that day. He would have felt better if Gora had
reprimanded him for it. A storm would have cleared the air,
restoring their old friendship, and he would have felt relieved.
There was something else that bothered him. When Gora
arrived suddenly at Poresh's house for the first time and saw
Binoy present there on such familiar terms, he must have
concluded that Binoy was a regular visitor there. Not that
there was anything wrong with being a frequent visitor there,
of course. Whatever Gora might say, the opportunity of
becoming intimately acquainted with Poreshbabu's well-
educated family seemed to Binoy a great advantage. If Gora
saw anything wrong in mingling with such people, his orthodox
attitude was entirely to blame. But since he had previously
heard that Binoy was not in the habit of frequenting
Poreshbabu's house, Gora might suddenly assume now that
this was not true. In particular, it had not eluded Gora's sharp
gaze, that Borodasundari had specially invited Binoy indoors,
to introduce him to her daughters. Binoy was inwardly proud
and delighted at such familiarity with the girls and such
intimacy with Borodasundari, but he was also privately troubled
at the difference between Gora's reception in this household,
and his own. Until now, nobody had hindered the deep
friendship between these two classmates. Only once, Gora's

enthusiasm about the Brahmo Samaj had cast a temporary shadow upon their friendship; but as I have said before, opinions did not carry much weight with Binoy. For all his arguments over opinions, people mattered more to him. Now, he was apprehensive because people threatened to come between the two of them. Binoy valued his relationship with Poresh's family because he had never before tasted such joy. But Gora's friendship was an organic part of Binoy's existence; he could not imagine life without it.

Until now, Binoy had not allowed any human being to come as close to him as Gora. Until today, he had only read books, argued with Gora, quarreled with Gora, and loved Gora, without the opportunity of paying any attention to anyone else in the world. Though he had no lack of devoted followers, Gora, too, had no other friend save Binoy. There was a solitary streak in Gora's nature. It was not beneath his dignity to mingle with ordinary people, yet he found it impossible to form close relationships with all and sundry. Most people could not help sensing a certain aloofness in him.

Binoy now realized that his heart was profoundly drawn to Poreshababu's family. Yet, he had not known them long. This made him feel guilty, as if he had wronged Gora in some way. He could clearly visualize Gora's contempt at Borodasundari's display of maternal pride to Binoy that evening, when she exhibited her daughters' English handwriting and artistry, and flaunted their prowess at recitation. There was indeed something ridiculous about it, and in a sense, something demeaning too, in Borodasundari's pride at her daughters having a smattering of English, receiving praise from an English mem, and being briefly patronized by the Lieutenant Governor's wife. But even though he understood these things, Binoy could not scorn them in accordance with Gora's ideals. He was rather enjoying the whole affair. That a girl like Labanya—there was no denying that she was quite pretty—

should take pride in showing him Moore's poem inscribed in her own hand, was also quite gratifying for Binoy's own self-esteem. Not that Binoy had failed to observe the incongruity of Borodasundari's excessive attempts at being up-to-date when she had not quite acquired the right shade of modernity; but he rather liked her, all the same. The simplicity of her vanity and intolerance had disarmed him. The way these girls filled the room with the sweetness of their laughter, prepared and served tea to visitors, decorated the walls with their own handiwork and relished English poetry—however trivial these things might be, Binoy was captivated by them. Never before in his rather lonely life had Binoy savoured such pleasures. These girls, with their attire and adornments, laughter and conversation, their chores and activities, conjured up countless lovely visions in his mind's eye. Immersed only in books and intellectual debate, this boy who had entered adolescence without being aware of it, now discovered a wonderful new world in Poresh's humble abode! When Gora walked away in a huff, Binoy could not regard his anger as unwarranted. Finally, their long friendship was threatened by a real obstacle.

Clouds began to rumble, causing vibrations in the dark silence of that rainy night. Binoy's heart felt very heavy. It seemed to him that his life had taken a new turn, abandoning the course it had always followed. In this darkness, where had Gora disappeared, and where was Binoy himself going? The prospect of separation makes love more intense. Now, when it had suffered a blow, Binoy realized the magnitude and force of his love for Gora.

Back home, the darkness of the night and the solitariness of his chamber filled Binoy with a heavy feeling of emptiness. He stepped out once, ready to go to Gora's house. But he could not hope, tonight, for a meeting of hearts with Gora. So he went back indoors, and lay down wearily.

When he awakened the next day, his heart felt lighter. At

night, his imagination had needlessly exaggerated his own pain. In the light of day, his friendship with Gora did not appear so directly contrary to his intimacy with Poresh's family. Binoy now wanted to laugh at the previous night's agony, dismissing it as not so grave after all!

Throwing a chador over his shoulders, he hurried to Gora's house. Gora was downstairs, reading the newspaper. He had spotted Binoy coming down the street, but did not raise his eyes from the paper when his friend arrived. Without a word, Binoy snatched the paper from Gora's hands.

'I think you are making a mistake,' Gora observed. 'I am Gourmohan, a superstitious Hindu.'

'It is you who are mistaken. I am Srijukta Binoy, the superstitious friend of the aforementioned Gourmohan.'

'But Gourmohan is so obdurate, he never feels ashamed of his superstitious nature.'

'Binoy is exactly the same. But he doesn't aggressively attack others with his own convictions.'

In no time at all, the two friends were embroiled in a heated argument. The entire neighbourhood became aware that there was a confrontation between Gora and Binoy.

'Why did you deny the other day, that you were a regular visitor to Poreshbabu's house? What was the need?' Gora demanded.

'It was not from any need, but because I am not a regular visitor there, that I denied it. After all this while, I finally set foot in their house for the first time yesterday.'

'I suspect that like Abhimanyu, you know only the way in, but not the way out.'

'That's as it may be. Perhaps that is my inborn nature. I can't abandon someone I love or respect. You, too, have encountered this trait in my nature.'

'So, from now on your visits there will continue?'

'Why should I be their only visitor? You are mobile too; it's not as if you are a motionless object.'

'I may come and go, but judging from your symptoms, you seem committed only to going there. So, how did you relish the hot tea?'

'The brew was rather bitter.'

'So?'

'Rejecting it would have felt more bitter still.'

'Is adherence to social norms merely a matter of observing civilities then?'

'Not always. But look here, Gora, where society clashes with matters of the heart, it's difficult for me to . . .'

Impatiently, Gora cut Binoy short.

'Matters of the heart!' he roared. 'It's because you belittle society that your heart feels afflicted at every juncture. If you realized how far the pain travels when you attack the community, you'd be ashamed to mention that heart of yours. It pains you to cause the slightest offence to Poreshbabu's daughters, but it pains me that you should so casually attack the entire nation for so slight a reason.'

'Bhai Gora, let me speak the truth, then. If drinking a cup of tea wounds the entire nation, then the nation must benefit from this assault. If shielded from such a blow, the nation would be enfeebled, like an effeminate babu of the respectable class.'

'I am familiar with all those arguments, mister! Don't think me so obtuse. But these things are not new. When a sick boy refuses his medicine, his mother takes the medicine herself though she is in good health, just to signal that she shares his plight; it is not a rational argument, but a show of love. Without such love, despite all the arguments in the world, the mother-son bond would suffer. Then the medicine wouldn't work either. I too wouldn't quibble about that cup of tea, but I can't bear to be alienated from the nation. Easier by far to refuse the tea, for offending Poreshbabu's daughters is a matter of far less significance. At present, it's our primary duty to unite wholeheartedly in the nation's cause. Once such unity is achieved, all arguments about accepting or refusing tea will be settled in no time.'

'I must wait very long for my second cup of tea, it seems!' Binoy observed.

'No, you need not wait too long. But, Binoy, why continue with me? Along with many other unpleasant features of Hindu society, it's time to discard me, as well. Else, you would offend Poreshbabu's daughters.'

At this moment, Abinash entered the room. He was Gora's disciple. He would broadcast whatever he heard Gora say, demeaned by his own intellect and distorted by his own use of language. Those who could not comprehend Gora's words found it easy to understand and praise what Abinash said. Abinash was extremely jealous of Binoy. Hence, he would foolishly take every opportunity to draw Binoy into an argument. Binoy would lose patience with his idiocy. Then, Gora would take up cudgels on Abinash's behalf and fight Binoy. Abinash would imagine that Gora was acting as his mouthpiece.

Abinash's arrival interrupted Binoy's exchange with Gora on the subject of union. He rose to his feet and went upstairs. Anandamoyi was chopping vegetables on the veranda outside the larder.

'I have been hearing your voices for a long time,' she remarked. 'What brings you here so early? I hope you had a snack before you set out?'

On another occasion, Binoy would have said, 'No, I haven't eaten,' and relished being fed in Anandamoyi's presence. But today, he declared:

'No, Ma, I shan't have anything to eat. I ate before I left home.'

Today, Binoy had no urge to aggravate his guilt in Gora's eyes. He was inwardly troubled at the thought that Gora was keeping him at arm's length, unable to forgive him for socializing with Poreshababu. Taking a knife from his pocket, he busied himself peeling potatoes.

About fifteen minutes later, he went downstairs to find that Gora had left with Abinash. For a long time, Binoy lingered quietly in Gora's room. Then, picking up the newspaper, he glanced through the advertisements absently. Presently, he left with a sigh.

~13~

At noon, Binoy again felt the urge to visit Gora. He had never felt ashamed of bending to Gora's will. But even in the absence of personal pride, the pride born of friendship is hard to withstand. In yielding to Poreshbabu, Binoy had felt guilty indeed, about failing to live up to his long-term loyalty to Gora. But he had expected only that Gora would mock and reprimand him, never imagining that his friend might try to keep him at arm's length in this fashion. Having walked some distance from his house, Binoy turned back, unable to proceed to Gora's house lest his friendship be spurned.

After lunch, Binoy settled down with pen and paper to write to Gora. Needlessly cursing the pen for its bluntness, he began to sharpen it with a knife, slowly, with excessive care, when someone called out to him from downstairs. Flinging down his pen, Binoy hurried downstairs.

'Come, Mahimdada!' he cried. 'Please come upstairs!'

In the room upstairs, Mahim made himself comfortable on Binoy's bed and carefully scrutinized the furnishings.

'Look, Binoy,' he said, 'not that I don't know your house, and occasionally I do feel the urge to look you up, but I know you boys are well-behaved, in the present-day mode.

There's no hope of finding any tobacco in your homes, so except for some special purpose . . .'

'If you're thinking of immediately sending for a new hookah from the market for my sake, please give up the idea,' Mahim continued, seeing Binoy rise hastily to his feet. 'I can forgive you for not offering me tobacco, but I can't tolerate tobacco inexpertly stuffed into a new hookah.' With these words, Mahim picked up a fan from the bed and began fanning himself.

'There is a reason why I have come to you, sacrificing my Sunday afternoon nap,' he observed. 'You must do me a favour.'

What was the favour, Binoy wanted to know.

'Give me your word first, then I'll tell you what it is.'

'Only if it's something within my power.'

'Only you have the power. You just have to say "yes", that is all.'

'Why beg me in this fashion? You know I'm one of the family. I can't deny you a favour that is within my means.'

Taking a leaf-wrapped package from his pocket, Mahim extracted a couple of paans which he handed to Binoy before stuffing the remaining three paans into his own mouth.

'You know my Shashimukhi, of course,' he remarked, chewing on the paan. 'She's not bad looking, meaning she hasn't taken after her father. She's almost ten now. It's time to arrange a match for her. I can't sleep nights, worrying about the rascally hands she might fall into.'

'Why worry? There's plenty of time.'

'If you had a daughter of your own, you'd understand my concern. Age advances automatically as the years pass, but prospective grooms don't automatically appear! So, as time passes, the heart grows ever more anxious. Now, if you were to give me some assurance, I could even wait for a while.'

'I don't know too many people,' Binoy responded. 'In

Kolkata, I know virtually no family but yours. But still, I shall make enquiries.'

'You know all about Shashimukhi's nature and temperament.'

'Indeed I do. I have known her since childhood. She is such an angel.'

'Then why look far, my boy? I shall place the girl in your hands.'

'How can you say that!' cried Binoy, in agitation.

'Why, have I said something unfair? True, your family is much more highly-placed than ours. But Binoy, what use is all your education, if you still insist on caste distinctions?'

'No, no, there's no question of caste distinctions here, but in age, she is so . . .'

'What's this you say! Shashi is hardly young! After all, a Hindu girl is not a mem. One can't afford to ignore the community, can one?'

Mahim was not one to give up easily. He pestered Binoy beyond endurance.

'Please give me some time to think!' Binoy begged, finally.

'I'm not about to fix the wedding date tonight, am I!'

'Still, consulting family members . . .'

'Indeed, that is a must. We must seek their consent, for sure. With your khuromoshai still alive, nothing can be decided against the wishes of your father's elder brother.'

Emptying the contents of the second sachet of paan from his pocket, Mahim took his leave, his manner indicating that the matter was all but clinched.

A few days earlier, Anandamoyi had indirectly hinted at a match between Shashimukhi and Binoy. But Binoy had paid no attention. Even now, it was not as if the proposal struck him as apposite, but at least the matter registered somewhere in his consciousness. Binoy felt that if this marriage were to take place, Gora could never spurn him for relying too much on matters of the heart. So far, he had always derided the idea of a love-marriage as an anglicized fetish, hence marrying Shashimukhi did not seem an impossible prospect. Meanwhile, he was pleased only that he now had a pretext to consult Gora regarding Mahim's proposal. Binoy desired some persuasion from Gora. If he did not readily consent to Mahim's proposal, he had no doubt that Mahim would try to get Gora to convince him. Thinking of these things, Binoy's lethargy evaporated. He set out at once for Gora's house, with his chador draped over his shoulder. He had walked only a short distance before he heard someone call out from behind:

'Binoybabu!' Turning around, he saw Satish. Binoy re-entered his house, accompanied by Satish

'Guess what's inside!' From his pocket, Satish produced a handkerchief knotted into a bundle.

Naming several impossible things, such as a skull or a puppy, Binoy was admonished by Satish's wagging finger. Satish then proceeded to undo the handkerchief, from which he produced four or five blackened fruits.

'Do you know what these are?' he asked.

Binoy attempted some random guesses. When he finally gave up, Satish told him that the fruits were a gift from an uncle in Rangoon to his mother, who in turn had sent five of them as a present for Binoybabu.

Mangosteens from Myanmar were not easily available in Kolkata then. Hence, feeling the fruits, Binoy asked:

'Satishbabu, how are these to be eaten?'

'Watch out! You'd better not bite into them,' laughed Satish, scornful of Binoy's ignorance. 'You're supposed to pare them with a knife.'

Satish himself had just been derided by his relatives for his futile attempts at biting into these fruits. So, he dispelled his agony by laughing knowledgably at Binoy's lack of experience.

Subsequently, after these two friends of unequal age had exchanged some banter, Satish declared:

'Binoybabu, Ma says you must drop by if you have the time today—it's Leela's birthday!'

'I have no time today, bhai. I'm going elsewhere.'

'Where?'

'To my friend's place.'

'That friend of yours?'

'Yes.'

That Binoy could visit other friends' houses but not their own seemed irrational to Satish, who had taken a particular dislike to this friend of Binoy's. He seemed harsher than a school headmaster; nobody was likely to earn any glory from playing the organ to him. That Binoy should feel the slightest need to visit such people was not to Satish's liking, at all.

'No, Binoybabu, you must come to our house,' he insisted.

Binoy had boasted to himself that he would go to Gora's house even if Poreshbabu invited him. He had decided that he would not hurt his friend's sentiments, that he would respect his friendship with Gora above all else. But it did not take him long to succumb. With a mind full of doubts and a heart full of objections, he ultimately allowed the boy to lead him by the hand towards House Number 78, as before. It was impossible for Binoy to ignore the sense of kinship expressed in the sharing of rare Myanmar fruits thoughtfully sent to him.

Approaching Poreshbabu's house, Binoy saw Panubabu emerge from within, accompanied by some unknown people. They had been invited to Leela's birthday lunch. Panubabu walked past Binoy, as if he had not noticed him at all. Entering the house, Binoy was greeted with sounds of laughter and running feet. Sudhir had stolen Labanya's keys; not only that, he was threatening devilishly to divulge to the vulgar world the comic details of the would-be-poetess' writings in the notebook within her drawer. The two sides were locked in battle when Binoy entered the arena. Seeing him, Labanya's group vanished at once. Satish ran after them, to take part in their merriment.

After a while, Sucharita came in. 'Ma has requested you to wait awhile,' she said. 'She'll join you in a few moments. Baba has gone to Anathbabu's; he won't be long, either.'

To quell Binoy's awkwardness, Sucharita spoke of Gora. 'I don't suppose he'd ever visit us again!' she smiled.

'Why not?'

'He must have been surprised that we appear before male company. He probably can't respect women if he sees them in any situation but a domestic one.'

Binoy found this hard to refute. He would have liked to contradict it, but how could he lie?

'It is Gora's belief that unless completely absorbed in housework, women lose their devotion to duty,' he replied.

'Then why not let men and women carve up the world into private and public spaces, once and for all?' demanded Sucharita. 'Perhaps it's because men have access into private areas that they fail in their public duties? Do you also subscribe to your friend's views?'

So far, Binoy had indeed supported Gora's views regarding rules for women. He had even published newspaper articles on the subject. But now, he found it hard to declare these views his own.

'In these matters, we are slaves of custom,' he insisted. 'That's why the sight of women venturing out in public makes us uneasy. We merely try to prove by forceful argument that it offends us as something improper, a violation of duty. The argument here is merely a pretext; it's the convention that is real.'

'Such conventions seem firmly ingrained in your friend's mind,' Sucharita observed.

'So it may seem momentarily, if viewed from outside,'

Binoy replied. 'But please bear in mind that if he clings to the traditions of our country, it's not because he thinks them the best. It's because we were ready to dismiss all our land's customs out of a blind disrespect for our country, that he has taken it upon himself to stem the tide. He says we must first possess and understand our nation as a whole, through respect and love. Subsequently, the process of reform will begin automatically from within, according to the natural rules of health.'

'If it was automatic, why didn't it happen in all these years?' Sucharita asked.

'It didn't happen because until now, we were unable to perceive our nation or our community as a unified whole. We may not have disrespected our own race then, but we showed them no respect either. In other words, we ignored them, hence their power was not aroused. The patient was neglected once, denied any treatment or medication. Now, he has been taken to the hospital indeed, but apart from amputating his limbs one by one, the doctor is too disdainful to patiently prescribe a long-term course of treatment based on nursing. Now another doctor, this friend of mine, insists: 'I cannot bear to allow my close relative to be utterly destroyed by such treatment. I shall stop these surgical procedures, and by means of a suitably wholesome diet, arouse the life-spirit within the patient's soul. Subsequently, the patient will be able to withstand surgery, or even recover without such procedures.' According to Gora, profound respect is the most potent diet for our nation's present predicament. It is lack of such respect that prevents us from a unified vision of our country, and it is due to lack of such awareness that all our attempts at redressal prove counterproductive. Without loving our nation, we can't have the patience to understand it properly. And without understanding it properly, we cannot benefit the country, despite all our good intentions.'

Unobtrusively, with her probing comments, Sucharita ensured that the discussion about Gora continued. Binoy also presented his defense of Gora in the best manner possible. He had never argued so cogently and with such vivid examples; it is doubtful whether Gora himself could have declared his own views with such clarity and brilliance. Exhilarated by his own cleverness and powers of expression, Binoy began to enjoy himself, and his face glowed with pleasure.

'*Atmanam biddhi*: know thyself, the scriptures say,' he argued. 'There is no other path to liberation. My friend Gora is Bharatvarsha's self-awareness incarnate, I tell you. I cannot take him for an ordinary man. While all our minds are scattered in the external realm, seduced by the petty lure of novelty, this man alone stands firm amidst all this frenzy, chanting in his leonine voice that same ancient mantra: *atmanam biddhi*.'

This discussion could have lasted much longer, and Sucharita too, was listening avidly, but suddenly, from the adjacent room, Satish began to recite in a loud voice:

> Say not in sorrow, without pausing to reflect,
> That the world's an illusion, and life but a dream.

Poor Satish never got to display his learning before visitors to the house. Even Leela could arouse the audience with her recitation of English verse, but Borodasundari never sent for Satish. Yet Leela and Satish were great rivals in every matter. It was Satish's foremost pleasure to somehow demolish Leela's pride. The previous day, Leela's talents had been tested in Binoy's presence. Uninvited there, Satish could have made no attempt to outshine her. Even if he had tried, Borodasundari would have quelled him immediately. Today, therefore, he made a show of reciting loudly from the next room, as if to himself. Hearing him, Sucharita could not refrain from mirth.

At this point, Leela came in, tossing her braids. Throwing

her arms around Sucharita's neck, she whispered something in her ear. Satish rushed in, close on her heels.

'Tell me, Leela, what does "monojog" mean?' he asked her, referring to the Bengali word for 'attentiveness'.

'I shan't tell you!' Leela replied.

'Ish! Not tell me indeed! Admit you don't know what it means!'

'You tell us what "monojog" means, then,' laughed Binoy, drawing Satish close.

'"Monojog" means "mononibesh,"' answered Satish proudly, head held high.

'And what is "mononibesh?"' Sucharita wanted to know.

Could anyone but a family member cause such embarrassment? Satish bounded out of the room as if he had not heard the question at all.

Today, Binoy had firmly resolved to leave early from Poreshbabu's house to go across to Gora's. Talking about Gora deepened his enthusiasm about visiting him. Hearing the clock strike four, he therefore rose quickly from his chowki.

'Must you leave now?' pleaded Sucharita. 'Ma is preparing some snacks for you. Can't you go a little later?'

For Binoy this was not a question, but an order. He at once resumed his place on the chowki.

'Didi, the snacks are ready,' announced Labanya, entering the room, all dressed up, in colourful silk. 'Ma wants us to go up to the terrace.'

On the terrace, Binoy had to accept the refreshments. Borodasundari began to recount the life-stories of all her offspring. Lalita dragged Sucharita indoors. On a chowki, Labanya bent her head over a piece of knitting. Somebody had once told her that when she knitted, the play of her delicate fingers was an exquisite sight; ever since, she had grown used to knitting unnecessarily in the presence of others.

Poresh arrived. It grew dark. As this was Sunday, they were supposed to go to the prayer-temple.

'Would you object to visiting the Samaj in our company?' Borodasundari asked Binoy.

After this, there could be no ifs and buts. They went to the prayer hall, all of them, in two carriages. On the way back, as they mounted the carriages, Sucharita suddenly remarked, in a startled voice:

'Look, there goes Gourmohanbabu!'

There was no doubting that Gora had spotted their group. But he hastened away as if he had not seen them at all. Gora's arrogant uncivility made Binoy cringe in shame before Poreshbabu's family. But privately, he clearly realized that it was the sight of Binoy in the group that had prompted Gora to rush away in such a hostile manner. The glow of pleasure in his heart was utterly extinguished. Sucharita instantly sensed Binoy's mood and its cause. She was again incensed at Gora for misjudging a friend like Binoy, and his unwarranted disrespect for Brahmos. She wished with all her heart that Gora could somehow be vanquished.

~14~

When Gora sat down to his meal at midday, Anandamoyi gently broached the subject:

'Binoy came by this morning. Didn't you meet him?'

'Yes, I did,' answered Gora, without looking up.

'I asked him to wait but he left, looking rather preoccupied,' resumed Anandamoyi, after a long pause.

Gora made no reply.

'Something has hurt him very deeply,' Anandamoyi asserted. 'I've never seen him like this before. I am extremely upset.'

Gora continued to eat in silence. Because she was so fond of him, Anandamoyi was also secretly a little in awe of him.

If he did not confide in her, she never pestered him about anything. On any other occasion, she would have desisted at this point. But now, because her heart was aching for Binoy, she persisted:

'Look Gora, let me tell you something. Please don't mind. Ishwar has created innumerable human beings, but he has not made just one path for everyone to follow. Because Binoy loves you with his heart and soul, he tolerates whatever you inflict on him. But if you insist that he must follow your path alone, it will not bode well.'

'Ma, please bring me some more milk,' was Gora's reply.

The conversation ended there. Meal over, Anandamoyi sewed in silence on her bed. After a futile attempt to draw her into a discussion of a particular servant's bad conduct, Lachhmia lay down on the floor and went to sleep.

Gora spent a long time over his correspondence. Amidst all his work, Gora listened for Binoy's footsteps, thinking it impossible that his friend would fail to come and pacify him, after having received a clear signal that morning that Gora was angry with him. The hours passed by, but Binoy did not come. Laying down his pen, Gora was about to rise from his desk when Mahim entered the room.

'What are your thoughts on Shashimukhi's marriage, Gora?' he asked as soon as he was seated.

Never having given the matter a single thought, Gora was forced to maintain a guilty silence. Highlighting the exorbitant price of bridegrooms in the marriage market and his own insolvency, Mahim begged Gora for a solution. When Gora failed to come up with a suggestion, Mahim sought to rescue him from his dilemma by proposing Binoy's name. Such a roundabout approach was not necessary, but whatever he might say, Mahim was privately afraid of Gora. Gora had never dreamt that Binoy's name could be mentioned in such a context. He and Binoy had resolved to remain bachelors, devoting their lives to the service of the nation.

'Why should Binoy marry?' Gora therefore expostulated.

'Is this what your Hindu beliefs are worth! For all your tikis and tilaks, your English ways are ingrained in your very bones. Are you aware that our holy shastras define marriage as an essential ritual for a Brahman boy?'

Mahim neither violated traditional customs like modern youths of today, nor cared much for the scriptures either. He considered dining in hotels to be excessively bold, but he also did not consider it normal to constantly dabble in the shastras like Gora. But one must adopt the customs of the land one's in, as the saying goes. With Gora, he was forced to use the shastras as a pretext.

Even a couple of days earlier, Gora would have dismissed this proposal out of hand. But today, the matter did not strike him as utterly dispensable. The proposal at least provided an excuse for going immediately to Binoy's house.

'Very well, let me find out what Binoy feels about this,' he agreed ultimately.

'There is nothing to find out. He can never reject a suggestion from you. The matter is virtually settled. A word from you is all that's needed.'

That very evening, though it was late, Gora arrived at Binoy's house. Storming into his friend's room, he found it empty. He summoned the bearer, who informed him that Babu had gone to House Number 78. Gora's spirits drooped. Binoy, for whom Gora had fretted all day, now did not even have the time to remember his friend! Gora might fret and fume, but it would not disturb Binoy's peace of mind at all!

Gora's soul rose in bitterness against Poreshbabu's family and the Brahmo Samaj. He rushed to Poreshbabu's house, a tremendous rebellion surging in his heart. He wanted to raise issues that would torment this Brahmo family, and make Binoy uncomfortable as well. Reaching Poreshbabu's place, he was told that no-one was home. They had all gone to the prayer hall. For a moment, he doubted that Binoy may have accompanied them. Perhaps, at this very moment, he had gone to Gora's house.

He could not restrain himself. Gora rushed to the prayer-temple at his usual stormy speed. At the entrance, he saw Binoy following Borodasundari into their carriage. In public, he was shamelessly entering a carriage in the company of women from another family! Fool that he was! To let himself be ensnared like this, in serpent-coils! So quickly! So easily! Friendship was no longer worthy of respect, then. Gora rushed away from the scene. And from the darkness of the carriage, Binoy gazed silently at the street.

Imagining that the Acharya's advice was taking effect on his mind, Borodasundari did not utter a word.

~15~

Back home, Gora paced up and down the terrace at night. He was angry with himself. Why had he wasted his Sunday in this fashion? He was not born into this world to get embroiled in one person's love affairs at the expense of all his other duties! To try holding Binoy back from the path he had taken would be a waste of time, and a painful experience as well. So, from now on, he must exclude Binoy from his life. Giving up his only friend, Gora would prove his faith true. With this resolve, Gora gestured violently with his arms, as if pushing away his association with Binoy.

At this moment, Mahim appeared on the terrace, panting.

'Why build a three-storey house when humans don't have wings?' he protested. 'The gods in the heavens don't like it if human beings, creatures of the soil, attempt to inhabit the sky. Did you see Binoy?'

'Binoy cannot marry Shashimukhi,' declared Gora, avoiding a direct reply.

'Why? Is Binoy unwilling?'

'I am unwilling.'

'How extraordinary!' exclaimed Mahim, spreading his hands. 'Here's a new twist, I see! So you are unwilling! May I know why?'

'I see clearly that it will be hard to keep Binoy within our community. We can't let him marry one of our girls.'

'I've seen a lot of Hindu fanaticism, but nothing to match this. You surpass even the Hindus of Kashi and Bhatpara! Your rulings are based on future predictions, I find. One of these days, you will prescribe swallowing cowdung to restore my caste purity, just because you've dreamt of my conversion to Christianity!'

After much ranting, Mahim said: 'I can't marry the girl to an illiterate, after all! An educated, intelligent young man is bound to circumvent the shastras sometimes. Argue with him, curse him if you like, but why punish my daughter by preventing his marriage? All your ideas are totally perverse!'

'Ma, please restrain this Gora of yours!' Mahim went downstairs and begged Anandamoyi.

'Why, what's the matter?' asked Anandamoyi anxiously.

'I had almost fixed a match between Shashimukhi and Binoy. I had even got Gora to agree to it. But meanwhile, Gora has understood clearly that Binoy is not Hindu enough, because he deviates occasionally from the views of Manu and Parashar. So Gora has dug his heels in, and you know what he's like when he chooses to be obdurate. In today's depraved world, this Kaliyug of ours, if Janak were to decree that he would offer Sita's hand only to a suitor who could make Gora unbend, I can wager that Shri Rama would have failed. After Manu-Parashar, you are the person Gora respects the most. Now, if you find a way, my girl's future will be assured. Search as we might, another such suitor is not to be found.'

Mahim proceeded to recount all that had passed between him and Gora on the terrace. Sensing the developing hostility between Binoy and Gora, Anandamoyi was distressed. Going upstairs, she found that Gora, having stopped pacing the terrace, was reading on one chowki, his feet propped up on another. Anandamoyi drew up a chowki close to him. Lowering his feet, Gora sat upright and glanced at her face.

'Gora, my boy, you must keep a request of mine,' Anandamoyi pleaded. 'Don't quarrel with Binoy. To me, you two are like brothers. I can't bear the prospect of a split.'

'If a friend wants to sever our ties, I can't waste my time running after him.'

'Baba, I don't know what has occurred between you two. But if you can believe that Binoy wants to sever his ties with you, then what's your friendship worth?'

'Ma, I prefer to be direct. I can't hold with those who equivocate. If it's in a person's nature to have one foot in each boat, he must step off the boat that is mine, even if it hurts me or the person concerned.'

'Tell me what the matter is,' Anandamoyi insisted. 'His only crime is having visited a Brahmo home occasionally, isn't it?'

'It's a long story, Ma.'

'So what? Let me tell you Gora, you are so obstinate in all matters, that no one can divert you from your chosen course. But why are you so detached only where Binoy is concerned? If your Abinash wanted to leave your group, would you let him go so easily? Is it because Binoy is your friend that he means least of all to you?'

Gora lapsed into a thoughtful silence. Anandamoyi's words made him clearly understand his own feelings. He had imagined all this while that he was ready to sacrifice his friendship for duty's sake, but now he realized it was quite the contrary. It was because his pride as a friend had been wounded that he was about to inflict on Binoy the ultimate punishment possible in a friendship. He had assumed that friendship alone would keep Binoy bound to him; any other method would be an insult to their mutual affection.

As soon as Anandamoyi sensed that her words had had some effect on Gora, she gently prepared to rise, without saying more. Gora too, jumped to his feet suddenly, and taking his chador from the alna, he flung it across his shoulder.

'Where are you going, Gora?' Anandamoyi enquired.

'To Binoy's.'

'Your meal is ready. Please dine before you set out.'

'I'll go get Binoy. He'll dine with us too.'

Anandamoyi went downstairs, without saying more. Hearing footsteps on the stairs, she stopped suddenly.

'Here comes Binoy!' she exclaimed.

As she spoke, Binoy arrived on the scene. Anandamoyi's eyes grew moist.

'Binoy, baba, haven't you dined yet?' she asked, patting him tenderly.

'No, Ma.'

'You must dine with us,' Anandamoyi insisted.

Binoy glanced at Gora.

'You'll have a long life, Binoy,' Gora remarked. 'I was just going to your place.'

Anandamoyi's felt light-hearted with relief. She hurried downstairs.

Once the two friends had moved indoors, Gora made a random remark:

'Do you know, I've found a good gymnastics coach for our boys. He's training them quite well.'

Neither of them dared raise the subject closest to their hearts. At dinner, Anandamoyi sensed from their conversation that the veil of constraint had not yet been lifted.

'It's very late, Binoy,' she observed. 'Sleep here tonight. I'll send word to your house.'

'*Bhuktwa rajabadacharet*,' quoted Binoy in Sanskrit, after darting a swift glance at Gora's countenance. 'One should not walk the streets after a meal. So one may as well sleep here tonight.'

After dinner, the two friends went to the terrace and settled on a madur. It was the month of Bhadra; moonlight flooded the sky, for it was the bright quarter of the lunar cycle. Flimsy white clouds floated gently across the sky, blurring the moon occasionally, like short spells of drowsiness. Rows of rooftops of varying shapes and sizes stretched to the horizon in every direction, their outlines sometimes merging with the treetops in the play of light and shade, the scene resembling a vast, needless fantasy. The church clock struck eleven; the ice-seller called out his wares for the last time, and departed. The hum of traffic had dwindled. In Gora's street, there was no sign of wakefulness. There was only the occasional sound of horse hooves on the wooden floor of the neighbour's stable, or every now and then, the barking of dogs.

Both of them were silent for a long time. Then Binoy, after some initial hesitation, ultimately poured out his inner feelings, in full force, without restraint.

'Bhai Gora, my heart is full to bursting. I know you have no taste for such things, but I'll die if I don't unburden myself. I can't tell good from evil anymore, but one thing is certain: no clever strategy will work here. I have read many things in books, and assumed, all these days, that I know everything: like looking at a painting of water and assuming that swimming would be easy, only to discover, once in the water, that staying afloat is no easy feat!'

So Binoy tried fervently to explain this extraordinary insight to Gora. Nowadays, he said, his days and night were too full to allow any space—as if there was no chink in the sky, it was so utterly dense—like a beehive in spring, full to bursting with honey. Formerly, much of the universe had been left out of his life, his gaze fixed only on the small part of it that met his needs. Today, he saw the entire universe, was touched by everything in it, and found everything imbued with a new meaning. He had not realized he loved the world so much, that the sky was so extraordinary, the light so exquisite, even the movement of unknown pedestrians on the street so intensely real. He longed to be of some service to all, to offer all his energy to the world forever, like the sun in the sky.

It was not immediately apparent that Binoy was saying all this with reference to any particular person. He could not bring anyone's name to his lips, embarrassed even to offer a hint, as if he had wronged someone even in discussing such things. It was wrong of him, and an insult, but tonight, by his friend's side, in the solitary darkness, under the silent sky, he found it impossible to avoid this guilty act.

What a face! How exquisitely her spirit glowed on her tender cheeks! How extraordinary her inner radiance that shone forth in her smile! What an intellectual brow! And what deep, unfathomable mysteries lurked in those eyes, beneath the shadow of those dense lashes. And those hands, so eloquently expressive, ready to fulfill with grace the promise of devotion and love! Binoy's heart seemed to swell with the joy of knowing that his life, his youth, were indeed worthwhile. That Binoy should see incarnate the vision that most people would die without ever beholding—what could be more amazing?

But what madness was this? How wrong of him! But, wrong or not, it could be checked no longer. If this tide should wash him up on some shore, all the better; and if it should sweep him away and drown him, there was no preventing it. The problem was, he did not even want to be rescued. As if being carried away, surrendering all long-cherished beliefs, all stability, was life's true fulfillment!

Gora listened in silence. Upon this terrace, on such solitary, drowsy moonlit nights, they had exchanged many thoughts on many other occasions: so many thoughts on literature, human nature, social good, the future course of their lives, so many resolves the two of them had made together. But never had they spoken of such things. Gora had never before been confronted with such truths about the human heart, expressed so cogently, in such a manner. All along, he had dismissed such things as romantic claptrap. But today, he saw them so closely that he could no longer disavow them. Not only that, these emotions jolted his heart, with a thrill that streaked like lightning through his body. Momentarily, the veil was lifted, as in a breeze, from an unseen part of his youth, and the Sharat moonlight entered that long-sealed chamber, suffusing it with magic.

The moon went down, beneath the line of rooftops. From the east came the faintest hint of light, like the smile on a face in sleep. At last, Binoy's heart felt light, and a certain embarrassment crept in.

'All my words must seem very petty to you,' he observed, after a short silence. 'In your heart you probably feel contempt for me. But tell me, what else can I do? I have never concealed anything from you. Today too, I have concealed nothing, whether you understand me or not.'

'Binoy, I can't say I understand these things correctly,' Gora said. 'Just a couple of days ago, you wouldn't have understood them, either. Nor can I deny that, until now, I have found such worldly obsessions to be extremely trivial. But that may not mean they are actually insignificant. They have struck me as insubstantial illusions because I have had no direct experience of their force and intensity. But how can I say this major insight of yours is false? The fact is, a man cannot function unless he belittles all things outside his own field of action as trivial. That is why Ishwar has made distant things appear small to the human eye, instead of placing man in grave trouble by presenting all truths in an equal light. We must choose a particular direction, relinquishing our desire to cling to everything at once, or else we shall never grasp the truth. I cannot transfer myself to your position to salute the image of truth that you have beheld, for that would mean losing what's true for my life. It's either one or the other.'

'Either Binoy, or Gora. I am ready for self-fulfillment, while you prepare for self-sacrifice.'

'Binoy, stop trying to compose a book with your pronouncements,' protested Gora, impatiently. 'I see clearly from your words that you are today confronted with a powerful reality which you cannot evade. Once you recognize a truth, you must surrender to it; there is no holding back. It is my desire that one day, I, too, shall similarly attain the truth of my chosen field. So far, you were satisfied with knowledge of love gleaned from books. I, too, know patriotism only from books. Now that love has revealed itself to you, you have instantly realized how much truer it is than book-learning. It has taken over your whole universe, and you can find no respite from it anywhere. The day patriotism confronts me similarly in its entirety, there will be no saving me either. It will effortlessly draw to itself my life and wealth, my blood, marrow and bones, my sky, and all my light. Listening to your words, I get an inkling of how wonderfully exquisite, how manifestly well-defined is the true image of our own nation swadesh, how tremendously powerful are its joys and sorrows, engulfing life and death in an instant, like a flood. Your experience affects my life, today. I don't know if I'll ever understand what you have found, but through you, I seem to have a foretaste of what I myself wish to achieve.'

As he spoke, Gora rose from the mat and began pacing about on the terrace. The glow of dawn in the east appeared to him like a statement or a message, like a mantra from the

Vedas chanted in some ancient meditation-grove. His hair stood on end. For an instant, he stood transfixed, and from his crown, a ray of light seemed to rise like a fine stem, blossoming into a thousand-petalled lotus that filled the whole sky. His entire spirit, consciousness and strength seemed to extinguish themselves in surrendering to this supreme bliss.

'Binoy,' Gora suddenly exclaimed when he was himself again, 'you must transcend this love of yours as well. You can't stop there, I tell you. One day, I shall demonstrate to you how immensely real is the great power that summons me. My heart is overjoyed today. Now I cannot relinquish you to anyone else.'

Rising from the madur on the floor, Binoy came and stood close to Gora, who embraced him with both arms in extraordinary enthusiasm.

'Bhai,' he said, 'if we die, we die together. We two are one. Nobody can separate us, or come between us.'

The force of Gora's passionate enthusiasm rocked Binoy's heart as well. Wordlessly, he surrendered to Gora's magnetism. Side by side they roamed the terrace together, in silence. A rosy hue appeared in the eastern sky.

'Bhai,' said Gora, 'I see my devi, the female deity I worship, not in a beautiful setting, but where there is famine and poverty, pain and humiliation. There, one does not worship with music and flowers, but with one's life and blood. To me, that seems the greatest joy. There, no pleasure exists to delude you; by one's own strength, one must awaken fully and give oneself completely. This is no sweetness, but an invincible, unbearable manifestation, cruel and terrible. It has a harsh resonance that strikes all seven notes at once, causing the strings of the instrument to snap. The thought of it thrills me. This indeed, is the joy of manhood, I think—the tandava-dance of destruction. It is to see the exquisite image of the new appear above the violent sacrificial flames of the old, that men must strive. In the blood-red sky, I see a free, radiant future—I see it in today's impending dawn. See how my heart vibrates to the rhythm of some unknown tabor!'

As he spoke, Gora pressed Binoy's hand to his heart.

'Bhai Gora, I'm with you,' declared Binoy. 'But never let me hesitate, I tell you. Draw me in your wake, relentless as destiny itself. We are destined for the same path, but the two of us are not equal in strength, after all!'

'Our natures differ, but an immense bliss will merge our disparate temperaments,' Gora asserted. 'A love even greater than our mutual affection will unite us. Until that love materializes, there will be many clashes between us at every step, many conflicts and separations. Then, one day, forgetting everything, our differences and even our friendship, we shall be able to stand together, united in unshakable strength, in a great, magnificent act of self-surrender. That terrible bliss will be our friendship's final outcome.'

'Let it be so!' cried Binoy, grasping Gora's hand.

'But until then, I shall trouble you a lot,' warned Gora. 'You must put up with all the torment, for we can't regard friendship as life's ultimate goal, nor dishonour our friendship by trying to keep it alive at any cost. It can't be helped if our friendship collapses as a result; but should it survive, it will indeed be worthwhile.'

Sudden footsteps startled them. Turning, they saw that Anandamoyi had come up to the terrace.

'Come, it's time to sleep now,' she insisted, dragging them by the hand towards the room.

'We can't sleep now, Ma!' both of them protested.

'You can!' declared Anandamoyi. She forced the two friends to lie in bed side by side, and shutting the door, she sat close to their headstead and began to fan them.

'Ma, we can't sleep if you start fanning us,' Binoy objected.

'We'll see about that,' she said. 'The moment I leave, the two of you will start talking again. We shan't allow it.'

When they had fallen asleep, Anandmoyi tiptoed out of the room. As she descended the stairs, she saw Mahim on his way up.

'Not now,' she told him. 'They didn't sleep at all last night. I have just put them to bed.'

'My goodness, that's called true friendship indeed,' responded Mahim. 'Do you know if they spoke of marriage?'

'I don't know.'

'Perhaps something has been decided. When will they wake up? If the wedding doesn't take place soon, there will be many problems.'

'No problems will arise from their falling asleep,' laughed Anandamoyi. 'They are bound to wake up in the course of the day!'

~16~

'Aren't you going to get Sucharita married?' Borodasundari demanded.

'Where is a groom to be found?' asked Poreshbabu gently, after stroking his beard in his usual quiet, grave manner.

'Why, her marriage to Panubabu is more or less fixed,' replied Borodasundari. 'At least, so we privately assume. Sucharita knows it, too.'

'I don't think Radharani quite fancies Panubabu.'

'Look, I don't like such ideas. I don't distinguish between Sucharita and my own daughters, but we must admit there's nothing very extraordinary about her either! If a learned, devout man like Panubabu fancies her, is that to be taken lightly? Say what you will, my Labanya is much prettier, but

I assure you she'll marry the man we choose. She will never say 'no.' If you encourage Sucharita's arrogance, it will be hard to find a match for her.'

Poresh said no more. He never argued with Borodasundari. Especially about Sucharita.

Sucharita was seven when her mother died at Satish's birth. Her father, Ramsharan Haldar, joined the Brahmo Samaj after his wife's demise. Hounded by his neighbours, he left his village and sought refuge in Dhaka. While deployed at the Post Office there, he developed a close friendship with Poresh. Since then, Sucharita had regarded Poresh as a father-figure. Ramsharan had died suddenly. Having bequeathed his savings in equal shares to his son and daughter, he had appointed Poreshbabu executor of his will. Since that time, Satish and Sucharita had become part of Poresh's family.

Borodasundari did not like it if relatives or outsiders showed Sucharita any special affection or attention. Yet Sucharita somehow won everybody's liking and respect. Borodasundari's daughters would fight like rivals for her affection. In particular, the second daughter Lalita seemed to cling to Sucharita day and night, with a jealous, possessive love. Borodasundari desired that her daughters should surpass all the learned women of their time in their reputation for educational prowess. It did not please her that Sucharita, raised along with her own daughters, should equal them in these things. Hence, Sucharita encountered all sorts of obstacles when it was time for school.

Sensing the reason for all these obstacles, Poresh withdrew Sucharita from school and began to tutor her personally at home. Not only that, Sucharita came to be a special companion to him. He discussed many subjects with her, taking her with him wherever he went. When he was forced to be away, he elaborated on many issues in his letters to her. In this way, Sucharita's mind matured far beyond her age and status. Her demeanour developed a gravity that made it impossible for anyone to think of her as a little girl, and though close to her in age, Labanya regarded Sucharita as her senior in every respect. In fact, even Borodasundari could not treat her lightly, even if she wished.

Readers have already realized that Haranbabu was a very enthusiastic Brahmo. As night-school teacher, newspaper editor and secretary of the girls' school, he had a hand in every Brahmo activity. He was utterly indefatigable. Everyone hoped that this young man would one day occupy a very high position in the Brahmo Samaj. Especially concerning his command of English and his philosophical expertise, his fame had spread beyond the Brahmo Samaj through the university student network.

Hence, like all other Brahmos Sucharita too had a very high regard for Haranbabu. When they arrived in Kolkata from Dhaka, she had also been very eager to make Haranbabu's acquaintance. Ultimately, she was not only introduced to the famous Haranbabu, but within a few days, he did not hesitate to express his attraction for Sucharita. Not that he had directly declared his love to her; but he concentrated so intensely on compensating for all her shortcomings, amending her errors, encouraging her interests and improving her personality, that it became obvious to everyone that he wanted to make this girl a suitable companion for himself.

This destroyed Borodasundari's former respect for him, and she tried to dismiss him as a mere schoolmaster. And Sucharita, sensing that she had won the famous Haranbabu's heart, secretly developed towards him a feeling of devotion mixed with triumph.

Although no proposal had been made by the dominant party, when everyone assumed the certainty of Sucharita's marriage to Haranbabu, she too had mentally consented to the match. She had become especially anxious to determine

how, through education and endeavour, she could also become
worthy of the Brahmo Samaj's benevolent activities, to which
Haranbabu had dedicated his life. In her heart, she could not
feel that she was marrying a human being; she seemed to be
preparing herself to be wedded to the great beneficence of the
Brahmo community—a beneficence made highly erudite from
extensive book-learning, and excessively profound in its
command of philosophy. In her imagination, this marriage
appeared like a stone fortress built of fear, deference and
overwhelming responsibility—not just a place to live in
comfortably, but a site for struggle, a space not domestic, but
historic.

If the wedding had taken place at this stage, the bride's
party at least, would have considered it a blessing. But so
important to Haranbabu were the responsibilities of his self-
created vocation that he considered it unworthy of himself to
marry merely on account of a personal attraction. He could
not proceed without calculating exactly how much the Brahmo
Samaj would benefit from this marriage. Hence, he began to
test Sucharita from this perspective. To test others in this way
is to submit oneself to similar trials as well. Haranbabu
became a familiar visitor to Poreshbabu's house. Here, too,
he came to be known as Panubabu, from his family nickname.
It was no longer possible to regard him simply as a storehouse
of English learning, a source of philosophy and an incarnation
of Brahmo altruism. It was primarily as a human being that
everyone regarded him. Now, instead of commanding respect
and deference alone, he became subject to the likes and
dislikes of others.

Strangely, Haranbabu's manner, which had formerly
attracted Sucharita's devotion from afar, now began to offend
her, when seen up close. As the guardian of all that was true,
good and beautiful about the Brahmo Samaj, Haranbabu, in
assuming the caretaker's role, seemed incongruously reduced

in stature. Man's real relationship with truth is based on devotion: it makes man naturally humble. Where man becomes arrogant and proud instead, his pettiness becomes readily apparent in comparison with that truth. Here Sucharita could not refrain from privately analyzing the contrast between Poreshbabu and Haran. Poreshbabu's head seemed always bowed in humility before all that he had received from the Brahmo Samaj. There was no trace of arrogance here; he had immersed his life in those profound depths. Poreshbabu's tranquil face revealed the greatness of the truth that he bore in his heart. But Haranbabu was not the same. His aggressive self-projection as a Brahmo manifested itself in an ugly way, in all he said and did, obscuring all else. This had raised his prestige within the organization; but Sucharita, unable to confine herself to the narrowness of community loyalties, thanks to Poresh's tutelage, found Haranbabu's extreme Brahmoism an assault upon her natural humility. Haranbabu believed that his spiritual pursuits had given him such clarity of vision that he could easily assess people's levels of morality and honesty. Hence, he was always judgemental about everyone else. Worldly folk are also given to criticism and gossip; but those who indulge in these things in religion's name combine a spiritual arrogance with this critical attitude, generating great trouble in the world. Sucharita could not stand this. Not that she took no pride in the Brahmo community; nevertheless, she had grave reservations about Haranbabu's notion that eminent members of the Brahmo Samaj had attained their distinctive status only through the special power of being Brahmo, while morally depraved persons outside the Brahmo Samaj had lost their integrity through the special weakness of not being Brahmo.

For the benefit of the Brahmo Samaj, Haranbabu would not spare even Poreshbabu, judging and condemning him. On such occasions, Sucharita would react instantly with the

ferocious intolerance of a wounded female serpent. The
Bhagavad Gita was not a subject of discussion among Bengalis
educated in English in those days. But Poreshbabu would
sometimes read the *Gita* to Sucharita. He had also read most
of Kalisingha's *Mahabharata* to her. This had displeased
Haranbabu. He was in favour of banishing such texts from
Brahmo families. He himself had not read these texts. He
wanted to segregate the *Ramayana-Mahabharata-Bhagavad Gita*
as Hindu property. The Bible was the only religious text to
which he had recourse. It troubled Haranbabu like a thorn in
the flesh that Poreshbabu, in studying the scriptures and in
other small matters, did not observe the boundaries between
Brahmo and non-Brahmo. Sucharita could never tolerate the
possibility that anyone should criticise Poreshbabu's behaviour
in any way, openly or in private. And when his arrogance in
this regard became apparent, Haranbabu lost his stature in
Sucharita's eyes.

So, for various reasons, Haranbabu was gradually losing
his lustre in Poreshbabu's household. Even Borodasundari,
though no less enthusiastic than Haranbabu about maintaining
the divide between Brahmo and non-Brahmo, and though she
too, often felt ashamed of her husband's behaviour, did not
regard Haranbabu as an ideal man. She detected a thousand
shortcomings in him.

Although Sucharita's secret aversion for Haranbabu
increased daily due to his communitarian zeal and narrow-
minded dullness, neither of the two questioned or doubted
that it was Haranbabu Sucharita would marry. When a man
puts a boldly inscribed, highly expensive price tag on himself
in the market of the religious community, others too,
eventually begin to acknowledge his priceless worth. So once
Haranbabu had selected Sucharita after suitably testing her
according to his noble vocation, neither he nor anyone else
doubted that everyone would bow to this decision. Even

Poreshbabu had not mentally dismissed Haranbabu's claims. Everyone regarded Haranbabu as the future hope of the Brahmo Samaj, and he too acquiesced, without any thoughts to the contrary. It was therefore a matter of concern for Haranbabu whether Sucharita would prove adequate to a man like himself. It had not occurred to him to consider how much he might appeal to Sucharita. Just as nobody had deemed it necessary to think of Sucharita's views regarding this marriage proposal, she too had not thought about herself. Like all other members of the Brahmo Samaj, she had also assumed that the day Haranbabu said, 'I am ready to take this girl as my wife,' she would accept this marriage as her noble duty.

So things had continued, up until now. But that day, overhearing the heated tone of Haranbabu and Sucharita's brief argument about Gora, Poresh began to suspect that Sucharita did not respect Haranbabu sufficiently, that perhaps there were reasons why their natures clashed. Hence, when Borodasundari pressed for an early wedding, Poresh could not acquiesce as before. That very day, Borodasundari called Sucharita aside.

'You have caused your father great anxiety!' she declared.

Sucharita was startled. Nothing could pain her more than to give Poreshbabu cause for anxiety, even unintentionally.

'Why, what have I done?' she asked, turning pale.

'I don't know, child! He thinks you don't approve of Panubabu. Everyone in the Brahmo Samaj knows your marriage to Panubabu is more or less fixed. In this situation, if you . . .'

'Why, Ma, I haven't said a word to anyone about this!'

Sucharita had reason to be surprised. True, she was frequently irritated at Haranbabu's behaviour, but she had never nursed any objections to the marriage. Nor had it occurred to her to question whether this marriage would make her happy or unhappy, for she knew only that it was not to be judged in terms of happiness or grief. Then she remembered having clearly expressed her exasperation with Panubabu, in Poreshbabu's presence the other day. Her heart ached to think that this had made Poreshbabu anxious. Indeed, she had never shown such lack of restraint before, and she privately vowed not to do so in future, either.

Meanwhile, Haranbabu also arrived there that very day, not long afterwards. His heart had grown restless too. He had believed until now that Sucharita worshipped him in private; his share of her devotional offerings would have been fuller if Sucharita's blind faith had not made her incongruously devoted to old Poreshbababu. Even if the many shortcomings in Poreshbabu's life were pointed out to her, Sucharita still seemed to regard him as a deity. Haranbabu had privately derided this, and also been offended by it, but he had hoped that at a suitable time, he would eventually be able to steer this unwarranted devotion into a single, proper channel.

At any rate, as long as Haranbabu considered himself an object of Sucharita's devotion, he had constantly criticized her minor actions and behaviour, and striven always to mould her personality with his advice, but he had never clearly mentioned marriage. But that day, when he realized from some of Sucharita's remarks that she, too, had begun to judge him, it became difficult to retain his unruffled gravity and composure. Since then, the couple of times he had met Sucharita, he had failed to experience or display his own glory as before. A discordant note had entered his conversation and behaviour with Sucharita. He fussed over her conduct, either without reason or on trivial pretexts. Sucharita still maintained a calm indifference that forced him to privately admit defeat, and back in his own home he regretted his own loss of face.

When Sucharita showed signs of having lost her respect for him, it became hard for Haranbabu to sustain his exalted position as her examiner. Earlier, he never visited Poreshbabu's house very frequently. Lest anyone suspect that love for

Sucharita had made him desperate, he visited only once a week, and acted with gravity, as if Sucharita was his pupil. But something had come over him these last few days, for on the smallest pretexts, Haranbabu had been turning up more than once a day, and trying on even flimsier pretexts to engage Sucharita in conversation. This also gave Poreshbabu the opportunity to observe the two of them closely, and his doubts continued to intensify.

When Haranbabu arrived that day, Borodasundari immediately took him aside.

'Tell me, Panubabu,' she demanded, 'everyone says you're going to marry our Sucharita, but we never hear you say a word about it. If you really have such intentions, why don't you declare them clearly?'

Haranbabu could not delay any more. All he wanted now was to somehow secure Sucharita. Her devotion to him and her worthiness of the Brahmo cause could be tested later.

'I didn't mention it because it was so obvious,' he assured Borodasundari. 'I was only waiting for Sucharita to turn eighteen.'

'You are rather extreme, I must say,' she complained. 'We think fourteen is old enough.'

At teatime that evening, Poreshbabu was astonished at Sucharita's manner. She had not attended upon Haranbabu in this way for a very long time. In fact, when Haranbabu prepared to depart, she requested him to stay a little longer, for Labanya to show him one of her new creations. Poreshbabu felt reassured. He had been mistaken, he thought. He was privately a little amused, even. He assumed that the two had been involved in some secret lovers' quarrel, which had now blown over. That day, while taking his leave, Haran placed his marriage proposal before Poreshbabu, saying he did not favour any delay.

'But you say it's wrong to marry off girls before they're

eighteen!' protested Poreshbabu, rather surprised. 'You have even published these views in the newspapers!'

'Such views don't apply to Sucharita, for she is mentally more mature than girls who are much older.'

'Be that as it may, Panubabu,' said Poreshbabu with quiet firmness. 'Since there is no particular danger to be feared, it is our duty to abide by your convictions and wait until Radharani comes of age.'

'Indeed it is!' cried Haranbabu, embarrassed that his weakness had been exposed. 'I would only like us to invite everyone to confirm this match in the name of the Almighty, one of these days.'

'That is a wonderful idea,' Poreshbabu declared.

~17~

After sleeping for a few hours, when Gora awakened to find Binoy asleep beside him, his heart brimmed over with joy. It was like dreaming of having lost something precious and then awakening to find that it was not lost, after all. How much abandoning Binoy would cripple his life, Gora realized tonight, when he awoke to see Binoy by his side. Restless with joy, he shook Binoy awake.

'Let's go, there's something we must do,' he announced.

Ritually, every morning, Gora would visit the lower-class homes in his neighbourhood. He went there not to offer charity or advice, but to actually meet and mingle with the people. He was scarcely on similar visiting terms with members of the educated class. The poor addressed Gora as their respected elder brother, Dadathakur, and greeted him with shell-adorned hookahs. Gora had forced himself to take to tobacco, just to accept their hospitality.

In this crowd, Gora's chief admirer was Nanda, a

carpenter's son. He was twenty-two. He built wooden chests in his father's workshop. No hunter in the marshy rubbish dumps could match him in marksmanship. He was also a matchless bowler in cricket games. In his hunting group and cricket team, Gora had merged these boys, sons of carpenters and cobblers, with trainees from respectable bhadra families. In these mixed groups, Nanda outshone everyone else in every form of sport and physical exercise. Some of the bhadra pupils were jealous of him, but under Gora's discipline, they all had to acknowledge Nanda as their leader.

Wounded in the foot by an accident with a chisel, Nanda had been absent from the playing field for a few days. Depressed about Binoy, Gora had not been able to visit their home these last few days. Today, at the crack of dawn, he arrived at the carpenters' colony, accompanied by Binoy. As soon as they neared the two-storey dwelling where Nanda's family lived, they heard women wailing. Nanda's father was away, and so were all other adult males.

'Nanda died early this morning; they have taken his body for cremation,' the nearby tobacco-shop owner informed them.

Nanda dead! So healthy, so strong, so fiery, so full of warmth, so young—Nanda had died that morning! Gora stood silent and rigid. Nanda was the son of an ordinary carpenter. Few people would notice the shortlived void that his absence had caused. But today, Nanda's death struck Gora as terribly inappropriate and impossible. Gora had seen how spirited he was, after all. So many people were alive, but it was hard to find such abundance of spirit anywhere.

Inquiries about the cause of his death revealed that he had developed tetanus. Nanda's father had suggested sending for a doctor, but the boy's mother had insisted that her son was possessed by some evil spirit. The ojha had spent the entire night scorching and beating the boy and chanting mantras to exorcise the demon. When he fell ill, Nanda had begged that Gora be informed. But, lest Gora demand proper medical treatment, Nanda's mother had not allowed it.

'What stupidity, and what a terrible penalty!' exclaimed Binoy, on their way back.

'Don't console yourself Binoy, that you can distance yourself from this stupidity,' Gora warned him. 'If you could clearly discern the enormity of such stupidity and the magnitude of its repercussions, you wouldn't try to brush it off with a mere expression of regret!'

Gora's pace increased with his agitation. Without answering, Binoy tried to match his speed.

'Our entire breed has sold out to falsehood,' Gora continued. 'There is no end to the things they fear—gods, demons, tetanus, sneezes, Thursdays, the conjunction of three lunar days on one calendar day. How would they understand the boldness with which one must tackle the realities of this world? And you and I imagine that we are not of their party, simply because we have studied a few pages of science! Know this for certain: a select few can never protect themselves with textbook knowledge from the seductions of self-debasement all around them. So long as they fail to recognize the supremacy of tradition in worldly life, so long as they remain bound by false fears, even our educated members cannot escape their influence.'

'And what if educated members were indeed able to escape such influences?' demanded Binoy. 'How many educated people do we have, indeed! Not that others must progress in order to promote the educated. Rather, the glory of the educated lies in using their education for the advancement of others.'

'That's exactly what I want to say!' cried Gora, grasping Binoy's hand. 'But I've repeatedly observed that your respectability and education makes all of you arrogant enough to remain very comfortable with your distance from the masses. That's why I wish to caution you that without freeing the people beneath you, there can be no freedom for yourselves, either! If there's a hole in the hull of a boat, its mast, however high, can never wander free of care!'

Binoy marched beside Gora without replying.

'No, Binoy, I can never accept this easily!' Gora exclaimed suddenly, after walking in silence for a while. 'That ojha who killed my Nanda—his assault wounds me, wounds my entire nation. I cannot view such matters as minor, scattered incidents.'

Binoy still made no reply.

'Binoy, I quite understand what you're thinking!' roared Gora. 'You think there is no remedy for such things, or that the time for such remedies is far away. You think no power on earth can shake the burden of the fear and falsehood, heavy as the Himalayas, oppressing all of Bharatvarsha! But I can't think like that. If I did, I wouldn't survive. There must be a remedy for whatever hurts my country, however massive and strong the assailant might be. And it's because I firmly believe that the remedy lies in our hands, that I can withstand all the sorrows, adversities and humiliations all around me.'

'I lack the courage to sustain my belief in front of this vast, tremendous, nationwide suffering,' confessed Binoy.

'Darkness is vast, the lamp's flame tiny. I have more faith in this tiny flame than in that vast darkness,' Gora asserted. 'I can never believe in the permanence of misery. It's constantly assailed from within and without, by the entire world's powers of knowledge and vitality. However small each of us might be, we shall side with the supporters of this knowledge and vitality. If that kills us, we'll die with the certainty that our side will win. We shall not rest in comfort upon the nation's moribund state, taking it to be supreme and all-powerful. I believe banking on the devil and fearing ghosts are exactly the same, for they leave us with no urge to seek true treatment for our malaise. False fears and false ojhas—both together are out to destroy us. Binoy, I urge you repeatedly, not for a single moment, even in your dreams, to think it impossible that our nation will definitely gain freedom, that it will not always remained shackled by ignorance, and that the merchant ships of the British will not always hold us in tow. Bearing this firmly in mind, we must be ever-ready. You are content, all of you, to bank upon some future date when Bharatvarsha will start fighting for independence. I tell you the fight has already begun, and it rages, every moment. There can be nothing more cowardly than for you to remain complacent at such a time.'

'Look, Gora,' argued Binoy, 'one difference I see between you and the rest of us is that you seem to discover anew, every day, all that occurs daily in the streets and alleys of our nation, things that have been happening for a long time. Like our own breathing process, these things don't draw our attention; they arouse neither hope nor despair in us, neither joy nor sorrow. My days pass in utter emptiness; amidst my surroundings, I feel neither my own presence nor my nation's.'

Suddenly, Gora's face reddened, the veins swelling on his forehead. Fists clenched, he began to run down the middle of the street, chasing a coach and pair. 'Stop the carriage!' he thundered, startling all the pedestrians. With a single backward glance, the babu sporting a heavy watch-chain, who had been driving the carriage at speed, lashed his spirited horses and vanished from sight in an instant.

An elderly Muslim had been carrying on his head a basketful of fruit, vegetables, eggs, bread, butter and other provisions for his English master's kitchen. The babu with the watch-chain had sounded his horn, warning him to move out of the carriage's path. But as the old man did not hear, the carriage almost crushed him. He escaped with his life, but the basket, with all its contents, went tumbling across the street. The incensed babu, turning around in his coach-box, abused him as 'a damned swine,' and lashed him on the face, drawing blood. 'Allah!' sighed the old man, and began to gather some of the still-intact items back into his basket. Gora walked back and began to collect the scattered things, returning them to the basket.

'Why bother, babu, these things are useless now,' protested the Muslim porter, acutely embarrassed at such behaviour from a respectable bhadra pedestrian. Gora understood the futility of his action, and also that it shamed the person being helped; in fact, such efforts meant little in terms of actual assistance. But then the man in the street could not understand that this was one bhadralok's attempt to restore equilibrium by coming down to the level of a common man who had been unjustly insulted by another bhadralok.

'You can't bear this loss,' said Gora, once the basket was full. 'Come home with me and I shall buy everything at its full price. But let me tell you baba, Allah will never forgive you for enduring this insult without a word.'

'Allah will punish the guilty one,' the Muslim declared. 'Why would he penalize me?'

'He who tolerates injustice is also guilty, for he generates injustice in the world. You will not understand my words, but remember still that meekness is not true religion, for it encourages evildoers. Because your Mohammad understood this, he didn't preach in the guise of a meek person.'

Since his own home was not close by, Gora brought the Muslim to Binoy's house.

'Take out some money,' he urged Binoy, standing near his chest of drawers.

'Why so anxious?' Binoy asked. 'You go make yourself comfortable, and I'll get the money.'

Suddenly, he couldn't find the keys. Impatiently, Gora

yanked at the fragile drawer, and the lock gave way. As the
drawer fell open, a photograph of Poreshbabu's family first
caught his eye. Binoy had procured it from his young friend
Satish. Having obtained the money, Gora dispatched the
Muslim, but said nothing about the photograph. Observing
Gora's silence, Binoy too was unable to mention it, although
exchanging a few remarks about it would have relieved him.

'I'm off,' announced Gora suddenly.

'Wah, how can you go alone!' protested Binoy. 'Ma has
invited me to dinner at your place, after all. So I'm off, too.'

They set out together, the two of them. Gora said
nothing, the rest of the way. The picture in the drawer had
suddenly reminded him once again that a major stream of
Binoy's emotional life had taken a course completely unrelated
to Gora's. That the main current might eventually flow this
way, diverted from their friendship which was its now
dwindling source, was a vague fear secretly weighing upon
Gora's innermost heart. All these days, the two friends had
not differed in their thought and behaviour, but now this was
hard to sustain. In one area of his life, Binoy was becoming
independent. Binoy realized why Gora had fallen silent, but
felt embarrassed to break down that wall by force. He, too,
felt that Gora's heart had come up against a real obstacle that
threatened to separate them.

Arriving at Gora's house, they immediately saw Mahim at
the door, gazing at the street.

'What's the matter?' he demanded, seeing the two friends.
'You stayed up all of last night. I wondered whether you two
had fallen asleep somewhere on the pavement! It's not early,
is it? Go, Binoy, have a bath.'

Having urged Binoy to his bath, Mahim turned to Gora.

'Look, Gora,' he importuned. 'Think about what I said.
If you suspect Binoy of being unorthodox, then where in
today's market shall we find a Hindu bridegroom? We want

not only a Hindu, but also an educated one, after all! True, the product of Hindu orthodoxy and education combined is not quite what the Hindu scriptures might decree, but it's not a bad thing either. If you had a daughter, your opinions on this would surely coincide with mine.'

'Very well,' replied Gora, 'Binoy will probably have no objections.'

'Listen to this! Who's afraid of Binoy's objections? It's your objections I fear. Ask Binoy yourself, just once: that's all I want, even if it proves useless.'

'Very well.'

'Now I can go ahead and order sandesh from the sweet shop and yoghurt and kheer from the milkman,' gloated Mahim to himself.

'Dada is really plaguing us about your marriage with Shashimukhi,' Gora said to Binoy when he found the opportunity. 'What do you say?'

'Tell me first what you would desire.'

'Not a bad idea, I'd say!'

'You didn't think it a good idea earlier! It was more or less understood that neither of us would marry.'

'It is now understood that you will marry, but I won't.'

'Why? Why must the same journey yield different outcomes?'

'It's to preclude different outcomes that the present arrangement is intended. Our Maker has created some of us to be easily weighed down, while others remain casually carefree. For two such beings to move in tandem, one must be loaded with some ballast, in order to balance their weight. If you marry and assume some responsibilities, you and I can match our steps.'

'If that is your intention, add extra weight to my side of the scales,' smiled Binoy.

'You have no objection to the weight itself, I hope?'

'For the sake of balance, one can manage with anything at hand. A stone, a clod, anything.'

Why Gora expressed enthusiasm about the marriage proposal, Binoy was left in no doubt. He felt privately amused, guessing that Gora was anxious lest his friend marry into Poreshbabu's family. Not for an instant had the idea or likelihood of such a marriage occurred to Binoy. It was totally impossible. Anyhow, he consented readily to marry Shashimukhi, thinking that such a move would completely uproot such bizarre fears, restoring the health and peace of his friendship with Gora, and removing all cause for embarrassment about his mingling with Poreshbabu's family. After lunch, they spent the day making up for lost sleep. There was no further discussion between the two friends that day. But as the veil of dusk descended, at the hour when lovers mutually unveil their hearts, Binoy observed, gazing directly at the sky from the terrace:

'Look Gora, I want to say something. I think there is a serious lack in our patriotism. We see only half of Bharatvarsha.'

'Why do you say that?'

'We see Bharatvarsha only as a land of men; we don't notice women at all.'

'So, like the English, would you like to see women everywhere, indoors and out, on earth, in water and in space, at meals, feasts and work, everywhere? As a result, you will notice women rather than men, and it will destroy your balance of vision.'

'No, no, you can't dismiss my words like that. Why ask whether I'll adopt the English point of view? I say it's true that in our own country, we don't give women enough place in our thoughts. About you, I can declare you don't spend a moment's thought on women. You know the nation as a place without women. Such knowledge can never be true.'

'In seeing and knowing my mother, I have simultaneously seen and known all the women of my country.'

'That was just a well-put statement to delude yourself with. When members of a household gaze with long familiarity at women performing domestic chores, they don't really see the women at all. If we could view our nation's women outside our domestic needs, we would perceive our nation in its beauty and wholeness. We would see an image of the nation easy to die for. At least we would never behave mistakenly as if the women of our country are nowhere to be found. I know you will be incensed if I attempt any sort of comparison with English society. That is not what I wish to do. I don't know how and to what extent our women can appear in public without loss of dignity, but we must admit the seclusion of women has reduced swadesh, our own nation, to a half-truth, incapable of infusing our hearts with love and power in their complete forms.'

'How did you make this sudden discovery, so recently?' Gora asked.

'Yes, it's indeed a recent discovery, and a sudden one,' Binoy acknowledged. 'I was blind to such an immense reality, for so long! I count myself fortunate to have discovered it. Because we see the peasant only as farm labour, and the weaver only as fabric producer, we dismiss them as lowly and uncouth, not recognizing them as complete human beings, and this rich-poor divide weakens the nation. For very similar reasons, our entire nation's growth remains stunted because we imprison the women of our country within their routine of cooking and grinding, regarding them reductively as merely the female sex.'

'Just as day and night are the two halves of time, so are men and women the two halves of human society,' Gora asserted. 'In normal social situations, woman remains invisible like the night, all her actions concealed and private. We exclude the night from our work-time. But that doesn't halt any of the night's profound operations. Behind the veil of rest, the night secretly heals our losses, and nurtures us. But in abnormal social situations, night is turned into day, with machines operated by the light of gas-lamps, nightlong revelry by lamplight—but what's the result? The night's natural, private processes are destroyed, fatigue sets in, there's no restoration of injury or loss, and people become overwrought. Similarly, if we drag women into the public workplace, it disrupts their private activities, ruining social health and peace, driving society into a kind of frenzy. This frenzy may be mistaken for power, but it is only the power to destroy. Power has two aspects, one manifest, the other not manifested, one involving effort, the other rest, one productive, the other abstemious. If this balance is destroyed, power grows turbulent, and such turmoil is not beneficial. Man and woman represent two aspects of social power; man is power manifest, but the magnitude of his strength does not lie in its visibility; woman's power remains unexpressed, and to try constantly to express this secret power is to propel society towards swift bankruptcy by expending all its stored-up capital. That is why I say, if we men perform the holy sacrifice while women take charge of the grain-store, the yajna ritual will be successful, despite the women's invisibility. Those who try to expend all forms of power for the same purpose, at the same place and in the same way, must be insane.'

'Gora, I don't want to contradict you. But you, too, have not contradicted what I said. Actually . . .'

'Look, Binoy, if we say much more on this subject, it will be merely for the sake of argument. I admit I'm not as aware of the opposite sex as you have lately become, hence you can never make me feel what you are experiencing. So, why not accept for now that on this subject, our opinions differ?'

Gora dismissed the matter. But seeds, even when blown

away, land on the soil, and then there is nothing to stop them from sprouting at a suitable time. Up until now, Gora had completely excluded women from his life's arena; even in his dreams, he had not regarded this as a lack or loss. Today, witnessing Binoy's change of attitude, he had become aware of women's special presence and influence in society. But because he could not determine the place of women or what purpose they served in society, he was reluctant to argue with Binoy about these things. He could neither ignore nor master this subject, hence he wanted to avoid discussing it.

'Binoy, I hear your marriage to Shashimukhi has been fixed?' asked Anandamoyi that night, calling Binoy aside when he was leaving for home.

'Yes Ma, Gora is the go-between in this auspicious matter,' smiled Binoy, embarrassed.

'Shashimukhi is a nice girl, but don't act impulsively, bachha. I know you, Binoy. You are acting in a hurry because you are somewhat doubtful. You still have time to think. You are old enough, baba—don't take such a serious step lightly.'

She gently patted him on the shoulder. Without a word, he walked away slowly.

~18~

On his way home, Binoy reflected upon Anandamoyi's words. Up until now, he had never disregarded anything she said. That night, his heart felt heavy.

Next morning, he awakened to a sense of freedom. He felt he had bought his freedom from Gora's friendship at a very price. In exchange for the lifelong bondage which he had accepted in agreeing to marry Shashimukhi, he had gained the right to loosen his ties in another area of his life. Gora had, very unjustly, suspected Binoy of being tempted to leave his own community to marry into a Brahmo family. Binoy obtained his freedom by offering his marriage to Shashimukhi as a permanent security against this false suspicion. After this, he began to frequent Poresh's house without any constraint.

It was not at all difficult for Binoy to make himself at home where the company was to his liking. Once he had discarded his qualms about Gora, he quickly grew intimate with everyone in Poreshbabu's household, as if he had long been part of the family. Only Lalita, as long as she suspected Sucharita of having developed a weakness for Binoy, seemed to have armed her heart for battle against him. But when she saw clearly that Sucharita was not particularly partial to Binoy, she dropped her resentment with immense relief. Now she had no reason not to regard Binoybabu as a remarkably decent person.

Even Haranbabu was not hostile to Binoy. He seemed rather too eager to acknowledge that Binoy knew all about respectable conduct, implying that Gora lacked this quality. Binoy never raised any topic of debate in Haranbabu's presence, and Sucharita, too, tried to ensure against it, hence Binoy had so far not disrupted the peaceful atmosphere at the tea-table.

But in Haran's absence, Sucharita would herself try to get Binoy to discuss his social views. How educated men like Gora and Binoy could support the ancient social evils of the country was a question that continued to arouse her curiosity. Had she not been acquainted with Gora and Binoy, Sucharita would have had no second thoughts about dismissing anyone who held such views as worthy of contempt. But ever since she met Gora, she had been unable to dismiss him with contempt. Hence, at every opportunity, in her conversations with Binoy, she would somehow raise the subject of Gora's views and lifestyle, and by contradicting every argument, try to stretch the discussion until she had extracted the minutest details. Exposure to the views of every community was the best education for Sucharita, Poresh felt; therefore, he never felt anxious about these arguments, nor tried to prevent them.

'Tell me,' asked Sucharita one day, 'does Gourmohanbabu really believe in caste difference, or is it an exaggerated form of patriotism?'

'Do you believe in the steps on your staircase?' Binoy retorted. 'They, too, are differently placed, some higher, some lower.'

'I recognize them only because I must climb from a lower level to a higher, or there would be no need to heed them. On level ground, stairs become redundant.'

'Quite so! Our society is a stairway, meant to enable mankind's ascent to a particular goal. If we took society or the world for an end in itself, there would be no need for hierarchies; like European societies we could continue snatching and killing, each individual trying to grab more than everyone else, allowing the successful to flourish, and failures to sink into oblivion. Because we want to transcend the world by worldly means, we have not based our duties on desire and competition. We have made worldly endeavour our dharma because through endeavour, we seek no success but liberation. Hence, keeping in mind both worldly activities and their outcome, our society has created caste distinctions and division of labour.'

'I don't understand you clearly, I must confess,' Sucharita said. 'My question is, do you see that the purpose of promoting caste discrimination has been fulfilled?'

'It's hard to encounter fulfillment in this world. Simply because the achievement of the Greek civilization is no longer found in Greece, we can't declare the idea of the Greek civilization to be mistaken or futile. The idea of the Greek civilization continues to bear fruit in different forms within the human world. The caste system, India's answer to the problems of society, has not yet died out. It still remains, for the world to see. Even Europe has not yet found any other answer to the problems of society; there you still find only jostling and wrestling. The answer provided by Bharatvarsha still awaits fulfillment in the human world. Don't expect it to evaporate simply because a small community, out of their blindness to reality, might wish to dismiss it. Our tiny communities will vanish like bubbles in the ocean, but this great solution born of Bharatvarsha's natural genius will survive unmoved, until its task here is accomplished.'

'Please don't mind,' asked Sucharita hesitantly, 'but are you simply echoing Gourmohanbabu's words, or do you believe wholeheartedly in all these things?'

'I have told you truly that my convictions are not as strong as Gora's,' smiled Binoy. 'I often voice my doubts when I observe the mess caused by caste discrimination and the aberrations of society. But Gora says doubts are born when we view great things in a reductive light; it is intolerant to mistake broken branches and dry leaves for the tree's essence. I don't ask you to praise the broken branch, he says, but try to see the tree in its wholeness, and to understand its significance.'

'Even if we overlook the dry leaves, the fruits of the tree must be considered,' Sucharita insisted. 'What are the fruits of caste discrimination, for our country?'

'What you call the fruits of caste discrimination are also the products of a situation, not only of casteism. If it hurts to chew with loose teeth, it's not the teeth that are to blame, but their shakiness. Because a variety of causes have damaged and weakened us, we have distorted the idea of Bharatvarsha instead of fulfilling its promise. But that distortion is not intrinsic to the idea. Once we achieve plenitude of energy and health, everything will be set right. That's why Gora insists we must not dismiss the head because we have a headache. Grow healthy, grow strong, he urges us.'

'So, you'd want us to view Brahmans as living deities?' demanded Sucharita. 'Do you really believe that dust from a Brahman's feet can purify people?'

'Many honours in this world are man-made, after all. As long as a monarch is necessary for some reason, men declare him extraordinary. But a monarch is not really extraordinary, is he? Yet, he must transcend his ordinariness to become extraordinary, or he cannot rule. We project a monarch as extraordinary to ensure that we receive proper administration under his rule. The monarch must respect the demands of the honour we bestow on him; he must become extraordinary. Such artificiality affects all human relationships. In fact, it's our idealization of parenthood and not just natural parental love that determines parents' role in society. Why, in a joint family, does an elder brother tolerate and sacrifice so much for his younger brother? Our society, unlike others, has constructed this special image of the dada. If the Brahman's image were also similarly constructed, that would be no mean advantage for our society! We desire a living deity. If our desire for this human deity is really heartfelt and intelligent, then we shall have him. And if ours is a foolish desire, we shall add the world's burdens, increasing the number of anti-gods who indulge in all sorts of wrongdoing and survive by scattering on our heads the dust from their feet.'

'Does your human deity exist?' inquired Sucharita.

'He exists as the tree lives in its seed, in Bharatvarsha's deepest purposes and needs. Other nations want generals like Wellington, scientists like Newton, millionaires like Rothschild, but our nation wants Brahmans. Brahmans who are fearless, who despise avarice, conquer grief, ignore deprivation, who are *param brahmani jojitachittah*, unshakable, calm, and free. That is the kind of Brahman Bharatvarsha wants, and only when he is found can Bhratvarsha really become free. Our society needs Brahmans to constantly provide a song of liberation for every group, every form of labour, not to cook or to sound the prayer bell. We need Brahmans to keep our society's value constantly in view. The greater our ideal of Brahmanism, the more highly we must honour Brahmans. Such honour is greater by far than that accorded to kings, it amounts to honouring the gods. When the Brahmans of our country become truly worthy of such honour, nobody can dishonour our nation. Do we bow to kings, or allow despots to enchain us? We bow to our own fear, entangled in the net of our own avarice, enslaved by our own folly. Let the Brahmans pray; let them liberate us from that fear, avarice and folly. We don't ask them to wage war, engage in trade, or serve any other purpose; let them actualize the pursuit of liberation in our society.'

Poreshbabu had been listening in silence. Now, he spoke up gently: 'I can't say I know Bharatvarsha, and I certainly don't know what Bharatvarsha desired or whether that desire was ever fulfilled. But can we ever return to our bygone days? Our endeavours must focus on present possibilities. What use wasting time in groping for the past?'

'What you say echoes my line of thinking, and what I've often said as well,' Binoy responded. 'Gora says, is the past really over because we dismiss it as such? It does not become obsolete simply because it may be out of sight, screened by the turmoil of the present; it survives in the very marrow of Bharatvarsha's bones. No truth can ever become obsolete. That is why this truth about Bharatvarsha has begun to impinge upon us today. One day, if even one of us recognized and accepted this truth, it would unlock the door to our mine of strength, and the treasures of the past would become the possessions of the present. Do you imagine that a man of such significant destiny has not appeared on Bharatvarsha's horizon?'

'You phrase these things differently from ordinary people,' observed Sucharita. 'Hence one hesitates to accept your views as a reflection of the entire nation.'

'Look, scientists describe sunrise in one way and ordinary people in a different way. That does not harm the sunrise much. But we do gain something from understanding the truth in its proper form. Gora has the amazing capacity to take a unified, coherent view of the truth about our nation, which we regard in scattered, fragmented ways. But would you, therefore, regard Gora's vision as an optical illusion? And is the fragmented vision of others to be taken for the truth?'

Sucharita remained silent.

'Don't count my friend Gora among our ordinary countrymen who pride themselves on being supreme Hindus,' Binoy continued. 'If you knew his father Krishnadayalbabu, you would have perceived the difference between father and son. Krishnadayalbabu is anxious day and night to keep himself pure, constantly changing his clothes, sprinkling Ganga water, studying the holy almanac and the scriptures. Regarding food, he doesn't trust even the best Brahman cook, lest there be some flaw in the man's Brahmanhood. He doesn't let Gora anywhere near his own room. If he ever has reason to visit his wife's quarters in the house, he purifies himself upon his return. His days and nights in this world are spent in extreme detachment, lest he be touched, knowingly or unknowingly, by the minutest impurity arising from a violation of sacred rules. Just like the dandy Ghor Babu, constantly anxious to maintain the radiance of his complexion, the glory of his hair and the neatness of his dress, by avoiding the sun and screening himself from exposure to dust. Gora is not like that at all. He does not disrespect the rules of Hindu orthodoxy, but he can never be so petty and fastidious. He views the Hindu religion from within, and with great regard for its magnitude. He never thinks of the Hindu spirit as something very delicate, shrivelling at the slightest touch, destroyed by the merest contact.'

'But he seems very cautious about observing the purity and impurity of touch!' said Sucharita.

'That caution of his is a strange thing,' Binoy explained. 'If asked, he at once says: "Yes, I believe in all this. That touch can taint our caste purity, that eating certain things is sinful: these are unshakable truths." But I know for sure that these are mere overstatements; the more inappropriate they are, the more loudly he seems to proclaim them for everyone to hear. Gora wants to observe all orthodox rules indiscriminately, lest rejecting minor features of present-day Hinduism should lead other unwise people to disrespect even its major features, and lest this give the detractors of Hinduism a sense of victory. He wouldn't slacken his stance, even before me.'

'There are many such among the Brahmos as well,' remarked Poreshbabu. 'They would indiscriminately reject all contact with Hinduism, lest outsiders mistakenly imagine that they endorse Hindu malpractices as well. Such people can't lead a natural life; they either pretend or exaggerate. Thinking that the truth is weak, they consider it part of their duty to protect it, through either force or strategy. "I don't depend on truth, the truth depends on me": those who believe this become fanatics. Those who believe in the power of truth keep their own aggressiveness under control. If outsiders temporarily misunderstand us, there's not much harm done; far worse is the harm resulting from inability to acknowledge the truth because of petty hesitations. I always pray to the Almighty that, be it a Brahmo prayer hall or a Hindu chandimandap, let me in every situation be able to salute the truth easily, with bowed head, and without resistance. Let no external hindrance restrain me.'

Poreshbabu fell silent, as if briefly immersing himself in introspection. These few words uttered by him in a low voice seemed to lend a certain harmony to the entire discussion, arising not merely from those words, but from the tranquil depths of Poreshbabu's own life. A glow of blissful devotion lit up the faces of Sucharita and Lalita. Binoy remained silent. He, too, was privately aware of a tremendous aggressiveness in Gora's nature. The easy, simple tranquility to be expected in the mind and conduct of purveyors of the truth was lacking in Gora. This fact struck Binoy afresh and more clearly, upon hearing Poreshbabu's words. Of course, Binoy had so far argued with himself in Gora's defence that when one's community is precariously placed and in conflict with the external political atmosphere, soldiers of the truth cannot preserve their natural demeanour. At such times, temporary necessities demand even the fragmentation of truth itself. Today, Poreshbabu's words made Binoy wonder momentarily, that if it was natural for ordinary persons to be tempted to distort the truth in serving their temporary needs, did Gora too belong to that same order of people?

When Sucharita retired for the night, Lalita came and perched at one end of her bed. Sucharita sensed that Lalita was brooding over something. Realizing also that it must be something concerning Binoy, she brought up the subject herself.

'I must say I rather like Binoybabu,' she remarked.

'You like him because he talks about Gourbabu all the time.'

Sucharita grasped the insinuation, but ignored it.

'True indeed,' she admitted, feigning innocence. 'I enjoy hearing him speak of Gourbabu. He brings Gourbabu to life.'

'I don't enjoy any of it! It annoys me.'

'Why?' asked Sucharita in surprise.

'It's only Gora, Gora, Gora, day and night!' protested Lalita. 'His friend Gora may be a very eminent man, that's all very well. But Binoy is a person in his own right, too!'

'Indeed he is,' smiled Sucharita, 'but what's the problem?'

'His friend has overshadowed him to such an extent that he is unable to express himself. Like a cockroach captured by a green glass beetle. In such situations, I feel angry with the beetle, but can't respect the cockroach either.'

The sharpness of Lalita's tone made Sucharita laugh, though she said nothing.

'You laugh Didi, but let me tell you, if someone tried to suppress me like that, I couldn't tolerate him for a single day!' Lalita declared. 'Take yourself, for instance. Whatever people may think, you don't overshadow me, it's not in your nature. That's why I love you so. Actually, it's what you've learned from Baba: he gives everybody their own space.'

Sucharita and Lalita were Poreshbabu's devoted followers in this family, the very mention of 'Baba' making their hearts swell with pride.

'Baba is beyond compare,' Sucharita agreed. 'But say what you will, Binoybabu has a way with words.'

'It's because the words are not his own that he can utter them with such grace,' Lalita insisted. 'If he spoke his mind, his words would sound quite natural; we wouldn't feel he'd made them up. I'd find that much better than wonderful words.'

'So what makes you angry, my dear? Gourmohan's words *have* become Binoy's own.'

'Then it's a terrible thing. Has the Almighty Ishwar given us brains to elaborate on other people's views, and mouths to utter other people's words in a marvelous way? I have no use for such marvelous words!'

'But why don't you see that Binoybabu loves Gourmohanbabu, that their views truly coincide?'

'No, no, no!' cried Lalita impatiently. 'Their views don't coincide entirely. He has become habituated to following Gourmohanbabu. That is slavery, not love. Yet, he would force himself to believe that their views are exactly similar.

That's why he tries so hard to present Gourmohanbabu's views in wonderful terms, to delude others as well as himself. He constantly wants to suppress the doubts and contradictions that arise in his own heart, lest he be compelled to reject Gourmohanbabu's ideas. He lacks the courage to disown Gourmohanbabu. Where there is love, acceptance is possible even where opinions differ; self-surrender is possible even without blindness. But that's not true in his case. He may follow Gourmohanbabu out of love, but cannot bring himself to acknowledge it. That's clear from his words. Well, Didi, haven't you realized that? Tell me honestly.'

Sucharita had not considered the matter in this way at all. For she was curious to understand Gora completely, but without any urge to regard Binoy separately in his own right.

'Very well, suppose we accept your argument,' she said, not directly answering Lalita's question. 'So what's to be done now?'

'I feel like extricating him from bondage to his friend, to set him free.'

'Why don't you try, bhai?'

'No use my trying. If you put your mind to it, it would work.'

Although Sucharita had privately sensed Binoy's attraction towards her, she tried to laugh off Lalita's suggestion.

'I like him because of the way he comes to surrender himself to you, flouting even Gourmohanbabu's authority,' Lalita asserted. 'Others in his place might write a play condemning Brahmo women, but his love for you and respect for Baba shows his mind is still open. Didi, we must make Binoybabu a person in his own right. I can't bear to see him merely promoting Gourmohanbabu.'

'Didi! Didi!' cried Satish, rushing into the room at this moment. Binoy had taken him to the circus at Gorer Maath. Late though it was, Satish could not contain his excitement at his first visit to the circus.

'I almost dragged Binoybabu to my bed tonight,' he informed them, after describing the circus. 'He entered the house, then left, saying he'll come tomorrow. Didi, I've asked him to take both of you to the circus one day.'

'What did he say to that?' Lalita inquired.

'He said the girls would be frightened by the tigers. I wasn't frightened at all, though.' Satish puffed up his chest in male arrogance.

'Indeed!' said Lalita. 'I can clearly see how brave your friend Binoybabu is! No, bhai Didi, we must take him to the circus!'

'But tomorrow's show is scheduled for the morning,' objected Satish.

'All the better!' Lalita declared. 'We'll go in the morning.'

As soon as Binoy arrived the next day, Lalita cried:

'Here's Binoybabu, just on time. Let's go!'

'Where?' asked Binoy.

'To the circus.'

To the circus! To visit the circus in broad daylight, in the company of women, in full public view! Binoy was dumbfounded.

'It will offend Gourmohanbabu, I suppose?' Lalita demanded.

Binoy was rather startled at Lalita's question.

'Does Gourmohanbabu have an opinion about escorting girls to the circus?' Lalita persisted.

'He certainly does,' answered Binoy.

'Please explain it to us,' Lalita demanded. 'Let me call Didi, so she can hear it too.'

Binoy smiled at her sarcasm.

'Why do you smile Binoybabu! You told Satish yesterday that women are afraid of tigers. Are you afraid of someone, too?'

Binoy took the girls to the circus that day. Perturbed, he wondered again and again how his relationship with Gora might appear to Lalita, and possibly to other women in this family.

'Did you tell Gourmohanbabu about the circus performance that day?' Lalita asked him the next time they met, feigning naïve curiosity.

This pointed question unsettled Binoy profoundly.

'No, I haven't told him yet,' he had to admit, flushing to the tips of his ears.

'Binoybabu, please come with me, will you?' called Labanya, coming in.

'Where?' asked Lalita. 'To the circus?'

'Wah, as if there's a circus performance today! I'm calling him to draw a border along the edges of my handkerchief, for me to embroider,' Labanya told her. 'Binoybabu draws so beautifully!'

Labanya dragged Binoy away.

~19~

In the morning, Gora was busy working when Binoy suddenly arrived on the scene.

'I went to the circus with Poreshbabu's daughters the other day,' he announced very abruptly.

'So I heard,' replied Gora, continuing to write.

'Who told you?' asked Binoy, surprised.

'Abinashbabu. He was also at the circus that day.'

Gora said no more. He scribbled away. From long force of habit, Binoy was terribly embarrassed that Gora should have heard the news already, and that too from Abinash, which meant there would have been no lack of description and detail. He would have been happier if the circus visit, and public knowledge of it, could have been avoided.

He now remembered having stayed awake the previous night, mentally quarreling with Lalita. She thought he was in awe of Gora, deferring to him as a small boy obeys his tutor. How could one human being so unfairly misjudge another! Gora and Binoy were soulmates after all! True, he respected Gora for his uniqueness, but what Lalita imagined was unfair to Gora and Binoy both. Binoy was not a minor, and Gora was not his guardian.

Gora continued to write in silence, and Lolita's pointed questions continued to haunt Binoy. He could not dismiss them easily. But soon, he grew indignant.

'So what if I went to the circus! Who is Abinash to raise the issue with Gora, and why, for that matter, should Gora discuss my activities with that good-for-nothing fellow? Am I under Gora's surveillance, answerable to him for the company I keep, and my movements? This is a grave assault upon our friendship!'

Had he not suddenly recognized his own cowardice, Binoy would not have felt so incensed at Gora and Abinash. He seemed to be privately trying to blame Gora for his own compulsion to conceal something from Gora, even momentarily. If Gora had said a few harsh things to Binoy about the circus visit, their friendship would have remained on an equal footing and Binoy would have felt consoled as well. But when Gora silently ignored Binoy, acting like a grave judge, Lalilta's barbs began to sting Binoy insistently.

At this moment, Mahim entered, hookah in hand. Lifting the damp cloth covering the casket, he handed Binoy a paan.

'Baba Binoy, everything is settled on our front,' he said. 'Now, all we need is a letter from your father's elder brother, to set our hearts at rest. You've written to him haven't you?'

This pressure to marry struck Binoy as deeply offensive at

this time, yet he knew Mahim was not to blame, for he had received a promise. But Binoy felt that this promise was inadequate somehow. After all, Anandamoyi had virtually forbidden him, and the idea of marriage did not attract him at all either. So how, amidst all this confusion, had the matter ripened so quickly? Not that Gora had actually urged him to hurry. Nor would he have importuned Binoy if the latter had objected strongly. But still! Still, it was on this account that Lalita's barbed remarks pierced his heart. Behind it lay no particular recent development, but a long history of domination. Purely out of affection and simplicity, Binoy had grown accustomed to tolerating Gora's supremacy. Hence, this relationship of dominance had overwhelmed their friendship. Binoy had not felt it all these days, but now it could no longer be denied. Must he marry Shashimukhi, then?

'No, I haven't written to Khuromoshai yet,' he said.

'I'm to blame for that,' Mahim declared. 'It's not a letter you should write. I shall write it. Tell me, what's his full name, baba?'

'Why are you in such a hurry?' asked Binoy. 'The wedding can't happen in the months of Ashwin and Kartik, after all. That leaves only Agrahayan, but even that is problematic. Long back in our family history, somebody suffered a mishap in Agrahayan. Ever since then, our family has avoided weddings and other auspicious events during that month.'

'Binoy,' said Mahim, propping his hookah against the corner wall, 'does your education amount to mere rote-learning, that you should believe in such things? It's hard enough to find auspicious dates in this wretched country, and then if every family starts following a private almanac, how would our business proceed?'

'Then why do you believe in the inauspiciousness of Bhadra-Ashwin?' Binoy demanded.

'As if I do! Never! What's to be done baba—in these

parts, you can manage quite well without believing in God, but unless you believe in Bhadra-Ashwin, the planets Brahaspati-Shani, and what the stars decree, they won't let you survive. Besides, though I may refute these things in theory, violating the almanac in practice makes the mind uneasy. Fear pervades the air of our nation, just like malaria. I can't overcome it.'

'Our family's fear of Agrahayan can't be overcome, either. Khurima, at least, will never agree.'

So Binoy managed to suppress the matter for that day. From his tone, Gora guessed that he had developed some doubts. For a few days, Binoy had not been visible at all. Gora had realized he had started visiting Poreshbabu's house oftener than before. Now this attempt to evade the marriage proposal roused Gora's suspicions. Just as a snake cannot relinquish the victim it has begun to swallow, Gora too was virtually incapable of giving up a resolve or discarding parts of it. Any resistance or slackness on the part of others only aggravated his obstinacy. He became determined, heart and soul, to cling to the wavering Binoy by force.

'Binoy,' said Gora, looking up from his writing, 'having given your word to Dada, why torment him needlessly by keeping him in a state of uncertainty?'

'Did I give him my word, or was a promise hastily extracted from me?' demanded Binoy, suddenly losing patience.

'Who extracted a promise?' asked Gora harshly, surprised at Binoy's sudden show of indignation.

'You did!'

'Me! I'd barely exchanged a few remarks with you on the subject—is that called extracting a promise?'

Indeed, Binoy had no clear evidence to support his claim. Gora was right, they had exchanged very few remarks, hardly involving the kind of urging that could be termed as insistence. But still, it was Gora who had taken Binoy's consent, virtually by force. People are especially resentful about allegations regarding lack of external evidence. Hence Binoy sounded unduly angry when he said:

'It doesn't take many words to extract a promise.'

'Take back what you said!' demanded Gora, rising from the table. 'This promise is not so valuable that I must beg you for it or extort it from you.'

'Dada!' he thundered, calling to Mahim in the adjacent room. 'Dada!' Gora exploded, as soon as the flustered Mahim rushed in, 'didn't I tell you at the outset that Shashimukhi cannot marry Binoy, that I don't approve of the match?'

'Of course you did,' Mahim confirmed. 'No one but you could have said such a thing. Any other brother would have been enthusiastic from the beginning about a marriage proposal for his niece.'

'Why did you make me seek Binoy's consent?' Gora persisted.

'Only because I imagined it would work.'

'I'll have nothing to do with all this,' announced Gora, flushing. 'Matchmaking is not my trade. I have other things to do.'

With these words, Gora marched out of the room. Before the stupefied Mahim could question him on this, Binoy too walked directly out into the street. Retrieving the hookah from the corner, Mahim began to puff away in silence.

Gora and Binoy had quarreled many times previously, but never before had such a sudden, terrible eruption taken place. At first, Binoy was stunned at what he had done. Afterwards, once he was home, pain seared his heart. Thinking of the grievous blow he had inflicted on Gora in so short a time, he could not eat or sleep. He was especially troubled by remorse at the utter unreasonableness of blaming Gora for the present situation.

'It was unjust, unjust, unjust!' he repeated.

At two in the afternoon, when Anandamoyi had just taken up her sewing after lunch, Binoy came and perched close to her. She had heard some news of the morning's developments from Mahim. At lunch, she had also guessed from Gora's expression that there had been a storm.

'Ma, I have acted wrongly!' declared Binoy as soon as he arrived. 'There's no justification for what I said to Gora this morning about my marriage to Shashimukhi.'

'Never mind, Binoy,' Anandamoyi consoled him. 'When we try to suppress something painful, it comes out in this way. This was for the best. A couple of days, and both you and Gora will forget this quarrel.'

'But Ma, I have no objection to marrying Shashimukhi. That's what I've come to say.'

'Bachha, don't get into another mess in your haste to overcome a quarrel. Quarrels last only a couple of days, but marriage is forever.'

Binoy refused to be persuaded. He could not go to Gora immediately with his proposal. He went to inform Mahim that there was nothing to hold up the wedding. It would take place in Magh itself. Binoy would himself ensure that Khuromoshai raised no objections.

'Why not go ahead with the betrothal then?' suggested Mahim.

'Good idea. Please consult Gora first.'

'Consult Gora again?' exclaimed Mahim, flustered.

'No, we can't proceed otherwise,' Binoy insisted.

'Then we have no choice. But . . .' He stuffed a paan in his mouth.

~20~

Mahim said nothing to Gora that day. The next day, he went to his house, anticipating another struggle to persuade Gora again. But when he announced that Binoy had consented to the marriage the previous evening and asked for Gora to be consulted about the betrothal, Gora at once expressed his own approval:

'Very well, let the betrothal take place.'

'Now you say "very well"!' exclaimed Mahim in amazement. 'But you won't throw a spanner in the works again later, will you?'

'If I did, it was by way of a request, and not by posing obstacles,' Gora reminded him.

'Therefore I entreat you to neither pose obstacles nor make requests. I have no use for Narayani sena, Krishna's troops, on the Kaurav side, nor for Narayan, Krishna himself, on the side of the Pandavas. Best to manage with my own resources. I made a mistake. I did not know earlier that even your assistance could be so perverse. Anyway, you wish this betrothal to take place, don't you?'

'Yes I do.'

'Let it remain a wish then; no need to try converting it into action.'

Gora was hot-tempered, no doubt, and capable of anything when incensed; but it was not in his nature to nurse his anger and destroy his own resolve. He wanted to tie Binoy down by any means; this was no time for sulking. Gora was privately pleased at the previous day's episode, realizing that it was in reaction to yesterday's quarrel that the wedding had been finalized, and it was Binoy's rebellion that had confirmed his bondage. Gora wasted no time in restoring the natural relationship between Binoy and himself that had existed all along. But this time, there was a slight deviation from their utterly direct manner towards each other.

Gora had now realized it would be hard to restrain Binoy from afar. He must guard the danger-zones. 'If I visit Poreshbabu's house regularly, I can keep Binoy within proper limits,' he thought.

The very day after their quarrel, Gora arrived at Binoy's
house in the late afternoon. Binoy had never imagined Gora
would visit him that very day. Hence he was as pleased as he
was surprised. Even more surprisingly, Gora raised the subject
of Poreshbabu's daughters, yet without any air of hostility. It
did not take much to excite Binoy when this subject came up.
He began to recount in detail to Gora all the things he had
discussed with Sucharita. He tried to enthuse Gora by informing
him that Sucharita herself raised these subjects with special
eagerness, and that despite all her arguments, she was
unconsciously acquiescing, little by little, to Gora's point of
view.

'When I recounted what you and I said about Nando's
mother sending for the ojha and causing his death,' Binoy said
conversationally, 'Sucharita said, "You people think women
have fulfilled their duties if they are confined within the home
and allowed to cook and clean. On the one hand you stunt
their mental growth like this, but on the other, when they
send for the ojha, you don't spare them either. Those for
whom a couple of families constitute the whole world can
never become complete human beings. And if denied their
full humanity, they are bound to destroy and retard all major
male undertakings, dragging men down to avenge their own
plight. The way you have moulded Nando's mother and kept
her circumscribed, you couldn't make her see sense even if
your life depended on it, because you wouldn't get through
to her." I've tried hard to argue about this, but truly, Gora,
because I secretly agreed with her, my arguments didn't carry
any force. With her, one can at least argue, but I dare not
argue with Lalita. When Lalita arched her brows and said—
"You think you will serve the world while we serve all of you!
That's not possible! Either we, too, must serve the world, or
we must remain a burden. If we become a burden, you grow
angry and say women are expendable. But if you allowed

women to advance, outside or in the home, 'there'd be no need to discard them!"—her words rendered me speechless. Lalita doesn't open her mouth easily, but when she does, one must respond with care. Whatever you say Gora, I too am deeply convinced that our work will make no progress if our women's development remains stunted like Chinese women's feet.'

'But I've never said women should not be educated!' Gora protested.

'Does Part Three of the primer *Charupath* amount to an education?'

'Very well, from now on we can introduce Part One of *Binoybodh*.'

That evening, the two friends kept returning to the subject of Poreshbabu's daughters, until it grew quite late. On his way home alone, Gora mulled over these things, and once back home in bed, could not drive the thoughts of Poreshbabu's daughters from his mind, until he fell asleep. Such complications had never occurred in Gora's life. He had never spared women a single thought. Now Binoy had proved that this too, was a significant part of life. One could not dismiss it; it called for resistance, not compromise.

The next day, when Binoy proposed, 'Come on, let's go to Pareshbabu's, it's been long since you visited them. He keeps asking after you'—Gora agreed without demurring. Moreover, he was inwardly not as indifferent as before. At first, Gora had been totally detached about the very existence of Sucharita and Poreshbabu's daughters; then, lately, he had developed a contemptuous hostility towards them; but now, a certain curiosity had arisen in his mind. He felt a special urge to understand what it was that had so captivated Binoy.

It was dark when the two of them arrived at Poreshbabu's house. In the room on the first floor, Haran was reading one of his English pieces to Poreshbabu by the glass-shaded light

of a sej. Poreshbabu here was just a pretext, actually; Haran's
real target was Sucharita. At the far end of the table, shading
her eyes from the oil lamp's glare with a palmleaf fan,
Sucharita listened in silence. From habitual compliance, she
was trying hard to be attentive, but her mind wandered,
every now and then. When the attendant announced Gora
and Binoy, Sucharita started. As she rose from her chowki,
preparing to leave, Poreshbabu stopped her:

'Where are you going Radhé? It's only our own Binoy
and Gour.'

Sucharita sat down again, embarrassed. She was relieved
that Haran's prolonged reading of his English composition had
been interrupted. She was excited no doubt at news of Gora's
arrival, but the thought of seeing him there in Haranbabu's
presence unsettled her and made her very uneasy. Was it the
prospect of a confrontation between the two men, or was
there some other reason? It was hard to tell.

The very mention of Gora's name aroused deep hostility
in Haranbabu's heart. After somehow returning Gora's
namaskar, he remained silent and taciturn. As soon as he saw
Haran, Gora's aggressive instincts were aroused.

Borodasundari had been invited out with her three
daughters. Poreshbabu was supposed to fetch them in the
evening. It was time for him to go. The arrival of Gora and
Binoy at this time made things difficult for him. But knowing
he should delay no more, he left, whispering to Haran and
Sucharita:

'Please keep them company. I'll be back as soon as
possible.'

In no time, a terrible argument broke out between Gora
and Haranbabu. The quarrel was about Brownlow Saheb,
magistrate of a district not far from Kolkata, whom Poreshbabu
and his family had met during their stay in Dhaka. Because
Poreshbabu's wife and daughters came out of the antahpur to

socialize in public, the saheb and his wife showed them special respect. Every year on his birthday, the saheb held an agricultural fair. This time, when she met Brownlow Saheb's wife, Borodasundari spoke of her daughters' expertise in English poetry.

'The Lieutenant Governor and his wife will attend the fair this year,' the memsaheb suddenly observed. 'It would be very nice if your daughters could enact a short English verse drama for their benefit.'

Borodasundari was highly enthused by this proposal. Today, it was for a rehearsal that she had taken the girls to a friend's house. When asked if he could attend the fair, Gora had said 'No!' with unwarranted belligerence. Now Gora and Haran engaged in a violent altercation about Anglo-Bengali relations and the obstacles to mutual social intercourse between them.

'The Bengalis are to blame,' Haran declared. 'With all our social malpractices and evil customs we are not even worthy of social interaction with the British.'

'If that's true,' countered Gora, 'then it is humiliating for us to be tempted by the idea of mingling with the British despite our unworthiness.'

'But those who have made themselves worthy are sufficiently honoured by the British,' insisted Haran. 'Take everyone here, for instance.'

'Where honour for one highlights the dishonour of all others, I count such honour an insult,' Gora retorted.

In no time, Haranbabu flew into a rage, and Gora continued to sting him with a succession of barbed remarks. As they argued in this fashion, Sucharita, at the other end of the table, observed Gora intently from behind her fan. Though within listening range, she paid no attention to what was being said. Had she realized she was staring fixedly at Gora, she would have felt embarrassed; but she seemed to forget herself as she gazed at him. Gora was leaning forward, his

powerful arms resting on the table; the lamplight shone on his
broad, fair forehead; sometimes a contemptuous smile,
sometimes a frown of disgust, would play upon his face; every
fluctuating mood expressed proud self-esteem. Not only his
voice, but his face and entire body seemed to exude the
strong conviction that his words expressed not passing thoughts
or emotions, but attitudes born of long cogitation and practice;
his words bore no trace of hesitation, weakness or randomness.
Sucharita watched him in wonder, as if, for the first time in
all her life, she saw someone as a special human being, a
special man. She could no longer compare him with other
ordinary persons. In contrast to Gora, Haranbabu now seemed
insignificant. His own bodily and facial contours, his expression
and mannerisms, even his outfit and chador, seemed to mock
Haranbabu. All these days, in her repeated conversations with
Binoy regarding Gora's character, Sucharita had taken Gora
for an unusual man who belonged to a certain group and held
a certain set of beliefs. She had imagined merely that he might
serve to accomplish some special goal for the nation's benefit.
But today, gazing at him with rapt attention, Sucharita saw
Gora as himself alone, independent of all groups, all belief-
systems and all goals. Like an ocean that surges in unaccountable
turmoil when it sees the moon rise above all everyday needs
and actions, Sucharita's heart also filled to overflowing, its
flood engulfing everything, all her thoughts and beliefs, her
entire life. For the first time, she experienced what it meant
to be human, to possess a human soul, and in this exquisite
sensation, she forgot herself completely.

Haranbabu had noticed Sucharita's total absorption. This
weakened the force of his arguments. Ultimately, he lost his
patience, and rising to his feet, he called to Sucharita with an
air of deep intimacy:

'Sucharita, step into this room for a moment, there is
something I must tell you.'

Sucharita started, as if someone had struck her. Not that Haranbabu's relationship with her precluded his calling her aside in this way. At any other time, she would have thought nothing of it; but today, in the presence of Gora and Binoy, she felt insulted. Gora, in particular, glanced at her with such an expression that she could not forgive Haranbabu. At first she remained silent, as if she had not heard.

'Do you hear me, Sucharita?' demanded Haranbabu, a hint of annoyance in his voice. 'I have something to tell you. We must step into the other room.'

'Let it be for now,' Sucharita answered, without meeting his eyes. 'Let Baba join us first.'

'We should be going,' said Binoy, rising.

'No, Binoybabu, please don't get up!' Sucharita quickly intervened. 'Baba wants you to stay. He'll be here any moment.' There was a desperate plea in her voice, as if they were proposing to abandon a female deer to the hunter's clutches.

'I can't take this anymore! I'll take your leave, then.' With these words, Haranbabu rushed from the room. Having left precipitately in the heat of the moment, he regretted it instantly, but could find no other excuse to return.

After Haranbabu's departure, as Sucharita sat with bowed head and flushed countenance in a state of acute embarrassment, Gora found a chance to take a good look at her face. In Sucharita's expression there was no sign of the arrogance and garrulity that Gora mentally expected of educated women. Her face shone with intelligence no doubt, but how gentle it appeared now, softened by modesty and shame! How delicately graceful were the contours of that face! Above those eyebrows, how pure and clear her forehead, like the Sharat sky in early autumn! Those lips were mute, but the sweetness of unspoken words nestled between them like a tender, unopened bud. Never before had Gora noticed the attire of a nabina, a modern young lady, having spurned such things without even having seen them. But today, he saw with special approval the new style in which Sucharita had draped her body in a sari. Her arm rested on the table. To Gora's eyes, that arm, emerging from the folds of her sleeve, seemed like a beneficent message from her tender heart. On this tranquil, lamplit evening, Sucharita's chamber appeared to him as a special, unified vision, encircling her with its light, its picture-embellished walls, its décor and its orderliness. In a single instant, Gora realized that this was a home, adorned by the care, affection and grace of a woman skilled at nurture, the room's atmosphere far exceeding its physical dimensions, its walls, beams and ceiling. Gora sensed the presence of a living spirit in the environment around him, his heart rocked by surging tides of emotion, held captive by a deep intimacy. Never before in his life had he experienced anything so exquisite. As he gazed at her, everything about Sucharita, from the unruly tendrils of hair above her forehead to the sari border at her feet, gradually assumed for him a very special significance. Gora felt simultaneously attracted to Sucharita's personality as a whole, and also to every separate aspect of it.

For a while, all of them were embarrassed, at a loss for words. Then, glancing at Sucharita, Binoy said, to start a topic of conversation:

'As we were saying, the other day . . .' He continued: 'I've told you earlier, I once believed there was no hope for our nation and our society, that we would remain immature forever, the English always deployed as our custodians, that things would remain exactly the same, that we had no means whatsoever of resisting the tremendous power of the British and the moribund state of our own culture. Most of our compatriots share a similar attitude. In such situations, people either immerse themselves in selfish pursuits or live in a state of detachment. That's why middle class folk in our country think of nothing but professional advancement, and the rich feel gratified simply with titles conferred by the government. Our life's journey comes to a halt after just a small distance, so distant goals don't even arise in our imagination, and we deem it unnecessary to equip ourselves for such ventures. I, too, had once decided to get myself a job, with Gora's father as my patron. But then Gora forbade me, saying "No, a government job is not for you".'

'Please don't imagine I made that remark because I was angry with the government,' Gora clarified, seeing a hint of surprise on Sucharita's face. 'Those who serve the government arrogantly mistake the government's power for personal authority, and form a class apart from their fellow-countrymen. With each passing day, this attitude is becoming increasingly evident among us. I know a relative, a deputy in earlier times, but now living in retirement after he resigned from the post. The district magistrate had asked him: "Babu, why are so many persons acquitted in the trials you conduct?" "Saheb, there's a reason for that," he had answered. "Those you send to prison are mere animals in your eyes. But those I condemn to imprisonment are my brothers, after all." Those days, one could still find deputies capable of making such a major statement, nor did we lack British magistrates willing to listen. But day by day, the trappings of service are becoming mere decorations, the deputy of today increasingly treating his own countrymen as mere animals. And they are even losing the awareness that, in ascending the professional ladder by such means, they are constantly falling downwards on the moral scale. No good can ever come from condescension born of heights attained with someone else's support, for we immediately start being unjust to those we despise.'

As he spoke, Gora smashed his fist on the table, making the oil lamp tremble.

'Gora, this table doesn't belong to the government,' Binoy reminded him, 'and this sej is Poreshbabu's.'

Gora burst into a loud guffaw. The sound of his laughter filled the entire house. Sucharita was surprised that Gora could respond to sarcasm with such effusive childlike mirth. Privately, she was delighted. She had not known earlier that people who think about grave matters can also be capable of heartfelt merriment. Gora spoke of many things that day. Although Sucharita remained silent, the approval he saw on her face filled his heart with enthusiasm.

'Please remember one thing,' he said in conclusion, as if addressing Sucharita, 'if we mistakenly believe that because the British have assumed power, we too can never become powerful unless we ape them, then the impossible can never become a possibility, and blindly imitating them, we shall be neither here nor there. Know this for sure: Bharat has a special character, a special power, a special reality, and only through a complete flowering of these elements can Bharat be saved, its aims fulfilled. If we have not learned this from studying British history, then all our learning is false. I request you to enter the arena of Bharatvarsha with all its virtues and flaws, and if there are any imperfections, correct them from within. But observe, understand, and reflect upon Bharatvarsha, confront it, merge with it. Opposing it from outside, steeped to your very bones in Khristani ways right from your childhood days, you will not understand Bharat at all. You will continue to attack the nation, and will be of no service to it.'

Gora called it a request no doubt, but this was no request, more like an order, too forceful to depend on anyone else's consent! Head bowed, Sucharita heard him out. These words, specially addressed to her by Gora with such intense urgency, threw her heart into turmoil. She had no time then to analyze the nature of this turmoil. Never, for a single moment, had Sucharita imagined the existence of a vast, ancient entity called Bharatvarsha. Today, listening to Gora's powerful words, Sucharita suddenly realized that this entity, controlling the

distant past and remote future, was secretl
of distinctive hue, in a distinctive pattern,
of human destiny. How fine that strand w
and how profoundly connected with
instant Sucharita realized how petty we beco̶m̶
blind to our surroundings as we pursue our activities, if we do
not remain aware that every Indian's life is encompassed and
possessed by an entity of such magnitude. Shedding all her
inhibitions in that wave of sudden elation, Sucharita confessed
with simple humility:

'I had never thought about the nation like this, with such
breadth of vision, such verity. But I have a question: what is
the connection between dharma or religious duty, and the
nation? Isn't religion the nation's past?'

Sucharita's query, voiced so gently, was music to Gora's
ears. Reflected in her wide eyes, the question appeared even
more exquisite.

'The nation's past, greater by far than the nation itself,
manifests itself through the nation,' he replied. 'The Almighty
Ishwar has expressed his eternal image in this motley form.
Those who claim there is only one truth, and therefore, that
only one faith is true, that only one form of faith is true, are
believers only in a single truth, but unwilling to acknowledge
that the truth is infinite. The infinite One manifests itself in an
infinite multiplicity: that is the play of realities we encounter
in this world. That is why faith acquires diverse forms,
offering us manifold routes to sensing the presence of the One
who is the monarch of faith. I assure you that you can glimpse
the sun through the open windows of Bharatvarsha. For that
you need not cross the seas to look out of the window of a
Christian church.'

'You suggest that Bharatvarsha's mantra of faith leads us
to the Almighty by a distinctive route,' Sucharita said. 'What
is distinctive about that route?'

it's the fact that Brahma, the divinity without attributes, manifest within the particular and the definable. But there is no end to his special manifestations. Water, land, air, fire, life, intellect, love—all manifest his existence in special ways. He cannot be quantified, for he is infinite, and this has endlessly baffled science. The formless assumes countless forms without end; his eternal flow contains everything within it, large or small, abstract or concrete. The One with infinite attributes is also the One without attributes; the One who assumes infinite forms is also the One without form. Other nations have reduced Ishwar's stature, trying to confine Him to a single particularity. In Bharatvarsha, too, there is an attempt to see Ishwar within the limits of the particular, but Bharatvarsha doesn't count that particularity as the sole or ultimate truth. No devotee in Bharatvarsha would deny that Ishwar, with his infinite attributes, transcends even that particularity.'

'The knowledgeable may not, but what about the ignorant?' Sucharita asked.

'I have already said that the ignorant will distort every truth in every country!'

'But hasn't such distortion gone too far in our country?' Sucharita persisted.

'Perhaps,' conceded Gora. 'But that's because Bharatvarsha wants to fully acknowledge both aspects of religion: concrete and abstract, internal and external, bodily and spiritual. So, those who can't embrace the abstract accept only the concrete, and out of ignorance, they create strange distortions within that material image. But it is unthinkable that we should foolishly dishonour Bharatvarsha's extraordinary, diverse and tremendous effort to apprehend comprehensively, in body, mind and deed, the One who exists in form as well as formlessness, the concrete as well as the abstract, in contemplation as well as in manifest reality. Or that we

should, instead, embrace as our sole religion a narrow, dry,
featureless eighteenth century European faith, a hybrid mix of
theism and atheism. Owing to convictions imbibed since
childhood, you will not even understand me properly; this
man's English education has proved futile, you will think. But
if ever you should develop respect for Bharatvarsha's true
nature, its true endeavour, if you can penetrate the deep
secret of Bharatvarsha's success in manifesting itself, despite a
thousand obstacles and distortions, then—then, what can I
say? Having regained the Indianness of your nature and abilities,
you will be liberated.'

'Don't take me for a fanatic,' persisted Gora, observing
Sucharita's long silence. 'Please don't interpret my arguments
as the language of Hindu orthodoxy, especially of those who
have suddenly assumed a new orthodoxy. I have glimpsed a
vast, profound unity in the many manifestations and multiple
endeavours of Bharatvarsha, a unity that drives me wild with
joy. Rejoicing at such unity, I have no hesitation in mingling
with the most ignorant of Bharatvarsha's inhabitants, taking
my place beside them in the dust. Some understand this
message of Bharatvarsha, others don't, but never mind—I am
one with everyone in Bharatvarsha—they are all my own
people—within all of them, I have no doubt, eternal
Bharatvarsha's concealed presence is constantly at work.'

The words, uttered in Gora's powerful voice, seemed to
vibrate in the walls, tables and all the furniture in the room.
Sucharita could not be expected to readily understand such
words, but the first, vague stirrings of experience are also
extremely powerful. Sucharita was now tormented by the
realization that life was indeed not confined to four walls or
a single party.

At this juncture, swift female footsteps were heard near
the staircase, mingled with sounds of uproarious laughter.
Poreshbabu was back with Borodasundari and the girls. The

laughter concerned some prank Sudhir had played upon the girls as they mounted the staircase. Entering the room, Labanya, Lalita and Satish composed themselves as soon as they saw Gora. Labanya left the room. Standing beside Binoy's chowki, Satish began a whispered tete-à-tete with him. Drawing up a chowki behind Sucharita, Lalita all but hid herself from view.

'I really got delayed,' apologized Poresh, entering the room. 'Has Panubabu left?'

Sucharita did not reply.

'Yes,' said Binoy. 'He couldn't wait.'

'We'll take leave, as well,' said Gora, rising to his feet.

He bowed deferentially to Poreshbabu, joining his hands in a namaskar.

'I had no time to chat with all of you today,' said Poreshbabu. 'Visit us sometimes, when you have some spare time, baba.'

As Gora and Binoy prepared to leave, Borodasundari arrived on the scene. They greeted her with a namaskar.

'Are you leaving right away?' she asked.

'Yes,' Gora replied.

'But Binoybabu, you can't leave,' she insisted. 'You must dine with us tonight. I have something urgent to discuss with you.'

'Yes Ma, don't let Binoybabu leave!' cried Satish, springing to his feet and grasping Binoy's hand. 'He'll stay with me tonight.'

'Do you want to take Binoybabu away?' Borodasundari asked Gora, seeing that Binoy was too embarrassed to reply. 'Do you need him?'

'No, not at all,' answered Gora. 'Binoy, why don't you stay on? I'll take my leave.' He rushed from the scene.

When Borodasundari asked Gora's permission for Binoy to remain, Binoy could not help stealing a glance at Lalita's face. Lalita turned away with a suppressed smile. Binoy could not counter these small barbs she directed at him, yet they pierced him like thorns. As soon as he came inside, Lalita said:

'Better, Binoybabu, if you had managed to escape tonight.'

'Why?' he wanted to know.

'Ma is conspiring to get you into trouble. They're short of an actor for the performance at the magistrates' fair. Ma has decided you're the right person.'

'What a disaster!' exclaimed Binoy, flustered. 'I can't take it on!'

'I've already said so to Ma,' Lalita assured him with a smile. 'Your friend will never permit you to participate in this performance.'

'Leave my friend alone,' said Binoy, stung. 'I've never acted in my life, not since I was born. Why me?'

'It's not as if we have been actors all our lives either, through all our different births!'

At this moment, Borodasundari entered the room.

'Ma, it's no use your asking Binoybabu to join the performance,' Lalita told her. 'If you can first get his friend to agree . . .'

'This has nothing to do with my friend's consent!' pleaded Binoy. 'Acting isn't child's play. I just don't have the talent.'

'Don't worry about that,' Borodasundari assured him. 'We can train you up. If little girls can act, why can't you?'

There was no way out for Binoy.

~21~

Gora walked home slowly in a preoccupied state, abandoning his usual brisk pace. Instead of taking the direct route to his house, he made a detour via the Ganga shore. At that time, the land and water of the Ganga riverside in Kolkata had not yet been assailed by the hideousness of mercantile greed, the river's edge was not shackled by railway lines, nor the water by bridges. On winter evenings, the city's dark breath did not blacken the sky so intensely. The river carried a message of peace from the lonely peaks of the remote Himalayas into the dust-filled turmoil of Kolkata.

Nature had never found a chance to attract Gora. His mind was constantly in upheaval, caused by his own enthusiasm. He had not even noticed stretches of water, land and sky that were not related to his field of activity.

But today, the sky above the river began to silently stir Gora's heart, insistently, with its darkness steeped in starlight. No ripple disturbed the river. At the ghaat on the Kolkata rivershore some boats twinkled with lights, while others remained unlit and still. In the dense trees on the opposite shore, an inky blackness had congealed. Above them glowed the planet Jupiter, its unblinking gaze piercing the night like the all-knowing god of darkness.

Nature, great and silent, seemed to overwhelm Gora's mind and body tonight. The darkness of the vast night sky began to pulsate to the rhythm of his heart. All this while, Prakriti, the force of Nature, had waited patiently. But now, finding a door to Gora's heart unlocked, it instantly conquered this unguarded fortress. For so long, Gora had remained very independent, engaged with his own intellect, ideas and activities. But what happened tonight? When did he acknowledge Nature's presence! And all at once, how did these deep dark waters, this dense black shore, that great black sky, embrace and welcome him! How did Gora surrender to Prakriti tonight?

From the roadside, the delicate fragrance of some unknown flower wafted across from a foreign vine in the garden surrounding a commercial office, seeming to gently stroke Gora's agonized heart. The river diverted his attention from the tireless workspaces of human habitation, pointing towards some indistinct, far-off place; there, upon the solitary shore, what blossoms those interlocking tree-branches produced! What shadows those trees had cast! There, beneath the pure blue sky, the days resembled someone's wide-eyed gaze, and the nights were like the shade of her bashfully lowered lashes. Never before had Gora experienced anything like the attraction of the unfathomable eternal force that swept him away suddenly, engulfing him in a whirlwind of sweetness. It simultaneously seared his mind with extremes of pain and joy. On this cool Hemanta night, on the rivershore, amidst the city's inarticulate babble and the indistinct starlight, Gora forgot himself as he stood before a veiled enchantress whose presence filled the whole universe. Because he had not previously greeted this empress with bowed head, the magic web of her authority suddenly bound Gora tonight, its multicoloured strands fastening him to land, water and sky. Amazed at himself, Gora sank down to one of the steps of the solitary ghaat. Repeatedly he asked himself what this new apparition signified, and why it was necessary to his life! Where was its place in the resolve by which he had always determined and mentally arranged his life? Was it opposed to such a resolve? Must he struggle to vanquish it? With these thoughts, as Gora clenched his fists, he saw in his mind's eye the questioning gaze of a pair of moist eyes, bright with intelligence, tender with modesty. The fingers of a flawlessly beautiful hand disrupted his reflections with the promise of the untasted heavenly nectar of their touch. Rapture streaked like lightning through Gora's entire body. In the solitary darkness, this profound experience demolished all his questions and hesitations. He began to enjoy this new sensation with all his mind and body, reluctant to relinquish it.

'You're so late baba, your food has gone cold!' Anandamoyi remarked when Gora came home late at night.

'I don't know, Ma, what got into me tonight,' replied Gora. 'I spent a long time at the Ganga ghaat.'

'Binoy was with you, I suppose?' she asked.

'No, I was alone.'

Anandamoyi was secretly rather surprised. Never before had Gora unaccountably lingered at the ghaat so late, lost in his thoughts. It was not his nature, at all, to brood in silence. As he ate absentmindedly, Anandamoyi noticed a strange, animated glow on his face.

'You went to Binoy's house, I suppose?' she asked him gently, after a short silence.

'No, both of us went to Poreshababu's place today,' Gora replied.

Anadamoyi reflected in silence for a while.

'Have you got to know all of them?' she now wanted to know.

'Yes, I have.'

'Their daughters come out to meet everyone, I suppose?'

'Yes, they follow no restrictions.'

Seeing no sign of the intense emotion that would normally have accompanied such an answer, Anandamoyi again lapsed into a thoughtful silence.

When he got up the next morning, Gora did not immediately proceed to wash and dress for work, as on other days. Absently, he opened the bedroom door facing east, and stood there for a while. Their alley opened onto a major road, at the east end of which was a school. Above an ancient jamun tree in the school grounds floated a wisp of white mist, and behind it one could see the rosy haze of approaching dawn. Slowly, as Gora watched in silence, the fragile mist evaporated, bright sunshine penetrating the tree-branches like so many glittering bayonets, and in no time, the streets of Kolkata filled with crowds and babble. Just then, seeing Abinash and some other students approach his house from the corner of the alley, Gora ripped the magic web in a single violent move.

'No, all this means nothing. It won't do, at all!' he told himself, striking a great blow at his own heart.

He rushed out of his bedroom. For Gora's gang to arrive at his house and not find him ready well in time, was unprecedented. This minor lapse struck Gora as utterly contemptible. He privately resolved not to visit Poreshbabu's house anymore, and to try putting a stop to more such discussions by avoiding Binoy for a few days as well.

When he went downstairs, it was determined after mutual consultation that Gora, accompanied by two or three others, would proceed on a walking tour on the Grand Trunk Road. He would carry no funds, accepting the hospitality of homes along the way. Armed with this wonderful resolve, Gora felt a sudden surge of extreme enthusiasm. He was gripped by a powerful exhilaration at the prospect of breaking all bonds to set out on the open road like this. He felt as if the very idea of his setting forth had ripped the web in which his heart had secretly become entangled. Reminding himself resonantly that such emotional obsessions were merely illusory and that duty alone was real, Gora rushed from the ground floor sitting room like a schoolboy after class, to prepare himself for the journey.

At that moment, Krishnadayal was returning from his bath in the Ganga, his small round ghoti filled with Ganga water, shoulders wrapped in a namavali inscribed with the deity's name, chanting the holy mantra to himself. Gora all but collided with him. Embarrassed, Gora hastily greeted him with a pranam. 'Never mind, never mind!' cried Krishandayal, flustered, and hastened away awkwardly. Gora's touch had erased the purifying effect of his bath in the Ganga before his daily puja. Gora did not quite realize it was his touch that Krishnadayal particularly tried to avoid. He thought it was an obsession with purity that made it Krishnadayal's sole aim, always, to avoid all contact with everybody. After all, he spurned Anandamoyi as a non-believer, and Mahim being a working man, Krishnadayal hardly had the opportunity to interact with him. Mahim's daughter Shashimukhi was the only family member he sought out, to teach her Sanskrit stotras and initiate her into the rituals of prayer.

After Krishnadayal had escaped in dismay at Gora having touched his feet, the cause of his embarrassment dawned upon Gora, who felt privately amused. In this manner, his ties to his father had been virtually severed, and for all his criticism of her lack of orthodoxy, Gora worhipped his unconventional mother with full devotion. After his morning meal, Gora came to his mother, carrying a small bundle of clothing on his back as British travelers do.

'Ma, I'm going away for a few days.'

'Where are you going, baba?'

'I can't say for sure.'

'Do you have some task to accomplish?'

'Nothing that would qualify as a task. This journey is a task in itself.' Then, seeing that Anandamoyi was silent, Gora pleaded: 'Please, Ma, you can't forbid me. You know me after all. There is no fear of my becoming a sanyasi. I can't stay away from my mother for long.'

Never before had Gora articulated his love for his mother in this way. As soon as the words were out of his mouth, he felt embarrassed.

'Binoy will go with you, I suppose?' asked Anandamoyi, hastily concealing her delight.

'No, Ma, he won't be going with me,' Gora told her. 'Just look—Ma is immediately worried, wondering who will protect her Gora on the way! If you consider Binoy my bodyguard, that's your blind faith. If I come back safe this time, I'll dispel that false belief of yours.'

'I'll hear from you every now and then, won't I?' Anandamoyi inquired.

'Assume that you won't. Then you'll be pleased if you do hear from me. There's nothing to fear; nobody will snatch

away your Gora. Ma, nobody values me as you do. But
if anyone fancies this bundle, I'll hand it to him and come
away. I shan't stake my life trying to safeguard it, that's for
sure!'

Gora touched Anandamoyi's feet. She stroked his head
and kissed the hand with which she had blessed him, without
forbidding him in any way. Anandamoyi never forbade anyone
anything simply because she herself might suffer, or from any
imaginary misgivings. Having overcome many obstacles and
mishaps in her own life, the outer world was not unknown to
her and fear was alien to her mind. She had not entertained
any apprehensions that Gora might come to some harm. But
since the previous day, she had been wondering what revolution
had taken place in Gora's heart. Today, hearing that Gora was
off on a tour for no reason, her anxiety increased.

Gora had barely stepped out into the street, bundle on his
back, when he met Binoy, carefully carrying a pair of blood-
red Basra rosebuds.

'Binoy, now we can test whether seeing your face augurs
well or ill for my journey,' Gora remarked.

'Are you going away?'

'Yes.'

'Where?'

'"Where?" the echo replies.'

'Is there no better answer than an echo?'

'No. Go to Ma, she'll tell you everything. I'm off.'

Gora rushed away.

Entering the interior space of the antahpur, Binoy greeted
Anandamoyi with a pranam and placed the roses at her feet.

'Where did you find these, Binoy?' she asked him.

'When one obtains something of value, one's first desire
is to offer it to one's mother in devotion,' he replied evasively.
Then, settling on Anandamoyi's taktaposh, her wood-plank
bed, he observed: 'Ma, I must say you are preoccupied.'

'Why do you say that?'

'You've completely forgotten to offer me the usual paan.'

Embarrassed, Anandamoyi fetched some paan for Binoy. They spent the afternoon chatting, the two of them. Binoy could shed no clear light on Gora's random travels.

'Yesterday you went to Poreshababu's with Gora, I believe?' asked Anandamoyi, conversationally.

Binoy recounted all that had taken place the previous day. Anandamoyi drank in all his words.

'Ma, now my puja is over, may I reverentially carry away the flowers that your feet have blessed?' said Binoy, while taking his leave.

Anandamoyi handed the roses to Binoy with a smile. These roses are valued for more than their beauty, she thought: surely they conceal some truths too deep for botany to define.

In the evening, after Binoy had left, she grew very thoughtful. Again and again she prayed to the Almighty that Gora should not be unhappy, and that nothing should separate him from Binoy.

~22~

Those roses have a history.

The previous night, Gora had come away from Poreshbabu's house, but Binoy had to suffer an ordeal regarding his proposed participation in the performance at the magistrate's house. Not that Lalita was particularly enthusiastic about this performance; rather, she had a distaste for such occasions. But she seemed stubbornly determined to involve Binoy in this performance, somehow. She was bent on making Binoy do things that were against Gora's wishes. Why she found Binoy's devotion to Gora so intolerable, Lalita herself could not understand. As if breaking all bonds to liberate Binoy would bring her great relief.

'Why, sir, what's the harm in acting?' Lalita demanded, tossing her braids.

'There may be no harm in acting,' Binoy replied, 'but the thought of performing at that magistrate's house makes me uneasy.'

'Are those your thoughts, or someone else's?'

'It's not my brief to speak for others and in any case that would be difficult. You may not believe me, but it's my own thoughts I express, sometimes in my own words, sometimes in others'.'

Lalita smiled faintly, offering no reply. 'Your friend Gourbabu probably considers it extremely heroic to ignore the magistrate's invitation, as effective as fighting the British,' she observed after a while.

'My friend may not think so, but I do!' declared Binoy heatedly. 'What is it, but a form of battle? If a man treats me with utter disregard, thinking I'd be grateful if he just beckoned me with his little finger, then how can I preserve my self-esteem unless I return his contempt?'

The injured pride in Binoy's words appealed to Lalita, herself proud by nature. But for that very reason, realizing the weakness of her own argument, Lalita began to inflict Binoy with the sharpness of her unwarranted sarcasm at the slightest provocation.

'Look, why are you arguing with me?' Binoy ultimately protested. 'Why don't you say, "I want you to join our performance"? Then I would have the pleasure of sacrificing my own convictions to keep your request.'

'Wah, why should I say any such thing? If you truly have convictions of your own, why should you sacrifice them at my request? But they must be true convictions.'

'Very well, let that be so. I have no true convictions. I

agree to perform, not at your request, but because you have defeated me in argument.'

At this moment, Borodasundari entered the room. Rising at once, Binoy went up to her.

'Please tell me how I must prepare for the performance,' he said.

'Have no worries on that score,' replied Borodasundari proudly. 'We'll get you into shape. But you must come regularly for practice every day.'

'Very well. I'll take leave of you now.'

'That's out of the question! You must dine with us.'

'Not tonight, let it be.'

'No, no, that's not possible.'

Binoy stayed for dinner, but lacked his usual cheerfulness. Sucharita, too, was strangely silent and preoccupied. She had been pacing the veranda while Lalita and Binoy were engaged in their war of words. Tonight, the conversation flagged.

'I failed to please you, even after admitting defeat,' Binoy remarked, observing Lalita's grave expression when it was time for him to leave.

Lalita walked away, without offering any reply. She was not given to weeping, but tonight her eyes were brimming with unshed tears. What was the matter? Why did she provoke Binoybabu repeatedly, hurting her own self? As long as Binoy remained averse to joining the performance, Lalita's obduracy had kept increasing, but as soon as he consented, all her enthusiasm disappeared. All the arguments against his participation in the show now gathered strength in her heart.

'Binoybabu should not have consented like this, just to keep my request!' her heart protested in torment. 'Request! Why must he keep my request? Does he think he's being civil, keeping my request? As if I'm dying to receive this bit of civility from him!'

But was it any use making such tall claims now? She had

indeed importuned Binoy continuously, to drag him into the theatre troupe. How could she be angry with Binoy for conceding her request out of sheer politeness? Lalita was overcome with contempt and shame at her own behaviour, emotions acute beyond all reason. On any other day, she would have gone to Sucharita at this moment of inner turmoil. But today she didn't go to her, and why her eyes overflowed with tears that choked her heart, she herself could not fathom.

The next morning, Sudhir had brought Labanya a bouquet. In the bouquet, a pair of ready-to-bloom Basra rosebuds grew on a single stem. Lalita extracted the stem from the bouquet.

'What are you doing?' Labanya demanded.

'It hurts me to see fine blossoms tied into a bundle with a mass of common flowers and leaves,' Lalita told her. 'It is barbaric to forcibly bind everything into a single category, like that.'

With these words, Lalita untied all the flowers and arranged them separately in different parts of the room, reserving only the pair of roses, which she took away.

'Didi, where did you get those flowers?' asked Satish, running up to her.

'Won't you visit your friend today?' Lalita inquired, without answering his question.

Satish had forgotten about Binoy all this while, but at the mention of his name, he jumped up.

'Yes, I will.' He declared, impatient to leave at once.

'What do you do there?' asked Lalita, restraining him.

'We chat,' answered Satish, briefly.

'He gives you so many pictures, why don't you ever give him anything?'

Binoy would cut out all sorts of pictures for Satish, from English papers and other such sources. Satish had begun pasting the pictures into a notebook. He was now so obsessed with filling up the pages that even when he saw a proper book, he would long to cut out pictures from it. He had suffered many reprimands from his sisters on account of this greed.

Today, suddenly confronted with the awareness that acts of kindness must be reciprocated, he became very worried. It was not easy to renounce his attachment to any of the personal belongings stored in his broken tin trunk.

'Never mind,' laughed Lalita, seeing Satish's anxious expression. She pinched his cheek. 'You needn't get so worried. Just give him this pair of roses.'

He brightened at such an easy solution to his problem. Carrying the twin rosebuds, he set off at once to repay the debt of friendship. On the way, he ran into Binoy.

'Binoybabu! Binoybabu!' called Satish from a distance, rushing up to him with the flowers concealed under his clothing. 'Guess what I've brought for you!'

When Binoy admitted defeat, Satish produced the flowers.

'Oh, how wonderful!' exclaimed Binoy. 'But, Satishbabu, these don't belong to you, after all. I hope I won't end up in police custody for harbouring stolen goods?'

Satish was suddenly doubtful whether he could actually describe the flowers as his own property.

'No! Wah, Lalitadidi asked me to give them to you, after all,' he disclosed, after some thought.

The matter ended there, and Binoy dispatched Satish with the assurance that he would come by that evening.

Binoy was unable to forget his pain at Lalita's barbed comments the previous night. As he rarely rubbed anyone the wrong way, he never expected such a sharp onslaught from anybody. Before this, he had merely regarded Lalita as Sucharita's follower. But for some time now, Binoy's feelings for Lalita had resembled the plight of a goaded elephant unable to ignore his keeper, the mahout, even for an instant. It had become Binoy's chief concern to determine how to find peace by pleasing Lalita ever so slightly. When he returned to his lodgings in the evening, Lalita's sarcastic, piercing remarks would resonate in his mind, one by one, keeping him awake.

'Lalita despises me as Gora's shadow, thinking I lack substance of my own, but that is utterly untrue!' He would mentally accumulate all sorts of counter-arguments. But all these arguments were of no use to him, for Lalita had never explicitly charged him with this accusation. In fact, she had not given him a chance to debate the issue at all. Binoy had so many arguments to answer her with, but because he could not articulate them, his inward resentment grew even more intense. Ultimately, seeing no pleasure on Lalita's countenance even after he acknowledged defeat, he felt extremely restless when he came back home. 'Am I really so despicable?' he began to wonder. So, when he learnt from Satish that it was Lalita who had sent the flowers, he felt exhilarated. He thought Lalita had given him the roses as a token of reconciliation because she was pleased at his agreeing to participate in the performance.

'Let's leave these flowers at home,' he thought, at first. Then he reconsidered: 'No, let me purify them with the touch of Ma's feet, because these flowers are a peace offering.'

When Binoy arrived at Poreshbabu's that evening, Satish was reading his school homework aloud to Lalita.

'Red is the colour of war,' said Binoy to Lalita. 'So the flowers of truce should have been white.'

Lalita gazed at him in incomprehension. Binoy drew a bunch of white oleanders from beneath the folds of his chador, and held them out to her.

'Lovely though your flowers might be,' he declared, 'they still retain shades of anger. These flowers of mine can't match them in beauty, but they present themselves to you humbly, in the white hue of peace.'

'My flowers? What are you referring to?' asked Lalita, flushing to the roots of her ears.

'I must have misunderstood, then,' said Binoy, rather taken aback. 'Satishbabu, did you deliver the right flowers to the right person?'

'Why, Lalitadidi asked me to present them, didn't she?' Satish protested loudly.

'Who did she want them given to?' Binoy asked him.

'To you.'

'I've never seen someone so stupid!' exclaimed Lalita, reddening. She rapped Satish on the shoulder. 'Didn't you want to offer flowers to Binoybabu in return for those pictures?'

'Yes, that's true, but wasn't it you who suggested I give them to him?' asked Satish, stupefied.

In trying to argue with Satish, Lalita found herself entangled even more securely in a web of words. Binoy clearly understood that the flowers were indeed sent by Lalita, but she had intended the gift to be anonymous.

'I relinquish all claims to your flowers,' he said, 'But that doesn't mean there's something wrong with the flowers I've brought. On the auspicious occasion of our reconciliation, these flowers . . .'

'What is our quarrel about, and how is it resolved, for that matter?' asked Lalita, shaking her head.

'Is the whole thing an illusion then, from beginning to end? The quarrel, the flowers, the reconciliation, is everything a lie? Is this merely a case of mistaking an oyster shell for silver, or is the oyster itself an illusion? What about that proposal regarding a performance at the magistrate saheb's?'

'That's no illusion,' said Lalita. 'But why quarrel about it? Why do you imagine that I have stirred up a great dispute just to make you agree to this performance, or that I am gratified at your consent? If you consider acting a sin, why should you agree to it simply at someone else's urging?'

With these words, Lalita left the room. Things had turned out completely contrary to her expectations. Today, Lalita had resolved that she would concede victory to Binoy, and persuade him to withdraw from the performance. But the way the topic was broached, and the way it developed, the outcome was exactly the opposite. Binoy thought Lalita still chafed with the desire to retaliate against his prolonged reluctance to perform. He felt she could not overcome her indignation because Binoy had accepted defeat only outwardly, remaining inwardly negative about the idea. He was full of anguish that the matter had hurt Lalita so deeply. Privately, he resolved never to discuss the matter even in jest, and to perform his promised task with such skill and dedication that nobody could accuse him of indifference.

That morning, in the seclusion of her bedroom, Sucharita had been struggling since dawn to read an English religious text called *Imitations of Christ*. She had not taken up her other routine chores. At times, when her mind wandered from the book, the words on the page seemed to her mere shadows; but the very next moment, angry with herself, she would forcibly concentrate on her book, refusing to give up. Presently, hearing voices from afar, she sensed Binoybabu's arrival. She gave a start, at once feeling the urge to put her book aside and move to the outer room. Then annoyed at her own restlessness, she sank back onto the chowki and took up her book. She tried to block her ears as she read, to shut out all sounds.

At this juncture, Lalita came into her room.

'Tell me, what's the matter with you?' Sucharita asked, glancing at her face.

'Nothing at all!' insisted Lalita, vigorously shaking her head.

'Where were you?'

'Binoybabu is here. I think he wants to chat with you.'

Today, Sucharita could not bring herself to ask if anyone else had accompanied Binoybabu. Had there been another visitor, surely Lalita would have mentioned him, but still, Sucharita could not rest content. Giving up her attempts at self-restraint, she went towards the outer chamber to do her duty by their visitor.

'Won't you come?' she asked Lalita.

'Go ahead, I'll join you later,' replied Lalita rather impatiently.

Entering the outer room, Sucharita found Binoy chatting with Satish.

'Baba has gone out,' said Sucharita. 'He'll be back soon. Ma has taken Labanya and Leela to Mastermoshai's house to help them memorize a poem for that show of ours; but Lalita simply refused to go. Ma has asked us to keep you here when you arrive; today, you will be tested.'

'Are you not involved in all this?' Binoy asked her.

'If everyone became an actor, who on earth would the spectators be?'

Borodasundari excluded Sucharita from such matters, as far as possible. This time, too, Sucharita had not been called upon to display her talents.

On other days, Sucharita and Binoy were never at a loss for words when they met. But today, there were such obstacles on both sides that all their efforts at conversation failed. Sucharita had vowed not to mention Gora. Binoy also could not bring up Gora's name easily, as before. He found it difficult to speak of Gora, imagining that Lalita, and perhaps everyone else in this house, regarded him as Gora's minor satellite.

It had often happened before that Binoy arrived first and Gora joined them later. Imagining that the same might happen

today, Sucharita remained restless and alert. She was afraid
that Gora might come, yet also tormented by the fear that he
may not arrive. After exchanging a few desultory remarks
with Binoy, Sucharita found no option but to take up Satish's
notebook and discuss it with him. She annoyed Satish, finding
fault sometimes with his arrangement of pictures. Highly
agitated, Satish began to argue loudly. And Binoy, humiliated
and aggrieved at the sight of the rejected oleander-bunch on
the table, began to think, 'Lalita should have accepted these
flowers of mine, out of civility, if nothing else.'

Startled by a sudden footfall, Sucharita turned around to
see Haranbabu entering the room. Because she had started so
visibly, she blushed.

'Why, isn't your Gourbabu here?' asked Haranbabu,
taking his place on a chowki.

'Why, do you have some need of him?' asked Binoy,
annoyed at Haranbabu's needless query.

'You're not often seen without him,' observed Haranbabu.
'That is why I ask.'

Binoy was privately incensed. Lest his anger become
apparent, he answered curtly: 'He is not in Kolkata.'

'Has he gone on a preaching tour?' asked Haran.

Binoy's fury increased. He made no reply. Sucharita also
rose and left the room without a word. Haranbabu rushed
after her, but could not catch up.

'Sucharita, I have something to tell you,' he called from
a distance.

'I'm not well today,' she replied. As she spoke, the bar
slammed down on her bedroom door.

Borodasundari now arrived, and summoned Binoy to
another room to rehearse his lines for the show. Not long
after, the flowers suddenly vanished from the table. That
night, Lalita did not appear at Borodasundari's rehearsal, and
Sucharita also stayed up very late, gazing out at the darkness

of the night, the *Imitations of Christ* lying folded on her lap, the lamp in her room turned to face the corner. Like a mirage, a strange, exquisite land seemed to arise before her eyes, a terrain somehow utterly divorced from everything she had seen and known until now. Hence the lights burning at the windows there frightened her with their remote mysteriousness, like a garland of stars in the dark night sky. Yet, she felt, 'My life is insignificant, all my long-held certitudes riddled with doubt, my regular daily activities utterly meaningless. Perhaps, in that other place, I shall gain complete knowledge, perform deeds that are noble, and make my life worthwhile. Who has brought me to the unknown gateway of that exquisite, unfamiliar, terrifying land? Why does my heart tremble so? Why are my feet frozen immobile when they try to advance?'

~23~

Binoy came daily for rehearsals. Sucharita would glance at him once, then concentrate on the book in her hands or go away to her own room. Every day she suffered the frustration of seeing Binoy arrive unaccompanied, but she asked no questions. Yet, the longer this state of affairs continued, Sucharita's heart grew ever more reproachful against Gora, with each passing day. As if, on that previous occasion, there had been an understanding that Gora was bound to visit them. Ultimately, learning that Gora had unaccountably gone away to some unknown place for a few days, Sucharita tried to dismiss the matter as a trifling piece of news, but it continued to pierce her heart. While performing her daily chores, she would suddenly remember it. When preoccupied, she would realize suddenly that it was this matter that she had secretly been thinking of.

After her discussion with Gora the other day, Sucharita had never expected him to vanish suddenly like this. Despite the great divide between Gora's views and her own convictions, there had been no contrary currents of resistance in her heart that day. Whether she understood Gora's opinions clearly it is hard to say, but she seemed to have arrived at a certain understanding of Gora as a human being. Whatever Gora's views might be, they had not reduced his human stature, nor rendered him contemptible; rather, they had made his strength of character visible. This she had felt deeply, that day. She could never have tolerated such words from another person's mouth; she would have been furious, regarded the person as a fool, and her mind would have felt a strong urge to mend his ways by teaching him a thing or two. But that day, with Gora, none of these things happened; combined with Gora's nature, the sharpness of his intellect, the firmness of his unquestioning faith, and the penetrating force of his thunderous voice, his words had acquired a life and a reality of their own. Sucharita herself might not accept all these opinions, but if someone else embraced them like this with all his life and soul, there could be no cause to spurn him. In fact, it was even possible to respect him, beyond one's own reservations. Such was the feeling that had completely overwhelmed Sucharita that day. This state of mind was entirely new to her. She was extremely impatient about differences of opinion; despite the example of Poreshbabu's detached, steady, tranquil lifestyle, she regarded opinions in an exclusive light, because she had been surrounded by communalism since childhood. That day she had for the first time seen ideas in relation to human beings, sensing the mysterious presence of something alive and whole. She had forgotten that day, the divisive vision that saw human society in black and white alone, separating my side from yours. She had been able to regard a person of different views as primarily a human being, so his opinions became secondary.

That day, Sucharita had felt that Gora had enjoyed his discussion with her. Was it merely the joy of expressing his own opinions? Did she contribute nothing to that joy? Perhaps not. Perhaps no human being had any value for Gora, perhaps he had moved far away from everyone else, absorbed in his own ideas and intentions. Perhaps human beings, to him, merely served as occasions for the application of his ideas.

Of late, Sucharita had been concentrating on her prayers. She seemed to be trying, harder than ever, to make Poreshbabu her refuge. One day, when Poreshbabu was reading alone in his room, Sucharita silently came in and joined him.

'What is it, Radhé?' asked Poreshbabu, placing his book on the table.

'Nothing,' she replied. She began to rearrange the books and papers on the table, although they were already arranged quite neatly.

'Baba, why don't you teach me as you used to before?' she blurted out, after a while.

'But my pupil has graduated from my school,' Poreshbabu smiled affectionately. 'Now you can grasp things by reading on your own.'

'No, I can't grasp anything,' declared Sucharita. 'I'll read under your guidance, as before.'

'Very well, I'll tutor you from tomorrow,' Poreshbabu consented.

'Baba,' resumed Sucharita suddenly after a short silence, 'The other day, Binoybabu said a lot of things about caste discrimination. Why don't you explain such matters to me?'

'Ma, you know I have always encouraged all of you to try to think and understand things for yourselves, instead of merely making a habit of parroting my opinions or someone else's. To offer advice on a subject before the question has formed properly in your mind is like offering food before you have developed an appetite: it only creates distaste and indigestion. Whenever you ask me a question, I'll answer as best I can.'

'It's a question I ask you,' Sucharita persisted. 'Why do we condemn caste discrimination?'

'There is no harm in a cat approaching our plate and devouring rice from it, but if a certain human being enters the room, we must throw away the rice. If caste discrimination causes men to treat other men with such humiliation and contempt, how can I call it anything but anti-religion? Those who can treat human beings with such contempt can never attain greatness. They must suffer the contempt of others.'

'There may be many flaws in the malpractices prevalent in our community today,' argued Sucharita, echoing Gora. 'But then such flaws have pervaded all aspects of the community. For that, is the original community itself to blame?'

'If I could locate the original element, I would have an answer,' replied Poreshbabu with his customary tranquility. 'When I see with my own eyes that people in our country are treating other people with intolerable contempt, tearing us apart, how can I in such circumstances console myself with thoughts of an imaginary original element?'

'Tell me,' said Sucharita, echoing Gora's party again, 'It was our nation's ultimate philosophical ideal to regard everyone equally, wasn't it?'

'Equality concerns knowledge, not emotions of the heart. It includes neither love nor contempt, for it is beyond anger and jealousy. The human heart can't sustain such a state, shorn of everything the heart must believe. That is why, in our country, despite such an egalitarian philosophy, low-caste people are not even allowed into temples. If our country does not permit even equality of worship, how does it matter whether such ideas exist in philosophy?'

For a long time, Sucharita mulled over Poreshbabu's words in silence, trying to comprehend them.

'Tell me, Baba,' she finally said, 'Why don't you try explaining these things to Binoybabu and the others?'

'It's not as if Binoybabu and the others lack the intellect to understand these things,' smiled Poreshbabu. 'Rather, it's from an excess of intellect that they don't want to understand, only to explain. When they develop a heartfelt desire to understand all these things from the perspective of religion, the greatest truth of all, they won't have to depend on your Baba's intellect. At present, they are viewing things from a different perspective. My words will be of no use to them now.'

Sucharita had listened to Gora and the others with respect, but their views, clashing with her convictions, had been inwardly troubling her. She could not rest in peace. Today, her conversation with Poreshbabu brought her temporary relief. Sucharita did not want to entertain the slightest possibility that Gora, Binoy, or anyone else, knew more on any subject than Poreshbabu. She could not help being angry with anybody who contradicted Poreshbabu. Of late, since her acquaintance with Gora, it was because she could not completely dismiss his words in anger or contempt, that she suffered such mental agony. That was why she had grown desperate to seek refuge again in Poreshbabu, like his shadow, as in her childhood days. Rising from the chowki, she went to the door, then came back again, and standing behind Poreshbabu, leaning against the back of his chowki, she said:

'Baba, let me join you at your prayers today.'

'Very well.'

Afterwards, going into her bedroom, Sucharita closed the door and tried to remove Gora's words from her mind. But Gora's image, glowing with intelligence and conviction, lingered before her mind's eye. She began to feel that his words were not words alone, but Gora himself; those words had a form, a motion, a life of their own, brimming with the strength of his convictions and the pain of his patriotism. They were not mere opinions to be countered; they comprised an entire being, and no ordinary one. It was hard indeed to spurn this being. Caught in an intense inner conflict, Sucharita felt like weeping. Her heart was full to bursting at the thought that someone could cast her into such a major dilemma and then so easily grow remote, like someone utterly detached. Yet there was also no end to her self-castigation at her own agony.

~24~

It had been determined that Binoy would dramatically recite a poem about music by the English poet Dryden, while the girls, appropriately attired, would mime the accompanying actions onstage. In addition, the girls would also recite English poems and sing English songs. Borodasundari had repeatedly assured Binoy that they would somehow groom him for the performance. She herself had only a smattering of English, but she could rely on a couple of experts in her troupe. But when they assembled for rehearsals, Binoy astounded Borodasundari's team of experts with his recitation. Borodasundari was denied the satisfaction of moulding this outsider to their coterie. Those who had formerly treated Binoy with scant respect now could not help privately admiring him. In fact, even Haranbabu requested him to write occasionally for his paper. And Sudhir started pestering Binoy to deliver occasional lectures in English at their students' assembly.

Lalita found herself in a peculiar situation. She felt pleased, yet privately rather dissatisfied, that Binoy did not require any help from anybody. Binoy was not inferior to any of them;

rather, he was superior to them all, and secretly aware of his own superiority, he would not expect any guidance from them. This thought tormented her. Regarding Binoy, she herself could not understand what she desired, what might ease her mental discomfort. Meanwhile, her unhappiness constantly expressed itself sharply in trivial ways, always targeting Binoy in the end. Realizing that such conduct towards Binoy was neither fair nor civil, she felt remorseful and tried hard to restrain herself, but she could not understand why, at the slightest pretext, some unwarranted inner anguish would suddenly burst forth, snapping her self-control. She now pestered him to desist from the very activity which she had earlier ceaselessly urged him to join. But now, how was it possible for Binoy to abscond without reason, throwing the entire plan into jeopardy? There was not much time left, either; and having discovered a new skill, he had himself become enthusiastic about it.

'I'm dropping out,' Lalita ultimately told Borodasundari.

'Why?' asked Borodasundari very anxiously, for she knew her second daughter.

'Because I'm not good at it!'

In fact, ever since it became impossible to regard Binoy as a novice, Lalita never wanted to recite or rehearse her role in his presence. 'I'll practice on my own,' she would declare. This would hinder everybody's practice, but Lalita was impossible to handle. Defeated, they ultimately had to manage their rehearsals without Lalita. But finally, when Lalita wanted to opt out altogether, Borodasundari was thunderstruck. Knowing she could not find a solution, she sought Poreshbabu's help. Poreshbabu never interfered in his daughters' minor preferences. But considering that they had made a commitment to the magistrate, that the hosts would also have made arrangements accordingly, and that time was also very short, he sent for Lalita and inquired, stroking her head:

'Lalita, it would be wrong of you to withdraw now.'

'But Baba, I'm not good at it,' answered Lalita, her voice choked with unshed tears. 'I can't.'

'If you can't perform well you won't be to blame, but if you withdraw, it will be wrong on your part.'

Lalita hung her head.

'Ma, my little one, having taken it on, you must complete this undertaking. It's too late now to escape lest your pride suffer a blow. Even if your pride is hurt, you must ignore it to perform your duty. Can't you do that, ma?'

'I can!' declared Lalita, raising her face to her father's.

That very evening, especially for Binoy's benefit, she seemed to set about her task with excessive force and daring, casting aside all inhibitions. Until now, Binoy had never heard her recite. Today, listening to her, he was amazed. Binoy was thrilled beyond his expectations at such clear, spirited pronunciation, no trace of indistinctness anywhere, and such unhesitating power of expression. Her voice continued to ring in his ears long after.

In recitation, a good elocutionist casts a spell on the listener's mind. The poem's emotions lend an aura of glory to the one who recites, blending with her voice, appearance and nature. Like a flower on a tree-branch, the poem blossoms in the speaker's personality, enriching her. Lalita, too, began to appear to Binoy in a poetic light. All these days, she had troubled him continuously by her sharpness. Just as we tend to feel only the sore spots on our body, Binoy, too, had been unable lately to think beyond Lalita's sharp words and pointed mockery. He had been compelled to wonder repeatedly, why Lalita had acted or spoken in a certain way; the more he failed to penetrate the mystery of her displeasure, the more his mind grew obsessed with thoughts of her. Awakening suddenly at dawn, he would be reminded of those thoughts, and every day, on his way to Poreshbabu's, he would wonder what

Lalita's mood that day would be. When Lalita showed the slightest sign of pleasure, Binoy would heave a sigh of relief, and wonder how to make the feeling last, but he had failed to find a way.

After the mental turmoil of the last few days, the beauty of Lalita's recitation moved Binoy with particular force. It delighted him so much that he could not find suitable words of praise. He was afraid to say anything, good or bad, directly to Lalita's face, for the general human tendency of being pleased by a compliment may not apply to her. In fact, it may not apply precisely because it was the general rule. Hence, Binoy effusively praised Lalita's talents to Borodasundari. This deepened Borodasundari's respect for Binoy's learning and intellect.

There was another surprising development. As soon as Lalita herself realized that her recitation and acting had been flawless, that she had handled her difficult duty with the ease of a well-built boat riding a wave-crest, her bitterness towards Binoy evaporated. She made no further attempts to discourage him. Her enthusiasm for the task at hand increased, and the rehearsals brought her closer to Binoy. In fact, she had no objections now to seeking Binoy's advice about recitation or any other matter.

This transformation in Lalita removed a load from Binoy's mind. So overjoyed was he, that he began visiting Anandamoyi at odd hours to indulge in playful antics, just like a little boy. He stored up many things to prattle about to Sucharita, but nowadays, he did not get to see her at all. He conversed with Lalita whenever he had the chance, but with her he had to guard his tongue. Because he knew Lalita was sharply judgemental about him and everything he said, his words lacked their spontaneous flow in her company.

'Why do you speak as if your words are taken from a book?' Lalita would ask, sometimes.

'Because I have only read books all these years, my mind now resembles a printed book,' he would reply.

'Please make no effort to say things very gracefully,' she would urge. 'Just utter your own thoughts directly. You speak such fine language, I suspect you are using someone else's words, thoughtfully rearranged.'

So, if his natural talent spontaneously presented him with a finely worded idea, Binoy would have to struggle to shorten and simplify it for Lalita. If ever an ornate phrase rose to his lips, he would feel embarrassed.

Lalita's heart glowed as if a cloud had inexplicably lifted from it. Even Borodasundari was amazed at her transformation. Now Lalita did not resist all suggestions, as before; she would participate enthusiastically in all activities. She drove everyone to distraction, coming up with new ideas every day regarding costumes and other arrangements for the forthcoming event. However enthusiastic Borodasundari might be about such things, she also had an eye on the expenses. Hence, she felt as concerned about Lalita's present enthusiasm as she had been earlier about her aversion to acting. But she did not dare to oppose Lalita's active creative instincts either, for at the slightest hurdle in any task she had enthusiastically undertaken, Lalita would become utterly disheartened, unable to participate at all.

In this effusive mood, Lalita had often rushed eagerly to Sucharita. Sucharita had smiled, indeed, and spoken to her, but Lalita repeatedly came up against some hidden inner obstacle that made her turn away, secretly offended at the rebuff.

One day, she went up to Poreshbabu and said: 'Baba, Suchididi can't be left to read alone in a corner while we go off to perform. She must join us.'

Of late, Poreshbabu had also been feeling that Sucharita was drifting away from her female companions. He feared that this mental state was not healthy for her nature. Lalita's words convinced him that unless Sucharita could participate in the general merriment, this aloofness would grow more pronounced.

'Go speak to your mother,' he instructed Lalita.

'I'll speak to Ma, but you must to take the responsibility of persuading Suchididi,' Lalilta insisted.

When Poreshbabu asked her, Sucharita could not refuse. She set forth to do her duty. As soon as Sucharita emerged from her corner, Binoy tried to engage her in conversation as before, but something had happened in the last few days, for she seemed beyond his reach. In her face, in her glance, was a remoteness that made him hesitate to approach her. Even earlier, Sucharita's social interaction and everyday activities had revealed a certain detachment, but now it had become extremely apparent. Even in joining the rehearsals her independence had not been affected. Immediately after completing the bare requirements of her task, she would go away. At first, Binoy was deeply hurt at this aloofness. Gregarious by nature, he found it hard to accept any resistance from those he found congenial. In this family, it was Sucharita who had so far shown him a special regard; now, spurned without reason, he was deeply wounded. But when he realized that Lalita was also similarly offended at Sucharita's behaviour, he felt comforted and his relationship with Lalita grew more intimate. Without giving Sucharita a chance to avoid him, he forsook her company. In this way, Sucharita soon drifted far away from Binoy.

During Gora's brief absence, Binoy had been able to mingle very freely with Poreshbabu's family in every way. Everyone in Poreshbabu's household felt a special satisfaction at this uninhibited revelation of Binoy's true nature. Binoy, too, felt an unprecedented delight at achieving this unobstructed, natural state of mind. The feeling of being liked by all these people further enhanced his capacity to please. As his personality blossomed, as he sensed his own independent strength, Sucharita drifted away from Binoy. This loss, this blow, would have been intolerable at any other time, but now he could overcome it easily. Surprisingly, Lalita, too, had not expressed any reproach at Sucharita's change of heart, this time. Was it only the enthusiasm for recitation and drama that had completely possessed her soul?

Meanwhile, seeing Sucharita join the performance, Haranbabu suddenly became very enthusiastic. He volunteered to recite an extract from *Paradise Lost*, and to deliver a short lecture on the enchantment of music, as a prelude to the recitation of Dryden's verse. Privately, Borodasundari was extremely annoyed at this. Lalita was also displeased. Haranbabu had already met the magistrate to confirm this plan. When Lalita protested that the magistrate might object prolonging the show like this, Haranbabu silenced her by producing from his pocket a letter of thanks from the magistrate.

Gora had set out on a journey without a mission; nobody knew when he would return. Although Sucharita had decided not to give this matter any place in her thoughts, she hoped in her heart, each day, that Gora might arrive that very day. Her heart could never suppress such thoughts. When she was excruciatingly tormented by Gora's indifference and the unruliness of her own heart, when her soul was desperate to escape this net, Haranbabu requested Poreshbabu once again in the name of the Almighty Ishwar, to confirm his betrothal to Sucharita.

'But the wedding is a long way off,' Poreshbabu demurred. 'Is it a good idea to commit yourselves so soon?'

'I consider it very essential for our maturing sensibilities for both of us to spend some time in this state of commitment before the wedding takes place,' declared Haranbabu. 'Between early acquaintance and the wedding itself, such a spiritual relationship, a bond without worldly responsibilities, would be particularly beneficial.'

'Very well, let me ask Sucharita,' said Poreshbabu.

'She has already given her consent,' Haranbabu reminded him.

Poreshbabu still had doubts about Sucharita's feelings for Haranbabu. So he sent for her and placed Haranbabu's proposal before her. Relieved at the possibility of surrendering her fraught, divided life to some ultimate cause, Sucharita gave her consent so instantly and decisively, that all Poreshbabu's doubts were dispelled. He begged her to consider carefully whether it was advisable for her to be forsworn so long before her marriage. Still, Sucharita raised no objection to this proposal. It was decided that, once Brownlow Saheb's invitation was taken care of, they would invite everyone to the betrothal on a special date.

For a brief moment, Sucharita felt as if she had emerged from the devouring maws of the malign planet Rahu. She privately resolved to harden her heart, preparing herself to marry Haranbabu and join the activities of the Brahmo Samaj. She decided to read some English theological texts with Haranbabu every day, and to follow his guidance. Having vowed to accept what was difficult, even unpleasant for her, she experienced a great sense of elation.

For some time now, she had not read the English paper that Haranbabu edited. Today, she received the paper as soon as it appeared in print. Perhaps Haranbabu had sent it especially for her. Carrying the paper to her room, Sucharita sat motionless and began to read it from the very first line, as if it was her sacred duty. Respectfully, she began to absorb the advice offered in the journal, as if she was a student. The ship in full sail suddenly keeled over when it touched a mountain. In the present issue of the paper, there was an article entitled

'Breathing the air of olden times,' attacking people who remained backward-looking even in the present age. Not that the arguments were unreasonable; in fact, Sucharita had been looking out for such ideas. But as soon as she read the article, she realized that Gora was its target. Yet, there was no mention of his name, nor any reference to any of his published articles. Every line of this essay exuded the vicious joy of spearing live flesh, like the satisfaction of a soldier when every bullet finds its mark.

This article was too much for Sucharita to bear. She longed to shred its every argument to bits. 'Gourmohanbabu could reduce this essay to dust, if he wished,' she thought to herself. The image of Gora's glowing face arose before her mind's eye, and his powerful voice echoed even within the recesses of her heart. So trivial did this essay and its author's meanness appear, in comparison with the extraordinariness of that face and those words, that Sucharita flung the paper to the ground.

After a long time, Sucharita approached Binoy of her own accord. 'Tell me,' she remarked conversationally, 'you had promised to bring me the papers in which you people have published articles. Then why haven't you given them to me?'

Binoy did not tell her that he had not dared to keep his promise, observing Sucharita's change of heart. 'I've put them together,' he said instead. 'I'll get them tomorrow.'

The next day, Binoy brought a bundle of books and papers and left them with Sucharita. Having obtained them, Sucharita put them away in a box without reading them. Because she was dying to read them, she did not do so. Vowing that she would not allow her mind to be diverted under any circumstances, she once again sought consolation in surrendering her rebellious heart to Haranbabu's authority.

~25~

On Sunday morning, Anandamoyi was stuffing rolled up paan with spices. Beside her, Shashimukhi was shredding supari into a tiny heap. At this moment, Binoy came in. Shashimukhi immediately ran from the room, scattering the betelnut gathered in her lap in the corner of her sari aanchal. Anandamoyi suppressed a smile.

Binoy could get along with everybody. So far, he had enjoyed a very friendly relationship with Shashimukhi. They would tease each other a lot. Shashimukhi had invented the strategy of stealing Binoy's shoes in order to extract stories from him. Binoy had invented a couple of tales, highly coloured versions of some trifling events in Shashimukhi's life. If he began recounting one of those stories, Shashimukhi would be outwitted. First she would loudly accuse the narrator of lying; then, admitting defeat, she would flee the room. To counter this, she too had tried to create stories that were distortions of Binoy's biography; but as she could not match Binoy's creativity, she had not achieved much success in this matter. Anyway, whenever Binoy visited this house, Shashimukhi would drop all her work and rush to attack him. Sometimes she troubled him so much that Anandamoyi would scold her, but Shashimukhi was indeed not solely to blame. Binoy would provoke her beyond endurance. When the same Shashimukhi quickly escaped from the room upon catching sight of Binoy, Anandamoyi smiled, but it was not a happy smile.

Binoy, too, was so offended at this trifling matter that he remained speechless for a while. It was apparent from such trivial instances how inappropriate it would be for him to marry Shashimukhi. When consenting to the match, Binoy had thought only of his friendship with Gora; he had not imagined what the experience of marriage might actually be like. Besides, he had taken pride in publishing many newspaper articles about the fact that marriages in our country are primarily family affairs rather than a matter of personal choice. As for himself, he had never entertained any personal likes or dislikes in this matter. Today, when Shashimukhi bit her tongue and ran away upon seeing Binoy because she saw him as her would-be husband, he witnessed an aspect of his future relationship with her. At once, his whole heart rebelled. He felt furious with Gora for forcing him to act in a way so contrary to his own nature. He cursed himself, and recalling that Anandamoyi had been against this marriage from the start, his heart was filled with respect mixed with wonder at the subtlety of her perception.

Anandamoyi sensed Binoy's mood. To divert his mind, she said:

'Binoy, I received a letter from Gora yesterday.'

'What does he say?' asked Binoy, rather absently.

'He doesn't say much about himself. He writes in sorrow about the plight of the lower classes in this country. He recounts the injustices committed by the magistrate at some village called Ghoshpara.'

'Gora only notices what others are doing,' Binoy blurted out impatiently, provoked into opposing Gora. 'And when we ourselves oppress society, straddling its body and stifling its breath, that must always be pardoned, as the holiest task ever undertaken.'

Seeing Binoy suddenly attack Gora in this way, contradicting him in order to establish his own credibility, Anandamoyi smiled to herself.

'You smile, Ma,' said Binoy. 'You wonder why Binoy should suddenly grow so angry. Let me tell you why. The other day, Sudhir had taken me to a friend's garden estate at their Naihati station. As soon as we pulled out of Sealdah, it started raining. When the train stopped at Shodpur station, I saw a Bengali in Western attire, sporting an umbrella, helping his wife off the train. The wife had a baby boy in her arms. Covering the child somehow with her heavy wrap, the poor thing stood at one end of the open platform, huddled in cold and embarrassment, getting drenched. Her husband, carrying the umbrella, attended to the luggage, creating a commotion. I was instantly reminded that, in the whole of Bengal, rain or shine, among the elite or uncultured, no woman carries an umbrella. I saw the husband shamelessly protecting his head with the umbrella while his wife silently got drenched in her wrap, without condemning his own behaviour even in his private thoughts, and nobody at the station found anything wrong with this. I have vowed ever since not to utter poetic falsehoods claiming that we revere our women greatly, regarding them as Lakshmi, as devi, and so on. We call the nation our motherland, but if we don't see the greatness of that female image manifest in our womenfolk, if we don't see our women as mature, spirited, and direct in their intelligence, physical strength, sense of duty and largeness of heart, if we find only weakness, narrowness and immaturity in our homes, then we shall never experience the glory of our nation.'

Suddenly embarrassed at his own fervour, Binoy continued in his normal tone: 'Ma, you are thinking, sometimes Binoy tends to launch into lectures, making tall claims, and today as well he is obsessed with the urge to hold forth. By force of habit, my words begin to sound like lectures, but today, this is no public speech. I had not understood properly, never considered, how far ahead of the nation our nation's women might be. Ma, I won't say more. Because I talk too much, nobody believes my words to be my own. From now on, I'll say less.'

Binoy left without further delay, his heart aflame with enthusiasm.

'Baba,' Anandamoyi sent for Mahim and said, 'Binoy can't marry our Shashimukhi.'

'Why? Do you have any objection?'

'It's because this match won't work in the long run that I am against it. Otherwise, why should I object?'

'Gora is in favour of it, so is Binoy. Why shouldn't it last? Of course if you withhold your consent, Binoy won't proceed. Of that I'm well aware.'

'I know Binoy better than you do.'

'Better even than Gora?'

'Yes, I know him even better than Gora does. That's why, all things considered, I can't give my consent.'

'Very well, let Gora return.'

'Mahim, listen to me. If you are too persistent in this matter, it will ultimately create trouble. I don't want Gora to say anything about this to Binoy.'

'Well, we shall see,' declared Mahim, stuffing a paan in his mouth. He rushed from the room in fury.

~26~

When Gora set out on his journey, he was accompanied by four people: Abinash, Matilal, Basanta and Ramapoti. But they could not keep pace with Gora's relentless enthusiasm. Within four or five days, Abinash and Basanta returned to Kolkata on the pretext of poor health. Purely out of devotion to Gora, Matilal and Ramapoti could not bring themselves to abandon him. But there was no end to their sufferings, for Gora never tired of walking, nor did a sedentary existence exasperate him. However inconvenient the diet and lifestyle, he would spend day after day in the home of any village householder who offered him hospitality out of respect for his

Brahmanhood. All the villagers would gather about him to listen to his discourses, reluctant to let him go.

For the first time, Gora saw what our country is like, outside the social worlds of the respectable bhadralok, the educated, and the Kolkata-dwellers. How fragmented, narrow-minded and feeble was this vast, concealed realm of rural Bharatvarsha—how utterly unaware of its own power, how completely ignorant and indifferent about its own interests! How extreme were the social differences between places only five or seven krosh, ten to fifteen miles apart—how many self-created and imaginary obstacles constrained the land from advancing in the world's giant workspace—how much importance it attached to trivialities, how moribund it had grown, clinging to every prejudice and superstition—how somnolent was its mind, how faint its heart, how feeble its efforts! Had he not dwelt among the villagers in this way, Gora could never have imagined all this. During his stay at a village, a fire broke out in one of the localities. Even in the face of such a grave disaster, Gora was amazed to see how poor was their capacity to band together and fight the danger wholeheartedly. They ran about in confusion, all of them, weeping and wailing, but unable to do anything in an organized fashion. There was no water-body near that neighbourhood. The women would fetch water from far away to perform their household chores, yet even the more well-to-do villagers had not thought of reducing that daily inconvenience by digging an inexpensive well in their backyard. There had been fires in this locality on earlier occasions as well, but the people passively took them for acts of God, making no effort to arrange some supply of water near at hand. Gora thought it a mockery to discuss the state of the entire nation with people who were mentally so inert, even about their urgent local needs. What amazed him most was that Matilal and Ramapoti felt no consternation at witnessing such scenes; on the contrary, they found Gora's rage inappropriate. This was how poor folks always behaved, such was their mindset. They did not regard these hardships as hardships at all. To imagine that things should be any different for the poor folk was taking things too far, they thought. Gora's heart was tormented day and night because he now realized clearly the terrifying enormity of the burden of such ignorance, stasis and suffering, a burden oppressing the educated and the illiterate, rich and poor, allowing nobody to progress.

Matilal left, claiming he had news of illness in the family; now Gora had only Ramapoti with him. Travelling on, the two of them arrived at a Muslim settlement beside the river. Searching for hospitality, they heard of only one family of Hindu barbers in the entire village. Seeking refuge there, the two Brahmans noticed that the old barber and his wife had adopted a Muslim boy. Ramapoti, very devout, became highly agitated. When Gora reprimanded the barber for his sinful act, he said:

'Thakur, we say Hari and they call Him Allah, but there's no difference.'

The sun beat down upon their heads, the sand-bank was vast, the river far away. Desperate with thirst, Ramapoti asked:

'Where can we find some water for a Hindu to drink?'

There was an unpaved well in the barber's house, but unable to drink from a well polluted by such irreligious conduct, Ramapoti felt dejected.

'Is this boy an orphan?' Gora inquired.

'He has parents, but for him, they're as good as dead,' the barber replied.

'How's that?'

The gist of the background narrated by the barber was as follows:

The zamindari they belonged to was leased by sahebs,

traders in indigo. There were endless disputes between the
tenants and the owners of the factory, the nilkuthi, over the
indigo fields on the chors or sandbanks. All the other tenant-
farmers had yielded, but the sahebs had not been able to
subdue the tenants of this sandbank named Chor-Ghoshpur.
All the subjects here were Muslims and their leader, Pharu
Sardar, feared no-one. He had served a couple of jail sentences
for thrashing the police after being harassed by the nilkuthi
owners. He was virtually starving now, but giving up was
alien to his nature. This season, farming on the zigzag sandbanks
of the river, the villagers had managed to grow some boro
paddy. But a month ago, the nilkuthi manager had arrived in
person to rob his tenant-farmers, accompanied by strongmen
armed with staves. During that attack, Pharu Sardar had dealt
such a blow to the saheb's right hand that it had to be
amputated at the clinic. Never had this area witnessed such a
daring feat. Ever since, police torture had spread like wildfire
through every neighbourhood. They left nothing intact in the
tenant-farmers' homes, and the honour of women in their
homes was jeopardized. Pharu Sardar and many others were
behind bars; most of the villagers were absconding. Pharu's
wife was starving; in fact, her only garment was so tattered
that she was ashamed to emerge from her house. Her only son
Tamiz used to address the barber's wife as his aunt, as fellow
villagers do. Seeing that he was starving, the barber's wife had
taken him in. One of the courthouses of the nilkuthi was
about a krosh and a half away; the police superintendent was
still stationed there with his team. There was no saying when
he might show up in the village and what he might do there,
in connection with the investigations. The previous day, the
police had arrived at the doorstep of old Nazim, the barber's
neighbour. A young brother-in-law of Nazim's had come
there from another village, to visit his sister. Without any
provocation, the superintendent declared: 'I must say this is a

strapping young fellow, look at his puffed up chest!' And he attacked him so violently with his stave that the youth began to bleed from the mouth, his teeth smashed. Witnessing such torture, his sister rushed up to him, but the policeman pushed the old woman aside. Formerly, the police would not dare create such trouble in the locality, but now every able-bodied youth in the area was either behind bars or absconding. It was to capture the fugitives that the police still roamed the village. There was no saying when the dominance of this malign planet would end.

Gora showed no inclination to leave, but Ramapoti meanwhile was growing desperate. The barber had barely ended his narrative, when he demanded:

'How far away is the Hindu neighbourhood?'

'You know the nilkuthi courthouse a krosh and a half away? The tehsildar there is a Brahman named Madhab Chatujje,' the barber informed him.

'What's he like?' Gora inquired.

'Like the devil's own messenger,' answered the barber. 'It's hard to find someone so heartless, yet so devious. He'll make us pay for the superintendent's stay with him as his guest, with some profit added too.'

'Let's go,' pleaded Ramapoti. 'That's enough.' Especially when the barber's wife began to bathe the Muslim boy near the well, drawing water from it in her small ghoti, he flew into a rage and lost all desire to linger in this house.

'How is it that you have remained in this locality, amidst all this oppression?' Gora asked the barber while taking his leave. 'Don't you have relatives elsewhere?'

'I've lived here a long time,' the barber told him. 'I have grown attached to these people. I am a Hindu barber. Because I have no landed property to speak of, the nilkuthi folks leave me alone. Among the men in this locality, there is no elderly person left. If I leave, the women will die of apprehension.'

'Very well,' said Gora, 'I'll return after my meal.'

Faced with this prolonged description of the oppressive conduct of the nilkuthi owners, at a time when he was acutely hungry and thirsty, Ramapoti became incensed at the villagers. It seemed to him an extreme instance of the daring and folly of staunch Muslims that these fellows should rise against those in power. He did not doubt that it would be all for the best if their arrogance were to be demolished through appropriate disciplinary action. He considered it customary for the police to oppress such lawless wretches for such things were inevitable, and these people were primarily responsible for them. After all, they could always compromise with the owners. Why create trouble? Where was all their fire and mettle, now? As a matter of fact, Ramapoti privately sympathized with the saheb who owned the nilkuthi.

All the way, traversing the scorching sand under the midday sun, Gora uttered not a word. Ultimately, they spotted the thatched courthouse roof through the foliage, from a distance. Gora suddenly declared:

'Ramapoti, please go ahead and have your meal. I am going to that barber's house.'

'How can you say that!' expostulated Ramapoti. 'Won't you have something to eat? You must proceed on your way after stopping for a meal at Chatujje's.'

'I'll take care of my duties,' responded Gora. 'Now after your meal, please proceed to Kolkata. I might have to stay on at the Ghoshpur Chor for a while. It would be too much for you.'

Ramapoti's hair stood on end. He could not imagine how a devout Hindu like Gora could even propose staying with that infidel. He began to wonder whether Gora had resolved to renounce food and drink, to fast unto death. But this was not the time to ponder; every moment seemed an age to him. He did not need much persuasion to escape to Kolkata, abandoing Gora. Glancing at him briefly, Ramapoti saw the small shadow of Gora's tall frame trudging back alone amidst the desolate, scorching sands, in the heat of the midday sun.

Hunger and thirst had overwhelmed Gora, but the more he thought about having to accept the hospitality of the vile, unjust Madhab Chatujje just to preserve his caste purity, the more intolerable the prospect appeared. His face reddened, his temper flared, and a tremendous sense of rebellion arose in his heart. He thought, 'What a great heresy we are committing in Bharatvarsha, making purity a matter of appearances alone! It would save my caste purity to dine at the home of a man who torments Muslims by creating all sorts of trouble, but I would lose my caste status in the home of a person who accepts such torment to protect a Muslim boy, and is even ready to suffer social condemnation for it. Anyway, I'll reflect later upon the pros and cons of such discriminatory practices, but at present, I have no choice.'

The barber was surprised to see Gora returning alone. When he arrived, Gora first scrubbed the barber's ghoti thoroughly with his own hands, then collected water from the well to drink.

'If there's some rice and dal in the house, please let me have some,' he requested. 'I'll cook for myself.'

Flustered, the barber made arrangements for him to cook.

'I'll stay with you a few days,' Gora informed him, after he had eaten.

Terrified, the barber pleaded with folded hands: 'I cannot be more fortunate than to have you stay with someone as humble as myself. But the police have their eye on us, you see; there's no saying what problems might transpire if you remain here.'

'As long as I am present here, the police won't dare trouble you,' declared Gora. 'If they do, I shall protect you.'

'I beg you,' urged the barber, 'if you try to protect us, we shall have no rescue. Those fellows will think that I have conspired to get you here as a witness against them. I have survived somehow, all these days, but I cannot continue here if that happens. If I, too, am uprooted from here, the village will be trampled underfoot.'

Having grown up in the city, Gora found it hard to even understand the barber's apprehensions. He thought taking a strong stand on behalf of justice was sufficient to combat injustice. His conscience refused to let him abandon an endangered village, leaving it helpless. Now the barber prostrated himself at his feet.

'Look, sir, you are a Brahman,' he pleaded. 'On the strength of my punya, the accumulated virtue of my past lives, you have become our guest. It is wrong of me to ask you to leave. But because I know your sympathy for us, I can tell you that if you stay here and try to prevent police harassment, you would place us all in grave danger.'

Taking the barber's anxieties for baseless cowardice, Gora was rather annoyed. He left their home and set out in the late afternoon. He even began to regret having accepted food and other hospitality at this heretic's dwelling. Physically exhausted and mentally embittered, he arrived at the nilkuthi courthouse in the evening. Ramapoti had wasted no time in setting off for Kolkata after his meal, so there was no sign of him. With a special show of cordiality Madhab Chatujje offered Gora his hospitality.

'I shall not even taste the water in your house,' declared Gora, flying into a rage.

When a surprised Madhab asked him why, Gora abused him for being an unjust oppressor. He remained standing, refusing to take a seat. The police officer was lolling against a bolster, puffing upon his gurguri, the hookah with its long flexible tube.

'Who are you, mister?' he asked belligerently, sitting up.
'Where are you from?'

'Are you the superintendent?' Gora inquired, without
answering his question. 'I have learnt all about your assaults
on Ghoshpur Chor. If you don't take heed now, . . .'

'Will you send me to the gallows?' laughed the
superintendent. 'A fine fellow, I must say. I thought he had
come to beg for favours, but he threatens us instead! O
Tewari!'

Flustered, Madhab grasped the superintendent's hand.
'Arré, what are you doing?' he said. 'Don't insult him, he's
a bhadralok!'

'What sort of bhadralok is he!' fumed the superintendent.
'When he was so rude to you, wasn't that an insult, too?'

'What he said was not untrue,' said Madhab. 'So how can
we be angry? We make our living as agents of the nilkuthi
sahebs; need we say more? Don't mind Dada, but you're a
police superintendent, after all; would it be infamy to call you
an agent from hell? It's well understood that the tiger is a
man-eater, no vegtetarian boshtom ascetic. What's the tiger
to do? He must survive, mustn't he?'

No one had seen Madhab angry without reason. When
someone might prove useful—or when crossed, what harm
they might do—who could tell? Extremely careful about
injuring or insulting anybody, he did not waste his destructive
powers by making others the target of his wrath.

'Look here baba,' said the superintendent to Gora, 'we
are here to serve the government. If you object to that, or
make a nuisance of yourself, you'll be in trouble.'

Gora left the room without a word.

'Moshai, what you say is true,' admitted Madhab, rushing
after him. 'Our job makes butchers of us, and as for that
superintendent, it's a sin even to share the same divan with
him. I can't bring myself to mention all the misdeeds I've

made him perform. It won't take much longer—if I work for just two or three years more, I'll acquire the means to marry off these daughters of mine, and after that, my wife and I will head for Kashi, renouncing the world. I don't relish all this anymore, moshai; sometimes I want to hang myself. Anyway, where else will you go tonight? Please dine with us and spend the night here. You need not come anywhere near that superintendent fellow. I'll make separate arrangements for you.'

Gora's appetite was above the ordinary, and he had not had a proper meal in the morning, either. But his entire body seemed to be on fire. He could not remain here under any circumstances.

'I have some urgent work,' he declared.

'Wait, then, I'll organize a lantern.'

Gora rushed away without offering any reply.

'Dada, that man is on his way to the headquarters,' said Madhab, returning to his room. 'Send a messenger to the magistrate while there is still time.'

'Why, what must we do?' asked the superintendent.

'Nothing, just let him inform them that a bhadralok has surfaced from somewhere and is at large, trying to subvert witnesses.'

~27~

At sunset, Magistrate Brownlow was walking along the riverside path. With him was Haranbabu. Not far away, his wife, the mem, was savouring the air in the motor car, along with Poreshbabu's daughters.

From time to time, Brownlow Saheb would invite the Bengali bhadraloks to garden parties at his house. It was he who acted as chief guest at prize distribution ceremonies at the district entrance school. If invited to wedding rituals at some well-to-do person's house, he would accept the householder's hospitality. In fact, when invited to a jatragaan performance of songs from indigenous popular theatre, he would recline on a large armchair and for a while, patiently try to listen to the music. During the last puja, he had particularly appreciated the performance of the two lads who had played the bhisti or water-carrier and the methrani or scavenger-woman, in the jatra enacted at the house of the government pleader at his court. At his request, their scene had been replayed for his benefit more than once.

His wife was a missionary's daughter. Sometimes, they hosted a tea for missionary women at their house. He had established a girls' school in the district, and tried very hard to ensure that it had no shortage of students. He always encouraged the educational discussions he had witnessed among the female members of Poreshbabu's house. He would drop them a line every now and then, even when he was far away, and send them religious books for Christmas.

The mela was on. Borodasundari and the girls, accompanied by Haranbabu, Sudhir and Binoy, were present at the occasion, all of them. They had been offered accommodation at the Inspection Bungalow. Poreshbabu had no patience for such noisy events; he had stayed behind in Kolkata, by himself. Sucharita had tried very hard to remain with him, to give him company, but advising her strongly that it was her duty to respect the magistrate's invitation, Poresh sent her away. It had been decided that on the penultimate day, in the presence of the Commissioner Saheb and the Lieutenant Governor and his wife, at the after-dinner party at the magistrate's house, Poreshbabu's daughters would perform and recite. Many of the magistrate's British friends from the district as well as from Kolkata had been invited to the event. A few select Bengali bhadraloks were also to attend. There would even be snacks prepared for them by Brahman cooks in a garden tent, so it was rumoured.

In a very short time, Haranbabu had succeeded in winning the heart of the magistrate saheb by virtue of his lofty conversation. The saheb had been amazed at Haranbabu's extraordinary knowledge of Christian theology, and he had even asked Haranbabu why he had the slightest hesitation in embracing the Christian faith. This afternoon, pacing the riverside path, he was deeply engaged in discussion with Haranbabu about Brahmo and Hindu practices. At this juncture, Gora appeared before him.

'Good evening, sir,' he said.

Trying to meet the magistrate the previous day, he had realized that he must grease the sentry's palm to cross the saheb's threshold. Unwilling to tolerate such subjugation and insult, he had come to meet the saheb during his outing today. During this action, Haranbabu and Gora showed no sign of mutual recognition.

The saheb was rather perplexed when he saw this man. He could not recall having encountered such a person in Bengal, more than six feet tall, heavy boned, sturdy. Even his complexion was unlike that of the ordinary Bengali. Khaki shirt, coarse, faded dhoti, bamboo stave in hand, chador wound around his head like a turban.

'I've just come from Ghoshpur Chor,' Gora told the magistrate.

The magistrate gave a surprised whistle. He had received news the previous day, that an outsider was obstructing the investigations at Ghoshpur. So this was the man! 'What is your caste?' he asked Gora, surveying him once from top to toe.

'I am a Bengali Brahman.'

'Oh! Do you have any connections with the press?'

'No.'

'Then what are you doing at Ghoshpur Chor?'

'I took shelter there during my wanderings. Having witnessed the predicament of the village under police torture, and realizing the likelihood of further trouble, I have come to you to ask for redress.'

'Are you aware that the people at Ghoshpur Chor are utter scoundrels?'

'They're no scoundrels. They're bold and independent, unable to endure unjust oppression in silence.'

The magistrate was incensed. He concluded privately that this new Bengali had learned to parrot some words gleaned from history books. This was insufferable!

'You understand nothing of the present situation!' roared the magistrate.

'You know much less than me about the situation here,' thundered Gora in reply.

'I warn you,' declared the magistrate, 'if you interfere in the Ghoshpur matter in any way, you will not get off easily.'

'Since you have decided not to counter the injustice that is taking place, and since your attitude towards the villagers is predetermined and unshakable, I have no choice but to incite the villagers against the police, by my own efforts.'

'What!' The magistrate stopped suddenly in his tracks. 'How dare you!' he shouted, wheeling about to face Gora.

Gora stalked away slowly, without uttering another word.

'Haranbabu,' said the magistrate, 'what does the behaviour of your countrymen signify?'

'It's due to lack of in-depth study, especially due to the total absence of spiritual and ethical education in our country that all this is happening,' Haranbabu asserted. 'They have not yet earned the right to receive the best of English education. If these ungrateful people are reluctant even now to acknowledge British rule in India as God's decree, it's only because they have merely learned by rote. Their religious sense is extremely underdeveloped.'

'Without embracing Christianity, people's religious sense will never develop to maturity in India,' the magistrate declared.

'In a sense, that is true,' Haranbabu assented. He had then engaged the magistrate in a discussion of his possible conversion to Christianity, making fine distinctions between where his opinions coincided with or differed from a Christian's. So deeply had he kept the magistrate engrossed that when the memsaheb, returning in the carriage after dropping Poreshbabu's daughters at the dak bungalow, called to her husband: 'Harry, we must go home,' the magistrate started, took out his watch and exclaimed: 'By Jove, it's eight twenty!'

Before stepping into the car, he wrung Haranbabu's hand. 'Our discussion has made this evening very enjoyable,' he said, by way of farewell.

Back at the dak bungalow, Haranbabu recounted his interchange with the magistrate in detail. But he made no mention of his encounter with Gora.

~28~

Forty seven accused persons had been condemned to prison without being tried for any crime, just to keep the village under control. After his meeting with the magistrate, Gora set out in search of a lawyer. Someone told him that Satkori Haldar was a good lawyer.

'Wah, it's Gora , isn't it?' exclaimed Satkori, as soon as Gora arrived at his house. 'What brings you here?' It was as Gora had thought: Satkori was his classmate.

'The accused at Ghoshpur must be released on bail and their cases fought in court,' Gora declared.

'Who will stand security for bail?' Satkori asked.

'I will.'

'What resources do you possess, to stand guarantor for forty seven persons on bail?'

'If all the mukhtars, the legal representatives, collectively offer security, I shall pay their fees.'

'It won't be a small amount.'

The next day, they applied for bail at the magistrate's court. Looking askance at the previous day's hero dressed in his faded garments and turban, the magistrate ignored the request. From a fourteen year old boy to an old man of eighty, all the accused were condemned to rot in jail.

Gora requested Satkori to defend their case.

'Where will you find witnesses?' Satkori asked him. 'All potential witnesses are among the accused. Moreover, the people of this area are overwrought due to the investigation into the case of those murdered sahebs. The magistrate is convinced there is a secret bhadralok hand in this whole affair. Who knows, perhaps he even suspects me! The English papers keep saying that if the local people are incited to such daring, the unprotected, helpless British can't survive in the provincial areas any more. Meanwhile, things have reached a stage where our countrymen can't survive in their own land. I know there is oppression, but there's nothing we can do.'

'Why not?' thundered Gora.

'You're exactly as you were in school, I see,' smiled Satkori. 'When I say there's nothing we can do, I mean we have wives and children at home. If we don't earn our daily bread, many will go hungry. There aren't many in this world willing to give up their lives shouldering other people's burdens, especially in a country where the family is not taken lightly. Those with many dependants have no time for the problems of all and sundry.'

'So you'll do nothing for these people?' said Gora. 'If, by a motion in the high court, we . . .'

'Arre, they've killed Englishmen, don't you see!' cried Satkori impatiently. 'Every Englishman is a raja, after all. To murder even an ordinary Englishman amounts to a minor act of treason. I can't let myself fall into the magistrate's bad books in a false bid to achieve something futile.'

Gora set out the next morning, planning to catch the ten-thirty train to Kolkata, to see if he some lawyer there could help him with the case, when he encountered an obstacle. To coincide with the local mela, a cricket tournament had been scheduled, between students from Kolkata and the local students' team. The Kolkata boys were playing amongst themselves, to hone their skills. One of the boys was severely hurt when the cricket ball hit him on the leg. There was a large pond at the end of the field. Carrying the injured boy to the pond's edge, a couple of students shredded a chador, soaked the strips and began to bandage his leg with them. Suddenly, a watchman appeared from nowhere, and shoved a student by the shoulder, abusing him in obscene language. The Kolkata students did not know that it was forbidden to enter this pond because it was reserved for drinking water. Even had they known, they were not used to accepting such sudden humiliation from a watchman. Being physically strong as well, they began to suitably avenge the insult. Witnessing this spectacle, four or five constables rushed to the spot. At that very moment, Gora arrived on the scene. The students recognized Gora, for he had often played cricket with them.

'Don't hit them! I warn you!' cried Gora, unable to bear the sight of the students being beaten and dragged away.

When the watchman's party swore abominably at Gora as well, he created such a commotion, hitting and kicking them, that a crowd collected on the street. Meanwhile, the students quickly formed a cluster. When they attacked the police at Gora's urging and command, the watchman's party at once beat a hasty retreat. Onlookers in the street found this highly amusing. But needless to say, this spectacle did not remain a mere piece of entertainment for Gora.

At around three or four in the afternoon, when Binoy, Haranbabu and the girls were busy rehearsing at the dak bungalow, a couple of students known to Binoy came and reported that Gora and a few students had been arrested by the police and put in the lockup. The following day, the case would come up at the magistrate's very first session in court. Gora in the lockup! Everyone but Haranbabu was dumbfounded. Binoy immediately rushed to their classmate Satkori Haldar and having first told him the whole story, took him along to the lockup. Satkori offered to defend Gora in court, and to try getting him out on bail at once.

'No,' said Gora. 'I won't engage a lawyer, and there's no need to try and get me out on bail either.'

How could he say that!

'Look at this!' expostulated Satkori, turning to Binoy. 'Who would think Gora is out of school! His mindset remains exactly the same.'

'I don't want to be free of lockup and handcuffs simply because I'm fortunate enough to have money and friends,' declared Gora. 'According to our nation's religious law, we know it is the ruler's responsibility to ensure justice; it's the ruler who must be blamed if his subjects suffer injustice. But in this kingdom, if subjects must rot in the lockup and die in jail because they can't afford the lawyer's fee, if even under a king's rule one must go bankrupt trying to buy a fair verdict with money, I wouldn't spend a paisa on such justice.'

'But in the days of the kazis, one had to sell one's soul to afford the bribes,' Satkori pointed out.

'But bribery was not the ruler's decree,' Gora insisted. 'Corrupt kazis would demand bribes, and that continues even in the present regime. But now, to seek justice at the ruler's door, the subject must suffer, be he plaintiff or defendant, guilty or innocent. For the destitute, both victory and defeat spell disaster in their fight for justice. And where the ruler is the plaintiff and the defendant is a man like me, lawyers and barristers would all take his side, and as for me, I'd be lucky to find someone, or else I'm at the mercy of my fate! If a court case doesn't need a lawyer's assistance, why have government lawyers at all? If legal help is necessary, why must the party opposing the government have to find his own lawyer? Does this make the government an enemy of the nation's subjects? What sort of political ideology is this?'

'Bhai, why are you so angry?' asked Satkori. 'Civilization doesn't come cheap. For fine judgement, fine laws must be formulated, and to create fine laws, one must become a trader in law. To run a business you must buy and sell, hence the court of justice called civilization automatically becomes a market where judgements can be bought and sold. And it will remain likely that a person without money will get a raw deal. Tell me, what would you do if you were king?'

'If I created laws impenetrable even for a judge on a salary of a thousand rupees or a thousand-and-a-half, I would employ government-paid lawyers for both unfortunate parties, plaintiff and defendant alike. I wouldn't insult the Pathans and Mughals, vaunting the fairness of my own judgement while forcing my subjects to bear the costs of a well-conducted trial.'

'Good idea,' said Satkori, 'but since that auspicious day has not yet arrived, since you have not become king, since at present you are the defendant in a civilized monarch's court, you must either spend from your own pocket or seek the help of a lawyer friend. The third option would not be pleasant for you.'

'Let my fate be that which comes of making no effort,' said Gora obstinately. 'Let me share the fate of those who are utterly helpless in this kingdom.'

Binoy tried very hard to persuade him, but Gora paid no heed to his pleas.

'How did you suddenly turn up here?' he asked Binoy.

Binoy flushed slightly. Had Gora not been confined in the lockup, Binoy might have explained his presence in defiant terms. But now he could not offer an outspoken reply.

'We'll talk about my affairs later . . .' he demurred. 'Now as for you . . .'

'Today, I am a royal guest,' declared Gora. 'Today, the king himself is concerned about me, so none of you need have any concern.'

Knowing it was impossible to sway Gora, Binoy had to relinquish his efforts to engage a lawyer.

'I know you can't swallow the food here,' he said. 'I'll arrange to have some food sent to you from outside.'

'Binoy, why do you struggle in vain?' cried Gora, losing his patience. 'I don't want anything from outside. I want nothing more than what's meted out to everyone in the lockup.'

Binoy went back to the dak bungalow with a heavy heart. In a bedroom facing the street, Sucharita was awaiting his return, with her door shut and window open. She could not bear the company and conversation of others. Seeing Binoy approach the dak bungalow looking worried and dejected, her heart lurched in fear. Forcing herself to remain calm, she picked up a book and made her way to the drawing room. Lalita did not enjoy needlework, but today she was sewing silently in a corner. Labanya was playing a spelling game with Sudhir, with Leela as her audience. Haranbabu was discussing the next day's festivities with Borodasundari.

Binoy gave them a detailed account of Gora's confrontation with the police early that morning. Sucharita sat frozen still. The sewing fell from Lalita's lap and her face grew flushed.

'Have no fear, Binoybabu,' Borodasundari assured him.

'This evening, I shall personally petition the magistrate saheb and his mem on Gora's behalf.'

'No,' said Binoy, 'please don't do that. If Gora hears of it, he will never forgive me, all his life.'

'But we must make some arrangements for his defense,' Sudhir insisted.

Binoy told them all about Gora's objections to seeking bail or engaging a lawyer.

'This is too much!' exclaimed Haranbabu impatiently.

Whatever Lalita's opinion of Haranbabu, she had shown him deference up until now, and had never argued with him. But now she burst out, shaking her head violently:

'It's not too much at all! Gourbabu has done the right thing. If magistrates entrap us, are we supposed to defend ourselves? Must we provide taxes for them to receive a fat salary, and then pay a lawyer from our own pocket to escape their clutches! Better go to jail than receive such justice.'

Haranbabu had known Lalita since she was very young; he had never dreamt that she had opinions of her own. He was amazed to hear such sharp words from her lips.

'What do you understand of such things?' he admonished her reprovingly. 'You are carried away by the irresponsible, frenzied delirium of those who have just cleared college by learning a few books by rote, those who have no religion, no considered opinions.'

He proceeded to recount Gora's meeting with the magistrate the previous evening, and his own discussion about it with the magistrate. Binoy was unaware of the incident at Ghoshpur Chor. Hearing about it, he was filled with apprehension, realizing that the magistrate would not easily forgive Gora. Haran's purpose in telling this story was completely thwarted. Sucharita was wounded by the secret pettiness of his having kept his meeting with Gora a total secret until now. Haranbabu's personal envy of Gora, evident in every word he uttered, elicited the disrespect of all present, at such a time when Gora was in trouble. Sucharita had remained silent, but now she felt the urge to say something. Controlling herself, she opened her book and began to turn the pages with trembling hands.

'However closely Haranbabu's views might match the magistrate's, the Ghoshpur affair has demonstrated the greatness of Gourmohanbabu!' declared Lalita with pride.

~29~

Because the Lieutenant Governor was expected that day, the magistrate arrived at the courthouse punctually at half past ten, and tried to dispense with the day's legal business as early as possible.

Satkoribabu tried to save his friend by defending the schoolboys. Given the circumstances, he had realized that pleading guilty was the best strategy here. He pleaded for mercy, arguing that boys were naturally mischievous, that they had acted immaturely and foolishly, and so on. The magistrate ordered that the boys be taken to jail, and caned five to twenty times, according to their age and the gravity of their offence. Gora had no lawyer to defend him. In his own defense, he tried to say something about police torture. The magistrate at once silenced him with a sharp reprimand, sentenced him to a month's rigorous imprisonment for obstructing police activities, and acclaimed this light sentence as extremely lenient.

Sudhir and Binoy were present in the courtroom. Binoy could not bear to meet Gora's eyes. Feeling suffocated, he rushed from the courtroom. Sudhir begged him to return to the dak bungalow for his bath and breakfast, but he would not listen. He walked some distance down the path that skirted the field, and collapsed under a tree.

'Go back to the bungalow,' he told Sudhir. 'I'll come after a while.'

Sudhir went away. How long he remained in this state, Binoy had no idea. When the sun that had been directly overhead was declining westwards, a carriage stopped just in front of him. Raising his head, Binoy saw Sudhir and Sucharita dismount and approach him. Quickly, he rose to his feet.

'Come, Binoybabu,' pleaded Sucharita tenderly, coming up close.

Binoy suddenly realized that people on the street were highly entertained at this spectacle. He quickly stepped into the carriage. Nobody said a word, all the way back. Arriving at the dak bungalow, Binoy found that a fight had broken out there. Lalita had stubbornly refused to participate in the magistrate's programme that evening, under any circumstances. Borodasundari was in a grave dilemma. Haranbabu was outraged at such inappropriate rebelliousness in a girl so young. 'How depraved today's youngsters have become!' he kept exclaiming. 'They won't observe any discipline! This is the outcome of discussing all sorts of ideas in the company of all sorts of people.'

'Forgive me Binoybabu,' Lalita blurted out as soon as Binoy arrived. 'I have wronged you greatly. I had not understood any of your words before this. It's due to our total ignorance about the outside world that our notions are so mistaken. Panubabu says it's by God's decree that magistrates rule Bharatvarsha. In that case, it's by the same God's decree that one feels a heartfelt desire to curse this rule.'

'Lalita, you . . .' began Haranbabu angrily.

'Please be quiet!' Lalita interrupted, turning her back on Haranbabu. 'I am not speaking to you. Binoybabu, please ignore all requests. The show cannot be allowed to take place today.'

'Lalilta, you are quite amazing, I must say!' Borodasundari hastily intervened, to silence Lalita's outburst. 'Won't you give Binoybabu a chance to bathe and eat today? It's one-thirty already, do you realize? See how drained he looks!'

'Here we are guests of the magistrate,' declared Binoy. 'I can't bathe or dine in this house.'

Borodasundari pleaded with Binoy, trying hard to persuade him. Observing the girls' silence, she scolded them angrily:

'What's the matter with all of you? Shuchi, why don't you try to explain to Binoybabu? We have given them our word. People have been invited. We must somehow manage this occasion, or what will they think, tell me! We could never face them again.'

Sucharita bowed her head in silence.

Binoy left by steamer from the riverside not far away. The steamer with its passengers would depart for Kolkata in a couple of hours, to arrive there at approximately eight o'clock the next day.

Haranbabu began to criticize Gora and Binoy agitatedly. Quickly rising from her chowki, Sucharita went into the adjacent room and slammed the door. Soon afterwards, Lalita pushed the door open and came in. She saw Sucharita lying on the bed, both hands covering her face. Locking the door from within, Lalita gently sat down beside her, and began to run her fingers through Sucharita's hair. After a long while, when Sucharita had calmed down, Lalita prised away the arms shielding her face, and bent close to whisper in Sucharita's ear:

'Didi, let's go back to Kolkata. After all, we can't go to the magistrate's tonight.'

For a long time, Sucharita offered no answer. When Lalita persisted, she sat up in bed.

'How is that possible my dear?' she said. 'I had no wish to come here. But since Baba has sent me here, I can't leave without completing my undertaking.'

'But Baba knows nothing of what has transpired. Had he known, he would never have asked us to stay on.'

'That I couldn't say, bhai!'

'Didi, can you really bring yourself to do it?' asked Lalita. 'Tell me, how can you go there? And then, we must don our costumes to recite poems on stage! Even if I bit my tongue till it bled, I couldn't utter a word!'

'I know that bon, sister of mine! But even hell must be endured. There's no way out now. I'll never forget this day, all my life!'

Incensed at Sucharita's compliance, Lalita left her room.

'Aren't all of you going, Ma?' she asked.

'Have you lost your mind?' said Borodasundari. 'We're supposed to go there after nine.'

'I'm talking about going to Kolkata.'

'Listen, just listen to this girl!'

'Sudhirda, will you remain here as well?' Lalita demanded.

Sudhir's heart was broken at Gora's conviction, but he lacked the capacity to resist the temptation of displaying his learning before all those powerful sahebs. He uttered something inarticulate, signifying that although he was hesitant, he would stay back, after all.

'With all this confusion, it's already very late,' Borodasundari interrupted. 'We can't delay any longer. Now nobody must arise from bed before five-thirty—you have to rest. Otherwise you'll get tired and look haggard in the evening, and what an ugly sight that would be!'

She firmly propelled everyone to their rooms and to bed. They all went to sleep. Only Sucharita could not sleep, and in another room Lalita remained sitting upright in bed.

The steamer horn sounded, again and again.

As the steamer was preparing to leave and the sailors were about to draw up the gangway, from the upper deck Binoy saw a woman, seemingly from a respectable bhadra family, rushing towards the vessel. From her attire and appearance she looked like Lalita, but Binoy could not immediately believe it. Ultimately, when she came closer, he was left in no doubt. For a moment he thought she had come to take him back, but it was Lalilta after all who had opposed their participation in the magistrate's programme. She boarded the steamer. The sailors pulled up the gangway. Full of foreboding, Binoy descended from the upper deck to face Lalita.

'Take me to the upper deck,' she said.

'But the steamer is about to leave,' protested Binoy.

'I know.'

Without waiting for Binoy she ascended to the upper deck. Sounding its horn, the steamer set out.

Having offered Lalita an armchair on the first class deck, Binoy looked at her questioningly without saying a word.

'I'm going to Kolkata,' she said. 'I found it impossible to stay on.'

'What about all of them?'

'They don't know as yet, any of them. I've left a letter; as soon as they read it, they will know.'

Binoy was astounded at Lalita's daring.

'But . . .' he faltered.

'The steamer has left, so there's no room for ifs and buts!' she interrupted quickly. 'I don't understand why I must bear everything in silence just because I'm born a woman. Even women are capable of distinguishing between just and unjust, possible and impossible. I'd rather kill myself than perform at tonight's event.'

Binoy realized that now the deed was done, it was no use brooding over the pros and cons of having taken such a step.

'Look,' Lalita resumed after a short silence, 'privately, I had gravely misjudged your friend Gourmohanbabu. I don't know why, from the moment I saw him and heard him speak, my heart grew averse to him. He spoke too forcefully, and all of you seemed to comply. This used to make me angry. Such is my nature—if I see anyone use force in their speech and behaviour, I just can't tolerate it. Gourmohanbabu exerts force not only on others, though, but also on himself. That is real power. I have never seen such a person.'

Lalita prattled on in this fashion. Not that she was saying all this only from remorse about Gora. Actually, embarrassment at her impulsive act was constantly threatening to make itself felt. She was beginning to doubt whether she had acted wisely. Until now, she had never imagined how awkward it might be to confront Binoy alone on the steamer. But because the slightest expression of shame would at once make the whole affair utterly shameful, she desperately babbled on. Binoy found himself at a loss for words. For one thing there was Gora's misery and humiliation, then the shame of having come here to entertain himself at the magistrate's house, and to top it all, this sudden predicament created by Lalita. All this, taken together, had rendered Binoy speechless.

On earlier occasions, such daring on Lalita's part would have evoked Binoy's disapproval, but today that did not happen at all. In fact, the amazement roused in him was mingled with respect. There was the added satisfaction that, out of their entire group, only Binoy and Lalita had made the slightest attempt to oppose Gora's humiliation. For this, Binoy would not have to suffer too much, but Lalita's act would cause her great torment, for a long time to come. Yet Binoy had always regarded the same Lalita as hostile to Gora. The more he thought about it, the more he began to respect Lalita's courage, so heedless of her actions' outcome, and her extreme contempt for injustice. He could not think of a way to demonstrate or articulate this respect. Binoy was haunted by the feeling that Lalita's disdain for him as a spineless person constantly dependant on others' views, was entirely justified.

He could never have forcefully disregarded the approval and disapproval of all relatives and friends, to express his own views on any subject through courageous action in this fashion. Today, secretly acknowledging that he had often avoided following his own instincts for fear of hurting Gora's feelings or appearing weak in Gora's eyes, and that he had often used a web of subtle arguments to delude himself that Gora's ideas were his own, he admitted that Lalita was vastly his superior in her capacity for independent thought. He was ashamed to remember that he had often privately censured Lalita. Indeed, he wanted to apologize to her, but could not think of a way. Binoy saw Lalita's graceful feminine figure illumined by such inner glory, that he felt that this revelation of woman's uniqueness had made his own life worthwhile. Today he surrendered all his pride, all his pettiness, to this shakti, this power infused with sweetness.

~30~

Accompanied by Lalita, Binoy arrived at Poreshbabu's house.

Before he boarded the steamer Binoy was unsure about the nature of his feelings for Lalita. His antagonism with Lalita had kept his heart engaged. For some time now, it had become his daily preoccupation to devise some way of making some kind of truce with this irrepressible girl. It was Sucharita, with the pure radiance of her feminine charm, who had first appeared on Binoy's horizon like the evening star. His exquisite joy at her arrival had imparted wholeness to his nature, or so he had privately imagined. But that other stars had also meanwhile appeared, and that the first star having ushered in the festival of lights had slowly started to fade unnoticed from the horizon, was something Binoy had not clearly realized.

The day the rebellious Lalita came aboard the steamer, Binoy felt: 'Lalita and I are united in our stand against the rest of the world.' He could not dismiss the thought that, ignoring everyone else, it was to him that Lalita had come, seeking his support. Whatever the reason and whatever the purpose, today Lalita did not merely regard Binoy as one in a crowd; he alone was by her side, he was the only one; all her relatives and dear ones were far away, he alone was close. The rapture of this proximity throbbed in his heart like the rumbling of thunder clouds. When Lalita withdrew to the first class cabin Binoy could not tear himself away to retire to his own sleeping quarters. Removing his shoes, he began to silently pace up and down the deck outside that cabin. Lalita was not likely to face any harassment on board the steamer, but tempted to savour his sudden newfound rights to the full, Binoy could not resist exercising them even without need.

The night was intensely dark, the cloudless firmament covered in stars, the treeline on the shore still and silent like the night sky's deep ink-black base, the wide river's powerful current flowing silently beneath. In this setting, Lalita lay sleeping. This lovely, trustful sleep was all she had placed in Binoy's hands today. Binoy had assumed the responsibility of guarding her sleep like a priceless jewel. With neither parents nor siblings near her, Lalita was sleeping peacefully, resting her beautiful form on an unfamiliar bed, her breath rising and falling very gently, as if in rhythm with the poem that was her slumber; not one braid of her skillfully coiled hairknot had come undone; those hands, with their tender feminine grace, lay on the bed in a posture of complete repose; her feet with their lovely flowerlike soles rested on the bed, stilling all her charming restlessness, like music at the end of a festival. This image of tranquil repose filled Binoy's imagination. Like a miniscule pearl within an oyster, Lalita's tiny spell of sleep in the midst of this dark, silent firmament adorned with planets and stars, appeared to Binoy today as his only precious possession. 'I am awake, I am awake!'——like the fearless sound of a conchshell, these words arose from the expanded recesses of Binoy's heart, floating up to the vast, endless sky to merge with the wordless utterance of the ever-watchful, wakeful being who presides over the great universe.

On this night of the moon's dark quarter, another thought continued to torment Binoy. Tonight, Gora was in jail! Until now, Binoy had shared all Gora's joys and sorrows. This was the first time that it had happened otherwise. Binoy knew that for a person like Gora, the constraints of prison were of no consequence; but in this matter, from beginning to end, Binoy had not been involved with Gora at all; this important episode in Gora's life had occurred entirely without Binoy's participation. Once the course of their lives had diverged at this single point, could the two friends fill the gap when they were united again? Wasn't there a breach now in the completeness of their friendship? A friendship so perfect, so rare! Tonight, simultaneously experiencing emptiness on one account and fulfillment on another, having arrived at a moment in his life where the forces of creation and destruction merged, Binoy gazed silently into the darkness.

Had it indeed been purely due to circumstances that Binoy was unable to join Gora in his travels, or to share Gora's travails in prison after he was sentenced, their friendship could not have been damaged. But it was not mere happenstance that Binoy was acting in a show while Gora set forth on his journey. It was because Binoy's entire lifestream had deviated from the course of their former friendship that this outward separation had also become possible after so long. But now there was no denying the truth. It was no longer really possible for Binoy to singlemindedly adopt Gora's unswerving path. But would their lifelong mutual love be altered due to this change of direction alone? This doubt made Binoy's heart tremble. He knew Gora could not proceed without drawing all his friendship, his sense of duty, towards a single goal. How powerful Gora was! How fierce his desire! Fate had granted Gora's nature the royal splendour to draw all his relationships into a victory march in celebration of that single desire.

The hired cab stopped at Poreshbabu's door. Binoy could clearly sense how Lalita's legs trembled as she dismounted and how she braced herself when entering the house. Lalita herself was unable to gauge the extent of her guilt at the step she had impulsively taken. She knew Poreshbabu would not say anything that could be taken for a direct reprimand; for that very reason, it was his silence she feared most of all. Observing Lalita's hesitation Binoy could not determine exactly what to do in such a situation. To test whether his presence would aggravate Lalita's awkwardness, he said rather doubtfully:

'I'll take my leave then!'

'No,' said Lalita quickly. 'Come, let's go to Baba.'

Binoy was secretly delighted at this desperate plea. Thinking that his duty was not over as soon as he had brought her home after all, that these sudden developments had created a special bond between himself and Lalita, Binoy seemed to stand by her with added confidence. The thought of Lalita's dependence upon him was like a physical touch that electrified his entire body. He imagined Lalita was clutching his right hand. His male breast swelled at this contact with her. He privately expected that Poreshbabu would be incensed at Lalita's stubborn antisocial stance, that he would admonish her, at which point Binoy would take as much of the blame as possible. He would unhesitatingly accept his share of the reprimand and like a suit of armour, try to protect Lalita from every onslaught.

But Binoy had not understood Lalita's actual state of

mind. It was not merely because he could protect her from rebuke that she was reluctant to let him go. Truth be told, Lalita was incapable of subterfuge. She seemed to assume that all aspects of her action would be apparent to Poreshbabu and that she must accept the full consequences of her trial. Since that morning, Lalita had been secretly fuming at Binoy. She knew full well that her anger was unwarranted, but precisely for that reason, her fury increased instead of diminishing.

While on the steamer, Lalita's mood had been different. Since childhood, she had always managed to get into unimaginable scrapes, acting sometimes out of anger, sometimes out of stubbornness. But this time it was a serious matter. That Binoy should have been involved with her in this forbidden escapade caused her embarrassment on one hand and deep elation on the other. This elation seemed to be enhanced by its very forbiddenness. The way she had sought refuge with an outsider to her family, coming so close to him without her relatives as a protective barrier between them, could have caused great awkwardness. But Binoy's natural civility had created such a restrained aura of propriety, that in this risky predicament, the knowledge of his fine sense of decency had delighted Lalita. This was surely not the same Binoy who always laughed and joked with everybody in their house, who prattled on without pause, whose familiarity even with the servants was open and free! Binoy had maintained such a distance where he could easily have claimed more time in Lalita's company in the name of watchfulness, that this in itself had increased her secret sense of intimacy with him. At night, in the steamer cabin, all sorts of anxieties had kept her awake. As she tossed and turned, she presently felt sure that dawn must be approaching. Gently opening the cabin door she looked out and saw that the dew-drenched darkness of the late hours still enveloped the open sky above the river and the treeline along its shore. A cool breeze had just aroused gurgling sounds in the river, and below in the engine room there were signs of activity, as if the sailors were about to resume work. As soon as she stepped out of the cabin, Lalita found Binoy asleep on a cane chair not far away, a warm wrap around his shoulders. The sight at once set her heart racing. Binoy had stayed there all night guarding her! So near and yet so far! With trembling footsteps Lalita immediately left the deck and returned to her cabin. Standing at the door on that autumnal Hemanta dawn, she gazed at Binoy's solitary sleeping figure, within that darkness-enshrouded, unfamiliar riverine landscape. To her, the stars on the horizon before her seemed to encircle Binoy's slumber; her whole heart brimmed with an indescribable solemnity and sweetness; why her eyes so swiftly filled with tears she could not understand. The deity she had been taught by her father to worship seemed to bless her today. And on this sleeping rivershore dense with foliage, at the sacred moment of union when the night's darkness first secretly embraces the new light of dawn, at the full assembly of stars in the firmament, a divine melody rang out on the unstirred strings of the vast cosmic mahaveena, like unbearably exquisite pangs of joy. Just then Binoy's hand twitched slightly in his sleep. Lalita quickly shut the cabin door and lay down in her bed. Her palms and soles turned cold. For a long time, she was unable to quell the restlessness of her heart.

The darkness faded. The steamer was on the move. Having washed and dressed, Lalita came out and stood leaning on the railing. Binoy too, having already awakened at the sound of the steamer horn, was ready and waiting to watch the dawn break over the eastern shore. As soon as Lalita emerged, he grew embarrassed and prepared to leave.

'Binoybabu!' she called out at once.

'You probably didn't sleep well at night,' she observed when he came close.

'I didn't sleep too badly.'

After this, neither of them said a word. At the far end of the dew-moist kash fields with their tall feathery reeds, shone the golden radiance of approaching sunrise. Neither of them had ever witnessed such a sunrise before. The light had never touched them in this way. For the first time they realized that the sky was not empty, that it gazed steadfastly at Creation in silent wondrous bliss. Such an intense awareness had awakened in their hearts that they seemed to physically collide with the innermost consciousness of the entire universe. Neither of them uttered a word.

The steamer arrived at Kolkata. Hiring a cab at the ghaat, Binoy settled Lalita within and took his place beside the coachman. Travelling in the carriage on these Kolkata streets in the daytime, why Lalita's thoughts underwent a reversal, who could say! That Binoy was on the steamer at this time of crisis, that Lalita had become involved with him in this way, that he was escorting her home as if he was her guardian—all these things began to torment her. She now found it intolerable that Binoy should have acquired a certain authority over her by force of circumstance. Why should it be so! Why did that music of the night end on such a harsh note when confronted with the daytime workaday world! So when Binoy came to the door and asked hesitatingly, 'I'll take my leave then?' Lalita was even more annoyed.

'Binoybabu thinks I'm ashamed to face my father in his company,' she thought. To demonstrate emphatically that she had no qualms about this, and to present the complete facts of the case to her father, she was reluctant to let Binoy depart from the doorstep like a culprit. She wanted her relationship with Binoy to revert to its former transparent footing. She did not want to appear to Binoy in a reductive light by allowing any constraint or any hazy fantasy to linger as an obstacle between them.

~31~

As soon as he saw Binoy and Lalita, Satish rushed up, placed himself between them, and held their hands.

'Why, hasn't Borodidi come?' he demanded.

Binoy patted his pocket, looked all around and said: 'Borodidi! Really, what could have happened! She is lost.'

'Ish!' exclaimed Satish, giving Binoy a shove. 'Indeed! I don't believe you! Lalitadidi, please answer me!'

'Borodidi will come tomorrow' said Lalita, and headed for Poreshbabu's room.

'Come and see who is here,' Satish insisted, dragging Binoy and Lalita by the hand.

'It doesn't matter who's here,' said Lalita, pulling her hand away. 'Don't bother us now. We're going to Baba.'

'Baba is out. He'll be back late.'

Hearing this, both Binoy and Lalita felt a temporary sense of relief.

'Who is our visitor?' Lalita wanted to know.

'I shan't tell you. Achchha Binoybabu, can you guess who is here? You can never guess. Never never!'

Binoy began to suggest some preposterously impossible and inappropriate names: Sirajuddaula, Raja Nabokrishna, at one point even Nandokumar. Satish protested loudly, offering irrefutable reasons why such an assembly of guests was utterly impossible.

'True indeed,' conceded Binoy, acknowledging defeat. 'It hadn't occurred to me before that there might be some serious reasons why Sirajuddaula would find it inconvenient to visit this house. Anyway, let your didi investigate the matter first. Then, if necessary, I'll come as soon as you send word.'

'No, both of you must come,' Satish persisted.

'Which room must we go to?' asked Lalita.

'The room on the second floor.'

In a corner of the second floor terrace was a small attic with a jutting tiled roof sloping southwards to keep out the sun and rain. There beneath that sloping sunshade, the duo following in Satish's wake found a bespectacled elderly lady reading Krittivasa's *Ramayana* on a small mat. The broken end of her spectacle frame was tied with a string, secured behind her ear. She would be about forty-five. The hair had thinned in front, but her fair countenance was still almost perfectly smooth, like a ripe fruit. Between her brows was a tattoo mark. She was in widow's garb, her form unadorned. Spotting Lalita first, she hastily removed her spectacles, and abandoning her book, she gazed at her face with special eagerness. The next moment, seeing Binoy following behind Lalita, she swiftly rose to her feet, pulled her sari aanchal over her head and prepared to retreat into the room. Satish rushed up to hug her.

'Mashima, why are you running away?' he demanded. 'This is our Lalitadidi, and this is Binoybabu. Borodidi will arrive tomorrow.'

This brief introduction to Binoybabu was enough; there had undoubtedly been plenty of discussion about him already. At the slightest opportunity Satish would hold forth on the few subjects in the world he was equipped to speak about, and he kept nothing back. Not understanding who the term 'Mashima' might refer to here, Lalita stood transfixed in amazement. When Binoy touched this elderly woman's feet in a pranam, Lalita followed his example. Mashima hurriedly fetched a mat from the room and spread it out.

'Sit, baba. Please sit down, ma.'

When Binoy and Lalita had settled on the mat, she resumed her place on her own mat with Satish close to her. Embracing Satish firmly with her right arm, she declared:

'You don't know me, all of you. I am Satish's mashi. His mother was my own elder sister.'

This brief introduction did not reveal much, but there was something in Mashima's face and voice that manifested a pure, tear-bright hint of the deep sorrows of her life. When she clasped Satish to her bosom declaring 'I am Satish's mashi,' Binoy's heart ached in sympathy even without knowing anything of this woman's life history.

'You can't be Satish's mashi alone, for then Satish and I will quarrel for the first time in all this while. As it is Satish calls me Binoybabu, not Dada. For him to deprive me of Mashima as well would be utterly unfair.'

It did not take Binoy long to win people over. In no time at all this young man with his charming appearance and pleasing speech had usurped part of Satish's dominion in Mashima's heart.

'Where is your mother, my son?' Mashima asked him.

'I lost my own mother long ago,' Binoy replied, 'but I can't say that I have no mother.'

As he spoke, he remembered Anandamoyi and his eyes instantly grew moist, as if misted over by emotion. The conversation between the two of them became very animated. One could never have guessed that they were new acquaintances. Satish began to interrupt this dialogue with utterly irrelevant opinions of his own. Lalita remained silent.

Lalita seemed to find it difficult to express herself easily, even if she tried. She took very long to break the inhibitions of a first meeting. Besides, she was not in a good mood today. She did not like the way Binoy was effortlessly chatting with this unknown woman; privately, she condemned his frivolity in remaining so free of anxiety, heedless of the gravity of Lalita's predicament. Not that Binoy could have escaped Lalita's displeasure if he had remained morose and silent, with a grave expression; for then, surely, Lalita would have angrily said to herself: 'It is I who must confront my father, but Binoybabu is behaving as if he must shoulder all the blame!' Truth be told, in the broad light of day the impact that had struck a musical note last night now only produced chords of pain. Nothing was as it should be. That was why Lalita was mentally taking Binoy to task at every step. Nothing he did could have prevented this quarrel. The Almighty alone knew the root cause that must be addressed, for the problem to be solved.

Alas, why should women, who deal solely in matters of the heart, be condemned as irrational? If the heart is in the right place to begin with, it functions so easily and beautifully that all rational arguments bow to it in defeat. But should the slightest trouble occur in the beginning, it is beyond the brain's capacity to repair that instrument. It is fruitless then to even try gauging how anger and indifference, laughter and tears, lead from one thing to another.

Meanwhile it was not as if Binoy's heart-machine was functioning quite normally either. If its condition had remained exactly as before, he would have rushed to Anandamoyi this very moment. Who but Binoy could break the news of Gora's jail sentence to his mother? Who else did she have to console her! This painful thought was like a huge weight grinding away constantly at the bottom of his heart. But it had become impossible for him to part from Lalita immediately. He was trying to convince himself that he was now Lalita's sole protector against the whole world, and that if any intervention was required when Lalita faced Poreshbabu, he must discharge those duties before departing. His heart was easily convinced; it had no capacity to resist. However deep his anguish for Gora and Anandamoyi, Lalita's close proximity delighted Binoy so much, made him feel so expansive, made the whole world seem so glorious, gave him such a distinctive sense of identity, that his pain remained buried in the lower reaches of his heart. Today he could not meet Lalita's eyes. Even the tiniest glimpses that caught his eye every now and then—a corner of her clothing, a hand resting quietly on her lap—instantly made him ecstatic.

It grew late, but Poreshbabu did not return. Binoy's heart prompted him with increasing urgency to rise and take his leave. To suppress it, he continued to concentrate on his conversation with Satish's mashi. Ultimately, Lalita could no longer contain her annoyance. Suddenly interrupting Binoy, she blurted out:

'For whose sake must you delay so long? There's no saying when Baba might return. Won't you see Gourbabu's mother once?'

Binoy was startled. He was only too familiar with Lalita's angry tone. Glancing at her face, he instantly sprang upright like a bow when its string is snapped. For whose sake had he delayed his departure? After all, the arrogant assumption that he was urgently needed here had not occurred to Binoy on its own. He had been about to depart from their very doorstep, and it was Lalita who had requested him to accompany her inside. And now, for Lalita to ask him such a question! So suddenly had Binoy sprung up from the mat that Lalita stared at him in surprise. She saw that his natural cheerfulness had been extinguished at a single puff, like a lamp. Never before had she seen such pain on his face, nor such a sudden change of mood. Looking at him, Lalita at once felt the stinging whiplash of acute regret, striking repeatedly at her heart.

Quickly scrambling to his feet, Satish clung to Binoy's arm, pleading: 'Please stay Binoybabu, don't leave just now. Please have dinner with us. Mashima, why don't you ask Binoybabu to stay for dinner! Lalitadidi, why did you tell Binoybabu to leave!'

'Bhai Satish, not today,' Binoy demurred. 'If Mashima remembers, I'll come another day to taste her prasad, food sanctified by her touch. Today it's too late.'

There was nothing extraordinary about his words, but there were tears in his voice. The pathos did not escape Satish's Mashima's ear either. Swiftly glancing at Binoy and then at Lalita, she understood that this was a game of destiny.

Not long after, Lalita got up and went to her room on some slight pretext. How often had she brought herself to tears in this way!

~32~

Binoy at once headed for Anandamoyi's house. He was inwardly tormented by a mixture of shame and pain. Why had he not gone to Ma all this time! What a mistake he had made! He had imagined that Lalita needed him urgently. The Almighty Ishwar had punished him suitably indeed, for not rushing to Anandamoyi as soon as he reached Kolkata, irrespective of all other needs. Ultimately, he was forced to hear such a question from Lalita's lips: 'Won't you see Gourbabu's mother once?' Could such an aberration ever be possible, that Lalita should care more about Gourbabu's mother than Binoy did! After all, Lalita only knew her as Gourbabu's mother, but to Binoy, she was the sole image of motherhood personified.

Anandamoyi had just bathed. Immobile on her floormat, she was probably meditating silently. Binoy rushed to her and fell at her feet.

'Ma!'

'Binoy!' Anandamoyi stroked his bowed head with both her hands.

Was there anyone with a voice such as Ma's! At the very sound of that voice, Binoy's entire body felt the touch of sympathy flow over it. Restraining his tears with difficulty, he murmured:

'Ma, I have come too late!'

'I have heard all about it, Binoy.'

'You've heard all about it!' exclaimed Binoy, startled.

From the lockup itself, Gora had written a letter to Anandamoyi, which he had forwarded through the lawyer. He must have anticipated that he would be sent to prison.

In conclusion, the letter said:

Imprisonment will not succeed in harming Gora in the least. But it will not do for you to suffer at all. Your sorrow is the only thing that could be my punishment; it is beyond the magistrate's power to inflict any other penalty on me. Don't think of your own son alone, Ma! The sons of many other mothers serve jail sentences for no fault of theirs. I want to share an equal footing with them, for once; if this wish is fulfilled now, please don't grieve for me.

Ma, I don't know if you remember, but the year there was that famine, I had left my money pouch on the table in the room facing the road, and gone into the next room for five minutes. I returned to find the pouch had been stolen. It contained eighty-five rupees I had saved from my scholarship; I had privately resolved to have a silver ghoti made for you to wash your feet if I saved a little more. Finding the money stolen, as I seethed with futile rage against the thief, the Almighty Ishwar suddenly planted a good thought in my mind. I told myself that at this time of famine I had donated the money to the very man who had taken it. As soon as the words were said, all my fruitless indignation subsided. Similarly, I have now made my heart declare that I am going to prison of my own free will. There is no pain in my heart, no anger against anybody. I am going to accept the hospitality offered by the prison. There will be inconveniences with food and amenities; but after all, when I accepted the hospitality of many homes during my recent travels, I did not find there the comforts I was accustomed to or needed. The suffering I accept willingly is not suffering at all; today I shall voluntarily accept the jail as my refuge. Know this for sure: as long as I remain in prison, not for a single day will anyone keep me there by force.

When we remained at home, effortlessly enjoying our food and amusements, we were not conditioned to even feel the tremendous magnitude of our right to move freely in the daylight under the open sky. Until today I had neither thought about nor maintained any contact with the majority of human beings in this world who at that very moment were suffering bondage and humiliation, deprived of their god-given right to the world, deservedly or undeservedly. Now I wish to emerge in public as a marked man like the rest of them. I don't want to preserve my social prestige by joining the falsely virtuous men of this world, most of whom pretend to be civilized bhadralok.

Ma, this time my encounter with the real world has taught me a great deal. Ishwar knows that most of those responsible for passing judgement on others are themselves in need of mercy. Prisoners in jail pay for the sins of those who go unpunished while meting out punishments to others; the crime is committed by many, but these people alone are penalized. As for those who enjoy comfort and prestige outside the prison walls, I do not know how, when and where they will atone for their sins. Spurning such comfort and prestige, I shall emerge in public bearing on my breast the mark of mankind's guilt. Ma, please grant me your blessings, don't shed tears for me. Lord Krishna bore the mark of Bhrigu's kick on his chest, forever; in this world, wherever arrogance inflicts injustice, it deepens that scar on the deity's breast. If that mark becomes His ornament, what have I to worry about, and why should you grieve at all?

Upon receiving this letter Anandamoyi had tried to send Mahim to Gora. Mahim replied that he had to go to work,

and that his boss, the saheb, would never give him leave. He
then proceeded to curse Gora roundly for his arrogance and
lack of judgement, declaring that he too might one day lose
his job on Gora's account. Anandamoyi deemed it unnecessary
to apprise Krishnadayal of this matter. Regarding Gora, she
had a deep-seated grievance against her husband, knowing
that Krishnadayal had not given Gora the place of a son in his
heart. In fact, he was privately hostile to Gora. Like the
Vindhya mountain range, Gora stood as an obstacle to the
conjugal relations between Anandamoyi and her husband. On
one side of the breach was Krishnadayal, isolated by his
excessive vigilance about ritual purity; on the other side was
Anandamoyi, alone with her outcaste Gora. It was as if the
channels of communication were closed, between the only
two people in the world who knew Gora's life history. For all
these reasons, Anandamoyi's affection for Gora was solely her
treasure. She tried as far as possible to make light of Gora's
illegitimate presence within this family. It was her daily worry
lest someone should say, 'This was your Gora's doing', 'We
had to hear such things, thanks to your Gora,' or 'Your Gora
has caused us this loss.' After all, she alone was entirely
responsible for Gora. And her Gora was no ordinary
mischievous child, either! It was not easy, was it, to conceal
his existence, wherever he might be? Having spent all these
years bringing up her precious, unruly Gora in the midst of
this hostile family, managing him day and night until he was
now so grown up, she had faced many allegations she could
not answer, borne many ordeals she could not share.

Anandamoyi remained at the window, in silence. She saw
Krishnadayal enter the house, chanting mantras after his early
morning bath, marks of Ganga earth on his forehead, arms
and chest. Anandamoyi could not approach him. Forbidden,
forbidden, all was forbidden! Finally, with a sigh, she arose
and went to Mahim's room. He was reading a newspaper on

the floor while his servant gave his body an oil massage before
his bath.

'Mahim,' said Anandamoyi, 'give me an escort, let me go
and see what has happened to Gora. He has made up his mind
to go to prison; if he is imprisoned, can't I visit him once
before that?'

Whatever his outward manner, Mahim had a soft spot for
Gora. Verbally, he continued to growl:

'Let the wretch go to prison, then. Surprising it hasn't
happened before now!'

But having said this, the very next moment he sent for
Poran Ghoshal who was beholden to them. He gave him some
money for the lawyer's fees and dispatched him immediately.
He also decided to travel there himself, if the saheb at the
office gave him leave, and if his wife permitted.

Anandamoyi was also aware that Mahim could not rest
content without doing something for Gora. Once assured that
Mahim had made all the arrangements possible, she returned
to her room. She was well aware that at this difficult time,
amidst all the public mockery, curiosity and gossip, no one in
this family would escort her to Gora's unfamiliar location.
Eyes clouded with silent pain, she clenched her lips and
remained quiet. When Lachhmia burst into loud sobs she
scolded her and banished her to another room. It was her
lifelong habit to digest all her anxiety in silence. She calmly
accepted both joy and sorrow; only the all-knowing Lord
could see the grief in her heart.

Binoy did not know what to say to Anandamoyi. But she
never awaited words of consolation from anybody. Her nature
shrank from others who tried to talk about her sorrows,
which were beyond redress. Preventing any further discussion,
she said:

'Binu, I see you have not bathed yet. Go and have a bath
quickly, it's very late.'

When Binoy sat down to his meal after a bath, Anandamoyi's heart wept in grief at the sight of Gora's empty place beside him. Gora would have to eat prison food today, food with the bitter taste of heartless discipline, not sweetened by a mother's care. At one point, the very thought compelled Anandamoyi to rush from the room on some pretext.

~33~

When he returned home, as soon as he saw Lalita at this odd hour, Poreshbabu realized that this wild daughter of his had got into some unprecedented scrape. He looked at her inquiringly.

'Baba, I came away,' she blurted out. 'I couldn't remain there under any circumstances.'

'Why, what is the matter?' Poreshbabu asked.

'The magistrate has sent Gourbabu to jail.'

How Gour came into the picture and what exactly had occurred, Poreshbabu could not understand at all. When Lalita told him the whole story, he remained silent for a while. Immediately thinking of Gora's mother, his heart filled with anguish. He thought, 'if only the judge could sense how cruel was the punishment inflicted on several innocent people whenever one man was sent to prison, it could never be such an easy, routine matter to condemn someone to jail.' Only an extreme paralysis of the ethical sense could have generated the barbarity that enabled the magistrate to pronounce with equal ease the same punishment for Gora as for a common thief. The news of Gora's prison sentence made Poreshbabu recognize how much deadlier than other forms of violence was man's tyranny towards man, and also how social power and royal authority had combined to lend tremendous force and magnitude to such tyranny.

'Tell me, Baba, isn't this a terrible injustice?' demanded Lalita, encouraged by Poreshbabu's thoughtful silence.

'I don't quite know the extent and nature of Gour's actions,' replied Poreshbabu with his customary calm. 'But I can say this for sure: Gour may go beyond his rights when carried away by his strong sense of duty, but it is entirely against his nature to commit what the English language calls a crime. Of that I have not the slightest doubt. But what can we do, ma, the sense of justice in our times has not yet attained that level of moral discrimination. Even now, the same punishment is prescribed for mistakes as for crimes; both entail the same prison sentence, the same hard grind. We cannot blame any one person for this state of affairs. For this, all the sins of humanity are to blame.' Then, suddenly dropping the subject, Poreshbabu asked: 'Who did you come with?'

'With Binoybabu,' replied Lalita, drawing herself upright as if by some special effort. Whatever her outward display of strength, inwardly she was vulnerable. Lalita did not find it easy to declare that she had come with Binoybabu. From somewhere, a hint of embarrassment arose within her, and thinking that this embarrassment was visible in her facial expression, she grew even more self-conscious.

Among all his offspring, Poreshbabu loved this capricious, indomitable daughter of his the most. It was because her conduct seemed blameworthy to others that he had developed a special respect for the forthrightness of Lalita's behaviour. He knew that people would specially notice her faults but her virtues, however rare, would go unappreciated. Poreshbabu had carefully nourished her good qualities, all along; in the process of subduing Lalita's unruly nature, he had not wanted to trample upon her inner nobility as well. People acknowledged the beauty of his other two daughters at first sight; their complexion was fair, their facial contours flawless;

but Lalita's complexion was darker, and the extent of her facial charm was debatable. Hence Borodasundari constantly expressed anxiety to her husband about finding a match for Lalita. But the beauty Poreshbabu saw in Lalita's face was not that of complexion or of build, it was the profound beauty of the inner self. It had not only grace but also the fire of independence and the firmness of strength, a firmness not everyone would find appealing. It would attract a few special people, but repel many others. Realizing that Lalita would not be popular but that she would be genuine, Poreshbabu would draw her to him with a certain tender pain—because he knew that others were unforgiving, he judged her with compassion.

When he heard that Lalita had suddenly come away alone with Binoy, he instantly understood that she would have to undergo intense and prolonged suffering on this account. People would prescribe for her a punishment appropriate for a crime much greater than the minor one she had committed. As he pondered over this in silence for a while, Lalita blurted out:

'Baba, I have done wrong. But I have understood very clearly now that the relationship between the magistrate and our countrymen is such that his hospitality implies no honour for us, only condescension. Ought we to have stayed on, tolerating even this?'

The question did not strike Poreshbabu as an easy one.

'You crazy girl!' he smiled, patting her head with his right hand, avoiding any direct answer.

As Poreshbabu paced outside the house that afternoon, thinking about this episode, Binoy appeared and touched his feet respectfully. Poreshbabu spent a long time discussing Gora's imprisonment with him, but did not even mention Binoy's arrival with Lalita on the steamer. 'Come, Binoy, let's go inside,' he proposed when it grew dark.

'No,' said Binoy. 'I'll go home.'

Poreshbabu did not ask him a second time. Casting a swift, lightning glance at the upper storey, Binoy slowly walked away. Lalita had spotted Binoy from upstairs. When Poreshbabu entered alone, she assumed that Binoy would follow him in shortly. But even after a short while, Binoy did not appear. Then, after shuffling about some of the books and paperweights on the table, Lalita left the room. Poreshbabu called her back.

'Lalita, sing a Brahmo song for me,' he requested, looking tenderly at her downcast face.

He turned down the lamp, shading its light.

~34~

The next day, Borodasundari and the rest of her troupe came back. Unable to contain his disapproval of Lalita, Haranbabu accompanied them instead of returning to his own lodgings, and went directly to Poreshbabu. Angry and upset, Borodasundari went straight to her room without glancing at Lalita or saying a word to her. Labanya and Leela had also come back incensed with Lalita. The departure of Lalita and Binoy had so disabled their recitation and acting that their embarrassment was beyond description. Taking no part in Haranbabu's indignation, Borodasundari's tearful laments or Labanya and Leela's awkward indifference, Sucharita had fallen completely silent, mechanically performing her routine chores. Today as well, she followed everyone mechanically into the room. Cringing with shame and remorse, Sudhir went home from Poreshbabu's doorstep itself. Failing in her repeated attempts to invite him in, Labanya vowed not to speak to him anymore.

'Something terribly wrong has happened,' blurted out Haranbabu as soon as he entered Poreshbabu's room.

Lalita was in the adjacent room. As soon as these words entered her ears, she came and stood there, hands clasping the back of her father's chowki, gaze fixed on Haranbabu's face.

'I have heard all about it from Lalita,' said Poreshbabu. 'Now the deed is done, it is no use discussing it.'

Haran regarded the calm, restrained Poresh as extremely weak-natured. Hence he said, rather disdainfully:

'Episodes end once they have occurred, but character remains, after all. That is why even past events must be discussed. What Lalita has done today could never have been possible had she not always been pampered by you. How much you have harmed her will become apparent when you hear all about today's happening.'

Sensing a slight rocking movement at the back of his chowki, Poreshbabu quickly drew Lalita to his side and grasping her hand, he said with a faint smile:

'Panubabu, you will realize in due course that affection, too, is necessary for one's children's upbringing.'

Putting her arm round her father's neck, Lalita bent to whisper in his ear:

'Baba, your water is growing cold. Please go and have your bath.'

'I'll go a little later,' said Poreshbabu in an undertone, glancing at Haran. 'It's not so late.'

'No, Baba, please have your bath,' insisted Lalita tenderly. 'Meanwhile, we shall keep Panubabu company.'

After Poreshbabu had left the room Lalita firmly occupied a chowki and fixing her gaze on Haranbabu's face, she accused him: 'You think you have the right to say anything to anybody!'

Sucharita knew Lalita well. On any other day, the sight of Lalita in her present mood would have secretly aroused her anxiety. But today, she remained on her chowki by the window, staring silently at the open page of a book. By nature and habit, Sucharita was always self-restrained. In the last few days, the more she had felt the accumulated pain of all sorts of afflictions, the quieter she had become. Today, the burden of this silence had become intolerable, so when Lalita took it upon herself to express her views to Haran, it was as if the torrent imprisoned in Sucharita's heart found an opportunity for release.

'Do you think you know better than Baba what his duties towards us should be!' Lalita erupted. 'Are you sole Headmaster of the entire Brahmo Samaj!'

At first Haranbabu was stunned at such arrogance in Lalita. He was about to offer a very harsh reply when she interrupted:

'We have endured your superior airs all these days with great patience, but if you try to surpass Baba as well, nobody in this house will tolerate you—not even our bearer.'

'Lalita, you . . .' Haranbabu began to expostulate.

'Silence!' Lalita interrupted sharply. 'We have been hearing you at length, now listen to what I have to say. If you don't believe me, please ask Sucharita: my Baba is far more noble than you imagine yourself to be. Now you may give us all the advice you wish to offer.'

Haranbabu's face darkened. 'Sucharita!' he cried, rising from his chowki.

Sucharita looked up from her book.

'Can Lalita be allowed to insult me before your very eyes!' said Haranbabu.

'It is not her aim to insult you,' answered Sucharita calmly. 'Lalita wants to say that you should treat Baba with due respect. We don't know anyone more worthy of respect than he.'

For a moment it seemed as if Haranbabu would leave at

once, but he did not rise. He remained seated, his face very grave. The more he realized that he was gradually losing respect in this house, the harder he tried to establish his claim. He was becoming unmindful of the fact that the tighter one grasps a worn-out crutch, the faster it tends to crumble. Observing Haranbabu's solemn, offended silence, Lalita arose and went up to Sucharita. She began to chat with her in a low voice as if nothing serious had happened. Meanwhile, Satish came into the room.

'Borodidi, come with me,' he said, tugging at Sucharita's hand.

'Where must we go?' asked Sucharita.

'Just come with me, I'll show you something. Lalitadidi, you haven't told her have you?'

'No,' replied Lalita.

Lalita had promised Satish not to disclose his mashi's presence to Sucharita. She had kept her word. But Sucharita could not abandon their guest.

'I'll come in a little while, bakhtiar,' she said. 'Let Baba join us after his bath.'

Satish began to fret. If it had been within his power to somehow make Haranbabu disappear, he would have left no stone unturned. Being in awe of Haranbabu, he could not say anything to him. Haranbabu had not maintained any form of contact with Satish, apart from occasionally trying to mend his nature.

As soon as Poreshbabu appeared after his bath, Satish dragged his two sisters away.

'About that proposal concerning Sucharita,' declared Haranbabu, 'I wish to delay no further. I would like the ceremony to take place next Sunday itself.'

'I have no objection,' replied Poreshbabu, 'provided Sucharita agrees.'

'But we have already taken her consent.'

'Well then, the matter is decided.'

~35~

That day, after parting from Lalita, Binoy was haunted by a doubt that pierced his heart like a thorn. He began to think:

'I have been visiting Poreshbabu's house regularly without knowing for sure whether anyone likes or dislikes my going there. Perhaps that is not correct. Perhaps I have tested their patience frequently and at odd times. I don't know the ways of their culture, or the extent of my rights of access in this house. Maybe I am stupidly entering spaces forbidden to anyone but relatives.'

Considering these things it seemed to Binoy that Lalita may have seen something in his expression today that had affronted her. Until now, Binoy's own feelings for Lalita had not been clear to him. Today, they were no secret. He could not fathom how to handle these new revelations of his heart's inner state. A thousand times, he debated its links with the external realm, its relations with the world, whether it meant dishonour for Lalita or a betrayal of Poreshbabu. He felt like sinking into the earth, imagining that Lalita was angry at having caught him out. It became impossible for Binoy to go to Poreshbabu's house. The emptiness of his own house also weighed upon him. Early the next morning, he went to Anandamoyi.

'Ma, I'll stay with you for a few days,' he announced.

At heart, he also meant to console Anandamoyi to assuage her grief at separation from Gora. Realizing this, Anandamoyi's heart melted. Without a word, she stroked Binoy affectionately. Binoy made all sorts of demands upon her affection, concerning his meals and the attention he required. He quarreled with her on the false pretext that he was not being looked after properly there. With his diverting chatter he constantly tried to keep both Anandamoyi and himself distracted. In the evening, when it was hard to contain his emotions, he would pester her, dragging her away from all her housework to the mat spread on the veranda before the room. He would make her narrate stories about her childhood in her parents' house, stories about the days when she was an infant, extremely popular with the residential students at her grandfather's tol—his Sanskrit school—a special cause for anxiety for her widowed mother because as a fatherless girl, she was indulged by everyone in every way.

'Ma, I feel surprised to imagine a time when you were not our mother,' Binoy declared. 'I think the students at the tol saw you as a tiny mother, ever so small. As if it was you who had assumed the responsibility of bringing up Dadamoshai.'

One evening, placing his head upon Anandamoyi's outstretched legs upon the mat, Binoy said: 'Ma, I feel like returning all my learning and intellect to the Maker and to seek shelter in your lap as an infant. I wish there would be nothing in the world for me but you alone.'

Binoy's voice expressed such emotional fatigue that Anandamoyi was both moved and surprised. Shifting closer, she began to gently stroke his head. After a long silence she asked:

'Binu, is all well with Poreshbabu's household?'

Her question startled Binoy, making him suddenly embarrassed. 'There is no hiding anything from Ma,' he thought, 'she knows the secrets of my soul.'

'Yes indeed, they are all well,' he faltered.

'I really want to become acquainted with Poreshbabu's daughters. After all, Gora was not favourably disposed towards them at first, but since they have now won him over as well, they must be out of the ordinary.'

'I, too, have often wanted to introduce you to Poreshbabu's daughters somehow,' Binoy responded enthusiastically. 'I never proposed it lest Gora take offence.'

'What is the eldest daughter's name?' Anandamoyi wanted to know.

As introductions proceeded through such questions and answers, Binoy tried to abridge the discussion when Lalita's name came up. But Anandamoyi would brook no obstacle.

'Lalita is very intelligent, I am told,' she observed, privately amused.

'Who told you that?'

'Why, you did.'

There was a time when Binoy had felt no self-consciousness about Lalita. He had completely forgotten that in that unattached state, he had freely discussed Lalita's sharpness of intellect with Anandamoyi. Like a skilled oarsman Anandamoyi steered the conversation about Lalita past all obstacles so that almost all the significant details about the history of her acquaintance with Binoy were revealed. Now he even blurted out the fact that Lalita, anguished at Gora's prison sentence, had escaped alone with Binoy on the steamer. As he spoke, his animation increased; the dejection that had oppressed him in the evening evaporated without trace. He began to feel now that to get to know an extraordinary person like Lalita and to be able to speak of her in such terms was itself a great boon for him. When dinner was announced and the conversation ended, Binoy seemed to suddenly awaken from a dream, realizing that he had recounted to Anandamoyi all the secrets of his heart. Such was Anandamoyi's manner of listening to everything and accepting it, that Binoy did not even feel any cause for embarrassment. Up until today he had nothing to hide from Ma, confiding in her about the most trifling of things. But ever since he was introduced to Poreshbabu's family, a sort of communication block had appeared that was not healthy for Binoy. Now, sensing that his secret feelings for Lalita had been completely disclosed to the subtly perceptive Anandamoyi, Binoy felt overjoyed. Had he been unable to

offer up this development in his life to his mother, in all its
entirety, it would never have become pure and transparent.
It would have continued to taint his thoughts like an inkblot.

At night Anandamoyi had reflected upon this matter for
a long time. Thinking that a solution to the increasingly
complex problem in Gora's life could be found in
Porershbabu's household itself, she began to feel that she
must meet the girls once, by any means.

~36~

Mahim and his family had been proceeding on the assumption
that Shashimukhi's marriage to Binoy was more or less fixed.
In fact, Shashimukhi would not even approach Binoy. Binoy
was barely acquainted with Shashimukhi's mother. Not that
she was shy, exactly, but she was abnormally secretive. The
door to her room was often closed. Her husband apart,
everything else in her life was kept under lock and key. The
husband did not enjoy much access either: under his wife's
discipline, his movements were clearly charted and his sphere
of activity was extremely limited. Owing to this natural
tendency to circumscribe everything, Shashimukhi's mother
Lakshmimoni, had complete control over her own world;
entry for outsiders and exit for insiders was not unrestricted.
In fact even Gora did not receive much encouragement in
Lakshmimoni's domain. In the administration of this kingdom
there were no dichotomies. For the lawmaker here was
Lakshmimoni and from the lower court to the highest court
of appeal, she alone was all in all. Not only were the
executive and the judiciary unsegregated, but the legislative
was also combined with them. In his conduct towards outsiders,
Mahim seemed very firm indeed, but within Lakshmimoni's

territory, he had no power to exercise his own wishes. Not even in trivial matters.

Lakshmimoni had seen Binoy from behind the screen, and liked him as well. Since childhood, Mahim had regularly seen Binoy as Gora's friend; it was due to such excessive familiarity that he had been unable to think of Binoy as his daughter's suitor. When Lakshmimoni drew his attention towards Binoy, his respect for his wife's intelligence increased. Lakshmimoni firmly resolved that it was Binoy her daughter would marry. She impressed upon her husband a major advantage in this proposal: Binoy could not claim any dowry from them. For a few days, even when he found Binoy at home, Mahim had been unable to raise the subject of the marriage. He desisted because Binoy was dejected about Gora's imprisonment.

Today was a Sunday. The lady of the house did not allow Mahim to complete his weekly daytime siesta. Binoy was reading aloud to Anandamoyi from Bankim's newly published *Bangadarshan*. Casket of paan in hand, Mahim approached them and slowly lowered himself onto the wooden taktaposh. First offering Binoy a paan, he expressed his annoyance at Gora's reckless stupidity. Then, in the process of discussing how much time remained for Gora's release, he very suddenly remembered that the month of Agrahayan was almost half over already.

'Binoy,' he said, 'It's impractical of you to say that Agrahayan weddings are forbidden in your family. As it is the holy books and almanacs are full of restrictions; to add to that, if you keep inventing family shastras as well, how will we preserve our family line?'

'Binoy has been seeing Shashimukhi ever since she was very tiny,' Anandamoyi interrupted, observing that Binoy was in difficulty. 'The idea of marrying her does not appeal to him, hence this pretext about Agrahayan.'

'He could have told us right at the outset,' complained Mahim.

'It takes time even to know one's own mind, after all,' Anandamoyi replied. 'Is there any shortage of suitors, Mahim? Let Gora come back. He knows many nice young men. He will be able to fix up a match.'

'Hm!' said Mahim, his face like thunder. After a short silence, he said, 'Ma, if you had not discouraged Binoy he would not have objected to this proposal.'

Flustered, Binoy was about to speak, but Anandamoyi interrupted: 'Well, truth be told Mahim, I couldn't bring myself to encourage him. Binoy is young. He might have unwittingly taken a step that would have ultimately led to no good.'

Shielding Binoy, Anandamoyi bore the brunt of Mahim's rage. Realizing this, Binoy was ashamed at his own feebleness. As he was about to clearly announce his rejection of the proposal, Mahim left the room without waiting any longer, telling himself that a stepmother can never truly belong.

Anandamoyi was aware that Mahim was capable of such thoughts, and that as a stepmother she would always be listed as a criminal in the world's law-court. But it was never her habit to let other people's opinion determine her actions. From the day she had adopted Gora she had made herself independent of the ways of the world and the views of other people. Since then, indeed, she had adopted ways that invited public blame. The concealment of a certain fact constantly tormented her at the very core of her being, but it was the blame heaped upon her by society that offered her some relief from that pain. When people called her a Khristan she would clasp Gora in her lap and declare: 'God knows being called a Khristan does not condemn me.' So, gradually, it had become part of her nature to detach her conduct from public opinion in every respect. Even if Mahim secretly or openly humiliated her for this by calling her a stepmother, she would not be diverted from her chosen path.

'Binu, you haven't gone to Poreshbabu's house in a long time,' Anandamoyi remarked.

'A long time, how is that?' asked Binoy.

'You haven't gone there even once since you returned on the steamer.'

That was not long ago. But Binoy knew that his visits to Poreshababu's house had once been so frequent that even Anandamoyi had scarcely got a glimpse of him. By that measure, he had not visited Poreshbabu's house for many days, and it had indeed become noticeable. Shredding a thread pulled from the end of his dhoti, Binoy remained silent.

'*Maji, kahanse mayilog aya,*' the bearer came and announced in Hindi at this point. 'Ma, some ladies have come to see you.'

Binoy quickly rose to his feet. While he was trying to ascertain who had come and from where, Sucharita and Lalita entered the room. Binoy did not get a chance to leave the room. He stood there, stupefied. Both girls touched Anandamoyi's feet in a pranam. Lalita scarcely looked at Binoy. Sucharita greeted him with a namaskar.

'How are you?' she asked. 'We have come from Poreshbabu's house,' she added, addressing Anandamoyi.

Receiving them warmly, Anandamoyi said, 'Such introductions are not required. I have not seen the two of you before, ma, but I consider you members of my own household.'

In no time, their conversation grew warm and animated. Observing Binoy's silence Sucharita tried to draw him into the discussion.

'Why haven't you come for so many days?' she asked him in a low voice.

'I am afraid of losing your affection from troubling all of you too frequently,' said Binoy, casting a glance at Lalita.

'Don't you know that affection also waits to be troubled again and again?' asked Sucharita with a faint smile.

'He knows it only too well, ma!' Anandamoyi assured her. 'What can I tell you—with all his whims and fancies, it's a miracle if I get any time to myself all day.' As she spoke, she looked tenderly at Binoy.

'The Almighty Ishwar has granted you patience,' retorted Binoy. 'He is using me to test it.'

'Do you hear that, bhai Lalita?' demanded Sucharita, nudging Lalita. 'Our own test is over, it seems. We couldn't pass the test, I suppose?'

'Now our Binu is putting his own patience to the test,' smiled Anandamoyi, observing that Lalita showed no reaction to this banter. 'Indeed, you have no idea of his high regard for all of you. In the evenings, you are the sole topic of conversation. And he melts at the very mention of Poreshbabu's name.' Anandamoyi kept her eyes on Lalita's face. Making a supreme effort to meet her gaze, Lalita flushed for no reason at all.

'He has sprung to your father's defence against so many people!' Anandamoyi continued. 'The members of his community are on the verge of declaring him an outcaste for becoming a Brahmo. Truly, Binu my boy, such impatience won't do. I see no reason to be ashamed about it either. Ma, what do you say?'

This time, Lalita dropped her gaze as soon as she looked at her.

'We are well aware that Binoybabu thinks of us as family,' said Sucharita. 'But that is not solely to our credit, it owes much to his own ability.'

'That I couldn't say for sure, ma!' replied Anandamoyi. 'After all I have seen him ever since he was little. All these days, my Gora was his only friend. In fact I have noticed that Binoy could not mingle even with the men of his own community. But such has been the effect of his brief acquaintance with all of you that we, too, cannot reach him anymore. I wanted to pick a quarrel with you about this but now I find I must take his side. You people will outdo everyone else.' With these words Anandamoyi touched Lalita's chin, then Sucharita's, and kissed her own fingers in a gesture of affection.

'Binoybabu, Baba is back,' said Sucharita compassionately, noticing Binoy's wretchedness. 'He is talking to Krishnadayalbabu in the outer room.'

At her words, Binoy hastened from the room. Now Anandamoyi began to speak of the rare friendship between Gora and Binoy. She was not unaware that her two listeners were not indifferent to the subject. To these two boys Anandamoyi had given all her devotion, the holy offering of all her mother-love; no one mattered more to her in all the world. Indeed she had moulded them personally like the shivalinga of a young girl's prayers, but they had been the sole recipients of all her devotional efforts. Her narration of the story of these two deities raised in her own lap was so vivid, so saturated with affection, that listening to her, Sucharita and Lalita longed for more. They did not lack respect for Gora and Binoy but through the loving eyes of a mother such as Anandamoyi, they seemed to see the young men in a fresh perspective.

After meeting Anandamoyi, Lalita seemed to grow even more incensed at the magistrate. Anandamoyi smiled at her heated remarks.

'Ma,' she said, 'the all-knowing Lord alone understands my anguish at Gora's imprisonment. But I could not be angry with the saheb. I know Gora after all; he has a total disregard for rules and laws when it comes to his beliefs. If he does not observe the law, the dispensers of justice will of course send him to jail, and why should I blame them? Gora has performed

his duty, they have performed theirs; if someone must suffer
for this, suffer they will. If you read my Gora's letter, ma,
you will realize that he was not afraid of misery, nor vainly
angry with anyone. He had acted with a definite awareness of
what the fruits of certain actions might be.'

With these words, she drew Gora's letter, carefully
preserved, from her box, and handed it to Sucharita.

'Please read it aloud, ma,' she requested, 'let me hear it
once again.'

When Gora's extraordinary letter had been read out the
three of them remained silent for a while. Anandamoyi wiped
the corner of her eye with her aanchal. Those tears contained
not only the pain of a mother's heart but also a mixture of joy
and pride. Her Gora was no ordinary person, indeed! Was he
the sort to be forgiven and set free by the magistrate! Had he
not acknowledged all his guilt and deliberately shouldered the
burden of all the sufferings of imprisonment? There was no
need to quarrel with anybody about his sufferings. Gora was
bearing them unflinchingly, and Anandamoyi, too, could bear
the pain.

Lalita gazed at Anandamoyi's face in surprise. The traditions
of a Brahmo family were very firmly entrenched in Lalita's
mind; she had no respect for women who had not received a
modern education, whom she knew as 'daughters of Hindu
households.' In their childhood, when Borodasundari scolded
them saying 'Even daughters of Hindu households don't do
such things,' Lalita would bow her head with a special sense
of shame for the misdeed in question. Today, hearing
Anandamoyi's words, she was repeatedly overwhelmed with
amazement. Anandamoyi's strength was as extraordinary as
her calmness and her astonishing soundness of judgement.
Compared to this woman, Lalita felt extremely small and
humble for her own lack of emotional restraint. Her mind
was in turmoil today, hence she had neither glanced at Binoy

nor even spoken to him. But gazing at Anandamoyi's face, graced with affection, tenderness and peace, the heat of rebellion in her heart seemed to subside, easing her relations with everyone around her.

'Having seen you now, I understand where all Gourbabu's strength comes from,' Lalita told Anandamoyi.

'You don't really understand,' Anandamoyi corrected her. 'Had my Gora been like other ordinary boys, where would I have found the strength? Could I have borne the thought of his misery in this way?'

It is necessary to offer a brief history of the cause for Lalita's present state of anguish. These last few days, her first thought upon leaving her bed every morning was that Binoybabu would not visit them today. Yet all day long, not for an instant did her mind cease to await Binoy's arrival. Moment to moment, she constantly imagined that perhaps Binoy had come, perhaps instead of coming upstairs he was talking to Poreshbabu in the room downstairs. There was no saying how many times in the day she needlessly went from room to room, on this account. Finally, when she went to bed at the end of the day, she didn't know how to deal with her own heart. She felt like crying, fit to burst her heart, but at the same time she also felt angry, but with whom, it was hard to say. As if she was angry with herself. 'What's the matter!' she asked herself constantly. 'How will I live! I see no way out. How long can this continue!'

Lalita knew Binoy was a Hindu. There was no possibility of her marrying him. Yet, unable to control her heart by any means, her spirit drooped in shame and fear. That Binoy was not averse to her was something she sensed; it was because she realized this that she now found it hard to contain herself. Hence, while she anxiously awaited Binoy's arrival, she also felt inwardly afraid that Binoy might arrive. Wrestling with her own emotions like this, her patience had collapsed this morning. Her heart seemed to be in constant turmoil at Binoy's failure to arrive, and she felt that if she could only meet him once, her restlessness would disappear. In the morning she dragged Satish to her room. These days, his mashi's presence had made Satish more or less forget about his friendly interchanges with Binoy.

'Have you quarreled with Binoybabu then?' Lalita asked him.

He strongly repudiated this slanderous suggestion.

'What sort of friend is he!' taunted Lalita. 'You keep speaking of Binoybabu, but he doesn't even spare you a glance.'

'Ish! As if that's true!' exclaimed Satish. 'Never!'

As the family's tiniest member, Satish often had to assert himself vociferously in this manner, to establish his prestige. Now, to demonstrate it even more definitely, he rushed to Binoy's house at once. Upon his return he said:

'He's not at home, that's why he couldn't visit us.'

'Why didn't he visit us these last few days?' Lalita wanted to know.

'Because he was away all these days.'

'Didibhai,' Lalita now proposed to Sucharita, 'we ought to visit Gourbabu's mother once.'

'But we don't know them,' Sucharita protested.

'Why, wasn't Gourbabu's father Baba's childhood friend, after all?' Lalita reminded her.

'Yes, indeed he was,' Sucharita now recalled. She too became very enthusiastic.

'Bhai Lalita,' she said, 'go speak to Baba about this.'

'No, I can't talk to him. You go ask him.'

Ultimately it was Sucharita who went to Poreshbabu.

'You're quite right,' he instantly agreed, when she broached the subject. 'We should have visited them long ago.'

After their meal, as soon as their visit had been planned, Lalita's heart rebelled. Petulance and doubt assailed her unaccountably, and began to pull her in a contrary direction.

'Didi, you go with Baba,' she told Sucharita. 'I'm not going.'

'How is that possible!' Sucharita expostulated. 'I can't go alone without you. Bhai, my angel, please let's go, don't make a fuss.'

After a lot of persuasion Lalita accompanied her. But she seethed at the humiliation of this defeat, for she had been outdone by Binoy. He could easily abstain from visiting their house, but here she was, rushing to meet him! In her heart she strove to deny outright that it was the hope of glimpsing Binoy there that had made her so enthusiastic about visiting Anandamoyi's house. Due to that stubborn desire, she neither glanced at Binoy nor returned his namaskar, nor spoke a word to him. Binoy concluded that because Lalita had detected his secret feelings, she was ignoring him like this by way of repudiation. He did not have the self-assurance to imagine that Lalita might actually be in love with him. He came and stood bashfully at the door.

'Poreshbabu wants to go home now,' he announced. 'He has asked me to inform everyone.' He made sure to remain beyond Lalita's range of vision.

'How is that possible!' Anandamoyi protested. 'How can he leave us without tasting some sweets! It won't take long. Wait a little Binoy, let me go and see. Why are you standing outside? Come and join us inside the room.'

Keeping his face averted, Binoy somehow found a place far away from Lalita,.

'Binoybabu,' said Lalita in a natural tone, as if there had been nothing unusual in her conduct towards him before this. 'Are you aware that your friend Satish went to your house this morning to find out whether you've completely abandoned him!'

Binoy jumped in amazement, as people do when they suddenly hear a divine prophecy from the heavens. Embarrassed that he had started so visibly, he failed to summon up a reply with his customary skill.

'Had Satish gone there, then?' he asked, flushing to the tips of his ears. 'But I was not in!'

These casual words from Lalita aroused great elation in Binoy's heart. In an instant, a vast cloud of doubt was lifted from over the whole universe, vanishing like a stifling nightmare. As if this was all he desired in this world. 'I am saved! I am saved!' his heart began to chant. Lalita was not angry, she did not mistrust him at all. In no time, all constraints were removed.

'Binoybabu has suddenly taken us for long-nailed, sharp-toothed, horned, armed demons, or something of the sort,' laughed Sucharita.

'In this world, those who keep quiet, unable to complain openly, are the ones who end up as the accused,' protested Binoy. 'Didi, such words don't become you. You have yourself become so remote, and now you imagine that others have grown distant.'

This was the first time Binoy had addressed Sucharita as Didi, his elder sister. It sounded sweet to her ears. From their very first acquaintance, she had developed a sisterly tenderness for Binoy, a feeling that assumed a concrete, affectionate shape as soon as he addressed her as Didi.

The daylight had almost waned when Poreshbabu took his leave, along with his daughters.

'Ma, I won't let you do any work today,' said Binoy to Anandamoyi. 'Let's go upstairs.'

He was finding it impossible to contain the turbulence in his heart. Taking Anandamoyi to the room upstairs, with his own hands he spread a mat for her on the floor.

'Binu, what is it?' asked Anandamoyi. 'What is it you want to say?'

'I have nothing to say,' he declared. 'You must speak to me.' It was to hear Anandamoyi's opinion of Poreshbabu's daughters that Binoy's heart was yearning so restlessly.

'So, is this why you called me here?' exclaimed Anandamoyi. 'I ask you, is there something you want to say?'

'If I hadn't called you here, you would have missed watching such a sunset,' Binoy replied.

That evening, above the Kolkata rooftops, the Agrahayan sunset looked rather pale. There was nothing unusual in the sun's radiance. In a corner of the sky, the golden glow blended indistinctly with dusty vapours. But even the dullness of this faded dusk had lent a rosy hue to Binoy's mind today. He began to feel that he was closely encircled in every direction, as if the sky was touching him.

'They are good girls, both of them,' remarked Anandamoyi.

Binoy did not let the discussion end there. He kept it alive from diverse perspectives, recalling sundry small incidents from long ago, involving Poreshbabu's daughters. Many of these were insignificant, but on that lonely, fading Agrahayan evening, owing to Binoy's eagerness and Anandamoyi's curiosity, these unknown fragments of minor domestic history were infused with a profound glory. Suddenly, at one point, Anandamoyi sighed.

'I would be very happy if Sucharita were married to Gora,' she blurted out.

'Ma, I've often thought of it,' cried Binoy, jumping up. 'She is just the companion for Gora!'

'But would it be possible?'

'Why not? I don't think Gora dislikes Sucharita.'

Anandamoyi was not unaware that Gora had been attracted by someone. That the woman in question was Sucharita, she had also gleaned from some of Binoy's remarks.

'But would Sucharita marry into a Hindu household?' Anandamoyi wondered aloud, after remaining silent for a while.

'Tell me, Ma,' said Binoy, 'can't Gora marry into a Brahmo household? Would you not approve?'

'I would approve wholeheartedly.'

'You would?' Binoy asked again.

'Yes indeed, Binu! Marriages are born when two hearts meet; who cares what mantras are chanted on the occasion, baba! As long as you take God's name in some form or other.'

A load seemed to lift from Binoy's mind. 'Ma, I feel very surprised to hear such words from you. Where did you acquire such largeness of heart?'

'From Gora,' smiled Anandamoyi.

'But Gora says the exact opposite!'

'What if he does? All that I know is imbibed from Gora. How real an entity is man, and how false are the causes that prompt men to partisanship, fighting and killing! That's something the Almighty made me realize the day He gave me Gora. Who is a Brahmo, baba, and who is a Hindu, for that matter? The human heart has no caste or creed; it is the site where the Lord brings everyone together and unites with them Himself. Can we afford to spurn Him and depend solely on mantras and opinions to bring about unity?'

Binoy touched Anandamoyi's feet respectfully.

'Ma, your words are music to my ears,' he declared. 'My day has proved worthwhile, indeed.'

~37~

Sucharita's mashi Harimohini posed a serious problem for Poreshbabu's family. Before describing it, an abridged version of Harimohini's self-introductory remarks to Sucharita is offered below:

I was two years older than your mother. The two of us received boundless affection in our parental home. For at that time, only the two of us, both girls, had been born into the family, and there was no other infant in the house. Our kakas pampered us so much, we never felt any hardship.

At the age of eight I was married off into the famous Roychoudhury family of Palsa, as distinguished in lineage as in wealth. But I was not destined to be happy. At the time of my marriage, my father had fallen out with my father-in-law over the wedding expenses and other related matters. For a long time, my in-laws could not forgive my father's family for that offence. 'We'll get our boy married again,' they would all say. 'Let's see the girl's plight then.' It was the sight of my misery that made my father vow never to marry his daughters into a rich family. That was why he had married your mother into a poor household.

Many families lived together in my marital home. At the age of eight or nine, I had to cook for almost fifty or sixty people. After serving everyone else, I had to survive on plain rice, or sometimes with rice and dal. Sometimes I would get to eat at two in the afternoon, sometimes at the very end of the day. As soon as I had eaten, I had to go and cook the evening meal. I could dine only at eleven or twelve at night. There was no clearly designated place for me to sleep. In the private quarters of the antahpur, I would sleep next to anyone, wherever and whenever it suited their convenience! Sometimes I had to place a pinri to sleep on the wooden seat.

The general neglect I faced from everyone in the house could not but affect my husband's attitude. For a long time he kept me at arm's length. When I was seventeen, my daughter Manorama was born. Having given birth to a girl-child, I was subjected to even greater humiliation by my in-laws. Amidst all the neglect and shame that I suffered, it was this girl who became my sole consolation, my only joy. Because Manorama had not received much affection from her father or anyone else, she became the object of my heartfelt love.

Three years later, when I produced a boy, my status began to change. Then I became worthy of being considered the mistress of the household. My mother-in-law was no more, and my father-in-law had also left us just a couple of years after Manorama was born. Immediately after his demise, we were involved in property disputes with my deors, my husband's younger brothers. Ultimately, having squandered much of our property on legal expenses, we broke off from the rest of the family. When Manorama was of marriageable age, fearing that she might be taken far away, that I should never see her again, I married her off into Simulé village, five or six krosh away from Palsa. The boy looked just like the god Kartika, as fair as he was handsome. And they had the means of subsistence as well.

I had suffered great degradation and hardship once, but before misfortune struck, providence had temporarily granted me happiness in equal measure. In his last days, my husband showed me great care and respect, never taking a step without first consulting me. How could I enjoy such an excess of good fortune without paying a price? My son and husband died of cholera, four days apart. Ishwar the Almighty kept me alive just to demonstrate that human beings can tolerate even the sort of pain that is unimaginable.

Gradually, I began to discover my son-in-law's true nature. Who would have imagined that such a venomous serpent could lie hidden within such a beautiful flower? That he had fallen into bad company and become an addict was something even my daughter never told me. My jamai, this son-in-law, would come to me at odd times and ask for money, citing all sorts of needs. I had no need to save for anyone else in the world, so when my jamai asked my indulgence, I rather liked it. Sometimes my daughter would dissuade me. She would scold me, saying: 'You are spoiling him by giving him money like this; when money comes his way, there's no saying when and how he squanders it.' I would imagine that Manorama was forbidding me to give him money because her in-laws would lose respect if her husband accepted money from me in this fashion.

Then I grew inspired to provide money for my jamai's addictions, unbeknownst to my daughter. When Manorama got to know of this, she came to me one day and wept, telling me all about her husband's scandalous behaviour. Then I struck my forehead in self-reproach. My grief was indescribable. It was one of my deors who had ruined my jamai with his evil company and wicked ideas. When I withdrew my monetary support, my jamai began to suspect that it was my daughter who had forbidden me. The matter could be concealed no longer. Now he began to torment my daughter so extremely, insulting her so publicly, that to prevent it I again started giving him money behind my daughter's back. I knew I was condemning him to hell, but I could not rest in peace when I heard that he was subjecting Manorama to unspeakable torture.

Ultimately, one day—I remember that day so clearly! Towards the end of Magh, the summer having set in early that year, we were saying: 'The trees in our back garden are already laden with mango-blossom!' One afternoon, that Magh, a palki came and stopped at our door. I saw Manorama approach us, smiling; then she came and touched my feet.

'Why Manu,' I asked, 'what news?'

'Can't one visit one's mother just like that, even if there is no news?' laughed Manorama.

My beyan, Manorama's mother-in-law, was not a bad person. She sent me a message that as Bouma, her daughter-in-law, was expecting, she would be better off staying with her mother until the child was born. I took that for the truth. But I had no inkling that my jamai had started assaulting Manorama even in her condition, and that it was from fear of a disaster that my beyan had sent her daughter-in-law to me. Manu and her mother-in-law kept me deluded in this way. If I tried to give my daughter an oil massage and a bath, Manorama would elude me on various pretexts; she did not want to expose the scars on her tender body, even to her mother's eyes.

Occasionally, my jamai would come and create a scene, wanting to take Manorama back with him. Because my daughter was staying with me, it prevented him from seeking my indulgence with requests for money. Gradually, even this obstacle ceased to deter him. He began to pester me for money even in Manorama's presence. 'You must not give him money under any circumstances,' Manorama would stubbornly insist. But I was extremely vulnerable; I could not refrain from giving my jamai some money, lest he become too annoyed with my daughter.

One day, Manorama said: 'Ma, I'll take care of all your money.' She now took charge of my keys, cashbox, everything. When my jamai found no further possibility of extracting money from me, and failed to make Manorama unbend by any means, he began to insist: 'I'll take Mejobou home.' 'Give him, ma, give him some money and get rid of him,' I would urge Manorama, 'or who knows what he might do!' But my Manorama could be as firm as she was tender. 'No,' she would declare, 'he must not be given money under any circumstances.' One day, my jamai came and announced, glaring at us:

'I shall send the palki tomorrow evening. If you don't let Bou go, I warn you of dire consequences.'

'Ma, let's delay no more,' I urged Manorama when the palki arrived before dusk the following day. 'I'll send for you again next week.'

'Not today, let it be,' pleaded Manorama. 'I don't feel like leaving today, Ma. Ask them to return after a couple of days.'

'Ma, will my insane jamai spare us if I turn away the palki?' I persisted. 'Let's not try that, Manu. Please go today itself.'

'No, Ma, not today,' Manu begged. 'My father-in-law is away in Kolkata. He is expected back in mid-Phalgun. I'll go back then.'

Still I said: 'No, ma, we'd best not do that.'

At this, Manorama went to prepare for her departure. I busied myself arranging meals for the attendants and palki-bearers from her in-laws' household. I did not get the opportunity to spend a little time with her before she left, to give her special care that day, to dress her with my own hands, to feed her some favourite dishes before bidding her goodbye. Just before she mounted the palki, she touched my feet and said:

'Ma, I'll take your leave, then.'

How was I to know that she was really leaving me! She had not wanted to go, but I forced her to depart—my heart burns with grief at that thought, even today. Nothing has quenched that fire!

That very night, Manorama died of a miscarriage. Before I received the news, she had already been hastily cremated in secret. You will not understand, any of you, the kind of grief that leaves nothing to be said, nothing to be done, no end to one's thoughts, nor any relief to be found in tears. Such grief is best not understood.

So I lost everything, but my problems did not end there. From the time I lost my husband and son, my deors had been eyeing my property. They knew they were sole heirs to my property after my demise, but they could not bear to wait so long. For this, nobody is to blame; it was truly a crime for a

wretch like me to remain alive at all. How could people with
diverse worldly needs tolerate it if people like myself, with no
needs at all, should unaccountably remain alive, occupying
their rightful space?

As long as Manorama was alive, I did not let myself be
deluded by any of my deors' arguments. I did my best to
defend my property rights against them. I had vowed, as long
as I lived, to save money for Manorama and bequeath it to
her. It was my effort to save for my daughter that had become
intolerable for my deors, who felt it was their wealth I was
stealing. Nilkanta, a trusted old retainer of my husband, was
my only support. If I tried to arrive at a mutual settlement by
surrendering my claim to something that was rightfully mine,
he would never agree. 'I'd like to see who touches a single
paisa that is ours by right,' he would declare. Amidst this
struggle over our rival claims, my daughter passed away. The
very next day my deor came to me and advised me to
renounce the world.

'Boudi,' he urged, 'Ishwar has placed you in such
circumstances now, that it would no longer be appropriate for
you to cling to a worldly existence. For the remainder of your
life, retire to a place of pilgrimage and turn your mind to holy
things. We shall arrange for your upkeep.'

I sent for our Guruthakur, our spiritual guide.

'Thakur,' I begged, 'please tell me how I may escape the
clutches of sorrow. Whatever I do, I can find no consolation
anywhere. I seem to be trapped in a fence of fire; wherever
I go, whichever way I turn, I cannot see the slightest way out
of my agony.'

My guru led me to the puja-room and said: 'This deity
Gopiballav is your husband, son, daughter, your all in all. In
his service alone can you fill the vacuum in your life.'

Day and night I sojourned in the puja-room. I began to try
to devote myself wholeheartedly to the deity, but how could

I give unless He was willing to receive? He did not accept my offering, did he?

Sending for Nilkanta, I said: 'Niludada, I have decided to sign over all my life's possessions to my deors. They will give me some money every month to take care of my needs.'

'That cannot be allowed under any circumstances,' Nilkanta declared. 'You are a woman; don't involve yourself in such matters.'

'What need have I of property anymore?' I inquired.

'How can you say such a thing?' exclaimed Nilkanta. 'Why should we give up our rights? Don't take such an irrational step.'

In Nilkanta's eyes nothing was greater than one's rights. I was in a quandary. Worldly matters were anathema to me, but Nilkanta was the only person I trusted in this world. How could I hurt him? After all, he had suffered a lot trying to protect those 'rights' of mine. Ultimately one day, unbeknownst to Nilkanta, I signed a document. I had not properly understood what was written there. Why should I be afraid to sign, I had thought; what did I wish to keep that I could not bear to be defrauded of? After all everything belonged to my father-in-law; if it went to his sons, let them have it.

When the legal procedures had been registered, I sent for Nilkanta and said: 'Niludada, don't be angry, I have signed over everything I had. I have no further need of anything.'

'What!' cried Nilkanta in agitation. 'What have you done!'

When he read the document drafted by the agent and realized that I had indeed surrendered all I possessed, Nilkanta's anger knew no bounds. Ever since his master's demise, protecting my 'rights' had become the mainstay of his life. All his thoughts and strength had been tirelessly devoted to this sole purpose. Litigation and court proceedings, trips to the lawyer's house, unearthing relevant legal clauses—he had found pleasure in these things alone. So much so, he did not even have the time to attend to his own personal affairs. When those 'rights' vanished at a single stroke of a woman's pen, Nilkanta could not be pacified.

'That's it, then,' he declared. 'My links with this place are broken. I'll take my leave.'

Was it my ultimate misfortune in my in-laws' home that Niludada would abandon me in such fury? I called him back, pleading:

'Dada, please don't be angry with me. Let me give you these five hundred rupees from my savings. When you acquire a daughter-in-law, give her my blessings and use this money to order some jewelry for her.'

'I have no further need of money,' Nilkanta asserted. 'Now that my employer has lost everything, accepting those five hundred rupees will bring me no happiness. Let it be.' With these words, my husband's last true friend left me and went away.

I took refuge in the prayer room.

'Go and take up lodgings in a holy place,' my deors urged me.

'My father-in-law's ancestral property is a holy place to me,' I declared. 'And where my deity resides, there I shall take refuge.'

But they could not bear to let me occupy any portion of the house. They had already decided who would use the rooms and how, once their belongings had been transferred to our house. Ultimately they said:

'You may carry your deity's image with you, we shall not object.'

'What will you live on if you stay here?' they demanded, when I demurred even at this suggestion.

'Why, the allowance you have assigned me will suffice for my needs,' I replied.

'But there's no mention of any allowance!' they told me.

At this, taking my deity's image with me, exactly thirty-four years after my marriage, I left my marital home and set out on my own one day. Enquiring after Niludada, I heard that he had already departed for Brindavan. I accompanied pilgrims from our village to Kashi. But my sinful heart found no peace anywhere. Daily I would call upon my deity and say, 'Thakur, please become as real for me as my own husband and children had once been!' But he didn't answer my prayers, did he? My heart finds no solace, ceaseless tears wrack my body and soul. Baap re baap, how harsh the human heart can be!

Ever since I entered my marital home at the age of eight, I could not visit my parents even for a day. I had tried very hard to attend your mother's wedding, but to no avail. Afterwards, I received news of your birth in a letter from my father, and news of my sister's death as well. Until now, Ishwar has not given me an opportunity to draw you two motherless children into my lap.

Travelling in holy places, when I found my heart still enslaved by the illusion called maya and my inner thirst for an object of love still unquenched, I began to enquire after all of you. I had heard that your father had abandoned his religion, abandoned his community and broken free. But what could I do about that! Your mother was my sister after all, born of the same womb.

I have come here after a gentleman in Kashi informed me of your whereabouts. Poreshbabu doesn't believe in deities I'm told, but you only have to see his face to realize that Thakur, the almighty Lord, is happy with him. Prayers alone do not melt Thakur's heart, as I know only too well; I shall find out how Poreshbabu won Him over. Anyway, bachha, it is not yet time for me to live in isolation—that is beyond my power. Thakur may grace me with his favour when He pleases, but without having all of you close to my lap, I cannot stay alive.

~38~

In Borodasundari's absence, Poresh had given shelter to Harimohini. Offering her the secluded room on the terrace, he had made all arrangements to ensure that her observance of orthodox rituals could proceed unimpeded. Upon her return, Borodasundari was aflame with fury at finding such an unimaginable presence in her household.

'I can't accept this,' she protested very sharply to Poresh.

'You can tolerate all of us, but not this widow who has no support?' Poresh reproached her.

Borodasundari knew that Poresh had no practical sense; every now and then, he would suddenly do something outrageous, never sparing a thought for matters of worldly advantage. Subsequently, one may rave or rant, scold or weep, but he would remain unmoved as a statue. Who could cope with such a man? Which woman could live with a man who could not even be provoked into a quarrel when necessary!

Sucharita was about the same age as Manorama. Harimohini began to feel that she even resembled Manorama a great deal. She appeared similar in temperament as well, calm but firm by nature. At times, when Sucharita's back was turned, Harimohini's heart would miss a beat, looking at her. When she sometimes wept silently in the evening, if Sucharita approached her, Harimohini would clasp her to her bosom, eyes shut tight, and say:

'Aha, I feel as if it is she herself I have found, here in my heart. She did not want to go but I forced her to leave. Can I ever, under any circumstances, be pardoned! I have suffered the punishment that was my due. Now she is here. Here she

is, back with me, back with the same smiling countenance.
Here's my ma, my jewel, my treasure!' Saying this, she
would stroke Sucharita's face all over, kiss her, shed floods of
tears. Tears would stream from Sucharita's eyes as well.
Throwing her arms around Harimohini's neck, she would
declare:

'Mashi, I too could not enjoy my mother's love for long,
but now my lost mother has returned. How often, when
things were difficult, when I lacked the strength to pray to
Ishwar, when my heart had shrivelled within, I would call out
to my Ma! Today, my Ma has come, in response to my call.'

'Don't, please don't say such things,' Harimohini would
plead. 'Your words bring me such joy that I feel apprehensive.
O Thakur, please spare us from the evil eye! I plan to avoid
any further attachments, wanting my heart to turn to stone,
but indeed I can't! I'm very weak. Have pity on me, strike me
no more. O my Radharani, go, go, go away from me. Don't
entangle me further, please don't! O my Gopiballav, Lord of
my life, my Gopal, my priceless jewel, what predicament
have you placed me in this time!'

'You can't get rid of me by force, Mashi,' Sucharita
would reply. 'I'll never let you go—I'm here to stay by your
side forever.' Like an infant she would nestle her head in
Harimohini's bosom, and fall silent.

In no time, a deep bond evolved between Sucharita and
her mashi, not to be measured by the yardstick of time. This
too irked Borodasundari.

'Just look at this girl's behaviour. As if we never looked
after her, all of us. Where was her mashi all these days, I'd
like to know? We raised her right from childhood, and now
she swoons at the very mention of her mashi! I've always told
my husband, this Sucharita you all laud as such a wonderful
person, makes an outward show of decency, but it's impossible
to win her heart. All we've done for her all along has indeed
proved futile!'

Borodasundari knew Poresh would not understand her
agony. Moreover, she also had no doubt that she would lose
respect in Poresh's eyes if she expressed her hostility to
Harimohini. That infuriated her even more. She began to rally
support to prove that whatever Poresh might say, most
intelligent people would be in agreement with her. She
started discussing the Harimohini affair with all members of
their social circle, eminent or otherwise. There was no end to
her laments and complaints about Harimohini's orthodox
Hindu views, her idol worship, and the bad example she set
for youngsters in the family.

Borodasundari not only complained to others, but also
began to trouble Harimohini in all sorts of ways. She would
choose her moment to assign other tasks to the milkman
deployed as bearer to draw water for Harimohini's cooking
and other chores. If the matter came up she would say, 'Why,
Ramdeen is available, isn't he?' Ramdeen being a low caste
Dosad, she knew Harimohini would not accept water drawn
from the well by him. If anyone pointed this out she would
retort: 'If she was so fussy about Brahmanical ways, why
come to our Brahmo household? Here, it won't do to be so
finicky about caste. I shall never encourage it.' On such issues
her sense of duty became very aggressively manifest. The
Brahmo Samaj, she felt, had gradually become very slack in
matters concerning the community; that was why it could not
accomplish enough. She would try her best not to participate
in such leniency. No, never. If someone misunderstood her,
she was ready to take it; if even her kinfolk turned against
her, she would humbly accept that too. She began to remind
everyone that all great men of the world who had performed
noble deeds had been compelled to tolerate criticism and
opposition.

No inconvenience could vanquish Harimohini. She seemed
to have vowed to attain the ultimate heights of self-

mortification. As if to match the rhythm of the unbearable suffering her heart had inwardly undergone, she seemed to constantly torment herself outwardly with her strict observance of rules. Her endeavour was to voluntarily embrace sorrow, in order to master it through intimacy. When Harimohini faced trouble obtaining water, she gave up cooking altogether. She began to live on milk and fruits that she had dedicated to her deity as holy prasad. Sucharita was extremely distressed at this. Her mashi tried hard to convince her:

'Ma, this has proved a boon for me. This is what I needed. It does not hurt me at all; rather, it brings me joy.'

'Mashi,' said Sucharita, 'if I don't accept food or water from members of other castes, will you let me attend upon you?'

'Why, ma,' expostulated Harimohini, 'please follow the dharma you believe in. There is no need for you to change track on my account. It is a source of joy to me that I have been allowed this proximity to you, to hold you close, to see you everyday. Poreshbabu is your guru, and like a father to you. Follow the path he has shown you, and for that alone, the Almighty will bless you.'

Harimohini began to endure all the torment inflicted upon her by Borodasundari as if she was totally unaware of it. In answer to Poreshbabu's daily queries—'How are you? I hope you are not finding things inconvenient?'—she would reply: 'I am very happy.'

But Sucharita was wounded every moment by Borodasundari's unjust behaviour. She was not a girl to complain, and in particular, could never bring herself to speak to Poreshbabu about Borodasundari's conduct. She began to endure everything in silence, too shy to express any unhappiness at this state of affairs. As a result Sucharita gradually drew very close to her mashi. Despite her mashi's repeated remonstrations, she began to follow her aunt's dietary habits completely. Ultimately, observing Sucharita's discomfort, Harimohini was obliged to resume her interest in culinary matters.

'Mashi,' said Sucharita, 'I'll live exactly as you advise me, but I shall personally draw water for your use. I shan't stop that on any account.'

'Don't mind, ma' Harimohini pleaded, 'but the ritual food offering, my Thakur's bhog,, is cooked in that water, after all.'

'Mashi,' argued Sucharita, 'does your Thakur observe caste laws too? Can He also be tainted by sin? Does He also belong to some community?'

Finally, Harimohini had to concede to Sucharita's dedication. She accepted Sucharita's service completely. Imitating his didi, Satish, too, started insisting, 'I'll eat food cooked by mashi.' In this way, the three of them formed a small, separate domestic unit in a corner of Poreshbabu's house. Only Lalita remained as a bridge between the two household units. Borodasundari did not allow any of her other daughters to approach that part of the house, but she lacked the power to forbid Lalita.

~39~

Borodasundari began to invite her female Brahmo friends frequently to her home. Sometimes they would congregate on the terrace. With her natural provincial simplicity, Harimohini would offer these women her hospitality, but she did not fail to realize that they held her in contempt. In fact, Borodasundari would begin criticizing Hindu ritual practices even in Harimohini's presence, and many ladies would join the attack with Harimohini as their special target. Clinging to her mashi's side, Sucharita would silently endure all these onslaughts. She only seemed anxious to demonstrate that she belonged to her mashi's party. On days when refreshments were offered, if invited to help herself, Sucharita would declare:

'No, I don't eat such things.'

'What! Won't you eat with all of us?'

'No.'

'Sucharita is now a staunch Hindu, don't you know?' Borodasundari would say. 'Indeed she will refuse food that we have touched!'

'Sucharita has also become a Hindu! What further blows will Time inflict on us, I wonder.'

'Radharani, ma, please go ahead!' Harimohini would plead in agitation. 'Ma, please go and have something to eat!'

She found it very painful that because of her, Sucharita was suffering such taunts from members of her own community. But Sucharita remained unshakeable. One day, when a Brahmo girl, out of curiosity, was about to enter Harimohini's room with her shoes on, Sucharita blocked her way, saying:

'Don't go into that room.'

'Why not?'

'Her Thakur is there.'

'Thakur! You worship the Thakur every day, do you!'

'Yes ma, I worship Him indeed,' Harimohini asserted.

'Do you feel any devotion for Thakur?'

'Curse my misfortune! Could I attain devotion after all? If I had, I would indeed have been saved!'

Lalita was present on that occasion. Red-faced, she asked the questioner:

'Do you feel any devotion for the One you worship?'

'Wah, how strange, what would I feel but devotion?'

'You feel no devotion at all,' Lalita declared, vigorously shaking her head. 'And what's more, you're not even aware that you feel no devotion.'

Harimohini struggled to ensure that Sucharita should not be alienated from her own group because of the rules she followed, but to no avail. Until now, Haranbabu and Borodasundari had secretly harboured a certain mutual hostility. In the present situation, the two of them found their stances very well matched. Borodasundari pronounced that, whatever others might say, if anyone had an eye to preserving the purity of Brahmo ideals, it was Panubabu. Haranbabu also declared to everyone that Borodasundari's single-minded, sensitive awareness of the need to keep the Brahmo community untainted in all respects was a good example for every Brahmo housewife. His praise for her contained a special barb directed at Poreshbabu.

'You have started taking prasad, food blessed by the deity, I hear,' Haranbabu once asked Sucharita in Poreshbabu's presence. Sucharita flushed, but pretending not to have heard this remark, she started rearranging the pens on the inkstand upon the table.

'Panubabu, whatever we eat is blessed by the Lord, isn't it?' protested Poreshbababu, casting a distressed glance at Sucharita's face.

'But Sucharita is all set to reject our Lord,' Haranbabu pointed out.

'Even if that were possible,' Poreshbabu argued, 'would making a fuss prevent it in any way?'

'Must we not even try to haul ashore a person adrift on the tide?' Haranbabu demanded.

'If we all try to stone her on the head, that can't be described as hauling her ashore,' replied Poreshbabu. 'Rest assured, Panubabu, I have observed Sucharita ever since she was little. Had she fallen into deep waters I would have known of it before all of you and I would not have remained indifferent.'

'Sucharita is here,' said Panubabu. 'Why not ask her

directly? She doesn't accept food touched by all and sundry, we hear. Isn't that true?'

'Baba knows I don't accept food touched by all and sundry,' responded Sucharita, giving up her unwarranted interest in the inkpot. 'If he could tolerate my behaviour, that is enough. If it displeases all of you, blame me as you please, but why torment Baba? Do you know how forgiving he is about your behaviour? Is this what he receives in return?'

Even Sucharita had learned how to talk back these days, marveled Haranbabu to himself.

Poreshbabu was a peace-loving man. He did not enjoy discussing himself or others at length. So far, he had not accepted a prominent position within any project of the Brahmo Samaj; he had led a secluded life, away from the public eye. Haranbabu took this for detachment and lack of enthusiasm on Poreshbabu's part, and had even taken Poreshbabu to task for this.

'Active and inactive: Ishwar has created substances of both categories,' Poreshbabu had replied. 'I happen to be utterly inactive. Ishwar will extract from me whatever service a person like me can render. It's no use fretting over what's not possible. I am sufficiently advanced in years; my strengths and deficiencies have already been identified. Now it's fruitless to push and prod me.'

Haranbabu believed that he could enthuse even an indifferent heart, that he had the natural ability to push the lethargic towards the path of duty and soften with remorse the lives of the fallen. He was convinced that nobody could withstand for long his extremely powerful and single-mindedly benevolent desires. He held himself chiefly responsible, in some way or other, for all positive changes in the personal character of members of his community. He had no doubt, either, that his invisible influence also had a secret effect. Up until now, whenever someone had specially praised Sucharita in his presence, he had acted as if the credit went entirely to him. Using advice, example and the reflected glory of his company, he had moulded Sucharita's personality so as to present her to society as a living example of his own extraordinary influence. At the deplorable moral decline of this very same Sucharita, his pride in his own abilities remained undiminished. He laid the entire blame on Poreshbabu. People had always praised Poreshbabu, but Haranbabu had never joined them. He hoped everyone would now recognize this as evidence of the extent of his own sagacity.

A man like Haranbabu could tolerate all else, but if those he had especially guided to the moral path used their own judgement to adopt an independent course, he could never forgive such a crime. It was impossible for him to let them off easily; the more he found his advice disregarded, the more obstinate he became, repeatedly renewing his assaults. Like a machine that cannot stop until it winds down completely, he too could not restrain himself. Parroting the same words a thousand times to unwilling ears, he still did not want to give up.

This tormented Sucharita greatly, not on her own account, but on Poreshbabu's. Poreshbabu had become the target of criticism among all members of the Brahmo Samaj. How could this distressing situation be overcome? On the other hand, Sucharita's mashi was also growing daily more conscious that the humbler and more self-effacing she tried to be, the more she became a nuisance for this family. Sucharita was constantly haunted by her mashi's intense shame and embarrassment. She could not think of any way out of this predicament. Meanwhile Borodasundari began to pester Poreshbabu to get Sucharita married off quickly.

'We can't take responsibility for Sucharita anymore,' she argued. 'She has now started following her own views. If her wedding is likely to be delayed, I'll go away somewhere else with my daughters. Sucharita's odd example is proving a source of great damage to the girls. You will regret this later, wait and see. Indeed, Lalita was not like this before. Now, when she does outrageous things randomly and willfully, obeying no one, who is at the root of the problem? Her escapade the other day, for which I am dying of shame, do you think Sucharita had no hand in that? I have never protested the fact that you have always loved Sucharita more than your own daughters, but I tell you plainly, we can't let this continue any longer.'

Poreshbabu had grown worried, not about Sucharita, but about the discord within his family. He had no doubt that Borodasundari would make a huge fuss, now that she had found a pretext. The more fruitless her agitation, the more obdurate she would become. In the present circumstances, it might doubtless be better for Sucharita's peace of mind as well, if her wedding could be quickly arranged.

'If Panubabu can persuade Sucharita,' he told Borodasundari, 'I shall not oppose the marriage.'

'How many times must she be persuaded?' Borodasundari demanded. 'You surprise me, I must say! And why all this persuasion? Where will her ladyship find a suitor like Panubabu, I ask you! Truth be told, whether you like it or not, Sucharita is not a bride worthy of Panubabu.'

'I haven't clearly understood Sucharita's feelings for Panubabu,' Poreshbabu observed. 'So until they mutually clarify these things, I can't interfere in any way.'

'Haven't understood! At last you admit it! That girl is not easy to understand. She's different on the outside and different within!'

Borodasundari sent for Haranbabu.

That morning, the newspapers carried a critique of the current predicament of the Brahmo Samaj. The article targeted Poreshbabu's family in such a way that even without names

being mentioned the real object of the attack was quite
apparent to everybody. And from the style, it was not difficult
to identify the author. After scanning the paper, Sucharita was
tearing it to shreds. Frenziedly she tore the pieces of paper,
as if bent upon reducing them to atoms. At this moment,
Haranbabu entered the room and pulled up a chair beside her.
Sucharita did not look up even once. She continued shredding
the paper as before.

'Sucharita, I have a serious matter to discuss with you
today,' Haranbabu declared. 'You must listen carefully to
what I have to say.'

Sucharita went on tearing the paper. When it became
impossible to shred it with her nails, she took scissors from
her drawstring pouch and used them instead. Just then, Lalita
came in.

'Lalita,' said Haranbabu, 'there is something I must discuss
with Sucharita.'

When Lalita made as if to leave, Sucharita clutched at her
sari aanchal.

'But you have to discuss something with Panubabu!'
protested Lalita.

Without answering, Sucharita clung to Lalita's aanchal.
Lalita sat down beside her on the mat. Haranbabu was not one
to be deterred by any obstacle. Without any further preamble
he went straight to the point.

'I don't think it wise to delay our wedding any longer,'
he declared. 'I have spoken to Poreshbabu. He says there will
be no further hindrance once we have your consent. I have
decided, the Sunday after next . . .'

'No,' said Sucharita, before he could finish.

Hearing this very curt, distinct and haughty 'No' from
Sucharita's lips, Haranbabu came up short. He knew Sucharita
to be extremely docile. He had not even imagined that she
might instantly shoot down his proposal in mid-air with this
single arrow, her 'No'.

'No! What is 'No' supposed to mean?' he demanded irritably. 'Do you want to delay even further?'

'No.'

'Then?' he asked, astonished.

'I don't consent to this marriage,' replied Sucharita, head bowed.

'Don't consent?' repeated Haranbabu, as if nonplussed. 'What does that mean?'

'Panubabu,' Lalita jibed, 'have you forgotten your Bengali today?'

'It is easier to admit that one has forgotten the mother tongue, than that one has misunderstood someone whose words one has always respected,' retorted Haranbabu, looking daggers at Lalita.

'It takes time to understand people,' replied Lalita. 'Perhaps that applies to you as well.'

'From the beginning until now, I have never been inconsistent in my words, opinions or behaviour,' declared Haranbabu. 'I can claim with emphasis that I have given no one any cause for misunderstanding, none whatsoever. Let Sucharita herself say whether I am right or wrong.'

Lalita was on the point of retorting again, but Sucharita interrupted:

'You are quite right. I have no desire to blame you.'

'If you won't blame me, why wrong me either?' Haranbabu protested.

'If you call this wrong, then I must wrong you indeed,' declared Sucharita firmly. 'But . . .'

'Didi, are you in?' called a voice from outside.

'Come, Binoybabu, please come in,' Sucharita quickly responded, delighted.

'You're mistaken, Didi, it's not Binoybabu. I'm just Binoy. Please don't embarrass me with such deference,' said Binoy, as he entered. At once he saw Haranbabu and noticed

the displeasure on his face. 'Are you angry because I haven't
visited, all these days?' he asked.

'I have reason to be angry, indeed,' responded Haranbabu,
trying to join in the banter. 'But today you have come at a
rather inappropriate time. I was discussing a special matter
with Sucharita.'

'There you are,' said Binoy, flustered. 'I still haven't
understood when it is inappropriate for me to visit! That's
why I don't have the courage to visit at all.' He prepared to
leave.

'Binoybabu, please don't go,' pleaded Sucharita. 'Our
discussion is over. Please stay on.'

Binoy realized his arrival had rescued Sucharita from some
grave danger. Pleased, he took a chowki and said, 'If you
encourage me, I can't resist. If you ask me to stay, then stay
I will. Such is my nature. So, I humbly request Didi to think
before she says such things, or she will find herself in trouble.'

Saying not a word, Haranbabu remained still as a gathering
storm. 'Very well,' he seemed to say silently, 'I shall wait. I
shall leave only after I have finally had my say.'

Hearing Binoy's voice outside the room, Lalita had felt
the blood surge within her heart. She had struggled to sustain
her normal manner, but without success. When Binoy entered
the room she was unable to address him with familiar ease. It
became hard to decide where to look, in what posture to
place her arm. She tried once to get up and leave but
Sucharita would not release her aanchal. Binoy, too, spoke
only to Sucharita throughout. It became difficult, expert
conversationalist though he was, to start any conversation
with Lalita today. So he began chatting with Sucharita with
redoubled volubility, allowing no gaps or silences.

But this new awkwardness between Lalita and Binoy did
not escape Haranbabu's notice. He smouldered inwardly,
observing that the same Lalita who was so sharply articulate

with him these days, became so constrained in Binoy's presence. Considering how Poreshbabu was leading his family on the path to moral ruin by letting his daughters mix freely with men outside the Brahmo Samaj, his disdain for Poreshbabu increased. Like a curse, the desire arose in his heart that Poreshbabu should regret this terribly some day.

After things had continued like this for quite a while, it became clear that Haranbabu would not leave.

'You have not met Mashi for a long time,' Sucharita now pointed out to Binoy. 'She often asks after you. Can't you go and see her once?'

'Please don't make the false allegation that I have forgotten Mashi,' said Binoy, rising to his feet.

When Sucharita had led Binoy away to meet her mashi, Lalita arose and said, 'Panubabu, I don't think there is anything you particularly need to say to me.'

'No,' replied Haranbabu. 'You must be urgently needed elsewhere. You may leave.'

Lalita understood the innuendo. Haughtily raising her head, she at once put the matter into words:

'Binoybabu has come after a long time. I'll go chat with him. Meanwhile, should you wish to read your own article—but oh no! I find Didi has torn the paper to shreds. If you can bear to read the writings of others, you may glance through these.' With these words, she brought Gora's writings from the corner table where they had been carefully preserved, and placing them before Haranbabu, she rushed from the room.

Harimohini was delighted to see Binoy. It was not just out of affection for this good-looking young man, but also because visitors to this house who had met Harimohini had seemed to regard her as a creature of an alien species. Residents of Kolkata, they were better versed in English and Bengali letters than she. Their aloofness and contempt made her feel extremely inadequate. In Binoy she seemed to find a refuge from all this. He too belonged to Kolkata, and Harimohini had heard that his scholarly prowess was not negligible either. Yet he showed her no disrespect, treating her as a member of the family. This shored up her self respect. Especially for this reason, even upon a slight acquaintance, Binoy acquired an intimate place in her affections. She began to feel that he would protect her like a suit of armour from the arrogance of others, that like a cover he would shield her from view since she had become too visible in this house.

Lalita would never have approached Harimohini readily so soon after Binoy had gone there, but now, goaded by Haranbabu's sarcasm, she seemed compelled to go upstairs, tearing aside all her hesitation. She not only went there, but also began at once to prattle ceaselessly to Binoy. Their conversation grew so animated, that every now and then, the sound of their laughter reached the ears of Haranbabu, alone in the room on the floor below, piercing him to the heart. Unable to remain by himself for long, he tried to quell his inner bitterness by conversing with Borodasundari. Upon hearing that Sucharita had rejected Haranbabu's proposal, Borodasundari could hold her patience no longer.

'Panubabu,' she exhorted him, 'you can't afford to behave so decently. She has repeatedly expressed her consent, and the entire Brahmo Samaj is awaiting this marriage. Now we can't let everything be turned topsy-turvy just because she has made a gesture of denial today. You must not relinquish your claims, I tell you. Let's see what she can do!'

Haranbabu needed no incitement in this matter. Stiff and wooden, head held high, he was saying to himself:

'On principle, this claim must not be relinquished. Giving up Sucharita is no great matter for me, but I can't bring embarrassment upon the Brahmo Samaj.'

To cement his intimacy with Harimohini, Binoy had made

a childlike demand for food. Flustered, Harimohini had at
once offered him soaked chickpeas, cottage cheese, butter, a
little sugar and a banana, arranged on a small platter, and
some milk in a small brass bowl.

'I thought I would hassle Mashi, demanding food at an
odd hour, but I have been outwitted,' smiled Binoy. He now
made a great show of settling down to a feast. At this
moment, Borodasundari arrived on the scene. Bending as low
over his thala as possible, Binoy greeted her with a namaskar
and said: 'I was downstairs for a long time, but did not get to
see you.'

Without answering him, Borodasundari addressed
Sucharita: 'So her ladyship is here! Just as I had thought.
There's a party going on! She is entertaining herself! Meanwhile
poor Haranbabu has been waiting for her since early morning,
as if he is merely her gardener. I've reared them from
childhood, but bapu, I never saw such behaviour, all these
days. I wonder where they are learning such things nowadays.
What was unthinkable in our family has started happening
now. Indeed, we can't face the members of our Samaj any
more. To destroy in a couple of days everything you were
always taught! What outrageous conduct!'

'I didn't know someone was waiting downstairs,'
Harimohini agitatedly protested to Sucharita. 'We have been
very unfair, I must say. Go, ma, please go quickly. I am to
blame for this.'

Lalita was instantly about to assert that Harimohini was
not at all to blame. Sucharita secretly gripped her hand to
silence her, then went away downstairs.

I have already said that Binoy had attracted Borodasundari's
affection. She had no doubt that he would eventually join the
Brahmo Samaj under the influence of their family. She took a
certain pride in moulding Binoy with her own hands, as it
were, and had even shared this pride with some of her

friends. Seeing this same Binoy now ensconced in the enemy camp, she seethed with indignation, and needless to say, her inner agony was redoubled at the sight of her own daughter Lalita aiding Binoy's second moral downfall.

'Lalita, do you have any business here?' she asked, brusquely.

'Yes,' answered Lalita, 'Binoybabu is here, so . . .'

'The person Binoybabu has come to see will look after him. You come downstairs now. There are things to be done.'

Lalita concluded that Haranbabu must have made some unwarranted remark to her mother concerning Binoy and herself. This surmise hardened her heart. With unnecessary garrulity, she declared: 'Binoybabu is here after so long, I'll come after chatting with him awhile.' From Lalita's tone it became clear to Borodasundari that force would not work here. Lest her defeat be exposed to Harimohini, she said no more and left without any farewell greeting to Binoy. To her mother, Lalita expressed enthusiasm for conversation with Binoy, but once Borodasundari had gone, there was no sign of that eagerness. They felt a certain constraint, all three of them, and soon afterwards, Lalita arose, went to her room and closed the door.

Binoy could clearly sense Harimohini's predicament in this house. He brought up the subject and bit by bit he gleaned all the details of Harimohini's past.

'Baba,' she finally said, 'the world is not a suitable place for an orphaned soul like me. Better if I could have gone to some holy place and devoted myself to my deity's service. I could have managed for a while on the little money I have left, and if I lived longer I could have somehow survived by cooking for others and being fed by them. I saw so many people managing quite well like this in Kashi. But sinner that I am, I could not adapt to those conditions. Whenever I am alone, thoughts of my own grief overwhelm me, keeping all gods and deities at bay. I fear for my sanity. For me, Radharani and Satish are like a raft for a drowning man—I find that the very thought of relinquishing them makes me choke for breath. So day and night, I fear that I must lose them—else why, having once lost all I had, would I again so quickly grow to love them so much? Baba, I have no qualms telling you, ever since I discovered the two of them, I've been able to concentrate wholeheartedly on my prayers to Thakur; if I lose them, my Thakur will instantly harden, turn to stone.'

Harimohini wiped her eyes with the corner of her sari.

~40~

Entering the room downstairs, Sucharita faced Haranbabu.

'Tell me what you have to say,' she said.

'Sit down,' said Haranbabu.

Sucharita did not sit. She stood immobile.

'Sucharita, you are being unjust to me.'

'You, too, are being unjust to me.'

'Why,' protested Haranbabu, 'I have given you my word, and that still . . .'

'Do justice and injustice reside in words alone?' interrupted Sucharita. 'By emphasizing your word, would you torment me in deed? Isn't a single truth larger than a thousand falsehoods? If I have made a hundred mistakes, would you forcibly give them first priority? Now that I have realized I was mistaken, I shall not go by anything I may have said earlier, for it would be unjust of me to do so.'

How Sucharita could be so transformed, Haranbabu failed to comprehend. He had neither the courage nor the humility to infer that he himself might be responsible for her loss of habitual quietness and modesty.

'What was your mistake?' he asked, privately blaming Sucharita's newfound companions.

'Why do you ask?' demanded Sucharita. 'Earlier I had consented, but now I no longer consent—does that not suffice?'

'We are answerable to the Brahmo Samaj after all. What shall we say, either you or I, to members of the Samaj?'

'I shall say nothing at all,' Sucharita declared. 'If you wish to speak, you may tell them that Sucharita is young, lacking brains, inconsistent by nature. Say whatever you please. But between us, this is the end of the matter.'

'It can't be the end. If Poreshbabu . . .'

As he spoke, Poreshbabu arrived on the scene.

'What is it, Panubabu, what were you saying about me?' he asked.

Sucharita was on her way out.

'Don't go, Sucharita,' Haranbabu called out, 'let's discuss the matter with Poreshbabu.' Sucharita turned around. 'Poreshbabu,' Haranbabu continued, 'after all these days, Sucharita now says she does not consent to the marriage. Should she have treated this grave matter so frivolously, for so long? Mustn't you also take responsibility for this ugly development?'

'Ma,' said Poreshbabu gently, stroking Sucharita's head, 'there is no need for you to remain here. You may go.' These simple words instantly brought tears to Sucharita's eyes and she rushed out of the room.

'Because I had long suspected that Sucharita had consented to the match without fully knowing her mind, I could not keep your request that we confirm your betrothal in the presence of Samaj members,' Poreshbabu explained.

'Doesn't it occur to you that Sucharita indeed knew her own mind when she gave her consent, and now declines because she no longer understands herself?'

'Both are possible, but in such a state of doubt, the wedding cannot take place.'

'Will you not give Sucharita good advice, then?'

'I am sure you know that I would never willingly give Sucharita bad advice.'

'If that were true, Sucharita could never have come to such a sorry state. I say this to your face: all the things currently happening in your family are the results of your own lack of judgement.'

'Indeed you are right,' smiled Poreshbabu. 'Who but me can be held responsible for the consequences of my family's actions?'

'You will repent this, I tell you.'

'Repentance is God's will, after all. It is sin I fear Panubabu, not repentance.'

Sucharita came in. 'Baba, it is time for your prayers,' she announced, taking Poreshbabu's hand.

'Panubabu, would you wait a while, then?' Poreshbabu inquired.

'No.'

Haranbabu strode out of the room.

~*41*~

Sucharita was frightened by the conflict that had broken out simultaneously within herself and with the outer world. Her feelings for Gora had intensified without her knowledge. This had become completely, transparently and irrefutably clear to her ever since he went to jail. What to do about her feelings and where they might lead her, she could not determine. She could not speak of this to anyone else, diffident about it even to herself. She had not even found a secret opportunity to come to terms with herself about this private anguish.

Haranbabu was threatening to rouse their entire community at her threshold; even the likelihood of newspaper publicity loomed large. Besides, her mashi's problem had grown so acute that a solution had to be found without a day's delay. Sucharita realized her life had reached a crossroads where it was no longer possible to traverse well-known paths in her habitual contented way.

At this difficult moment, Poreshbabu was her only recourse. She had not sought his counsel or advice. There were many things she could not reveal directly to Poreshbabu, things unfit for disclosure because they were shameful and degrading. Poreshbabu's lifestyle, his company itself, seemed sufficient to make her feel silently drawn into some paternal lap, or maternal bosom.

These days, because it was winter, Poreshbabu did not visit the garden in the evening. In a small chamber on the western side of the house, he would place his mat before an open door and prepare himself for prayer. The glow of the setting sun would fall upon his tranquil face, framed by white locks. At this time, Sucharita would quietly approach him and silently take her place by his side. She seemed to immerse her own unquiet, agonized spirit in the depths of Poresh's prayers. Nowadays, at the end of his prayers, Poresh would often find this daughter, this pupil of his, seated silently beside him. Seeing this girl enveloped in an indescribable spiritual grace, he would quietly bless her with all his heart.

Because he saw union with the sublime as his life's sole target, Poresh's spirit was always inclined towards what was worthiest and truest. Hence worldly life could never assume much importance for him. Because he had thus acquired a certain internal detachment, he could not exert any pressure on others about their opinions or conduct. Dependence on divine beneficence and patience with the world came very naturally to him. So pronounced were these qualities in him, that he was condemned by those who were communal; but he received blame in such a way that it might assault him but not injure him permanently. He would constantly repeat to himself: 'I shall accept nothing from anyone else, receiving everything from Him alone.'

To receive the touch of this deep, silent tranquility at the core of Poresh's life, Sucharita would come to him on a variety of pretexts nowadays. At this inexperienced stage in her life, when her contrary heart and a contrary world made her frantic, she would repeatedly think: 'If only I could prostrate myself, clasping Baba's feet to my head and lie there just awhile, my heart would find peace.' In this way, Sucharita hoped to summon up all her inner strength and to withstand all assaults with unshakeable patience. Ultimately, all hostility would be vanquished automatically. But that was not how things turned out. She found herself compelled to take an uncharted course.

When Borodasundari found it impossible to sway Sucharita by raving and ranting, and saw no hope either of finding an ally in Poreshbabu, her fury against Harimohini reached violent proportions. Harimohini's presence within her household began to torment her every moment. One day, she had invited Binoy to the prayers for her father's death anniversary. The ceremony was scheduled for the evening, but before that, she was decorating the hall where the gathering would take place. Sucharita and the other girls were assisting her.

Suddenly, she spotted Binoy going up to meet Harimohini by the staircase at the side. When the mind is under pressure, even trivial incidents assume major significance. Binoy's going upstairs became instantly so unbearable for her that she abandoned her room-decoration and immediately went to Harimohini. There she saw Binoy on the floormat, chatting familiarly with Harimohini like a member of the family.

'Look here,' Borodasundari blurted out, 'stay here as

long as you please, and I shall take good care of you. But I tell
you, that deity of yours can't be kept here.'

Harimohini had always led a provincial life. She had
imagined that Brahmos represented a particular branch of the
Christian faith, and therefore that it was their company one
might discriminate against. But in these few days, she had
gradually begun to realize that they, too, might hesitate to
associate with her. She had been agonizing over what she
ought to do, when hearing these words from Borodasundari
she understood there was no time left to think. She had to
take a decision, somehow. First she thought of taking up
residence somewhere in Kolkata, so she could see Sucharita
and Satish now and then. But with her limited resources, she
could not afford to remain in Kolkata.

After Borodasundari's sudden, stormy entry and exit,
Binoy hung his head in silence.

'I want to go on a pilgrimage,' Harimohini announced
after a brief pause. 'Could one of you escort me there, baba?'

'Of course we can! But it will take a few days to make
arrangements. Come along meanwhile Mashi, come and stay
with Ma.'

'Baba, I am a heavy responsibility. I don't know what
burden destiny has placed upon my forehead, for it is too
much for anyone to bear. I should have realized this when
even my in-laws' home failed to take the weight of my
burden. But my heart is blind, baba; my bosom is hollow, and
to fill the emptiness I wander from place to place, but my
wretched destiny tags along. Let it be, baba, I'd best not go
to anyone else's house. I shall seek refuge at the lotus-like feet
of the One who bears the burden of the entire universe. I
can't cope anymore.' She began to wipe her eyes again and
again.

'You can't say that, Mashi! My Ma is incomparable. For
someone who has surrendered her entire life's burden to the

Lord it is no ordeal to bear the burden of others. Take my mother for instance, or Poreshbabu here. I shall brook no arguments. I shall take you first to my place of pilgrimage, and only then shall I visit your holy place.'

'Then we should send word once . . .'

'When we arrive, Ma will know of it. That will be confirmation indeed.'

'Tomorrow morning, then . . .'

'Why? We can go tonight.'

In the evening, Sucharita came to him and said, 'Binoybabu, Ma has sent for you. It is time for the prayer ceremony.'

'I have things to discuss with Mashi. I can't attend tonight.' Actually, Binoy now could not bear to accept Borodasundari's invitation on any account. The whole affair struck him as a farce.

'Baba Binoy, please go,' begged Harimohini, flustered. 'We can discuss things later. Let your ceremonies first be over, then come to me.'

'It would indeed be best for you to join us,' Sucharita suggested.

Binoy realized that if he did not join the gathering, it would further aggravate the revolution taking place within this family. So he went to the prayer venue, but even that did not entirely accomplish the desired results. After prayers, there was food.

'I have no appetite today,' declared Binoy.

'Your appetite is not to blame,' retorted Borodasundari. 'After all, you have already dined upstairs.'

'Yes, such is the fate of the greedy,' smiled Binoy. 'Tempted by the present, one loses the future.' He prepared to leave.

'So you're going upstairs, are you?' Borodasundari inquired.

'Yes,' replied Binoy curtly, and left the scene. Sucharita was at the door.

'Didi,' he murmured in a low voice, 'please go to Mashi once. There's something urgent to be discussed.'

Lalita was busy attending to their guests. At one point, when she came near Haranbabu, he announced for no reason: 'Binoybabu is not here. He has gone upstairs.'

Hearing this, Lalita stood her ground, met his gaze and declared, unabashed: 'I know. He will not depart without seeing me. I shall go upstairs by and by, once my duties here are done.'

Having failed to embarrass Lalita in the least, Haranbabu's inner fury began to grow. It had also not escaped his notice that Binoy had suddenly whispered something to Sucharita, and that she had followed him shortly thereafter. Today, his repeated attempts to find pretexts for conversation with Sucharita had met with no success. A couple of times, she had evaded his explicit invitation in such a way that Haranbabu had felt himself insulted before the entire gathering. So he was not in a wholesome frame of mind.

Going upstairs, Sucharita found Harimohini waiting with all her things packed as if ready to depart immediately for some other place.

'Mashi, what is this?' Sucharita demanded.

Unable to reply, Harimohini burst into tears. 'Where is Satish?' she asked. 'Please send for him just once, ma!'

When Sucharita glanced at Binoy he explained: 'Mashi's presence in this house causes inconvenience to everybody, so I'm taking her to Ma.'

'From there, I have decided to proceed on a pilgrimage!' Harimohini declared. 'It is not appropriate for someone like me to remain in anyone's house. Indeed, why should people tolerate me like this forever?'

Sucharita herself had been thinking the same thing of late. She had sensed that it was humiliating for her mashi to remain in this house. Hence she was at a loss for a suitable reply. In silence she went to her mashi's side. It was late. The lamp in the room was unlit. In the blurred Hemanta sky above Kolkata, the stars were enveloped in a vaporous haze. In the darkness it was impossible to tell who was weeping.

'Mashima!' Satish's high-pitched voice resounded from the stairs.

'What is it, baba? Come, baba,' called out Harimohini, quickly rising to her feet.

'Mashima,' said Sucharita, 'there's no question of your going anywhere tonight. We can arrange everything tomorrow morning. Tell me, how can you depart without bidding proper farewell to Baba? That would be very wrong of you, indeed.'

In his agitation at Borodasundari's humiliation of Harimohini, Binoy had not thought of this. He had decided that Mashi should not spend another night in this house, and to dispel Borodasundari's notion that Harimohini put up with everything just to remain in this house because she had no other refuge, he was reluctant to brook the slightest delay in removing Harimohini from this place. Sucharita's words suddenly reminded Binoy that it was not as if Harimohini's only or primary relationship in this house was with Borodasundari. It was not right, after all, to give more importance to the person who had inflicted an insult, and to forget the one who had been large hearted enough to shelter her like a member of the family.

'True, indeed,' exclaimed Binoy. 'We certainly can't leave without informing Poreshbabu.'

'Mashima,' declared Satish as soon as he arrived, 'do you know that the Russians are coming to attack Bharatvarsha? What fun!'

'Whose side are you on?' Binoy enquired.

'I am for the Russians.'

'In that case the Russians have nothing to fear.'

When Satish had managed to liven up Mashima's circle in this fashion, Sucharita slowly arose and went downstairs. She knew that before retiring to bed, Poreshbabu would read from one of his favourite books. Often, at such times, Sucharita would go to him and at her request, he would read to her as well.

Tonight, too, Poreshbabu had lit the lamp in his secluded chamber, and was reading Emerson's book. Gently, Sucharita drew up a chair and sat by his side. Putting aside his book, Poreshbabu glanced once at her face. Sucharita's resolve wavered. She could not bring up any worldly subject.

'Baba, please read to me,' she said.

Poreshbabu began to read to her, and to explain. At ten in the night, the reading session ended. Even now, Sucharita prepared to leave quietly without saying anything, lest she arouse any distress in Poreshbabu's heart.

'Radhé!' called Poreshbabu, affectionately. She came back.

'Did you come to speak to me about your mashi?' he asked.

'Yes, Baba,' replied Sucharita, surprised that he had read her thoughts. 'But tonight let it be, we'll talk tomorrow morning.'

'Sit down.'

When she had obeyed, he said, 'I have considered the fact that your mashi is finding it difficult here. I had not realized clearly before this that her beliefs and rituals would assault Labanya's mother's convictions so strongly. When it is obviously causing her pain, keeping your mashi here would inhibit her freedom.'

'My mashi is ready to leave,' Sucharita replied.

'I knew she would leave. You two are the only people she can call her own. I'm also aware that you will be unable to abandon her to her fate. So I've been thinking about it, these last few days.'

Sucharita had no idea Poreshbabu had realized her mashi's predicament and was worrying about it. She had proceeded very cautiously all along, lest he sense the true state of affairs and be pained by it. Now, she was amazed to hear Poreshbabu's words. Tears glistened on her lashes.

'I have selected a house for your mashi,' Poreshbabu informed her.

'But she . . .' faltered Sucharita.

'She can't afford the rent,' said Poreshbabu. 'Why should she pay rent? You will pay it.' Sucharita gazed at his face in amazement. 'Let her stay in your own house,' he smiled. 'She won't need to pay rent.' Sucharita was even more amazed.

'Don't you know,' Poreshbabu continued, 'you own two houses in Kolkata, the two of you! One yours, the other Satish's. When he was dying your father left some money with me. Investing the capital to make it grow, I bought two houses in Kolkata. All these days I was receiving rent for them, which was also accumulating. The tenant has vacated your house recently. There will be no inconvenience if your mashi lives there.'

'Can she live there by herself?' Sucharita inquired.

'With you two as her very own relatives, why must she live by herself?'

'That is what I came to discuss with you tonight. Mashi is ready to leave, but I was wondering how I could let her depart alone. So I have come to you for advice. I shall do whatever you say.'

'Do you see this alley here, skirting our house?' asked Poreshbabu. 'Your house is just two or three buildings down this alley. If you stand at that veranda there, you can see the house. If you all live there, you won't remain entirely unprotected. I can look after you.'

Sucharita felt as if a huge boulder had rolled off her chest. She had been ceaselessly worrying, 'how shall I abandon

Baba?' But leave she must: that too had become a certainty.
Her heart too full for words, Sucharita sat silently beside
Poreshababu. He too remained silent, deeply self-absorbed.
Sucharita was his disciple, his daughter, his soulmate. She had
become a part of his life, even of his devotional path. His
prayers seemed to gain a special completeness on days when
she came and joined him quietly. Moulding Sucharita's life
daily with his benevolent affection, he had been bestowing a
certain fulfillment to his own life as well. No-one had come
to him before with Sucharita's devotion and utter humility.
Like a flower gazing at the sky, she had turned to him, laying
bare her entire being. When approached by someone with
such single-minded eagerness, the limits of human generosity
are extended of their own accord; the heart bows down in its
own fullness, like a cloud burdened by its own moisture.
There can be nothing more auspicious than the opportunity of
daily gifting one's truest and worthiest qualities to a heart that
is compatible. Such was the rare opportunity Sucharita had
given Poreshbabu. Hence, his relationship with her had grown
very intense. Today it was time to sever his outward bond
with Sucharita; having ripened the fruit with his own life-sap,
he must now free it from him. The pain he felt within at this,
he offered up to the all-knowing Ishwar. Sucharita was equipped
with resources for her journey; for some time now, Poresh
had been observing her preparations for the call to take the
path that stretched out ahead, aspiring to new experience on
her own strength, arriving at it through joy and sorrow,
blows and counter-blows. Privately, he was saying: 'My child,
proceed on your journey . . . it is impossible that I should
overshadow your entire life with my intelligence and my
protection alone. May Ishwar liberate you from me and draw
you to the ultimate goal through a diverse range of experiences.
May your life find its fulfillment in Him!' With these words
he was mentally surrendering Sucharita, so lovingly cherished

from her infancy, as an offering to Ishwar. Poresh was not
angry with Borodasundari; in his mind, he had not fostered
any hostility towards his own family. He knew that a deluge
unleashed by the new rains can create a tremendous upheaval
in a beach that is narrow; the only solution is to release the
waters into an open field. He was aware that sheltering
Sucharita had in a short time given rise to unforeseen situations
within this small family, disrupting their regular traditions.
He also sensed that setting her free, instead of clinging to her,
was the only way to restore peace and normalcy, in keeping
with her natural tendencies. Realizing this, he was quietly
trying to arrange things so that peace and harmony could
easily be restored.

As they sat there in silence, the two of them, the clock
struck eleven. Rising to his feet, Poreshbabu led Sucharita by
the hand to the terrace above the portico. The evening
vapours had evaporated, and the stars were shining in the
pure darkness. On that silent night, with Sucharita by his side,
Poresh uttered a prayer: 'Dispelling all the falsehoods of this
world, let the pure image of perfect truth manifest itself in
our lives.'

~42~

At dawn the next day, Harimohini knelt to touch Poresh's
feet in a pranam.

'What are you doing?' he protested, flustered, moving
aside at once.

'I can never repay my debt to you,' Harimohini replied,
with tears in her eyes. 'You have found help for someone as
helpless as myself. No one but you could have accomplished
this. I have seen that nobody can do anything for my benefit,
even if they want to. You are deeply blessed by the Lord, that
is why you can favour even a person such as me.'

Poreshbabu was acutely embarrassed.

'I have not done anything much,' he insisted. 'All this is Radharani's . . .'

'I know, I know,' Harimohini interrupted. 'But Radharani herself belongs to you; whatever she does is really your doing. When she lost her mother, and her father too was no more, I regarded her as a very unfortunate girl. But how was I to know that the Lord would transform her misfortune into something so gloriously worthwhile? Having met you, after all my wanderings, I now understand clearly that the Lord has been kind to me as well.'

'Mashi, Ma has come to fetch you,' announced Binoy as he arrived. 'Where is she?' asked Sucharita, springing to her feet.

'Downstairs, with your mother.'

Sucharita hastened downstairs.

'Let me go and arrange all the things in your house,' said Poreshbabu to Harimohini.

When he had departed, Binoy asked in surprise: 'Mashi, I didn't know about your house!'

'I didn't know about it either, baba! Only Poreshbabu knew. It's our Radharani's house.'

'I had thought Binoy would prove useful to at least one person in the world,' declared Binoy, after listening to the whole story. 'But even that opportunity has eluded me. Until now, I have not been able to do anything for my mother; it is she who does the needful for me. I can't do anything for Mashi either; I shall draw favours from her instead. It is my destiny to take, not to give.'

After a while, Anandamoyi arrived there, accompanied by Lalita and Sucharita.

'When the Lord shows kindness, he does so without stinting,' said Harimohini, advancing towards them. 'Didi, today I get to meet you as well.' She took Anandamoyi's hand and drew her to the madur on the floor.

'Didi,' said Harimohini, 'Binoy speaks of no one but you.'

'That has been his ailment since childhood,' smiled Anandamoyi. 'Once he takes up a subject, he doesn't drop it easily. Very soon it will be Mashi's turn, too.'

'That will happen, let me tell you in advance,' confirmed Binoy. 'I have found Mashi late in life, acquired her by my own efforts. I must find diverse ways to compensate myself for this long deprivation.'

'Our Binoy knows how to acquire what he lacks,' smiled Anandamoyi, glancing at Lalita, 'and having acquired it, he also knows how to cherish it with his heart and soul. Only I know how he perceives all of you—as if he has suddenly glimpsed a vision he could never have imagined possible. Ma, what can I say? How happy I am that he has made your acquaintance! The way Binoy has taken a fancy to this household of yours, it's done him a world of good. He knows it only too well and doesn't hesitate to admit it, either.'

Lalita tried to reply, but could not find the words. She began to blush. Observing her distress, Sucharita interposed:

'Binoybabu can detect the inner goodness in everybody, so he gets to enjoy the best in everybody. That is largely due to his special talents.'

'Ma, you assume Binoy is a major subject of discussion but he doesn't enjoy such eminence in this world,' protested Binoy. 'I want to explain this to you every time, but from pure vanity, I fail to do so. But now it won't do anymore. No more of this, Ma, no more talk of Binoy today.'

At this moment Satish came bounding up, clasping his newborn puppy to his breast.

'Baba Satish, my dearest boy, please take the dog away, baba!' cried Harimohini, highly flustered.

'He won't trouble you, Mashi!' Satish assured her. 'He will not go into your room. Just pet him a little, he won't object.'

'No baba, no,' said Harimohini, shrinkng away. 'Take him away.'

At this, Anandamoyi drew Satish to her, dog and all. 'You're Satish, aren't you? Our Binoy's friend?' she asked, as she took the puppy on her lap.

Satish saw nothing incongruous in being identified as Binoy's friend. So he confirmed, without any hesitation:

'Yes.' He gazed expectantly at Anadamoyi.

'I am Binoy's mother,' she informed him. The puppy proceeded to amuse itself by trying to chew upon Anandamoyi's balas, the thick bangles she wore.

'Bakhtiar,' prompted Sucharita, 'touch Ma's feet.'

Awkwardly, Satish somehow performed the task. At this moment, Borodasundari came upstairs.

'Will you join us for something to eat?' she asked Anandamoyi without so much as glancing at Harimohini.

'I don't discriminate about food, touch and so on,' Anandamoyi declared. 'But today, let it be. Let Gora come back, I'll dine with you after that.' She could not bring herself to do something in Gora's absence that would have displeased him.

'So here you are, Binoybabu!' remarked Borodasudari, glancing at Binoy. 'I thought perhaps you had not come.'

'Do you think I would go away without telling you I was here?' Binoy at once retorted.

'Yesterday you avoided the feast to which you were invited,' persisted Borodasundari. 'So today, perhaps, you could join us for a meal uninvited.'

'I find that much more tempting,' Binoy responded. 'Tips are more attractive than a salary.'

Harimohini was privately surprised. Binoy dined at this house, and even Anandamoyi did not observe such restrictions. She was not happy about this.

'Didi,' asked Harimohini diffidently, after Borodasundari had left, 'is your husband . . .'

'My husband is a staunch Hindu.'

Harimohini was dumbfounded. Sensing her thoughts, Anandamoyi said:

'My sister, when the Samaj was greater than all of us, it was the Samaj I followed. But one day, Ishwar visited our home in such a form that He made it impossible for me to follow the Samaj anymore. Once the Lord Himself snatched my caste status away from me, what have I to fear from anyone else?'

'Your husband?' faltered Harimohini, not understanding this explanation.

'My husband is angry with me.'

'And the boys?'

'The boys are not happy either. But must I live to please them alone? My sister, I can't explain my situation to anyone else—only the all-knowing One can understand it.' Anandamoyi folded her hands in reverence.

Harimohini imagined that some missionary's daughter had visited Anandamoyi and filled her mind with Khristani ideas. She now felt an acute sense of constraint.

~43~

Sucharita had felt very reassured when told that she could live close to Poreshbabu's house, constantly under his supervision. But as the time approached for them to move into her new home once it was furnished, she felt a catch in her heart. No matter if they lived close to each other; but now it was time to sever the all-encompassing link between their lives, she felt as if a part of herself would die. Her place within this family, however insignificant, her duties there, even her relationship with each member of their domestic staff, became a source of agony for her.

Upon learning that Sucharita had some resources of her own and that she was comfortably preparing for an independent life on the strength of those resources, Borodasundari repeatedly expressed her approval, indicating her relief at being freed of the burden she had borne so long and so carefully. But inwardly she developed a reproachful attitude, as if it was wrong of Sucharita to break away from them and become self-sufficient. She had often felt sorry for herself, considering Sucharita a burden on her family, imagining themselves to be Sucharita's sole recourse. But upon suddenly learning she would be relieved of Sucharita's burden, she felt no joy within her heart. Anticipating that Sucharita might pride herself on having no urgent need for their protection, that she might feel no obligation to acknowledge her indebtedness to them, Borodasundari condemned her in advance. During this period, she remained especially aloof from Sucharita. Completely dropping her former habit of summoning Sucharita to help with the housework, she now showed her an unnatural degree of respect. Before she left, Sucharita, in her distress, tried to participate even more actively in Borodasundari's household chores, following her around on various pretexts, but Borodasundari kept her at arm's length, as if to ensure Sucharita did not suffer any loss of respect. It pained Sucharita most of all that the one who had reared her like a mother should remain hostile when it was time for her to leave. Labanya, Lalita and Leela began to cling to Sucharita. With great enthusiasm they went to decorate her new home, but even that enthusiasm was suffused with unshed tears.

Up until now Sucharita had performed many small errands for Poreshbabu on a variety of pretexts. Arranging flowers in a vase or books on a table, sunning his bedclothes, reminding him when it was time for his bath—neither of them had attached any importance to these habitual daily tasks. But when it was time to leave, abandoning even these unnecessary chores, these tiny acts of service, which someone else can also easily perform, which even if neglected would not greatly matter—it was these acts that became a source of torment for both parties. Now, when Sucharita came into Poresh's room to perform some trivial task, it would assume great importance in his eyes and he would stifle a sigh. And the thought that this task would shortly be taken over by someone else would bring tears to Sucharita's eyes.

On the appointed day, when Sucharita and the others were to move into the new house after lunch, Poreshbabu entered his secluded room to pray at dawn and found Sucharita waiting for him in a corner. In front of his prayer mat, she had arranged flowers on the floor. Labanya and Leela had also conspired to be present there, but Lalita had prohibited them. Knowing that Sucharita, when she joined in Poreshbabu's solitary prayers, seemed to receive a special share of his bliss as well as his blessings, and that she had a special need to glean those blessings this morning, Lalita had not allowed the solitude of today's prayers to be disrupted. As the prayers ended, tears were flowing from Sucharita's eyes.

'Ma, don't look back,' Poreshbabu advised her. 'Advance on the path that lies ahead, without any hesitation. Set forth joyfully, vowing that whatever happens, whatever situation confronts you, you will use all your power to imbibe the best from it. Surrendering yourself completely to Ishwar, make him your sole support. Then, even through mistakes, errors and loss, you can progress in the right direction. And if you divide yourself in two, dedicating part to Ishwar and part to something else, then everything will become very difficult. May Ishwar ensure that you have no further need of our humble shelter.'

After prayers, the two of them emerged to find Haranbabu awaiting them in the outer chamber. Vowing not to harbour any resentment against anybody on this day, Sucharita greeted him politely with a namaskar. At once assuming a rigid posture on his chair, Haranbabu declared, very severely:

'Sucharita, today you are about to regress from the truth that had sustained you for so long. This is a sad day for us.'

Sucharita offered no reply. But a discordant note entered the music that had filled her heart today with a melodious blend of peace and compassion.

'Only the One who knows our hearts can say who is making progress and who is falling back,' answered Poreshbabu. 'We vainly grow anxious trying to judge things from outside.'

'Do you mean to say that your heart is free of anxiety?' demanded Haranbabu. 'And that you have had no cause for remorse either?'

'Panubabu,' Poreshbabu responded, 'I entertain no imaginary anxieties and I shall only know whether I have cause for remorse when remorse arises in my heart.'

'What about your daughter Lalita arriving alone on the steamer with Binoybabu, is that imaginary too?' retorted Haranbabu.

Sucharita's face grew flushed.

'Panubabu, you are agitated for some reason, so it would be unfair to you to discuss the matter with you now,' Poreshbabu observed.

'I never say anything in the heat of emotion,' declared Haranbabu, head held high. 'I am sufficiently responsible for whatever I say, don't worry. What I say to you is not personal, but spoken on behalf of the Brahmo Samaj, and I speak because it would be wrong to remain silent. Had you not been blind, you would have realized from this one instance of Lalita traveling alone with Binoybabu that this family of yours is about to drift away from its moorings in the Brahmo Samaj. This will not only inflict remorse upon you, but also dishonour upon the Brahmo Samaj . . .'

'Blame can be ascribed from outside, but to pass judgement one must penetrate the inner reality of things,' Poreshbabu asserted. 'Please don't condemn people on the basis of incidents alone.'

'Incidents don't occur randomly,' Haranbabu insisted. 'You bring them about through your inner compulsions. You are developing intimate ties with people who wish to take your family away from your own community. Indeed, they have already drawn them away, can't you see?'

'Our perspectives don't coincide,' replied Poreshbabu, rather annoyed.

'Your perspective may not coincide, but I call upon Sucharita to testify. Let her say truthfully whether Lalita's current relationship with Binoy is merely an outward link? Has it not touched their inner selves at all? No Sucharita, you can't leave, you must answer. It's very important.'

'However important, you have no right to discuss it,' Sucharita retorted harshly.

'Had I no right, I would not only have held my tongue but refrained from anxiety as well,' Haranbabu declared. 'You may disregard the Samaj, all of you, but as long as it exists, the Samaj must judge you.'

'If the Samaj has deployed you as a judge, then exile from the Samaj is our best recourse,' pronounced Lalita, storming into the room.

'Lalita, I am glad you are here,' said Haranbabu, rising from his chair. 'The charges against you should be judged in your presence.'

Sucharita's face and eyes were aflame with fury. 'Haranbabu, please go to your own home and summon your court there. We can never accept your right to enter a household and insult a family within their own home. Come bhai Lalita, let's go.'

Lalita would not budge. 'No Didi, I shan't run away,' she

insisted. 'I want to leave only after I have heard everything Panubabu has to say. Go ahead, please say what you will!'

Haranbabu was speechless in surprise.

'Ma Lalita,' pleaded Poreshbabu, 'Sucharita is leaving our home today. I cannot permit any disturbance this morning. Haranbabu, however guilty we might be, you must forgive us for today.'

Haran maintained a grave silence. The more Sucharita spurned him, the more determined he became to hold her captive. He firmly believed he was bound to win by the force of his extraordinary moral power. Not that he had given up even now, but he was tormented by the anxiety that if Sucharita moved into a different house with her mashi, his power would suffer constant rebuffs there. Hence, today, he had come armed with his ultimate weapons, properly honed. He was ready to force a very tough compromise that very morning. Indeed he had come there shedding all his hesitations that day, but that his opponents could also cast off their inhibitions in this way, that Lalita and Sucharita would also draw arrows from their quiver to suddenly join the fray, was something he had never imagined. He was convinced that when he began shooting his flaming moral shafts with resplendent force, the enemy would suffer abject defeat. Things did not turn out quite that way, and the opportunity was lost. But Haranbabu would not give up. He told himself that the truth was bound to triumph, in other words, that he, Haranbabu, was bound to win. But victory does not come of its own accord. One must fight. Bracing himself, Haranbabu entered the battlefield.

'Mashi,' said Sucharita, 'I shall eat with everybody today. You must not mind.'

Harimohini remained silent. She had privately assumed that Sucharita was entirely devoted to her. Now that Sucharita was free to live independently on the strength of her own property, Harimohini had thought that no further constraints were necessary, for she could now act entirely as she pleased. Hence, when Sucharita once again disregarded the laws of purity and proposed to eat with everyone else, Harimohini was displeased. She remained silent.

'Thakur will be pleased at this, I can assure you,' Sucharita told her, sensing her attitude. 'The same all-knowing Thakur of mine has ordered me to eat with everybody today. If I don't obey, He will be angry. I fear His anger more than yours.'

As long as Harimohini faced humiliation from Borodasundari, Sucharita had accepted her rituals to share her plight, but now it was time to be free of that humiliation, Sucharita had no hesitation in dissociating herself from restrictions concerning purity. Harimohini had not quite anticipated this. She had not understood Sucharita completely, and it was difficult, indeed, for her to do so. She did not openly forbid Sucharita but privately, she was annoyed. 'Oh ma,' she thought, 'I can't imagine how people might develop such tendencies. She was born into a Brahman home, after all!'

'Let me tell you something, bachha,' she said, 'do as you please, but don't accept water served by that bearer of yours.'

'Why Mashi,' protested Sucharita, 'it's Ramdeen the bearer who milks his own cow to supply you with milk!'

'You amaze me' exclaimed Harimohini, wide-eyed, 'is milk the same as water?'

'Tell me Mashi,' smiled Sucharita, 'let me not drink water touched by Ramdeen today. But if you forbid Satish, he is bound to do exactly the opposite!'

'Satish is a different matter,' said Harimohini.

Harimohini knew that when it came to the male sex, lapses in discipline must be forgiven.

~44~

Haranbabu entered the battlefield.

It was now fifteen days since Lalita had arrived on the steamer with Binoy. The rumour had reached a few ears, and little by little, it had been trying to gain ground. But in the last two days, the news had spread like wildfire.

Haranbabu had persuaded many people that it was one's duty to curb such misdemeanour to safeguard the morals of the Brahmo family. It was not hard to convince others of such things. When we respond to the 'call of truth' and the 'call of duty' by condemning and punishing the blunders of others, it is not too difficult to meet the demands of truth and duty. Hence when Haranbabu proclaimed the 'bitter' truth to the Brahmo Samaj and proceeded to perform a 'harsh' duty', most people were not averse to joining him enthusiastically, awed by the magnitude of such bitterness and harshness. Well-wishers of the Brahmo Samaj visited each other by hired cab or palki to declare that now such things had begun to happen, the future of the Samaj looked bleak indeed. Alongside, news also spread that Sucharita had become a Hindu, and having taken refuge in her Hindu mashi's house, was devoting her days to sacrificial rituals, meditation, and idol worship.

For a long time, a battle had raged in Lalita's heart. Every night, before going to bed, she would tell herself, 'I shall never admit defeat,' and every morning, when she awoke, she would sit up in bed and declare, 'I shall never admit defeat under any circumstances.' Thoughts of Binoy obsessed her; the awareness that he was chatting with people in the room downstairs would make her heart race; if he failed to visit their house for a couple of days, her heart would seethe with suppressed reproach; every now and then, on various pretexts, she would incite Satish to visit Binoy's house, and when he returned, she would try to extract a detailed account of Binoy's activities and their conversation from Satish. The more unavoidable this became for Lalita, the more she fretted at the degradation of defeat. Sometimes, she was even angry with Poreshbabu, for not opposing her interaction with Binoy and Gora. But she was determined to fight to the end, to die rather than concede victory. As for how she would pass the rest of her life, all sorts of possibilities drifted through her imagination. The biographies she had read, relating the exploits of female welfare workers in Europe, began to appear possible and achievable.

One day she went to Poreshbabu and said: 'Baba, can't I take up a teaching post in some girls' school?'

Glancing at his daughter's face, Poreshbabu saw her eyes, full of the anguish of a yearning heart, gazing at him beseechingly like a destitute.

'Why not, ma?' he replied tenderly. 'But where can we find such a girls' school?'

We speak of a time when schools for girls were scarce; there were only ordinary pathshalas, and women of bhadra families had not yet advanced into the field of education.

'Is there no such school, Baba?' asked Lalita in agitation.

'Indeed I haven't seen one.'

'Tell me, Baba, can't we start a girls' school?'

'It's a very expensive proposition and would require help from many people.'

Lalita knew it was hard to even arouse the will to do benevolent deeds, but she had never imagined accomplishing them might pose so many obstacles. After a short silence she slowly arose and left. What was the source of his favourite daughter's heartache, Poreshbabu wondered thoughtfully. He was reminded, too, of Haranbabu's insinuations about Binoy. Sighing, he asked himself: 'Have I done something unwise?' Had it concerned one of his other daughters, there would be no special cause for worry, Lalita saw her life only too literally; with her, there could be no half-measures; joy and sorrow were not half-truths to her.

How would Lalita live, bearing false condemnation every day of her life? She could see no stability, no positive outcome ahead. It was not in her nature to drift along helplessly like this. That very afternoon, she arrived at Sucharita's house. The house was sparsely decorated. A wall-to-wall mat covered the floor on which Sucharita's bed had been laid out at one end. Harimohini's was at the opposite end. Because Harimohini did not sleep on a bed, Sucharita had also arranged to sleep on the floor, in the same room. On the wall hung a picture of Poreshbabu. In a small adjacent room, Satish's bed had been placed, and beside it, on a small table, ink, pens, notebooks, books and papers lay randomly scattered. Satish was in school. The house was silent.

After their meal, Harimohini prepared to sleep on the madur, and on her own mat, Sucharita sat immersed in her reading, open tresses outspread across her back, a pillow on her lap. A few more books lay in front of her. Seeing Lalita suddenly enter the room, Sucharita first closed her book in apparent embarrassment, then opened it as before, even more embarrassed. She was reading the collected works of Gora.

'Come, come, ma,' called Harimohini, sitting up. 'Come in, Lalita. I know what Sucharita is feeling, having left your house. Whenever she is upset, she takes up those books. Just now, lying here, I was thinking how nice it would be if one of you came by, and here you are. You will have a long life, ma!'

Settling beside Sucharita, Lalita at once broached the subject on her mind. 'Suchididi,' she proposed, 'what if we were to open a school for girls in our neighbourhood?'

'Just listen to her!' exclaimed Harimohini. 'How can you start a school, the two of you?'

'Tell me, how would we accomplish it?' Sucharita asked. 'Who would help us? Have you told Baba?'

'The two of us can teach, after all,' Lalita declared. 'Borodidi might also agree.'

'But it's not simply about teaching after all,' Sucharita reminded her. 'We must formulate rules for the running of the school, locate a building, acquire students, and find the funds. How much of this can the two of us accomplish, as women?'

'Didi, you can't say that!' Lalita protested. 'Just because I was born a woman, must I remain confined at home, dashing my brains against the walls? Can I be of no use to the world?'

The anguish in Lalita's words resonated in Sucharita's heart. She began to think, without offering any reply.

'There are many girls in the neighbourhood, aren't there?' Lalita persisted. 'If we want to teach them free of cost, their parents would actually be pleased. Let it suffice for us to teach as many of them as possible, here in this house of yours. What would it cost us?'

At this proposal to gather innumerable girls from unknown families, to teach them here under this roof, Harimohini grew very agitated. She wanted to remain pure and unsullied, busy with her prayers and holy offerings in seclusion. She began to resist the possibility of disruption.

'Have no fear, Mashi,' Sucharita assured her. 'If we manage to procure pupils we shall deal with them in the rooms downstairs. We shall not disturb you upstairs. So, bhai Lalita, if we can find pupils, I am willing.'

'Very well, let's give it a try,' said Lalita.

'Ma, you can't imitate the Khristans in every respect, can you?' Harimohini protested repeatedly. 'Since my father's times, I have not heard of women from middle class households teaching in schools.'

From Poreshbabu's terrace, conversations took place with

women on the neighbouring terraces. One of the thorniest issues in these interchanges was the fact that the women next door often expressed curiosity and surprise that the girls in this house were still unmarried, even at such an advanced age. Hence Lalita tried her best to avoid these rooftop conversations. It was Labanya who was most enthusiastic about spreading friendship from terrace to terrace. There was no limit to her curiosity about the details of life in other homes. Discussions of many matters, significant or otherwise, concerning her neighbours' daily lives, would reach her through these airy channels. Comb in hand, tending her hair, she often enjoyed these afternoon colloquia under the open sky.

Lalita gave Labanya the responsibility of procuring students for her projected school for girls. When Labanya announced this proposal across the rooftops, many girls were fired with enthusiasm. Pleased, Lalita began to prepare the room on Sucharita's ground floor, sweeping, washing the floor, decorating the place. But her schoolroom remained empty. The male heads of households were incensed at the proposal to lure their daughters into a Brahmo house on the pretext of educating them. In fact, when they got to know, in this connection, that their daughters regularly chatted with Poreshbabu's daughters, they considered it their duty, indeed, to put a stop to the practice. Their daughters' freedom to climb up to the terrace was jeopardised, and the men were not very civil in the language in which they voiced their attitude towards the good intentions of the Brahmo girls. Poor Labanya, climbing to the terrace comb in hand at the usual time, found the young, modern nabinas replaced by congregations of mature, old-fashioned prabinas on the neighbouring terraces; and she did not receive a warm greeting from any of them.

Lalita was not daunted even by this. 'Many Brahmo girls find it impossible to go to Bethune School,' she declared. 'It would help if we took up the responsibility of educating them.' She applied herself to the hunt for such female students, and deployed Sudhir as well.

Those days, Poreshbabu's daughters were widely reknowned for their learning. In fact their fame had far exceeded the truth. Hence many parents were pleased to hear that the girls would teach female students free of charge. At the outset, Lalita's school established itself within just a few days, with five or six girls. She did not allow herself a moment of leisure, discussing the school with Poreshbabu, framing the rules by which it would be run, organizing everything. In fact, a proper quarrel broke out between Labanya and Lalita concerning the kind of prizes to be awarded to the girls after the annual examinations. The books that Lalita proposed Labanya did not like, but Labanya's tastes did not match Lalita's either. They even differed somewhat regarding the choice of examiners. Although Labanya detested Haranbabu on the whole, she was overwhelmed by his fame as a scholar. She had no doubt that it would be a matter of pride if Haranbabu were involved in their school, as examiner, teacher, or in some other capacity. But Lalita dismissed the suggestion out of hand—no connection could be allowed between Haranbabu and this school of theirs.

Within two or three days, the number of her students dwindled until the class became empty. Waiting in her vacant classroom, Lalita would start at the sound of footsteps, anticipating the arrival of female students, but no-one came. When several hours passed by in this fashion, she realized something was wrong. She visited a pupil who lived nearby.

'Ma won't let me go,' confessed the girl tearfully.

'It's inconvenient,' the mother asserted. It was not clear where the inconvenience lay. Lalita was proud; at the slightest trace of reluctance in others, she could neither insist nor ask the reason why.

'If it's inconvenient, why proceed?' she said. At the next house she visited, she faced some plain speaking.

'Sucharita has become a Hindu nowadays,' they said. 'She observes caste differences. Idols are worshipped at her house,' and so on.

'If that is your objection then we can run the school from our own house,' proposed Lalita. But even this did not allay their doubts. There was something more to it. Instead of visiting any other homes, Lalita sent for Sudhir.

'Sudhir, tell me honestly what the matter is,' she demanded.

'Panubabu is up in arms against this school of yours,' Sudhir replied.

'Why, is it because there is idol worship at Didi's house?' asked Lalita.

'Not just that.'

'What else is it? You may as well tell me!' demanded Lalita impatiently.

'That's a long story.'

'Am I to blame as well?' Lalita wanted to know. Sudhir remained silent.

'This is the price I must pay for that steamer journey!' exclaimed Lalita, flushing. 'Even if I acted thoughtlessly, does our Samaj permit no atonement through good deeds? Does this community forbid me to undertake any benevolent action? Is this the mode of spiritual upliftment all of you have prescribed for me and for our community?'

'Not quite,' said Sudhir, trying to soften the blow. 'They are afraid Binoybabu might eventually become involved with this school.'

'Would that be fearsome, or fortunate?' flamed Lalita. 'How many among them can compare with Binoybabu in personal worth!'

'True indeed!' admitted Sudhir, daunted by Lalita's rage. 'But then, Binoybabu . . .'

'Is not a member of the Brahmo Samaj! Therefore the Brahmo Samaj will punish him. I feel no pride in such a society.'

Observing how the students had vanished, Sucharita had realized what the matter was and who was behind it. Without saying a word about it, she was with Satish in the room upstairs, tutoring him for his approaching examinations.

'Have you heard?' demanded Lalita, going to Sucharita after her conversation with Sudhir.

'I haven't heard,' replied Sucharita with a faint smile, 'but I have understood everything.'

'Must we tolerate all this?'

'There is no humiliation in tolerance,' asserted Sucharita, taking Lalita's hand. 'You've seen, haven't you, how Baba puts up with everything?'

'But Suchididi,' protested Lalita, 'I often feel that tolerance amounts to accepting injustice. Refusing to tolerate injustice is indeed the right way to retaliate.'

'Tell me, bhai, what you would like to do.'

'I haven't thought about it at all,' confessed Lalita. 'I don't even know what I can do about it, but do something we must. Those who are persecuting women like us in such a vile fashion are cowards, regardless of their high opinion of themselves. But I shall never admit defeat at their hands— never! Let them do what they can.' Lalita stamped her foot. Without answering, Sucharita began to stroke her arm gently.

'Bhai Lalita,' she said after a while, 'try speaking to Baba once.'

'I'll go to him straightaway,' declared Lalita, rising to her feet.

Approaching the door to her house, Lalita saw Binoy emerge with bowed head. Seeing Lalita he stopped short for a moment, debating whether or not to exchange a few words

with her, but restraining himself, he greeted her with a
namaskar, eyes averted, and left, still hanging his head. Lalita
felt as if a white-hot stake had speared her body. Rushing
indoors, she went straight to her mother's room. Her mother
was at the table, poring over a long, slim ledger, trying to
concentrate on household accounts. Seeing Lalita's expression,
Borodasundari was alarmed. She tried to vanish quickly into
the depths of her ledger, as if her household would be utterly
destroyed if she did not immediately balance a particular
account. Lalita drew up a chowki close to the table. Still
Borodasundari did not raise her head.

'Ma!'

'Wait, bachha, I just . . .' Borodasundari bent excessively
low over her ledger.

'I shall not trouble you for long,' Lalita assured her.
'There is something I want to know. Was Binoybabu here?'

'Yes,' said Borodasundari, without lifting her head from
the ledger.

'What did you discuss?'

'That's a long story.'

'Did you speak about me or not?'

Seeing no way out, Borodasundari flung aside her pen,
and raised her head. 'Yes we did, bachha,' she admitted. 'I
found that things were going too far, with people of our
community casting aspersions on us everywhere, so I had to
warn him.'

Lalita's face grew red with shame. Her head seemed
ablaze with fury.

'Has Baba forbidden him to come here?' she demanded.

'As if he thinks about such things!' responded
Borodasundari. 'If he did, all this could have been prevented
from the very beginning.'

'Is Panubabu allowed to visit?'

'Just listen to this!' exclaimed Borodasundari, astounded.
'Why should Panubabu not visit us?'

'Why should Binoybabu not visit us, either?'

'Lalita, there's no arguing with you, bapu!' said Borodasundari, drawing the ledger to her once again. 'Go away, don't plague me now. I have a lot to do.'

In the afternoon, while Lalita was away at Sucharita's to work at the school, Borodasundari had taken the opportunity to send for Binoy and give him a piece of her mind. She had imagined Lalita would never get to know. Suddenly caught out in her intrigue, she now sensed danger. She realized that the outcome would not be peaceful, and that the matter would not be easily resolved. All her rage now directed itself against her utterly impractical husband. What an affliction for a woman to be compelled to live with this obtuse man!

Lalita left Borodasundari, carrying a cataclysmic storm in her heart. She went straight to the room downstairs where Poreshbabu was writing letters, and asked him directly:

'Baba, is Binoybabu unfit company for us?'

Her question at once made the situation clear to Poreshbabu. He was not unaware of the recent upheaval within their Samaj regarding his family. It had caused him a great deal of worry, as well. If he did not have doubts about Lalita's feelings for Binoy, he would have paid no attention to outside gossip. But he had repeatedly asked himself what his duty should be, if Lalita had developed romantic feelings for Binoy. After having openly adopted the Brahmo creed, his family now faced another difficult moment. Hence, while he was inwardly tormented by a certain apprehension and pain, simultaneously all his intellectual faculties were also aroused, declaring: 'I passed a difficult test when I adopted the Brahmo faith with my eyes fixed only on Ishwar, my life finding eternal fulfillment in valuing truth above happiness, property, society, everything. If I should now face a similar moment of reckoning, I shall overcome it by looking to Him alone.'

In answer to Lalita's question, Poreshbabu said: 'I know Binoy to be a very good person, in intellect as in character.'

After a short silence, Lalita said: 'Gourbabu's mother came by a couple of times recently. May I visit her today, along with Suchididi?'

For a while, Poreshbabu could not reply. He knew for sure that in the present climate of opinion, such visits would foster even greater social disapproval. But his heart protested: 'As long as it is not wrong, I cannot forbid it.'

'Very well, you may go,' he said. 'I have work to do, or I would have accompanied you myself.'

~45~

Binoy had not dreamt that beneath the terrain he had entered so nonchalantly as a visitor and a friend, smouldered such an active social volcano. When he first started mingling with Poreshbabu's family, he had been quite diffident. Unsure of the extent of his claims upon them, he trod carefully. Gradually, as his fears faded, he had not even suspected there could be the slightest hint of danger from any quarter. Today, when suddenly informed that Lalita had been condemned by members of the Samaj on account of his own behaviour, he was thunderstruck. What disturbed him most was his own awareness that the intensity of his feelings for Lalita had far exceeded the limits of ordinary friendship. In the present instance, given the gulf between their respective communities, he privately considered this excessive intensity an offence. He had often felt that he had not been able to keep to his proper place as a trusted visitor to this family, that he had somehow been dishonest. If his true feelings became known to them, it would be a matter of shame for him.

At this stage, when Borodasundari sent a note to summon Binoy one afternoon, and asked him, 'Binoybabu, you are a Hindu, are you not?'—and upon his answering in the affirmative, when she asked again: 'You can't abandon the Hindu community, can you?'—and upon Binoy's asserting that it would be impossible, when Borodasundari exclaimed, 'Then why are you . . .'—Binoy could find no answer to her query, ' Then why . . .?' He hung his head in silence. He felt he had been caught out, that something he had tried to conceal even from the moon, stars and wind had been publicly exposed here. He kept wondering what Poreshbabu must think, what Lalita must think, and what, indeed, must Sucharita think of him! He had briefly found a place in heaven due to some error on the divine messenger's part, but now he must suffer complete exile, bearing the stigma of unauthorized entry.

Afterwards, glimpsing Lalita as soon as he stepped out of Poreshbabu's door, he thought, 'At this moment of my final parting from Lalita, let me admit that I have brought great shame upon her, so the floodtides of our former acquaintance may subside.' But he could not think of a way. So, without meeting Lalita's gaze, he left with a silent namaskar.

Until very recently, Binoy had been an outsider to Poreshababu's household, and now he was back outside. But what a difference! Why did the outside seem so empty now? Nothing was missing from his former life after all; his Gora, his Anandamoyi, were still there. But still he began to feel like a fish cast ashore: wherever he looked, he found no support to keep him alive. On the crowded main streets of this densely built up city, Binoy began to detect everywhere a pale, shadowy image of the disaster that threatened his life. He was amazed at this all-pervading sense of dry hollowness. Why this happened, or when, or how it became possible, were questions he kept addressing to an unfeeling, unresponsive void.

'Binoybabu! Binoybabu!'

Binoy turned to find Satish behind him.

'What is it, bhai, what's the matter, my friend?' asked Binoy, embracing him. His voice seemed choked with tears. Binoy realized now, as never before, how much sweetness this boy had also added to Poreshbabu's household.

'Why don't you visit us?' demanded Satish. 'Labanyadidi and Lalitadidi are to dine with us tomorrow. Mashi has sent me across to invite you.'

Binoy realized that Mashi had not kept abreast of recent developments.

'Satishbabu,' he said, 'my pranams to Mashi, but I can't come.'

'Why not?' pleaded Satish, clasping Binoy's hand. 'You must come, I shan't take no for an answer.'

There was a special reason for the urgency of Satish's plea. In school he had been asked to compose a piece on 'Behaviour Towards Animals,' on which he had scored forty-two marks out of fifty, a piece he was very keen to show to Binoy. Knowing Binoy to be very learned and wise, he was convinced that such an accomplished man would appreciate the true value of his composition. If Binoy acknowledged the merits of Satish's work, then Leela, who lacked aesthetic sense, would be disgraced if she showed contempt for Satish's talent. It was Satish who had urged Mashi to issue the invitation. He wanted his sisters to be also present when Binoy evaluated his writings.

Learning that Binoy could not attend the social gathering under any circumstances, Satish was extremely disheartened.

'Satishbabu, come home with us,' proposed Binoy, hugging him.

As Satish was carrying that composition in his pocket, he could not ignore Binoy's invitation. The young would-be-poet went to Binoy's house, acknowledging that he was guilty of wasting time when his school examinations were so close. Binoy seemed reluctant to let him go. Not only did he listen to Satish's composition, but his words of praise also did not express a critic's neutral objectivity, and what was more, he fed Satish snacks ordered from the market. Then, escorting Satish almost to his home, he said with unwarranted agitation:

'Satisbabu, I'll take your leave then.'

'No, please come to our house,' begged Satish, tugging at his arm.

This time, such pleas proved futile

Walking like one in a dream, Binoy arrived at Anandamoyi's house, but could not meet her. He entered the empty room on the terrace where Gora used to sleep. How many happy days and nights of their childhood friendship had been spent in this room—such joyful conversation, such resolutions, such profound discussions—such romantic quarrels and such tendersweet reconciliations afterwards! Binoy longed to enter that former life, forgetting himself as before; but the new acquaintances formed in this short interim blocked his access to that same place. Until now, Binoy had not clearly understood when his life's focus had shifted, the route of entry changed; but now with all doubts dispelled, he grew afraid.

When the sun declined in the late afternoon, Anandamoyi came to take in the washing hung out to dry. Seeing Binoy in Gora's room, she was surprised. Quickly going to his side, she patted him and asked:

'Binoy! What's the matter, Binoy? Why do you look so pale?'

Binoy sat up. 'Ma,' he said, 'when I first began to frequent Poreshbabu's house, Gora used to be angry. I then thought his anger unjustified, but that was my foolishness, not his mistake.'

'I don't say you're the brightest of our boys,' replied Anandamoyi with a faint smile, 'but how in this case did the flaws in your intellect manifest themselves?'

'Ma, I had never considered the fact that our community is utterly different. I felt attracted by the sense of joy and advantage that their friendship, behaviour and example gave me. Not for a moment had any other considerations arisen in my mind.'

'They don't arise in my mind even after listening to you.'

'Ma, you have no idea, I have caused a great upheaval within the community regarding their family; people have started casting such slurs that I can no longer go . . .'

'Gora often says something that I find extremely sound,' responded Anandamoyi. 'He says, where there is something wrong within, outward calm is most dangerous. If their community is in a turmoil, I see no cause for remorse on your part. It will be for the better, you will see. As long as your own conduct remains above board, that's enough.'

But that was indeed Binoy's greatest doubt. Try as he might, he could not decide whether his own conduct was blameless. Since Lalita belonged to a different community, and marrying her was not a possibility, it was Binoy's tenderness for her that troubled him like a hidden sin, and he was tormented by the thought that he must now do terrible penance for it.

'Ma,' said Binoy suddenly, 'better if the proposed match between Shashimukhi and myself were finalized. I should somehow be confined to my proper place, so I don't stray from it under any circumstances.'

'In other words,' smiled Anandamoyi, 'you would make Shashimukhi the chain-latch on your door rather than the bride in your home. What a pleasant fate for Shashi!'

At this moment, the attendant announced the arrival of two ladies from Poreshbabu's house. Binoy's heart missed a beat. He thought they had come to complain to Anandamoyi, as a warning to him.

'I'll be off, Ma!' he cried, springing to his feet.

'Don't leave the house, Binoy,' Anandamoyi persuaded him, rising to grasp his hand. 'Wait in the room downstairs.'

'There was no need for this, really,' Binoy kept repeating to himself on his way down. 'What's done is done, but I would not have gone there again even if my life depended on it. Once the punishment for one's sins is under way, the fire refuses to subside even after the sinner is burnt to death.'

As Binoy was about to enter Gora's room on the ground floor overlooking the street, Mahim returned home from work, releasing his expansive paunch from the confinement of his chapkaan buttons.

'Here you are, Binoy! How nice to see you!' he exclaimed, grasping Binoy's hand. 'I've been looking for you.'

He drew Binoy into Gora's chamber and offering him a chowki, seated himself as well. Extracting a box from his pocket, he offered Binoy a paan.

'You there! Fetch us some tobacco!' he roared, then immediately turned to the matter at hand. 'What's the decision about that business? How long, after all . . .'

He found Binoy's attitude much softened. Not that Binoy expressed much enthusiasm, but he also made no evasive attempt to dodge the issue somehow. Mahim wanted to finalize the date and time immediately.

'Why not wait until Gora returns?' Binoy suggested.

'That's just a matter of a few days,' consented Mahim, reassured. 'Binoy, shall I send for some snacks? What do you say? You look very downcast today. You are not ill, I hope?'

When Binoy eluded the pressure to consume snacks, Mahim went inside to appease his own hunger. Pulling a book at random from Gora's table, Binoy began to turn the pages, then flinging the book aside, he began to pace the room from end to end.

'Ma has sent for you,' the attendant came and announced.

'Who has she sent for?' Binoy demanded.

'You, sir.'

'Are all the others there as well?'

'Yes, they are.'

Binoy made his way upstairs like a student heading for the examination hall. Approaching the room, he hesitated a little. At once, Sucharita called out to him in her usual natural, sisterly manner.

'Come, Binoybabu,' she invited him tenderly.

Her tone made Binoy feel that he had chanced upon an unhoped-for treasure. When he entered the room, Sucharita and Lalita were amazed at his appearance. In this very short time, his face already bore signs of the sudden, harsh blow he had suffered. His ever-cheerful countenance now resembled a lush green field suddenly devastated by a plague of locusts. Lalita secretly felt pain and pity, but also a hint of joy. On a different occasion, Lalita would not have suddenly launched into a conversation with Binoy. But now, as soon as he entered, she declared:

'Binoybabu, we have something to discuss with you.'

It was as if Binoy's heart had been struck by an arrow of joy that pierced the sound barrier. He was exhilarated. His pale, dejected face instantly lit up.

'We sisters want to jointly start a small school for girls,' Lalita told him.

'It has long been one of my life's resolves to create a school for girls,' cried Binoy enthusiastically.

'You must help us,' Lalita demanded.

'I shall spare no effort to do whatever is in my power,' Binoy assured her. 'Please tell me what I must do.'

'Because we are Brahmo, Hindu guardians don't trust us,' Lalita explained. 'You must try to assist us.'

'Have no fear,' said Binoy, aflame with eagerness. 'I can handle it.'

'Handle it he can,' remarked Anandamoyi. 'When it

comes to charming people with words, there is no match for Binoy.'

'You must handle all the work involved in running a school according to proper rules and procedures,' Lalita informed him. 'Forming timetables, allotting classes, prescribing textbooks—you must undertake all these things.'

This, too, was not difficult for Binoy, but he was baffled. Was Lalita utterly unaware that Borodasundari had forbidden him to mingle with her daughters, and that within their community there was a rising tide of hostility against them? Under such circumstances, would it be wrong, and harmful for Lalita, if Binoy agreed to her request? The question began to torment him. On the other hand, when Lalita sought his assistance in some worthwhile project, did Binoy possess the strength to avoid acceding wholeheartedly to her request?

Meanwhile, Sucharita was also amazed. She had not dreamt that Lalita would suddenly ask Binoy to assist with the girls' school, in this fashion. So many complications had already arisen concerning Binoy, and now, what was this new predicament! Seeing that Lalita was deliberately creating this situation, Sucharita felt apprehensive. She realized that Lalita's heart had grown rebellious, but was it right to involve poor Binoy in this turmoil?

'We must consult Baba about this once, mustn't we?' Sucharita blurted out anxiously. 'Let us not immediately arouse Binoybabu's hopes of acquiring the post of the inspector of a girls' school.'

Binoy realized that Sucharita had artfully stalled the proposal. This struck him as odd. Sucharita was obviously aware of the problems that had arisen, hence Lalita could not be in the dark about them either. Then why was Lalita . . .? Nothing was clear.

'Of course we must consult Baba,' Lalita affirmed. 'I shall speak to him as soon as Binoybabu confirms his willingness. Baba would never object. He, too, must be involved in this school of ours. We shan't let you off either,' she added, turning to Anandamoyi.

'I could go sweep your schoolrooms,' smiled Anandamoyi. 'What more would I be capable of?'

'That would be sufficient, Ma!' Binoy declared. 'The school would be completely purified.'

After Sucharita and Lalita had taken their leave, Binoy headed straight for the Eden Gardens on foot.

'I found Binoy much more amenable,' Mahim came to Anandamoyi and said. 'Now it's best to complete the ceremony at the earliest. Who knows when he might change his mind again?'

'What's this!' exclaimed Anandamoyi in astonishment. 'When did Binoy ever agree to the proposal? He hasn't told me anything about it.'

'We have discussed the matter today itself. He says we can fix a date as soon as Gora returns.'

'Mahim,' insisted Anandamoyi shaking her head, 'you have not understood him right, I tell you.'

'Thick-headed I might be, but please rest assured I am old enough to understand simple facts.'

'Bachha, I know you will be angry with me, but I can foresee complications ahead.'

'If you create complications, then complications are bound to occur,' retorted Mahim severely.

'Mahim, I shall tolerate anything all of you may say to me, but for your own good, I refuse to be party to something that may cause trouble.'

'If you leave it to us to decide about our own good, you will be spared unpleasant words, and we, too, might benefit,' Mahim declared harshly. 'Better you should think about our own good once Shashimukhi is married. What do you say?'

Offering no reply, Anandamoyi heaved a sigh. Chewing upon a paan he extracted from the box in his pocket, Mahim walked away.

~46~

'Because we are Brahmo no Hindu girl wants to come to us for tutoring,' Lalita came to Poreshbabu and said. 'So we feel it might facilitate our work if we involve someone from the Hindu community. What do you say, Baba?'

'Where would you find someone from the Hindu community?' Poreshbabu enquired.

Lalita had indeed braced herself for this meeting, but she suddenly found herself embarrassed at the prospect of mentioning Binoy's name.

'Why?' she said, forcibly shedding her awkwardness, 'it's not as if someone can't be found. There's our Binoybabu for instance, or . . .' This 'or' was utterly redundant, merely a grammatical excess. The sentence remained suspended, incomplete.

'Binoy!' exclaimed Poresh. 'Why would Binoy agree?'

Lalita's pride was hurt. Binoybabu not agree! She had realized only too well that it was not beyond her power to make Binoybabu agree.

'Well, he might consent,' she said.

'All things considered, he would never consent,' declared Poreshbabu, after a pause.

Lalita blushed to the roots of her ears. She began toying with the bunch of keys knotted at the end of her aanchal. Observing his daughter's tormented face, Poreshbabu's heart ached, but he could find no way to console her. After a while, Lalita slowly raised her head and said: 'Baba, our school can never be established, then!'

'I can see many hindrances that would prevent it from being established now,' Poreshbabu agreed. 'Any attempt would spark a lot of unpleasant discussion.'

Nothing was more painful for Lalita than the fact that

Panubabu would ultimately triumph and that she must silently let injustice win. In this regard she could not have accepted anyone else's authority save her father's, not for a single moment. She did not fear any form of unpleasantness, but how could she tolerate injustice? Slowly she arose and left Poreshbabu's side. Back in her own room she found that a letter had arrived by post, addressed to her. From the handwriting she realized it was from her childhood friend Shailabala, who was married, living with her husband in Bankipur. The letter said:

> I was upset to hear all sorts of rumours about all of you. For many days I have been thinking of writing to enquire about you, but could not find the time. But the day before yesterday, the news I received from somebody (he shall go unnamed) left me thunderstruck. I could never have imagined this possible. But it is also hard to disbelieve the person who wrote to me about it. Apparently you are likely to marry a Hindu boy. If that is true . . . and so on.

Lalita's whole being was aflame with fury. She could not wait a single moment. At once she replied:

> What amazes me is the fact that you have sent me a query to verify the news. Is it necessary to verify even the news received from a member of the Brahmo Samaj? Such lack of faith! Next, you are thunderstruck upon hearing that I am likely to marry a Hindu boy; but I can assure you, there is a well-known member of the Brahmo Samaj who is a worthy young man, and yet the prospect of marrying him fills me with a dread as terrible as a thunderbolt. And I know a couple of Hindu boys whose hand in marriage would be a matter of honour for any Brahmo maiden. Beyond this I have nothing more to say to you.

Meanwhile, Poreshbabu's work had come to a standstill for the day. For a long time he was silent, lost in thought. Then,

slowly and pensively, he went to Sucharita's room. The sight
of Poresh's worried face pained Sucharita's heart. She knew,
too, what he was worried about, and she herself had been
anxious about the same thing of late. Poreshbabu took Sucharita
aside to a secluded chamber and said:

'Ma, it is time for us to worry about Lalita.'

'I know, Baba,' she replied, gazing at him with compassion.

'I am not worrying about social slander,' he explained. 'I
am thinking . . . tell me, is Lalita . . .'

Observing his embarrassment, Sucharita took it upon
herself to clarify matters.

'Lalita always shares her thoughts with me,' she said. 'But
of late she has been rather evasive. I clearly sense . . .'

'Some feelings have been aroused in Lalita's heart, which
she does not want to admit even to herself,' Poresh interrupted.
'I can't think what we can do so she . . . Would you say we
have done Lalita any harm by allowing Binoy to visit us?'

'Baba, you know there are no flaws in Binoybabu's
character. He is pure of nature; one rarely comes across a
born bhadralok like him.'

'Quite right, Radhé, quite right,' exclaimed Poreshbabu
as if apprised of a new fact. 'It is his goodness of nature that
we must take into account. Ishwar, the all-knowing, does the
same. I offer him my pranams again and again, that Binoy is
a good man, and that I was not mistaken about him.'

Poreshbabu seemed relieved, as if he had broken free of
some net that would trap him. He had not sinned before his
deity. He had followed the same scales of justice on which
Ishwar weighed humans, the scales of daily duty. Because he
had not used the false weights created by society to tamper
with those scales, his mind was now free of self-blame. He
felt surprised he had been so tormented, unable for so long to
understand something so simple.

'I have learnt a lesson from you today, ma,' he told
Sucharita, patting her head.

At once she touched his feet, protesting, 'No! No! How can you say that, Baba!'

'The community makes us completely forget the simplest thing: our own humanity. Human beings create a complicated maze, questioning whether one is Brahmo or Hindu, making this socially-produced issue more important than the truth of the universe. All this time, I was vainly wandering in that maze.'

'Lalita is finding it hard to relinquish her resolve to start a school for girls,' continued Poresh after a short silence. 'She wants my permission to take Binoy's help in the matter.'

'No, Baba, let it wait for a while.'

Poresh's affectionate heart was deeply disturbed at the way Lalita had looked when she left his presence as soon as he forbade her, suppressing the turbulence of her troubled soul. He knew that his spirited daughter was less offended at the unjust harassment inflicted on her by her community than at being thwarted in her struggle against such injustice, especially since the cause of obstruction was her father. He was therefore eager to withdraw the prohibition he had imposed.

'Why Radhé?' he demanded, 'why let it be for now?'

'Or else Ma will be very annoyed.' Thinking about it, Poreshbabu realized she was right.

Satish came in and whispered something in Sucharita's ear.

'No bhai,' Sucharita responded. 'No bakhtiar, not now. Tomorrow.'

'But I have school tomorrow,' protested Satish, downcast.

'What is it Satish, what do you want?' smiled Poresh affectionately.

'He has a . . .' Sucharita began.

'No, no, please don't tell, don't tell!' pleaded Satish in agitation, clamping his hand on Sucharita's mouth.

'If it's a secret, why would Sucharita reveal it?' asked Poreshbabu.

'No Baba, he must be very keen for this secret to reach your ears,' Sucharita informed him.

'Never!' shouted Satish, 'not at all!' He ran off.

He was supposed to show Sucharita the composition that Binoy had praised so highly. Needless to say, Sucharita had correctly surmised why he had reminded her of the matter in Poresh's presence. Poor Satish did not know that such deep, secret motives could be detected so easily.

~47~

Four days later, Haranbabu came to Borodasundari with a letter. He had now given up all expectations of Poreshbabu.

'From the outset I have tried very hard to warn all of you,' declared Haranbabu, handing the letter to Borodasundari. 'That has made me unpopular here as well. Now from this very letter you will realize how far things have secretly advanced.'

Borodasundari read the letter Lalita had written to Shailabala.

'Tell me, how was I to know?' she lamented. 'The unthinkable is happening. But you mustn't blame me for this, I tell you. All of you have collectively turned Sucharita's head, praising her excessively for being such a good girl, as if there is no girl to match her in the Brahmo Samaj. Now you must deal with the handiwork of your ideal Brahmo girl. It is she who has brought Binoy and Gour into this household. Still, I had managed to a great extent to bring Binoy around to our way of thinking. But then she brought a mashi of hers and introduced idol worship into our own household. She even poisoned Binoy's mind, so now he avoids me. This Sucharita of yours is at the root of all that's happening now. I knew all along what that girl was really like, but I never said a word.

All along, I have brought her up so nobody could tell she wasn't my own daughter——and now see what rewards I have reaped! It's no use showing me this letter now. Now it's up to all of you.'

Openly acknowledging that he had once misunderstood Borodasundari, Haranbabu apologized very generously. Ultimately, Poreshbabu was sent for.

'Just look at this!' said Borodasundari, flinging the letter down on the table before him.

'So, what's wrong?' asked Poreshbabu after reading the letter two or three times.

'What's wrong!' exclaimed Borodasundari, outraged. 'What more do you want! Could there be worse to come? Idol worship, caste discrimination, everything has happened already; now it only remains for your daughter to be married off to a Hindu family. After that, you will perform penance and join the Hindu fraternity. But let me tell you . . .'

'You need tell me nothing,' Poreshbabu interrupted with a faint smile. 'At least, not yet. The question is, why have all of you concluded that Lalita's marriage into a Hindu family is already fixed? I see no hint of that in this letter, after all.'

'I have still not understood what might make you see anything clearly,' Borodasundari retorted. 'If you had seen things in time, the present calamity would not have occurred. Tell me, can a letter state things more plainly than this?'

'I think we should show this letter to Lalita and ask her what she intends. If you permit, I could ask her myself.'

At this moment, Lalita stormed in.

'Look, Baba,' she cried, 'we're receiving anonymous letters of this kind from the Brahmo Samaj these days!'

Poresh read the letter. Assuming that Binoy's marriage to Lalita had been secretly fixed, the writer had filled the letter with diverse reprimands and suggestions, along with assertions that Binoy's intentions were suspect, and that he would soon abandon his Brahmo wife to marry again into a Hindu family. After Poresh had finished with the letter, Haran read it through and said:

'Lalita, does this letter make you angry? But aren't you yourself not the cause for such letters to be written? Tell me, how could you write this letter in your very own hand!'

For a moment Lalita stood stock-still. 'So, have you been corresponding with Shaila on this subject!' she demanded.

'Bearing in mind her duty towards the Brahmo Samaj, Shaila felt obliged to return this letter of yours,' responded Haran, without answering her directly.

'Please tell me what the Brahmo Samaj would like to say now,' said Lalita, bracing herself.

'I can't bring myself to believe these current rumours about you and Binoybabu,' declared Haran, 'but still, I want to hear you clearly repudiate them yourself.'

Lalita's eyes began to blaze. Gripping a chair-back with trembling hands she asked:

'Why, can't you believe the rumours at all?'

'Lalita, your mind is not balanced now,' warned Poresh, patting her back. 'You and I can discuss this matter later. Let it be for now.'

'Poreshbabu, don't try to suppress the matter,' Haran interrupted.

'Would Baba try to suppress the matter!' Lalita erupted in fury, once again. 'Unlike the rest of you, Baba does not fear the truth. He places truth above even the Brahmo Samaj. I tell you, I don't consider my marriage to Binoybabu either impossible or sinful.'

'But is he to adopt the Brahmo faith?' Haranbabu demanded.

'Nothing is decided, and who says it is compulsory to adopt the faith?' Lalita retorted.

So far, Borodasudari had said nothing. Secretly she wanted

Haranbabu to triumph on this occasion, and Poreshbabu to feel guilty and repentant. She could contain herself no longer.

'Lalita, have you lost your mind!' she blurted out. 'What are you saying!'

'No Ma, these are not the ravings of a lunatic. I speak after much consideration. I cannot bear to be confined like this. I shall break free of this Samaj of Haranbabu's.'

'Do you mistake waywardness for freedom?' Haranbabu asked.

'No,' replied Lalita. 'Liberation from assaults of baseness and enslavement to falsehood—that's what I mean by freedom. Where I see no wrong, no breach of faith, why should the Brahmo Samaj hold me, or try to restrain me?'

'Poreshbabu, see for yourself!' declared Haran ostentatiously. 'I knew a calamity like this was inevitable. I have tried my best to warn you all, but to no avail.'

'Look here Panubabu,' retorted Lalita, 'we have reason to warn you as well. You should not be arrogant enough to caution those who are your superiors in every respect.' With these words she left the room.

'What a mess!' cried Borodasundari. 'Please think, what is to be done now?'

'It is duty that we must observe,' Poreshbabu answered. 'But we cannot identify our duty amidst such confusion. You must excuse me. Please don't discuss this matter with me now. I want to be left alone for a while.'

~48~

What a mess Lalita had created! Sucharita thought. After a short silence, she put her arm around Lalita's neck.

'I must say, bhai, that I feel afraid.'

'What are you afraid of?' Lalita demanded.

'The entire Brahmo Samaj is in turmoil, indeed, but what if Binoybabu turns down our request in the end?'

'He is sure to agree,' Lalita insisted, her head bent low.

'As you know, Panubabu has assured Ma that Binoy would never abandon his community to accept this marriage. Lalita, why did you speak of it to Panubabu without pausing to consider everything!'

'I still don't regret what I said,' Lalita asserted. 'Panubabu imagined that he and his Samaj had pursued me like a hunted animal to the edge of the bottomless ocean, where I must surrender. He doesn't realize I'm not afraid to plunge into this ocean; I fear being hounded into his cage by his pack of hunting dogs.'

'Let's consult Baba once,' Sucharita proposed.

'Baba will never join a hunting party, I can assure you. He had never wanted to shackle us, after all. If we have ever disagreed with his views, has he ever expressed the slightest annoyance? Has he tried to silence us by hounding us in the Brahmo Samaj's name? This has annoyed Ma so often, but Baba only feared we might lose the courage to think for ourselves. Having reared us like this, would he ultimately hand me over to a man like Panubabu, who acts as the community's prison warder?'

'Very well, presuming Baba poses no obstacle, what should we do next?'

'If you people don't do anything, I shall myself . . .'

'No, no,' cried Sucharita in agitation, 'you need not do anything, bhai! I'll find a way.'

Sucharita was preparing to approach Poreshbabu when he came to her himself that evening. Every evening at this hour, Poreshbabu would pace up and down in his garden, head bent low, lost in thought. It was as if he would slowly remove all the scars of the day's work by stroking his heart with the pure darkness of that evening hour, and prepare himself for the night's rest by filling his inner soul with pure tranquility. But tonight, having sacrificed the pleasant tranquillity of that solitary evening meditation, when Poreshbabu came to Sucharita's room with a worried expression on his face, her affectionate heart was moved, like a mother's heart when her usually playful infant falls ill and lies motionless.

'Radhé,' said Poreshbabu, 'you have heard everything, haven't you?'

'Yes, Baba, I have heard everything, but why are you so anxious?'

'I am not anxious about anything, save Lalita's capacity to bear the whole impact of the storm she has raised. Sometimes in the heat of excitement we are driven to blind daring, but when we begin to gradually experience the fruits of such daring, we lose the strength to bear them. Has Lalita carefully weighed all the consequences before determining what is best for herself?'

'I can say with emphasis that no form of social pressure can ever defeat Lalita,' Sucharita declared.

'I want to be completely sure that Lalita is not merely expressing rebellious defiance in a fit of rage.'

'No, Baba,' replied Sucharita, lowering her head, 'if that were so I would have paid no attention to her words. This sudden blow has exposed what lay concealed deep within her heart. If we now try to suppress the matter somehow, it would not be good for a girl like Lalita. Baba, Binoybabu is a wonderful person, after all.'

'Tell me,' asked Poreshbabu, 'would Binoy agree to enter the Brahmo Samaj?'

'I couldn't say for sure. Baba, should I go to Gourbabu's mother once?'

'I was also thinking that it might be a good idea for you to see her.'

~49~

From Anandamoyi's house, Binoy would drop by at his own home once, every morning. That day, he found a letter waiting for him. It bore no signature. It was full of lengthy advice, asserting that marriage to Lalita could never be a happy prospect for Binoy, and that it would prove inauspicious for Lalita. In conclusion it said that if Binoy still did not desist from marrying Lalita, then he must bear in mind that Lalita's lungs were weak, due to suspected tuberculosis.

Binoy was dumbfounded at receiving such a letter. He had never imagined that such things could even be conjured up as falsehoods. For nobody was unaware that Lalita's marriage to Binoy could never take place against the Samaj's wishes. Indeed, that was why he had always considered his weakness for Lalita a crime. But for such a letter to have reached him, the matter had doubtless been widely discussed within the Samaj. He was deeply agitated to imagine the humiliation Lalita must have suffered at the hands of her community members. He felt extremely ashamed and embarrassed that rumours had publicly linked his name with Lalita's. He was haunted by the feeling that Lalita was cursing and repudiating the fact that she knew him. He felt she could never again tolerate the sight of him.

But alas for the human heart! Even amidst this extreme feeling of rejection, a secret, profound, subtle, intense joy shot through Binoy's heart; it was unstoppable, denying all shame, all humiliation. To avoid encouraging that sensation in the least, he began to pace swiftly up and down his veranda, but the morning light sent a heady feeling through his heart. Even the hawker's call from the street aroused a deep restlessness in him. It was as if the tide of public slander had swept Lalita away and deposited her on the shore of Binoy's heart. He could no longer resist this image of Lalita having floated up to him, away from the social realm. 'Lalita is mine, mine alone!' his heart kept repeating. Never before had his heart dared to declare this so forcefully. But now that these words echoed so suddenly in the outer world, Binoy could no longer hush his own heart.

As he restlessly paced up and down the veranda, Binoy saw Haranbabu coming down the street. He realized at once that Haranbabu was coming to meet him, and became certain that there must be a major upheaval underlying that anonymous letter. Binoy did not display his natural loquaciousness as on other occasions. Offering Haranbabu a chowki, he silently waited for him to speak.

'Binoybabu, you're a Hindu, are you not?'

'Yes, indeed I am.'

'Please don't be offended at my question. Very often we act blindly without considering the situation around us, and that becomes a cause of misery. In such circumstances, should someone ask who we are, what are our limits, how far-reaching the consequences of our actions might be, however unpleasant this might seem, you should consider such a person your friend.'

'No need for such long preambles,' responded Binoy, trying to summon up a smile. 'It is not in my nature to react violently in any way out of anger at an unpleasant query. You may safely ask me all sorts of questions.'

'I don't want to accuse you of any deliberate offence. But needless to say, even errors of judgement may have poisonous effects.'

'You could avoid stating the needless,' answered Binoy, inwardly irritated. 'Please come to the point.'

'Since you belong to the Hindu community and since leaving the community is also impossible for you, should you frequent Poreshbabu's household in a way that may encourage rumours in the Samaj concerning his daughters?'

'Look Panubabu, how a community may construe certain facts depends largely on the nature of its members; I cannot take full responsibility for it. If even Poreshbabu's daughters can become targets of gossip within your community, that's a matter of shame for your community rather than for their family.'

'If an unwed girl is encouraged to leave her mother's side to travel in the same boat with a man outside her family, which community could be denied the right to criticize her, I ask you?' Haranbabu demanded.

'If you people also equate external events with internal sins, then why leave the Hindu community to join the Brahmo Samaj? Anyway Panubabu, I see no need to argue about all this. After due consideration I shall determine my appropriate course of action; you can be of no help to me in that regard.'

'I don't have much to say to you,' declared Haranbabu, 'but my last word to you is, you must now keep your distance. It would be very wrong of you to do otherwise. You people have only stirred up trouble by invading Poreshbabu's household; you have no idea how much harm you have done to their family.'

After Haranbabu had departed, Binoy's heart was pierced by a shaft of pain. Straightforward and open minded, how warmly Poreshbabu had welcomed the two of them into his home! Perhaps, unknowingly, Binoy had constantly overstepped the bounds of his rights within this Brahmo family, but still, he had never been denied Poreshbabu's affection and respect for a day. In this family, Binoy's nature had gained a safe haven such as he had not found anywhere else, as if, having got to know them, he had discovered a special aspect of his own identity. And here in this household, where he had received such care, such joy, such a sense of refuge, to think that Binoy's memory would forever prick like a painful thorn! For

him to have cast the shadow of indignity over Poreshbabu's
daughters! That he should have tainted Lalita's entire future in
this way! How could he compensate! Alas, alas! What an
immense contradiction this thing called community had
generated within the domain of truth! There was no real
obstacle against Lalita's union with Binoy; the Lord alone,
who lived within both their souls, knew Binoy's readiness to
surrender his whole life for Lalita's happiness and well-being.
It was He who had brought Binoy so close to Lalita through
the attraction of love; His eternal spiritual law had proved no
hindrance. Was it some other deity then, worshipped by the
Brahmo Samaj, by people like Panubabu? Was this deity not
the profoundest arbitrator of the human heart? If some law of
prohibition stood between Lalita and Binoy, baring its fangs at
them, if it obeyed only the dictates of society and not of the
Lord of all humanity, then was such prohibition itself not
sinful? But alas, perhaps this prohibition was powerful even in
Lalita's eyes! Besides, perhaps Lalita's feelings for Binoy were
not . . . So many doubts! How could they be resolved?

~50~

Exactly when Haranbabu arrived at Binoy's house, Abinash
had reported to Anandamoyi that Binoy's marriage to Lalita
was confirmed.

'This can never be true,' asserted Anandamoyi.

'Why not?' demanded Abinash. 'Is Binoy incapable of it?'

'That I cannot say, but Binoy would never conceal
something so important from me.'

Abinash repeated that it was from members of the Brahmo
Samaj that he had heard this news and that it was completely
believable. He had long known that Binoy was bound to end
up in such deplorable circumstances; in fact, he had warned

Gora about it. Having apprised Anandamoyi of these facts, Abinash gleefully proceeded downstairs to tell Mahim the news. When Binoy came to her that day, Anandamoyi could tell from his expression that his heart was disturbed by a particular anguish. Having fed him, she called him into her own chamber.

'Tell me Binoy, what is the matter with you?' she asked.

'Ma, read this letter and see for yourself.'

When Anandamoyi had read the letter, Binoy told her: 'This morning Panubabu came to my house. He rebuked me very sharply.'

'Why?'

'He says my conduct has aroused nasty rumours within their community about Poreshbabu's daughters.'

'People say your marriage to Lalita has been finalized. I see no cause for nasty rumours in that.'

'If marriage were possible there would be no cause for slander. But where there is no such possibility, how unjust to spread such rumours! It is particularly cowardly to spread such slander about Lalita.'

'If you have the slightest element of manliness in you Binu, you can easily shield Lalita from such cowardice.'

'How, Ma!' asked Binoy in astonishment.

'How? By marrying Lalita of course!'

'What's this you say Ma! I wonder what you imagine your Binoy to be! You think Binoy just has to say once, "I shall marry," and nobody in the world could contradict him—as if the whole world is awaiting a signal from me.'

'I see no reason for you to worry about so many things. Suffice it for you to do the little bit that is in your power. You could say, "I'm willing to get married."'

'Wouldn't it be humiliating for Lalita if I said something so improper?'

'Why do you call it improper? If there are rumours

linking the two of you, surely they have arisen because the idea is proper indeed. You have no cause for hesitation, I tell you.'

'But Ma, we must think about Gora as well.'

'No my dear child, this matter does not involve thinking about Gora at all,' replied Anandamoyi firmly. 'I know he will be angry. I don't want him to be angry with you. But it can't be helped! If you respect Lalita, you can't let society cast a permanent slur upon her name.'

But this was a very difficult proposition indeed. How could Binoy keep such a major blow in store for Gora, whose imprisonment had redoubled Binoy's affection for him! And then there was tradition. It is easy to cross society in theory, but to cross it in practice creates so many tensions, big and small! Terror of the unknown and rejection of the unaccustomed keeps pushing one back, without any rational cause.

'Ma, the more I observe you, the more amazed I feel,' Binoy declared. 'How is your heart so pure? Don't you need to tread on the ground? Has Ishwar given you wings? Is there nothing to confine you, anywhere?'

'Ishwar has left me with nothing to bind me,' smiled Anandamoyi. 'He has swept everything clear.'

'But Ma, whatever I may say outwardly, my heart still poses constraints. For all that I comprehend, read and study, or argue about, I still realize suddenly that my heart has remained uneducated, after all.'

At this point, Mahim entered the room and immediately subjected Binoy to such rude interrogation about Lalita that his heart cringed in humiliaiton. Controlling himself, Binoy hung his head and offered no reply. After making some extremely insulting remarks pointed sharply against all parties concerned, Mahim left the scene. He argued: 'There's a shameless conspiracy afoot in Poreshbabu's family to ensnare

Binoy like this and bring about his downfall. Binoy has been caught in such a trap only out of foolishness. Let them ensnare Gora, that will be something. That's difficult, indeed!'

Seeing such signs of humiliation everywhere, Binoy was stupefied.

'Do you know, Binoy, what you should do?' Anandamoyi asked him. He raised his head to look at her.

'You ought to meet Poreshbabu once. A few words with him and everything will become clear.'

~51~

Sucharita was surprised to see Anandamoyi so suddenly.

'I was just getting ready to visit you,' she exclaimed.

'I didn't know that,' smiled Anandamoyi, 'but hearing why you were getting ready, I couldn't wait. I just came along.'

Sucharita was astonished to learn that Anandamoyi had heard the news.

'Ma,' said Anandamoyi, 'I regard Binoy as my own son. Because of that relationship, how often I have mentally blessed you all, even without knowing you! How can I sit still upon being told that you have been wronged? I don't know whether I could be of any benefit to all of you, but I have rushed here because my heart was full of anguish. Ma, has Binoy done anything wrong?'

'Not at all. It is Lalita who is responsible for the matter that is causing such turmoil. Binoybabu had never imagined that Lalita might suddenly leave on the steamer without informing anybody. People are talking as if the two of them had hatched a secret conspiracy. And Lalita is such a spirited girl, she would never contradict the rumours or somehow explain what really took place.'

'We must find a solution,' declared Anandamoyi. 'Ever since all this reached his ears, Binoy has lost all his peace of mind; he has assumed himself to be the culprit.'

'Please tell me, do you think Binoybabu . . .' said Sucharita, lowering her flushed face.

'Look here, bachcha,' interrupted Anandamoyi, not letting the embarrassed Sucharita complete her words, 'I assure you Binoy would do anything you ask, for Lalita's sake. I have known him since he was a child. Once he surrenders himself, he can hold nothing back. That is why I must remain in constant dread, lest he give his heart where there's no hope of his receiving anything in return.'

Sucharita felt a load had been lifted off her mind. 'You need not worry about Lalita's consent,' she affirmed. 'I know her mind. But will Binoybabu agree to leave his community?'

'His community may reject him,' declared Anandamoyi, 'but why should he anticipate that by withdrawing from his community beforehand, ma? Is there any need for that?'

'How can you say that, Ma! Can Binoybabu marry into a Brahmo family while he is still part of the Hindu community?'

'If he is willing, why should all of you object?'

Sucharita found this extremely complicated.

'I can't see how that might be possible,' she confessed.

'To me it seems very simple, ma! Look, I can't follow the restrictions that prevail in my own household, hence many people label me a Khristan. When any rituals are performed, I deliberately remain aloof. You will be amused to know this, ma, but Gora doesn't accept the water served in my room. But why, therefore, should I say, "this is not my room, this community is not my own"? I can't bring myself to say that. Accepting all the abuse heaped upon me, I remain within this home and this community, with no undue hindrance. If the obstacles become too much for me, I shall take the path that Ishwar shows me. But to the end, I shall claim what is mine as my own; if others don't accept me, it is their problem.'

Sucharita was still not certain. She argued, 'The views of the Brahmo Samaj, if Binoybabu doesn't . . .'

'His views are similar too. The views of the Brahmo Samaj are not outlandish after all. He often reads to me the advice published in your journal; I can't see where the difference lies.'

'Suchididi,' called Lalita, entering the room. Seeing Anandamoyi, she immediately flushed in embarrassment. From Sucharita's expression she instantly guessed they had been discussing her. She would have been relieved to escape from the room, but it was too late.

'Come, Lalita ma, come,' cried Anandamoyi. Taking Lalita's hand, she drew her very close, as if they had developed a special intimacy. 'Look ma,' Anandamoyi now said to Sucharita, continuing in her earlier vein, 'it is hardest to combine the good with the bad, yet even that happens in this world, and we pull along somehow with a mixture of joys and sorrows. Not that it only causes harm: for sometimes, even good may come of it. If that too is possible, I fail to understand why a minor difference of opinion should keep two people apart. Are human affinities really a matter of opinions?'

Sucharita hung her head.

'Would your Brahmo Samaj also prevent two human beings from coming together?' Anandamoyi pursued. 'Would your Samaj outwardly divide people whom Ishwar has inwardly united? Ma, is there no community anywhere that would disregard minor differences and bring everyone together in a major union? Will human beings continue forever to oppose Ishwar like this? Were communities created only for that?'

Was Anandamoyi's fervour in pursuing this subject aimed solely at removing the obstacles blocking Lalita's marriage to Binoy? Was there not another motive in her wholehearted attempt to dispel the hint of doubt she sensed in Sucharita? It would not do, indeed, for Sucharita to remain trapped in such traditional ideas. If it was decided that the marriage could not take place unless Binoy converted to Brahmoism, the hopes Anandamoyi had nurtured of late, even in these difficult times, would be reduced to dust! That very day, Binoy had asked her:

'Ma, must I register with the Brahmo Samaj? Must I accept that as well?'

'No, no,' Anandamoyi had insisted, 'I see no need for that.'

'What if they pressurize me?'

'No, pressure would not work in this case,' Anandamoyi had replied, after a long silence.

Sucharita did not participate in Anandamoyi's discussion; she remained quiet. Anandamoyi realized that inwardly Sucharita was still not convinced.

'If my heart has broken free of all social prejudices, it is only because of my affection for Gora,' Anandamoyi thought to herself. 'Is Sucharita not attracted to Gora, then? If she were, this trivial issue would surely not seem so important.'

Anandamoyi felt rather downcast. There were just a couple of days for Gora's release from prison. She had privately imagined that the ground had been prepared for his happiness. Gora must somehow be pinned down this time, else there was no saying what predicament he might get into, or where. But it was not in every girl's power to pin Gora down. It would be wrong, though, to marry Gora to a girl from the Hindu community—hence she had rejected outright the proposals received from various families burdened with daughters. 'I shall not marry!' Gora would declare. People were surprised that as a mother, she never protested even once. But this time, observing some signs in Gora's behaviour, she had felt secretly overjoyed. That was why Sucharita's silent opposition to her views was a great blow to her. But she was not one to give up easily.

'We shall see,' she said to herself.

~52~

'Binoy, I don't want you to take a rash step, to rescue Lalita from a difficult predicament,' Poreshbabu declared. 'Social blame does not mean very much; in a couple of days, nobody will even remember what the fuss was all about.'

Binoy had no doubt that it was only to do his duty by Lalita that he had braced himself for battle. He knew such a marriage would cause awkwardness in the community, and more importantly, that Gora would be furious. But using only his sense of duty as a pretext, he had dismissed such unpleasant thoughts. Now that Poreshbabu suddenly sought to abjure that sense of duty completely, Binoy was loath to let it go.

'I can never repay all of you for your affection,' he responded. 'If I cause the slightest trouble for your family even for a couple of days, that too would be intolerable for me.'

'Binoy, you don't quite understand. I am delighted that you hold us in such high esteem, but if you are ready to marry my daughter only to repay that debt, it would not gain her much respect. That is why I was saying that the predicament is not grave enough to require the slightest sacrifice from you.'

So, Binoy was relieved of the burden of duty. But his heart did not rush out to embrace freedom like a bird that swiftly flaps its wings and flies away upon finding its cage door unbarred. He still did not want to move. For on the pretext of duty, he had demolished the dam of long-imposed self restraint, deeming it unnecessary. Where his mind would earlier advance very timidly and step back in shame like a culprit, it now firmly occupied a large space. Now it was hard to turn him back. When the sense of duty that had led him there now urged him: 'It's needless to remain here any longer bhai, let's turn back!' his heart replied: 'Return if you find it needless, but here I shall remain.'

When Poresh left no more room for subterfuge, Binoy blurted out: 'Don't imagine for a moment that I am ready to accept something painful to answer the call of duty. If all of you consent to it, there could be nothing more fortunate for me. My only fear is, lest . . .'

'Your fears are baseless,' the plainspoken Poreshbabu declared unhesitatingly. 'I have learnt from Sucharita that Lalita is not averse to you.'

Binoy felt a lightning flash of joy in his heart. A deep secret of Lalita's heart had been revealed to Sucharita. When and how had this happened? Binoy was pierced by a sharp, mysterious bliss upon learning that through hints and suggestions, such intimate knowledge had passed between these two women.

'If you all consider me worthy, nothing would bring me greater joy!' cried Binoy.

'Wait a little. I'll just go upstairs once.' He went to seek Borodasundari's consent.

'But Binoy must convert,' she said.

'Indeed he must,' Poreshbabu assented.

'Arrange that first,' she insisted. 'Why don't you send for Binoy?'

'So we must fix a date for the conversion,' Borodasundari said, when Binoy came upstairs.

'Is there any need for conversion?' Binoy asked.

'Any need? How can you say that! How else can you marry into the Brahmo Samaj?'

Binoy remained silent, hanging his head. Upon hearing that Binoy was willing to marry into his family, Poreshbabu had instantly assumed he would convert and join the Brahmo Samaj.

'I have a high regard indeed for the spiritual beliefs of the

Brahmo Samaj, and my conduct up until now has not contravened them either,' Binoy pointed out. 'So is formal initiation necessary?'

'If your beliefs are consonant, what harm in seeking initiation?' Borodasundari argued.

'It is impossible for me to declare that I have no connection with the Hindu community,' Binoy replied.

'Then it was wrong of you to bring up the subject at all,' Borodasundari declared. 'Have you consented to marry my daughter out of kindness, in order to help us?'

Binoy was deeply hurt. He realized that his proposal had indeed become humiliating for all of them. It was a while since the law sanctioning civil marriage had been passed. At the time, Gora and Binoy had sharply opposed it. For Binoy to accept civil marriage now and announce himself 'not a Hindu' was also very difficult.

Inwardly, Poresh could not accept the suggestion that Binoy should marry Lalita while still a member of the Hindu community. Sighing, Binoy rose to his feet and joining his hands in a namaskar, he said:

'Please forgive me. I shall not add to my wrongdoings.'

He left the room. Approaching the stairs he glimpsed Lalita alone at a small desk in a corner of the veranda ahead. She was writing a letter. Hearing his footstep, she raised her eyes to look at him. That momentary glance instantly set Binoy's heart in turmoil. His acquaintance with Lalita was not new after all; she had often raised her eyes to his face; but today, what mystery did her gaze unfold to him! Sucharita had learned a secret concealed Lalita's heart. That intimate secret appeared to Binoy's eyes today like a moisture-laden, gentle cloud that had gathered, full of pathos, under the shadow of Lalita's dark lashes. In Binoy's momentary glance, his heart's anguish also flashed across like lightning. With a farewell namaskar in Lalita's direction, he went down the stairs without addressing her.

~53~

When he came out of prison, Gora saw Poreshbabu and Binoy waiting for him at the gate.

A month was not a long time. Earlier, Gora had traveled for more than a month, away from relatives and friends. But seeing Poresh and Binoy as soon as he emerged from a month of separation in jail, he felt he had been reborn into the familiar world of his old friends. On the highway, under the open sky, in the glow of dawn, seeing Poresh's calm, affectionate, naturally dignified face, Gora touched his feet in an unprecedented ecstasy of devotion. Poresh embraced him.

'Binoy, I have shared my entire education with you, right from school,' smiled Gora, taking Binoy's hand. 'But at this school, I have given you the slip and outstripped you.'

Binoy could neither smile nor speak. His friend seemed to have emerged from his mysterious ordeal in prison with a stature far greater than that of a friend. In deep reverence, he stayed silent.

'How is Ma?' Gora enquired.

'Well enough,' Binoy replied.

'Come my dear boy,' said Poreshbabu, 'the carriage is waiting for you.'

As the three of them were about to mount the carriage, Abinash arrived there, panting for breath. He was followed by a crowd of boys. Seeing Abinash, Gora tried to hurry into the carriage, but Abinash blocked his way before he could succeed.

'Please wait a little, Gourmohanbabu,' he said. He had not finished speaking when the boys burst into song at the top of their voices:

Gone is the night of sorrow, the day has dawned.
Broken, broken, are our chains of bondage.

Gora flushed. 'Quiet!' he roared, in his thunderous voice. The boys were stunned into silence.

'What's all this, Abinash?' Gora demanded.

From the folds of his shawl Abinash produced a thick garland of kunda blossom, wrapped in banana leaf. Taking his cue, a young lad produced a piece of paper printed in gold lettering, and in a voice as shrill as a clockwork organ, started rapidly reading out a message congratulating Gora upon his release from prison.

Forcefully flinging aside Abinash's garland, his voice choked with suppressed rage, Gora exclaimed: 'Is this the first act of your show! Have you been practising all month to make me the clown in your jatra party here at the public roadside today?'

This had been Abinash's long standing plan; he had hoped to create a dazzling impression. Such annoying public spectacles were not current at the time we are speaking of. Greedy to take the entire credit for this extraordinary event, Abinash had not even discussed it with Binoy. In fact he had himself drafted a report for the newspapers, planning to send it off as soon as he got home, after filling in a couple of missing details.

'You are unfair,' protested Abinash, upset at Gora's reprimand. 'We have suffered no less than what you underwent in prison. Every moment, this last month, our ribs have been scorched by the inextinguishable flames of burning husks.'

'You are making a mistake Abinash,' Gora insisted. 'Look carefully and you will see at once that all the husks are still intact, and your ribs have suffered no fatal damage either.'

Abinash was not subdued. 'Those in power have insulted you,' he persisted, 'but today, on behalf of the entire land of Bharat, we offer this garland of honour . . .'

'This is becoming intolerable!' interrupted Gora. 'Poreshbabu, please get into the carriage,' he urged, brushing

Abinash and his party aside. Poreshbabu heaved a sigh of relief as he mounted the carriage, followed by Gora and Binoy.

Travelling by steamer, Gora arrived home early the next morning. He saw a large number of his party members assembled in the outer portion of the house. Somehow extricating himself from their clutches he went to Anandamoyi in the privacy of the antahpur. Having bathed early that morning, she was ready and waiting for him. When Gora came and fell at her feet in obeisance, tears gushed from Anandamoyi's eyes. The tears she had suppressed all these days could not be restrained anymore.

As soon as Krishnadayal returned from his bath in the Ganga, Gora met him, greeting him with a pranam from afar, without touching his feet. Embarrassed, Krishnadayal seated himself at a distance.

'Baba, I want to do penance,' Gora declared.

'But I see no need for that.'

'While in prison, I did not mind any other hardship, but I felt utterly impure. That sense of degradation has not left me yet. I must do penance.'

'No, no,' protested Krishnadayal in agitation. 'There is no need for such an extreme step. Indeed I can't agree to it.'

'Achchha, perhaps I shall consult the pundits about it.'

'No need to consult any pundit. I decree that you need not do penance.'

Gora had never been able to understand why a man like Krishnadayal, so obsessed with rites of purity, refused to accept that Gora should observe any restrictions—for he not only rejected, but obdurately resisted any such suggestion.

That day, Anandamoyi had placed Gora directly next to Binoy at mealtime. But Gora insisted:

'Ma, please move Binoy's mat a little further away.'

'Why, what crime has Binoy committed?' demanded Anandamoyi in surprise.

'The fault is not in Binoy but in me. I am unclean.'

'Never mind,' Anandamoyi assured him, 'Binoy is not so fussy about purity.'

'Binoy may not be, but I am,' Gora declared.

After their meal, when the two friends went to their secluded room upstairs, both felt rather tongue-tied. Binoy could not think how to broach to Gora the one subject that had assumed the greatest importance for him in this last month. Gora, too, secretly wanted to ask about Poreshbabu's family, but he said nothing at all. He was waiting for Binoy to raise the subject. True, Gora had asked Poreshbabu how all the girls in the family were doing, but that was just a polite query. Privately, he was eager for a more detailed account, beyond the mere assurance that they were all well.

At this point Mahim entered the room, and taking a seat, took some time to recover his breath after the effort of climbing the stairs. Then he said:

'Binoy, we have waited for Gora all these days. Now there is nothing to stop us. Let's fix the date and time now. What do you say, Gora? You understand what we are talking about, don't you?' Gora smiled faintly without saying a word. 'You smile!' exclaimed Mahim. 'Dada has still not forgotten the matter, you are thinking! But the girl is not a figment of the imagination—I see quite clearly that she is made of real stuff—so how can I forget the matter? This is no time to be facetious, Gora. Now let things be finalized somehow.'

'The one who must finalize things is here in person,' Gora pointed out.

'That would be disastrous!' cried Mahim. 'When he is not even sure of his own life, how can he fix anything! Now you're back, the entire responsibility is yours.'

Binoy remained grave and silent on this occasion, making no attempt to say anything even with his customary jocularity. Gora sensed that something was wrong.

'I may undertake to invite people, or to order the sweets, and may even be willing to serve the guests, but I cannot undertake to ensure that Binoy will marry your daughter. I am not well acquainted with the One who ordains such things, having always saluted Him from afar.'

'Don't imagine that He would keep away just because you remain aloof,' Mahim cautioned him. 'There is no saying when He might take you by surprise. I can't say for sure what He intends for you, but regarding Binoy I fear grave complications. If you don't involve yourself instead of leaving things entirely to Prajapati, the god of marriage, we may have cause for regret, I warn you.'

'I'm willing to regret an undertaking for which I am not responsible,' Gora replied, 'but it is harder if one must regret a responsibility after accepting it. I want to save myself from such a predicament.'

'Would you sit back and watch a Brahman's son lose his caste, blood ties and social respect?' Mahim demanded. 'You sacrifice your food and sleep to preserve your countrymen's Hindu beliefs, but if meanwhile your own best friend throws caste purity to the winds to marry into a Brahmo family, you will not be able to face the world. You may be angry, Binoy, but I have spoken to Gora in your presence, while many people might say the same things to him behind your back— they are dying to do so. It is best for everybody to be frank. If the rumours are indeed false, you just have to say so and the matter ends there; but if they are true, we must come to an understanding.' Mahim rose to his feet and left. Still, Binoy did not say a word.

'Why Binoy, what's the matter?' Gora enquired.

'It is very hard,' Binoy replied, 'to explain the situation accurately by merely offering some items of news. That's why I had thought I would gradually clarify the whole matter to you. But in this world, nothing tends to happen unhurriedly, according to one's convenience. Events, too, advance slowly and silently at first like a tiger on the prowl, then suddenly they pounce on you. News of such events also remains initially suppressed like a fire, but when it suddenly bursts into flames afterwards, it can no longer be controlled. That's why sometimes I feel that man's freedom resides in giving up all action and remaining utterly immobile.'

'How can freedom be possible if you alone are static?' smiled Gora. 'Unless the whole world also freezes, why would it let you remain still? On the contrary, it would create another problem. When the world is in action, if you do not act as well, you will be constantly cheated. Hence you must be careful not to let events get the better of your alertness. Let it not happen that you alone are unprepared while all else continues.'

'That's true. It is I who am unprepared. This time also I was not ready. I had no idea what was happening, and how. But when it has happened, one must take responsibility for it. Unpleasant though it is, one cannot now refuse to acknowledge what should not have happened in the first place.'

'Without knowing what happened, it is hard for me to discuss it theoretically.'

Binoy sat bolt upright and blurted out: 'Due to circumstances beyond our control, my relationship with Lalita has reached a stage where she must suffer unjust and baseless social humiliation all her life, unless I marry her.'

'What stage is that, may I know?'

'That's a long story. I shall narrate it to you in due course, but rest assured that the little bit I've told you is true.'

'Very well, suppose I accept it as true. I have this to say: if the event is inevitable, so are its painful consequences. If Lalita must suffer humiliation in the Samaj, there's no help for it.'

'But it is within my power to prevent it,' protested Binoy.

'If so, that is a good thing. But asserting the fact forcefully is not enough, after all. When in need, it is within the power of human beings to steal or even murder, but is that power real? You want to do your duty towards Lalita by marrying her, but is that really your supreme duty? Don't you have a duty towards your community?'

Binoy did not point out that it was his sense of duty towards the community that had made him reject a Brahmo wedding ceremony.

'I think you and I will perhaps differ on this issue,' he argued even more passionately. 'After all I am not opposing society in favour of individuals. I am saying that above both individual and society is something else, a spiritual ethic called dharma, and that must be kept in mind when we act. It is not my supreme duty to protect either a particular individual or my community. It is protecting my dharma that is my supreme duty.'

'A dharma that exists without either individual or society! I have no faith in such a dharma.'

Binoy grew even more obdurate. 'Granted,' he said. 'Dharma is not based on individual and society; rather, both individual and society are based on dharma. To be forced to accept society's wishes as one's dharma would ruin society itself. If society obstructs my legally and spiritually sanctioned freedom, it would be my duty towards society to flout such inappropriate prohibitions. If my marrying Lalita is not wrong, but in fact justified, then it would go against my dharma to desist simply because it violated social injunctions.'

'Are questions of justice and injustice confined to you alone? Will you not consider where you are placing your future progeny by agreeing to this marriage?'

'It is through such considerations indeed that people

perpetuate social injustices. Why then blame the clerk who accepts lifelong degradation, kicked around by the sahebs who are his masters? After all he, too, has his children's welfare in mind.'

His argument with Gora had brought Binoy to a point he had not reached before. Just a little while earlier, his whole being had shrunk from the prospect of severing his ties with society. He had not mentally debated the issue in any way, and but for this exchange with Gora, Binoy's heart would have followed its own accustomed prejudices and taken him on a course completely contrary to his present stance. But as he argued, his attitude, supported by his sense of duty, began to grow strong.

He and Gora started arguing heatedly. In such discussions Gora often expressed his views very forcefully, without relying on logic. Few could match his assertiveness. Now, he tried to demolish all Binoy's arguments by this aggressive force, but found himself thwarted. As long as their ideas alone had clashed, Binoy had always been defeated. But this was a confrontation between two real persons; instead of fending off airy weapons of its own kind, Gora's airborne verbal arrows now encountered a human heart full of pain.

Ultimately Gora said: 'I don't want to engage in a war of words with you. There is nothing much to argue about here; it's a matter for the heart to comprehend. It is your desire to disengage from the common people of the land by marrying a Brahmo girl: that is a source of great distress for me. You are capable of it, but I could never do such a thing. That is where we differ, not in learning or intellect. The target of my love is not the same as yours. You have no sympathy for what you would destroy in order to free yourself. But I have blood-ties with it. I want my Bharatvarsha; blame and curse it if you will, but it is Bharatvarsha I desire. I don't desire myself or any other human being above that. I would not take the slightest step that might create the minutest division between me and my Bharatvarsha.'

'No Binoy, you argue in vain,' Gora insisted when Binoy tried to reply. 'I want to share the degradation of the Bharatvarsha that the world has forsaken and condemned, this Bharatvarsha with its caste discrimination, social evils, idol worship. If you wish to distance yourself from it, you must distance yourself from me as well.'

Gora arose, went out of the room, and began to wander about on the terrace. Binoy remained where he was, silent and motionless. The attendant came to inform Gora that several babus were waiting for him in the outer chamber. Relieved to find an escape route, Gora went away.

Emerging into the outer room, he noticed Abinash among the motley crowd assembled there. Gora had assumed Abinash must be feeling offended. But he saw no signs of anger. In terms even more effusively laudatory, Abinash was recounting to everyone the way Gora had spurned him the previous day.

'My respect for Gourmohanbabu has grown immensely,' he declared. 'All these days I took him for an unusual man, but yesterday I realized that he is great. Yesterday we had gone to honour him, but the way he publicly spurned that honour—how many people in today's world could have done that! Indeed it is no ordinary matter!'

Gora's mind was already overwrought. Now Abinash's effusiveness made him furious. 'Look here Abinash,' he cried, losing his patience. 'It is your devotion that is offensive. If you people want to make me dance like a clown by the roadside, do you think I lack the decorum to refuse? Is this what you call a sign of greatness? Do you consider this land of ours a mere jatra party with everyone dancing about in order to collect the rewards of their performance? Is nobody doing any real work? If you want to join us, or even to pick a quarrel, that is acceptable; but I beg all of you not to laud me in this fashion.'

Abinash's reverence grew even more intense. He beamed at all present, as if to draw their attention to the wonder of Gora's words. 'Give us your blessing,' he pleaded, 'that we may selflessly surrender our lives to protect the eternal glory of Bharatvarsha, just like you.' With these words Abinash reached out to touch Gora's feet in a pranam. Gora at once recoiled. 'Gourmohanbabu,' Abinash declared, 'you will indeed accept no token of honour from us. But you cannot also remain averse to making us happy. We have planned a feast one day, where you will dine with all the rest of us. To this you must agree.'

'Until I have done penance I cannot dine with you,' Gora asserted.

Penance! Abinash's eyes lit up. 'That had never occurred to any of us,' he confessed, 'but no decree of the Hindu dharma can ever escape Gourmohanbabu's notice.'

It was an excellent idea, everyone agreed. The penance ritual itself would provide all of them an occasion to sit down together to a feast. That day they must invite all the great teachers and pundits of the area. The invitation to Gourmohanbabu's penance would make people aware that the Hindu dharma was alive and thriving, even now. The date and venue for the penance ceremony also came up for discussion. Gora declared that this house would not be suitable. A devotee proposed that the ritual be performed at his garden estate beside the Ganga. It was also decided that the group would collectively bear the expenses for the event. When it was time to depart, Abinash rose and addressed every one, gesturing like an orator:

'This may annoy Gourmohanbabu, but my heart is so full today that I cannot refrain from saying that just as the avatars, divine incarnations, were once born into this sacred land to protect the Vedas, so we have now found this avatar to rescue the Hindu dharma. In this world, our land alone has six seasons; in our land alone, through the ages, have avatars been born, and there are more to come. It is our glory that this truth has now been demonstrated. Come, bhai, let us all cry, 'Victory to Gourmohan!' Swayed by Abinash's eloquence all of them began chanting Gora's praises. Deeply offended, Gora rushed away from the scene.

On this day of his release from prison, a powerful sense of fatigue assailed Gora. In the confines of the jail, he had often imagined that he would work for the nation with renewed enthusiasm. But today he kept asking himself:

'Alas, where is my nation? Is it a nation to me alone! That my childhood friend, with whom I had discussed all my life's resolves, should be willing, after all this time, to ruthlessly abandon his nation's entire past and future, just to marry a woman! And as for those who are generally identified as members of my group, after all I have explained to them all along, that they should now conclude that I was an avatar born only to rescue the Hindu faith! Am I merely the shastras personified? And does Bharatvarsha have no place in their scheme of things? Six seasons! Bharatvarsha has six seasons indeed! If the six seasons have conspired to produce a man like Abinash, we could have done with a few seasons less!'

The bearer came to say that Ma had sent for Gora. Gora started. 'Ma has sent for me!' he exclaimed to himself. The words seemed to assume a new significance. 'Come what may, my mother is there,' he said. 'And it is she who has sent for me. It is she who will unite me with everybody, allowing no separation between people; I shall find my dear ones in her space. In prison, Ma had called me, and had appeared to me in a vision; out of prison, too, Ma is calling me; I shall set forth now to meet her.' With these words Gora gazed out at the wintry afternoon sky. The discordant note struck by Binoy on the one hand and Abinash on the other dwindled and faded away. Bharatvarsha seemed to open its arms to the afternoon sunlight. Before Gora's eyes the rivers, mountains, human habitations of Bharatvarsha lay outspread, extending to the sea; from the eternal realm, a free, pure light seemed to irradiate this Bharatvarsha everywhere. Gora's heart was full. His eyes began to blaze, and no trace of despair remained in any corner of his mind. His nature blissfully readied itself for ceaseless service of Bharatvarsha, with its distant goals. He felt no bitterness that he would not witness in his lifetime the glory of Bharatvarsha that he had seen in his contemplation. Again and again he told himself: 'Ma is calling me. I am on my way to the place where the mother goddess awaits me as Annapurna, as Jagaddhatri—to that distant time, yet at this very moment, to that other shore beyond death, yet within this present lifetime—to that glorious future which has brightened my humble present, making it completely worthwhile—I am on my way to that very place—to that place which is very distant, yet very near, Ma is calling me.' It seemed to Gora that Binoy, and even Abinash, were part of that bliss, that they too were no longer alienated from him. All the petty conflicts of the present were lost in a tremendous sense of achievement.

When Gora entered Anandamoyi's room his face was alight with joy, as if his eyes were gazing at some exquisite image, beyond the material things before him. When he suddenly entered the scene, he seemed not to quite recognize the person who was with his mother. Sucharita arose and greeted Gora with a namaskar.

'So you have arrived! Please make yourself comfortable,' said Gora. He spoke as if Sucharita's arrival was no ordinary event, but an extraordinary manifestation.

Gora had once avoided Sucharita's company. As long as he wandered, undergoing many hardships and performing diverse tasks, he had managed to keep thoughts of Sucharita at bay. But in the confines of prison, he had been unable to ward off memories of her. There was once a time when Gora had not even been aware that there were women in Bharatvarsha. At last, he newly discovered this fact in the shape of Sucharita; his nature, so robust, trembled at the impact of the sudden and immediate apprehension of such an important truth, so ancient and so great. In prison, when the sunshine and open breeze outside tormented his mind, he did not view that world as merely his workplace or as a male society. Whatever form of meditation he adopted, he could see only the faces of two founding deities, singled out by the light of sun, moon and stars, enveloped exclusively by the tender blue sky. One was the face of the mother he had known all his life, and the other gentle, lovely face, glowing with intelligence, was that of his new acquaintance.

In the joyless confines of prison, Gora had been unable to fight the memory of this countenance. The rapture of contemplating it brought a sense of the profoundest freedom into his jail cell. The harsh, physical bonds of prison would seem to him a shadowy illusion. From his pulsating heart emanated supranatural waves that penetrated all the prison walls unhindered, merging with the sky, swaying with the flowers and foliage, sporting in the world's workspaces. Imagining there was no reason to fear this fanciful image, Gora had for this last month given full rein to it. He feared only substantial things.

Seeing Poreshbabu as soon as he emerged from prison, Gora had felt overjoyed. His delight was not merely at the sight of Poreshbabu; Gora had not realized at first the extent to which his joy was infused with the magic of that imaginary figure who had lately become his companion. But gradually he understood. Travelling on the steamer he distinctly sensed that his attraction towards Poreshbabu was not on account of the latter's own virtues alone. At last, Gora again braced himself. 'I shall not admit defeat,' he declared. On the steamer he resolved firmly that he would again go somewhere far away, and not allow his mind to be fettered by any bonds, however subtle.

At this juncture he became involved in a debate with Binoy. When the two friends first met after their spell of separation, the argument would not normally have grown so intense. But now, concealed within this argument raged a debate with himself. Through this argument, Gora was clarifying his own premises even to himself. That was why he spoke so vehemently on this occasion, for it was he who particularly needed such vehemence. When this assertiveness aroused Binoy's antagonism, when Binoy mentally countered Gora's statements with his entire soul militating against the unjust fanaticism of Gora's strictures, he had not dreamt that Gora's onslaught might not have been so aggressive if it had not been directed against himself.

After his debate with Binoy, Gora decided: 'I cannot afford to quit the arena. If I abandon Binoy to save my own life, there will be no saving him!'

~54~

At this moment, Gora's mind was in a trance, regarding Sucharita not as an individual but an abstract idea. In the form of Sucharita the image of Indian womanhood manifested itself to him. It was to make the Indian home sweet and pure through virtue, beauty and love that this image had appeared. The goddess Lakshmi who nurtures the infants of India, tends to the sick, comforts the troubled, glorifies even the humble with her love, who has not abandoned or ignored even the poorest of us in times of trouble, who though herself venerable has devotedly worshipped even the unworthiest of us, whose lovely, skilful hands are dedicated to our service, and whose ever-sympathetic, merciful love we have received from the Almighty as an eternal gift—seeing her incarnate here before his very eyes, seated beside his mother, Gora was filled with profound joy. He began to think: 'We had not glanced at this Lakshmi-figure, pushing her completely into the background! There can be no greater sign of our degradation.' He now felt: 'She signifies the land itself, ensconced upon a thousand-petalled lotus in the soul's garden, at the heart of the entire nation Bharatvarsha. We are her servants. The country's plight is her dishonour; it is because we are indifferent to her humiliation that our virility is put to shame.'

Gora was privately astounded. Up until now he had not even realized how incomplete was his understanding of Bharatvarsha, as long as he had remained unaware of Indian womanhood. When the female sex had been an opaque mystery to him, he had felt something missing from his sense of patriotic duty. As if it had strength but no life, muscle but no nerves. In an instant Gora realized: 'The more we have kept women away and belittled them, the more our own virility has dwindled and wasted away.' Hence when Gora said to Sucharita, 'Here you are, you have arrived!' his words were not uttered merely as a customary polite greeting. They were loaded with a newfound joy and wonder.

Gora's body bore some marks of his prison days. He had become much thinner than before. Out of contempt and distaste for prison food, he had virtually fasted through this month-long period. His glowing, fair complexion had also grown somewhat dull. His extremely short-cropped hair made the haggardness of his countenance all the more apparent. It was this leanness that aroused pain and awe in Sucharita's heart. She longed to touch Gora's feet in obeisance. Gora appeared to her like a pure flame that burns so brightly, the wood and smoke become invisible. An intense devotion mingled with sympathy made her heart tremble inwardly. She could not utter a word.

'I now realize what joy a daughter could have brought me, Gora!' said Anandamoyi. 'How can I tell you what solace Sucharita offered me, when you were away! I didn't know their family before, but in times of trouble one discovers many great and good things in this world. I now recognize this glorious aspect of sorrow. We suffer only because we don't always realize where, in how many places, the Almighty Ishwar has left provision for our solace. You are embarrassed, ma, but how can I help mentioning in your presence the joy you have brought me during my difficult days?'

With profound gratitude, Gora glanced once at Sucharita's embarrassed face. 'Ma,' he said to Anandamoyi, 'she came to share your sorrows in your times of trouble, and is here again to enhance your joy in happier circumstances. Only those with largeness of heart are capable of such unwarranted sympathy.'

'Didi, once a thief is caught he is chastised by all concerned,' observed Binoy, noticing Sucharita's awkwardness. 'You are now suffering the result of being captured by all of them. Now there's no escape! I've known you a long time, but I never gave anything away. I have kept very quiet, knowing in my heart that nothing remains hidden for long.'

'You have kept quiet, indeed!' smiled Anandamoyi. 'As if you are the sort of boy to keep quiet! Ever since he met all of you, he has sung your praises continuously, but he can never say enough.'

'Pay heed, didi!' said Binoy. 'Here's direct proof that I appreciate the virtues of others and that I'm not ungrateful.'

'That only indicates your own virtues,' Sucharita retorted.

'But you will learn nothing about my virtues from me,' Binoy replied. 'If that's what you seek, please go to my mother and you will be dumbfounded. When I hear such praise from her lips, I am myself astonished. If Ma were to write my biography, I'd willingly die early.'

'Just listen to this boy!' said Anandamoyi.

'Binoy,' observed Gora, 'your parents indeed gave you a fitting name.'

'It was perhaps because they expected no other virtue of me that they claimed for me the quality of binoy or modesty, else I would have become a laughing-stock for everyone.'

In this way, the constraint of their first encounter melted away.

'Won't you visit our part of the town sometime?' Sucharita asked Binoy while taking her leave.

She invited Binoy but could not bring herself to ask Gora. Unable to quite understand what this meant, Gora was secretly hurt. So far he had never felt the slightest pang at the fact that he could not match Binoy's ability to easily make himself at home in everybody's midst. But today he felt this missing quality as a lack.

~55~

Binoy had realized that it was to discuss his marriage to Lalita that Sucharita had invited him. He may have dispensed with the proposal, but that did not mean the matter had ended there. As long as the issue remained alive, there could be no reprieve for either party.

All these days, Binoy's biggests worry had been, 'How can I hurt Gora's feelings?' By Gora he meant not just the man himself, but his attitude, his faith and the life he had adopted. To always keep in step with this had been Binoy's habit, his source of joy. Opposing it in any way seemed to him like rebelling against his own self. But his initial hesitation about striking that blow had vanished. Now that he had discussed the Lalita affair openly with Gora, Binoy felt heartened. Before his sore was lanced, there had been no end to the patient's fear and apprehension; but once the instruments were applied, he felt pain indeed but also relief, and found the procedure not as terrible as he had imagined.

All this while, Binoy had been unable to argue with himself, but now the doors to internal debate were also opened. Now, in his mind, he exchanged words with Gora. Mentally summoning up all the arguments one might expect from Gora, he began to counter them from diverse angles. If the entire debate with Gora could have taken place verbally, it would have aroused excitement but also quenched it. But Binoy realized Gora would not carry this particular argument to its conclusion. This, too, angered Binoy. 'Gora will neither understand nor explain, but only apply force. Force! I cannot submit to force.' 'Whatever happens, I am on the side of Truth,' he declared. With these words, he clutched the word 'Truth' to his heart. It was necessary to set up a very strong opposition to Gora; hence Binoy repeatedly told himself that Truth itself was his final recourse. In fact, he developed tremendous self-respect at having made Truth his refuge. So when Binoy headed for Sucharita's house that afternoon, he held his head high. Whether his strength came from his leanings towards Truth or whether his leanings lay elsewhere, he was in no state to determine.

Harimohini was preparing to cook. There, at the kitchen door, Binoy made her sanction the Brahman's claim to a midday meal, and proceeded upstairs. Fingers busy, eyes on a piece of embroidery, Sucharita raised the topic that was uppermost in their minds.

'Look here, Binoybabu,' she said, 'must external antagonisms matter where there is no internal obstacle?'

In his debate with Gora, Binoy had opposed him. But in his discussion with Sucharita, he again took the opposite side.

Who could tell, now, that there was any difference of opinion between Gora and him!

'Didi,' he argued, 'all of you are not minimizing the external obstacles either.'

'There's a reason for that Binoybabu! The obstacles we face are not exactly external. Our Samaj is based on our spiritual faith after all. But in your community, the restrictions are merely social. Hence it would not be as great a loss to you to renounce your community as it would be for Lalita to withdraw from the Brahmo Samaj.'

Binoy began to argue that religion is a personal pursuit, not to be associated with any community. At this juncture Satish entered, carrying a letter and an English newspaper. Seeing Binoy, he became very excited, eager to somehow convert Friday into Sunday. In no time, Binoy and Satish were deep in conversation. Meanwhile, Sucharita began to read Lalita's letter and the accompanying paper. This Brahmo paper carried the news that there was no longer any fear of a match between an eminent Brahmo family and the Hindu community, because the prospective Hindu groom had declined the proposal. In this connection, the pathetic weakness of the Brahmo family was decried, in contrast to the steadfastness of the aforementioned Hindu boy.

Sucharita privately resolved that Binoy and Lalita must be married, by whatever means. But that could not be accomplished by arguing with this young man. She sent a note to Lalita, inviting her home and mentioning that Binoy was present there. As no almanac offered any provision for turning Friday into Sunday by some planetary conjunction, Satish had to go and get ready for school. Sucharita also went away, saying she needed time to bathe.

Alone in Sucharita's secluded chamber, once the heat of the argument had evaporated, the young man in Binoy was aroused. It was about nine or nine-thirty in the morning.

There was no hubbub in the street. A clock was ticking on Sucharita's writing desk. The room exuded an influence that began to overwhelm Binoy. The small decorative items all around him seemed to set up a conversation with him. The neatness of the tabletop, the embroidered cover on the chair, the deerskin rug at the foot of the chair, the few pictures hanging on the wall, the small bookshelf at the back, with its books covered in red fabric—all this struck a profound chord in Binoy's mind. There seemed to be some beautiful mystery tucked away inside this chamber, as if all the intimate confidences shared here between sakhis on lonely afternoons still lingered in the room, scattered here and there. Binoy began to visualize the place and posture of the female companions during their conversations. The words spoken by Poreshbabu the other day—'I have learnt from Sucharita that Lalita is not averse to you'—appeared to his mind's eye in a myriad different ways, with a picture-like clarity. An unutterable anguish haunted his heart like a sad, melancholy melody. Because he lacked the capacity to express in any way the things that inhabit the recesses of one's heart in such secret, profound forms, like wordless hints—in other words, because Binoy was not a poet or painter—his whole inner being grew restless. He began to feel as if there was something that might bring him relief if only he could accomplish it, yet there seemed no way of doing so. The screen that hung before him, very close at hand yet keeping him at a slight distance—did Binoy not have the strength to arise and forcefully rip it apart, this very minute?

Harimohini looked in to ask if Binoy wanted a snack.

'No,' he replied.

Now Harimohini entered the room and sat down. While at Poreshbabu's, she had felt strongly drawn towards Binoy. But ever since she had set up house independently with Sucharita, these visits had become extremely distasteful to her. She had decided these companions were to blame for the fact that Sucharita did not completely follow Harimohini in observing orthodox restrictions nowadays. Though she knew Binoy was not a Brahmo, she clearly sensed that he inwardly lacked any firm convictions about Hindu tradition. So she no longer wasted the deity's prasad by enthusiastically inviting this Brahman's son to taste the consecrated food, as before.

'Tell me, baba, you are a Brahman's son after all, so don't you perform the sandhya prayer ritual, or offer any archana?' she asked Binoy conversationally that day.

'Mashi,' he answered, 'I'm so busy memorizing my lessons all day, I've forgotten gayatri, sandhya, everything.'

'Poreshbabu is also an educated man,' Harimohini protested. 'But he still performs some rituals, morning and evening, according to his faith.'

'Mashi, what he does cannot be accomplished by memorizing mantras alone. If I can ever become like him, I too shall follow his path.'

'Meanwhile,' said Harimohini rather sharply, 'why not follow the path of your forefathers? Is it a good idea to be neither here nor there? A person must have a religious identity after all. Neither Rama nor Ganga—O ma, what sort of conduct is this!'

At this moment Lalita entered the room. She started when she saw Binoy.

'Where is Didi?' she asked Harimohini.

'Radharani has gone for a bath,' Harimohini replied.

'Didi had sent for me,' said Lalita, by way of a needless explanation.

'Why don't you wait, she will join us very soon,' suggested Harimohini.

Harimohini was not favourably disposed towards Lalita either. She now wanted to bring Sucharita completely under her control, freeing her of all her former ties. Poreshbabu's other daughters did not visit here very frequently. Only Lalita would drop by at odd hours to chat with Sucharita, which Harimohini did not like. She often tried to disrupt their conversation, calling Sucharita away on some errand or other, or expressing regret that Sucharita's studies were no longer progressing unhindered as before. Yet when Sucharita applied herself to her studies, Harimohini would also not refrain from pointing out that excessive learning was unnecessary and harmful for women. Truth be told, because she could not succeed in bringing Sucharita as completely under her power as she wished, she would sometimes blame Sucharita's companions and sometimes her education.

Not that it pleased Harimohini to linger there with Lalita and Binoy; but there she remained all the same, because she was angry with both of them. She had sensed a mysterious relationship between Binoy and Lalita. Hence she told herself: 'Whatever the customs of your community, I shall not permit such shameless intermingling, such outrageous Khristani ways, in this house of mine!'

Meanwhile, Lalita's heart also bristled with rebellion. The previous day, she too had resolved to accompany Sucharita to Anandamoyi's house, but she could not force herself to go. Lalita respected Gora immensely, but her hostility towards him was also very intense. She could never dismiss the fact that Gora was opposed to her in every respect. Indeed, from the day Gora came out of prison, her attitude towards Binoy had also undergone a change. Even a few days earlier, she had arrogantly assumed that she had strong claims upon Binoy. But the very thought that Binoy could never overcome Gora's influence made her brace herself for battle with him.

As soon as he saw Lalita enter the room, Binoy's heart was flung into a turmoil. Try as he might, he could not maintain a natural demeanour towards her. Ever since rumours had spread within their social circle about the likelihood of their getting married, Binoy's heart would tremble at the very sight of Lalita, like a magnet within an electrical field. Seeing Binoy in the room, Lalita was incensed with Sucharita, assuming that Sucharita had been trying her best to persuade the reluctant Binoy and that it was to iron out this problem that she had been summoned here today.

'Please tell Didi I can't wait for her now,' she declared, addressing Harimohini. 'I'll come another time.' With these words, without so much as glancing at Binoy, she rushed from the room. Now that it was pointless for Harimohini to remain with Binoy any longer, she too departed to attend to her housework.

Binoy was not unfamiliar with this smouldering expression on Lalita's face. But he had not seen this look for a long time. He had thought with relief that those bad days were over when Lalita was constantly up in arms against him, but now he found her producing the same fiery arrows from her armoury. The arrows had not rusted at all. Anger could be tolerated, but for someone like Binoy, contempt was hard to bear. He recalled the sharp disdain Lalita had once felt for him, taking him for a mere satellite of Gora. He was tormented to imagine that even now, his hesitation made him appear cowardly in Lalita's eyes. He found it unbearable that though his sense of the constraints of duty may appear cowardly to Lalita, he would not have a chance to say even a few words in self-defense. To be denied the right to argue was a grave punishment for Binoy. For he knew he was a good debater, with an uncommon gift for presenting well-constructed arguments in support of a particular cause. But when Lalita quarreled with him she never gave him the chance to argue, nor would he have such a chance today.

The newspaper lay there still. Gripped by restlessness, Binoy pulled it towards him and suddenly noticed a certain section marked out in pencil. Reading, he realized that the

discussion and moralizing there was directed at them both. He
clearly understood the extent of the daily humiliation inflicted
upon Lalita by the members of her community. Yet Binoy was
making no effort to shield her from such dishonour,
preoccupied only with fine arguments about social philosophy.
Hence it seemed to him appropriate that a spirited woman
like Lalita should treat him with disdain. Remembering Lalita's
boldness in her complete disregard for society, and comparing
himself with this woman ablaze with fury, he began to feel
ashamed.

After her bath, having fed Satish and sent him off to
school, Sucharita came to Binoy and found him sitting in
silence. She did not raise the former subject. Before his meal
of rice, Binoy did not perform the gandush ritual of chanting
mantras over cupped handfuls of water.

'Tell me, bachha,' said Harimohini, 'you don't observe
any Hindu rituals after all, so what harm in becoming a
Brahmo?'

Binoy was privately rather offended. 'The day you take
Hinduism for mere observance of meaningless purity-rituals,
I shall adopt the Brahmo, Christian, Muslim or any other faith
you please,' he declared. 'But I still haven't developed such
disrespect for Hinduism.'

Binoy emerged from Sucharita's house in an extremely
dejected frame of mind, as if he had been buffeted about in all
directions and arrived at a void with no refuge. He could not
claim his former place by Gora's side, yet Lalita too was
keeping him at arm's length. Even with Harimohini, his close
relationship was on the verge of rapid dissolution.
Borodasundari had once cherished a heartfelt affection for him
and Poreshbabu loved him still, but in return for their
affection he had brought such turbulence into their home that
he had no place there either. Binoy was always hungry for the
respect and affection of those he loved, and he also had

considerable power to engage their hearts in diverse ways. How he came to be suddenly cast out now from his familiar trajectory of love and friendship, was something he began to privately ask himself. Now that he had left Sucharita's house, he could not think where to go next. Once he could have easily and unthinkingly made his way to Gora's home, but now he no longer had natural access there as before. If he went there he must remain silent in Gora's presence, and such silence was utterly unbearable. Meanwhile, Poreshbabu's home was not easy for him to access, either.

'How did I arrive at such an unnatural situation!' wondered Binoy as he walked slowly down the road with bowed head. When he reached the Hedua pond, he sank beneath a tree. So far, whenever a problem had arisen, large or small, he had solved it by discussing it with his friend, arguing about it. But now that path was not open to him, and he must think for himself.

Binoy did not lack powers of introspection. It was not easy for him to absolve himself by blaming everything on outward events. Hence, thinking in solitude, he concluded that he alone was to blame. 'In this world, I can't afford to be so cunning as to have something without paying its price,' he thought to himself. 'Whenever we seek to choose something, we must renounce something else. A person who can't decide to surrender any option will end up like me, rejected by all. Those who have firmly chosen their path of life are the ones who have found contentment. The unfortunate wretch who loves this path and that one as well, unable to deprive himself of either, is denied the destination itself, and is left wandering like a street dog.'

Diagnosing an ailment is difficult, but it is not as if treatment becomes easy as soon as the diagnosis is made. Binoy's understanding was extremely sharp; it was power of action that he lacked. Hence until now he had depended upon his friend, a person of much firmer resolve. Ultimately, at this very difficult moment, he had suddenly discovered that even if one lacks will-power, one can handle small matters by borrowing from others, but in times of real need, one can never do business by proxy.

As the sun declined, the shade was replaced by sunshine. He now left his shelter beneath the tree and took to the road again. He had not gone far when he suddenly heard someone call:

'Binoybabu! Binoybabu!' The next moment, Satish came and grasped his hand. He was returning home from school after his lessons.

'Come Binoybabu, come home with me,' Satish pleaded.

'How is that possible, Satishbabu?'

'Why not?'

'If I visit so frequently, how would your family members tolerate me?'

'No, come with me,' insisted Satish, deeming Binoy's argument utterly unworthy of any reply.

The boy had no inkling about the immense revolution that had occurred in Binoy's relationship with his family; he just loved Binoy. Realizing this, Binoy felt deeply perturbed. In the paradise that Poreshbabu's family had become for Binoy, it was only in this boy that the quality of bliss had remained complete and unaffected. In these stormy days, no cloud of doubt had shadowed his mind, no social onslaught had tried to destroy his moorings.

'Come bhai,' said Binoy, putting his arm around Satish's neck. 'Let's see you to your doorstep.' Embracing Satish, Binoy seemed to feel the sweet touch of all the love and affection that Satish had received from Sucharita and Lalita since his infancy. All along the way, Satish's unceasing, irrelevant chatter showered honey upon Binoy's ears. In contact with the boy's simplicity of heart, Binoy could briefly become oblivious to the complicated problems of his life.

They had to cross Poreshbabu's house on their way to Sucharita's. His sitting-room on the ground floor was visible from the road. When they arrived before that room, Binoy could not refrain from raising his head to glance at it once. He saw Poreshbabu at his table, but it was not clear whether he was speaking; and close to his chair on a small cane mora, her back to the street, was Lalita, silent as a pupil. Having no other means of quelling the petulance and wounded pride that had tormented her unbearably since she returned from Sucharita's house, Lalita had crept to Poreshbabu's side. There was such an air of perfect peace within Poreshbabu that the impatient Lalita sometimes came and sat quietly by his side, to control her own restlessness.

'What is it, Lalita?' Poreshbabu would ask.

'Nothing, Baba,' she would reply. 'This room of yours is very cool.'

On this occasion, Poreshbabu clearly sensed that Lalita had come to him with a wounded heart. A feeling of pain had also made him inwardly depressed. Hence he had gently broached a subject that could lighten the burden of trivial personal joys and sorrows.

The sight of this inaudible dialogue between father and daughter brought Binoy to a momentary halt. He did not hear what Satish was saying. The boy was asking him a very complicated question about war strategy. He wondered what the chances of victory might be if one's own side placed a pride of tigers in the frontline after giving them prolonged training. So far their question-and-answer session had proceeded unhindered; now, at this sudden interruption, Satish glanced at Binoy's face. Then, following Binoy's gaze, he looked towards Poreshbabu's room and cried out loudly:

'Lalitadidi, Lalitadidi, look! I have captured Binoybabu from the street!'

Embarrassed, Binoy broke out in a sweat. Within the room, Lalita instantly sprang to her feet. Poreshbabu turned around to look at the street. Altogether, the situation took a dramatically awkward turn. Having dispatched Satish, Binoy stepped into the house. Entering Poreshbabu's room, he found Lalita gone. Imagining that everyone saw him as a disruptive intruder, he awkwardly took a chair. As soon as they had finished exchanging customary polite queries about their mutual welfare, Binoy took the plunge:

'Since I don't respect the restrictions imposed by Hindu society and violate their laws daily, I consider it my duty to seek refuge in the Brahmo Samaj. It is from you I wish to receive my initiation.'

This desire and this resolve had not taken clear shape in Binoy's even fifteen minutes earlier.

'You have considered everything carefully I hope?' asked Poreshbabu after a moment's silence.

'There is nothing left to consider,' Binoy insisted. 'One need only consider the fairness or unfairness of it. That is a very simple matter. Given our education, I certainly cannot honestly accept that mere rituals and restrictions constitute inviolate faith. That is why at every step my conduct shows a lack of decorum; by remaining involved with those who respectfully follow Hindu custom, I only succeed in hurting them. I have no doubt that this is extremely wrong of me. In these circumstances, I must be ready to abjure such wrong conduct, without considering anything else. Otherwise I cannot retain my self-respect.'

There was no need to explain at such length to Poreshbabu, but he said all this only to fortify himself. Declaring that he was caught in a battle between right and wrong and that he must sacrifice everything to ensure victory for what was right, he puffed his chest in pride. After all, he must sustain the dignity of human life.

'In questions of religious faith, your opinions coincide with those of the Brahmo Samaj I hope?' Poreshbabu inquired.

'Truth be told,' confessed Binoy after a short silence, 'I used to believe earlier that I possessed religious faith of some sort, and I even quarreled with a lot of people on these issues. But now I have understood with certainty that in my life, the quality of spiritual faith remains imperfectly developed. This I have realized from observing you. I have never felt a true need for religion in my life and have developed no true belief in dharma. Therefore, all these days, I have used my imagination and debating skills to create fine arguments, reducing our community's religious practices to mere rhetoric. I never need to consider which form of faith is true; the faith that brings victory to me is the one I have propagated. The harder it is to prove, the greater my pride in proving it. Even now, I can't say whether spiritual belief will ever take root in my mind in a perfectly true and natural way, but given favourable circumstances and good example, I'm certainly likely to advance in that direction. At least, I shall be spared the degradation of forever carrying the insignia of something that inwardly perturbs my intellect.'

As he spoke to Poreshbabu, Binoy began to concretize the arguments favouring his own present situation. He spoke with much enthusiasm as if after long debate he had arrived at this firm, definite conclusion. Still Poreshbabu urged him to take some more time to consider. Imagining that Poreshbabu had doubts about the firmness of his resolve, Binoy grew even more obdurate. He reiterated that his thoughts had arrived at a point beyond all doubt, that there was no likelihood of his wavering in the slightest. Neither side mentioned the subject of his marriage to Lalita.

Borodasundari now entered the room to perform some

household chore. Completing the task at hand, she prepared to leave the room as if Binoy was not present there. Binoy had expected Poreshbabu to immediately send for Borodasundari to tell her the latest news. But Poreshbabu said nothing at all. Actually, he had not even judged the time ripe for disclosing the matter, still keen to keep it concealed from everyone. But when Borodasundari, exuding contempt and rage against Binoy, was about to leave the room, Binoy could not contain himself. With bent head he touched Borodasundari's feet as she was about to depart, and said:

'I have come to you all today with a request to join the Brahmo Samaj. I'm unworthy, but I depend upon all of you to make me worthy.' Hearing this, the astonished Borodasundari turned around, and slowly came into the room. She looked questioningly at Poreshbabu.

'Binoy requests intitiation,' Poreshabu informed her.

Hearing this, Borodasundari felt the triumph of victory indeed, but why was she not completely happy? Inwardly, she keenly desired that this time, Poreshbabu should really learn a lesson. Having repeatedly and vehemently predicted that her husband would have cause for deep remorse, she was privately losing patience with Poreshbabu for not being sufficiently perturbed at the turmoil within their community. At this point, Borodasundari did not feel unalloyed pleasure in finding all their problems so nicely solved.

'If this proposal had come a few days earlier, all of us would have been spared so much humiliation and suffering!' she pronounced severely.

'Our pain, suffering or humiliation is not the issue here,' Poreshbabu reminded her. 'Binoy wants to be initiated.'

'Initiation, is that all?' Borodasundari demanded.

'The all-knowing One knows that your suffering and humiliation are also entirely mine,' Binoy assured her.

'Look here, Binoy,' cautioned Poreshbabu, 'don't trivialize

the fact that you are seeking initiation into dharma. I have told you this once before—don't take any serious step just because you imagine we are caught in a difficult social predicament.'

'True indeed,' assented Borodasundari. 'All the same, it's not his duty either to sit idle after getting us entangled in a net.'

'If one struggles instead of remaining still, the knots in the net grow even tighter,' countered Poreshbabu. 'Not that action is itself a duty; often, our greatest duty is to do nothing at all.'

'That may be true,' said Borodasundari. 'I'm illiterate, not always able to understand everything properly. But I want to know what's been decided at present. I have lots to do.'

'I shall join the faith on Sunday itself, the day after tomorrow,' asserted Binoy. 'I hope Poreshbabu . . .'

'I can't perform an initiation rite where my family may expect to benefit from it,' demurred Poreshbabu. 'You must apply to the Brahmo Samaj.'

Binoy at once grew hesitant. He was in no frame of mind to apply formally to the Brahmo Samaj, particularly when so much had been said by the community about his relationship with Lalita. Did he have the humility, or the words, to write to them? When that letter was published in the Brahmo newsletter, how would he show his face in public? Gora would read that letter, and so would Anandamoyi. There would be no other background information accompanying that letter; it would only publicize the fact that Binoy's soul was suddenly thirsting for initiation into the Brahmo dharma. That was not entirely true after all. Unless this fact was seen in relation to other things, Binoy would be left with no shred of protection from shame. Observing Binoy's silence, Borodasundari grew anxious.

'But he knows nobody in the Brahmo Samaj,' she argued. 'We shall make all the arrangements ourselves. I shall send for

Panubabu right away. There's no time left, Sunday is the day after tomorrow.'

Just then they saw Sudhir pass by the room on his way upstairs.

'Sudhir, Binoy will join our Samaj the day after tomorrow,' Borodasundari called out to him.

Sudhir was delighted. Being secretly devoted to Binoy, he was greatly enthused to hear that he would become part of the Brahmo Samaj. Binoy's written English was so fluent, he was so well read and intelligent, that Sudhir used to consider it extremely inappropriate for him not to be a member of the Samaj. Having found proof that a person like Binoy was unable to remain outside the Brahmo Samaj, Sudhir swelled with pride.

'But what can we accomplish by the day after tomorrow?' he protested. 'The news would not have reached many people by then.' Sudhir wanted to proclaim Binoy's conversion to the general public, by way of example.

'No, no, it will be done this very Sunday,' Borodasundari insisted. 'Run along, Sudhir, fetch Panubabu quickly.'

As for the unfortunate wretch whose example Sudhir excitedly wished to publicize as proof of the Brahmo Samaj's invincibility, his heart was by then cringing in acute embarrassment. Seeing the outward appearance of something that he privately regarded as little more than mere rhetoric, Binoy grew desperate. As soon as Panubabu was sent for, he rose to take his leave.

'Wait a bit,' pleaded Borodasundari. 'Panubabu will be here in no time. He won't take long.'

'No,' insisted Binoy, 'please excuse me.' He was desperate to escape this confinement, for a chance to think things over carefully in private.

As soon as Binoy stood up, Poreshbabu arose as well. 'Binoy, don't do anything in a hurry,' he urged, placing a hand on his shoulder. 'Be calm, be steady, and think over everything. Don't proceed with such an important step in your life without fully understanding your own mind.'

'First, nobody thinks before acting!' protested Borodasundari, secretly very displeased with her husband. 'They create a mess, and then, once the situation becomes suffocating, you say, "sit down and think!" You people may think calmly, but we can't bear it anymore.'

Sudhir accompanied Binoy out into the street. He was restless, like someone longing to taste the food even before sitting down to a meal. He wished he could drag Binoy at once to his own circle of friends, to break the good news and begin the celebrations. But the onslaught of Sudhir's elation disheartened Binoy even further. When Sudhir proposed: 'Binoybabu, why not come with me? Let's go to Panubabu, the two of us together,' Binoy ignored his words and snatching his hand away, he left the scene. He had gone only a short distance when he saw Abinash hurrying somewhere with a couple of members of his group.

'Here you are Binoybabu,' exclaimed Abinash as soon as he saw him. 'Excellent! Come with us please.'

'Where are you going?'

'We are going to prepare the garden estate at Kashipur. A gathering will take place there for Gourmohanbabu's penance.'

'No, I can't get away now,' Binoy demurred.

'How is that possible!' protested Abinash. 'Do you realize, all of you, what a major event this is going to be? Else would Gourmohanbabu have made such a needless proposal? In today's world, the Hindu community must express its might. What an upheaval this penance of Gourmohanbabu's will create in the hearts of our countrymen! We'll invite great learned Brahman sages from all over the world. This will have a major impact on the Hindu community. People will realize

that we are still alive. They will understand that the Hindu
community is indestructible!'

Evading Abinash's allurements, Binoy went away.

~56~

When Borodasundari sent for Haranbabu and told him
everything, he remained gravely silent for a while, then said:

'It is my duty to discuss this with Lalita once.' When
Lalita appeared, Haranbabu put on his severest expression and
declared: 'Look here Lalita, you have arrived at a moment of
great responsibility in your life. Your faith on one side, and
your inclinations on the other—between these two, you must
choose your path.' Pausing, Haranbabu fixed his gaze on
Lalita's face. He was aware that this gaze of his, ablaze with
the fire of justice, made cowardice quail and deceit turn to
ashes. His radiant spiritual gaze was one of the precious
possessions of the Brahmo Samaj.

Lalita said nothing. She remained silent.

'Perhaps you have heard,' Haranbabu continued, 'that
either out of concern for your predicament, or for whatever
reason, Binoybabu has finally agreed to be initiated into the
Brahmo Samaj.'

Lalita had not heard this news before, nor did she express
her feelings upon hearing it. Her eyes lit up. She remained
still as a stone statue.

'Doubtless Poreshbabu is delighted at Binoy's compliance,'
Haranbabu observed. 'But it is for you to decide whether
there is any real cause for rejoicing in this. Therefore on
behalf of the Brahmo Samaj I request you now to set aside
your own wild inclinations and ask your heart, fixing your
gaze only on your dharma—is this any real cause for joy?'

Still Lalita was silent. Haranbabu thought his arguments

were working very well. 'Initiation!' he pursued, with
redoubled enthusiasm. 'Must I now explain how sacred is the
moment of initiation? Would you pollute that very idea of
initiation! Seduced by pleasure, convenience or attachment,
should we allow the untrue to enter the Brahmo Samaj and
invite deceit into our midst with pomp and ceremony! Tell
me Lalita, must your life be forever associated with this
history of the degradation of the Brahmo Samaj?'

Still Lalita said nothing. Gripping the chair handle, she
remained completely still.

'I have often witnessed how weakness attacks human
beings invincibly, using attachment as a loophole,' Haranbabu
continued. 'And I also know how to forgive human weakness.
But you tell me Lalita, can one for a single instant forgive the
weakness that attacks not only one's own life, but the very
foundation of a hundred thousand lives? Has Ishwar given us
the right to forgive such a thing?'

Lalita rose from her chair. 'No, no, Panubabu,' she cried,
'please don't forgive us. People the world over have grown
used to your attacks, but your forgiveness I think would be
too much for anyone to bear.' With these words Lalita left
the room.

Haranbabu's words made Borodasundari very anxious.
She could not release Binoy now, under any circumstances.
After many futile pleas, she ultimately lost her temper and
sent Haranbabu away. Her problem was that she had neither
Poreshbabu nor Haranbabu on her side. Nobody could have
imagined such an unthinkable situation. It was now time for
Borodasundari to change her mind again about Haranbabu.

As long as Binoy remained vague about the prospect of
initiation, he had been expressing his resolve very strongly.
But when he discovered that he must apply to the Brahmo
Samaj and that Haranbabu would be consulted in the matter,
he grew extremely perturbed at the threat of such open

publicity. He could not think where to go, or whom to consult. It even seemed impossible for him to approach Anandamoyi. Nor had he the strength to roam the streets. So he went to his empty home and lay down on the woodplank bed in the room upstairs.

It was almost dark. When the attendant brought a light into the dark chamber, Binoy was about to forbid him when he heard someone call from downstairs:

'Binoybabu! Binoybabu!'

Binoy heaved a sigh of relief, as if he had found water to quench his thirst in the desert. At this moment, no-one but Satish could have brought him solace. Binoy overcame his listlessness.

'What is it, bhai Satish?' he answered, jumping up from the bed and rushing downstairs without even putting on his shoes.

In his tiny courtyard, facing the stairs, he saw Borodasundari standing with Satish. Again the same problems, the same conflict! Flustered, Binoy led Satish and Borodasundari to the room upstairs.

'Satish, go sit in that veranda for a while,' ordered Borodasundari.

Pained at Satish's joyless exile, Binoy took out some picture books for him and settled him in the adjacent room, lighting the lamp there.

'Binoy, you don't know anyone in the Brahmo Samaj. Let me carry a letter from you, which I shall deliver personally to the editor tomorrow morning, to arrange everything so your initiation ceremony takes place this very Sunday, the day after tomorrow. You need have no further worries.'

Borodasundari's proposal left Binoy speechless. Under her directions, he wrote out a letter and handed it to her. He needed to take up some course of action, no matter what, so it would become impossible for him to retract or hesitate.

Borodasundari also left some hints about his marrying Lalita. When she had departed, Binoy began to experience a tremendous feeling of distaste. Even the memory of Lalita struck a rather discordant note in his heart. He began to feel that Lalita too had something to do with this unseemly haste on Borodasundari's part. Along with his own loss of self-esteem, his respect for everyone else seemed to diminish as well.

As soon as she was home, Borodasundari thought she would delight Lalita. That Lalita loved Binoy she had understood for certain. That was why their prospective marriage had stirred up such trouble within the community. At that time she had blamed everyone but herself. For a few days she had more or less stopped speaking to Lalita. So, now that a solution had been found, she was eager to take major credit for it, in order to achieve a reconciliation with Lalita. Lalita's father had virtually ruined everything, after all. Lalita herself had not been able to tackle Binoy. Nor had they got any help from Panubabu. Borodasundari had cut through all the knotty problems, all by herself. Yes, yes indeed! What a woman alone could accomplish was beyond the capacity of five men.

When she came home, Borodasundari was informed that Lalita had retired early tonight, as she was not feeling too well. 'I shall help her recover,' Borodasundari smiled to herself. Lamp in hand, she entered the dark bedchamber to find Lalita not yet in bed, but reclining instead in an armchair.

'Ma, where had you gone?' she demanded, sitting up at once. She had heard that Borodasundari had accompanied Satish to Binoy's house.

'I had gone to Binoy's place.'

'Why?'

Why! Borodasundari was privately rather annoyed. 'Lalita imagines that I am always working against her, as her enemy! How ungrateful!' she thought.

'See why!' she said, and held out Binoy's letter, letting it unfold before Lalita's eyes. As she read the letter, Lalita's face grew flushed. To publicize her own achievements, Borodasundari informed her with some exaggeration that extracting this letter from Binoy had been no easy matter. She could claim with confidence that such a feat was beyond the powers of any other human being.

Covering her face with both hands, Lalita fell back into her armchair. Borodasundari imagined she was too shy to express the intensity of her emotions in front of her mother. She left the room.

The next morning, when it was time to carry the letter to the Brahmo Samaj, Borodasundari found that someone had torn it to shreds.

~57~

As Sucharita was getting ready to visit Poreshbabu in the afternoon, the attendant announced a visitor, a babu.

'Which babu? Binoybabu?'

'No, a very fair, tall babu.'

Sucharita started. 'Bring the babu upstairs,' she said.

Until then, she had not even noticed what she was wearing or how she had draped her sari. But now, standing before her mirror, she found she did not like her own attire. There was no time to change. Hands shaking, she tidied her sari aanchal and her hair, then entered the room with a trembling heart. She had completely forgotten that Gora's collected works were lying on her table. Gora sat on a chair directly facing that very table. The books lay shamelessly, in front of his eyes; there was no means of concealing or removing them.

'Mashima has been anxiously waiting for you all these

days. Let me send for her.' With these words, Sucharita left
the room immediately after entering it. She could not find the
strength to converse alone with Gora. After a while she
reappeared, accompanied by Harimohini. For some time
now, Harimohini had been hearing Binoy's accounts of Gora's
convictions, devotion to duty, and way of life. Often, in the
afternoon, at her request, Sucharita had been reading Gora's
writings to her. Not that Harimohini completely understood
those pieces. Actually, they helped her to doze off. Still, she
could more or less gather that Gora was fighting in support of
the scriptures and social customs, against the present-day
disregard for rituals. For a modern, English-educated boy,
what could be more extraordinary, or more creditable! When
she had first seen Binoy in the midst of a Brahmo family, it
was he who had brought her a great deal of comfort. But
having gradually grown accustomed to this, when she began
to observe Binoy in her own household, what she noticed
with great displeasure were the lapses in his observance of
restrictions. It was because she had come to depend heavily on
Binoy that her rejection of him grew more pronounced with
each passing day. That was why she had been so eagerly
awaiting Gora's arrival.

As soon as she saw Gora, Harimohini was utterly amazed.
Here was a Brahman indeed! Like the sacrificial hom fire
personified. Like Lord Shiva with his white body. She felt
such a surge of devotion within, that when Gora touched her
feet in obeisance, Harimohini was embarrassed to accept his
pranam.

'I have heard a lot about you, baba!' Harimohini told him.
'Are you Gour? Gour indeed, so fair! I'm reminded of that
kirtan song:

With moon's ambrosia and sandal paste,
O who has polished Gora's form . . .

Today I see it with my own eyes. How did they have the heart to throw you jail, I wonder!'

'If people like you became magistrates, rats and bats would nest in our prisons,' smiled Gora.

'No baba,' protested Harimohini, 'is there any lack of thieves and scoundrels in this world? Didn't the magistrate have eyes in his head? One only has to glance at your face to see you're no ordinary person, that you're chosen by the Almighty Ishwar. Must you be sent to prison just because prisons exist? Baap re! What sort of justice is this!'

'Magistrates look only at law-books when they apply the law, lest they confront the Almighty's image in the faces of human beings,' Gora replied. 'Otherwise, having condemned human beings to flogging, imprisonment, exile or the noose, could they enjoy sleep or the taste of rice?'

'Whenever I get a chance, I make Radharani read aloud from your books,' Harimohini informed him. 'All these days, I was waiting hopefully for the day I could hear all sorts of wonderful words from your own lips. I am an illiterate woman, and very unfortunate; I don't comprehend everything, nor can I concentrate on all things. But I'm deeply convinced, baba, that I shall learn something from you.'

Gora maintained a polite silence, without contradicting her.

'Baba, you must have a bite before you leave,' Harimohini persisted. 'It's been a long time since I fed a Brahman's son like you. Today, just taste what sweets are at hand, but you are invited to dine properly at my place another day.' When Harimohini went away to arrange some refreshments, Sucharita's heart began to race.

'Did Binoy come here today?' Gora began directly.

'Yes.'

'I have not met Binoy since, but I know why he came here.'

Gora paused. Sucharita also remained silent.

'You people are trying to get Binoy married according to Brahmo customs,' Gora continued. 'Is that a good idea?'

At this jibe, all the constraints of diffidence or shyness vanished from Sucharita's mind.

'Do you expect me to consider a Brahmo wedding improper?' she demanded, lifting her eyes to look at him directly.

'I have no small expectations of you, that's for sure,' Gora retorted. 'I expect much more of you than what may be expected from a member of some community. I can assert with great certainty that you don't belong to the category of labour leaders who care only about swelling the numbers of a particular party. It is my desire that you too should understand yourself properly. Please don't be misled by others into underestimating yourself. You are not merely an ordinary member of some party: this you yourself must realize clearly, within your own heart.'

Sucharita summoned up all her mental strength to remain alert and firm. 'Aren't you a member of some party too?' she asked.

'I am a Hindu. Hindus are not a party after all. Hindus are a community. So immense is this community, it is impossible to express its essence by confining it to any label. Just as the ocean can't be described by its waves, Hindus can't be described as a party either.'

'If Hindus are not a party, why do they resort to party politics?'

'When you try to kill a man, why does he try to defend himself? Because he has a living spirit. Only a lifeless stone would lie passive in the face of all assaults.'

'If Hindus take for an assault what I understand to be my faith, what would you advise me to do?'

'I would urge you that, since what you consider your duty

is a painful assault on the great entity called the Hindu community, you must ponder very carefully whether there is some delusion or blindness within yourself, and whether you have contemplated everything from all angles, in every way. It is not proper to cause such a great disruption, taking the customs of one's own party to be the truth, through sheer force of habit or out of laziness. When a rat begins to nibble away at a ship's hull, it goes merely by its own convenience or natural instincts; it does not realize that boring a hole through such a great refuge will cause far greater harm to everyone else than the little bit of ease it will gain for the rat itself. Similarly, you too must consider whether you are thinking only of your own party or of humanity as a whole. Humanity as a whole—do you realize the magnitude of what that signifies? How diverse are the natures, tendencies and needs that it encompasses? All human beings do not occupy the same position on the same trajectory—some confront mountains, some face oceans, others open fields. Yet no-one can afford to remain idle; everyone must move on. Do you want to impose your own party's sole authority upon everyone else? Do you wish to turn a blind eye, imagining there's no diversity among human beings, that everyone is born into this world only to enlist with the Brahmo Samaj? Those brigand races who believe it's best for the world if they vanquish all other races to extend their sole empire, who are too arrogant about their own power to admit that the distinctiveness of other races is of priceless benefit to the world, who spread only slavery across the world—how are you people different from them?'

For a moment Sucharita forgot all her arguments. Gora's voice, deep as thunder, swayed her entire soul with an extraordinary force. She forgot Gora was arguing about something, aware only that he was speaking.

'It is not your Samaj alone that has created the twenty

crore people of Bharatvarsha,' Gora continued. 'On what
grounds do you seek to utterly flatten out this vast Bharatvarsha,
by forcibly seizing the responsibility of decreeing which course
of action is suitable for these twenty crores, or which beliefs
and practices would ensure sustenance and strength for all of
them! The greater the hindrances you encounter in your
impossible attempt, the more angry and disrespectful you will
feel towards your own country, and the more your contempt
will alienate the very people you wish to help! Yet, the Lord
who made human beings so diverse, who wishes to preserve
their diversity, is the very One you imagine that you worship.
If all of you truly believe in Him, why are you unable to
recognize his decree? Why does pride in your own intelligence
and your own party prevent you from accepting its
significance?'

Observing that Sucharita was listening in silence without
trying to offer any reply, Gora felt sorry for her. He paused,
then continued in a gentler tone:

'Perhaps my words strike you as harsh. But don't view
me with hostility as a member of the enemy camp. Had I
perceived you as an enemy I would not have spoken to you
at all. It pains me to see your natural broad-mindedness
confined within the limits of a party.'

Sucharita's face grew flushed. 'No, no,' she protested,
'don't worry about me at all. Please continue what you were
saying, and I shall try to follow your argument.'

'I have nothing more to say. View Bharatvarsha through
your natural intelligence and natural emotions. Love
Bharatvarsha. If you see the people of Bharatvarsha as non-
Brahmos you will distort their image and regard them with
contempt, and constantly misunderstand them. You will never
get to see them from the perspective that allows one to see
them whole. The Lord has made them human; they think in
many different ways, act in many different ways, follow many

different beliefs and customs, but underlying all this is a basic humanity; within all this is something that belongs to me, to Bharatvarsha, something that, when viewed from a true perspective, will pierce its outward shell of pettiness and incompleteness to present before us the vision of a great, noble entity. It is infused with the spirit of long endeavour; in it I can see the ancient sacrificial fire still burning amidst all the ashes, and I have no doubt that this fire will transcend its petty location in place and time to cast up its flame at the centre of this earth. The people of this Bharatvarsha have been saying many big things for a very long time; they have accomplished many great tasks; even to imagine that all that has become utterly futile is to show disrespect for the truth, and that itself is atheism.'

Sucharita had been listening with bowed head. Now she raised her head and asked:

'What are you asking me to do?'

'Nothing,' asserted Gora, 'I only say you must understand that the Hindu faith has tried to nurture people of many attitudes, many views; in other words, the Hindu faith alone has acknowledged people as human beings, not as members of some group. The Hindu faith accepts the illiterate as well as the learned—and not just a single facet of learning, but the growth of knowledge in many dimensions. Christians don't wish to acknowledge diversity; they say there's Christianity on one side and limitless destruction on the other, with no shades of difference in between. Because we follow those Christians, we feel ashamed of the diversity of the Hindu dharma, failing to recognize that Hinduism strives to perceive the One through the medium of the many. Unless our minds break free of the fetters of Khristani learning, we cannot claim the glory of understanding the true nature of the Hindu dharma.'

It seemed to Sucharita she was not merely hearing Gora's

words but seeing them manifest before her eyes; she felt
Gora's contemplative gaze, fixed upon the distant future,
merge with his words. Forgetting all shame, forgetting herself,
she raised her eyes to Gora's face, which glowed with the
intensity of his emotions. In that face Sucharita saw a power
that seemed to realize the greatest resolves through its own
spiritual energy. She had heard many philosophical discourses
from many learned and intelligent members of her community,
but Gora's utterance was no mere discourse, it resembled a
new creation. It was so tangible that over time it could
dominate one's whole mind and body. Today Sucharita beheld
Indra, the king of deities, armed with his thunderbolt; as the
words forcefully assailed her ears, shaking the very doors of
her heart, she felt flashes of lightning dance through her blood
from moment to moment. She no longer retained the strength
to determine how far her opinions coincided with Gora's.

At this juncture, Satish entered the room. Being in awe of
Gora, he avoided him and edged close to his didi. 'Panubabu
is here,' he informed her in an undertone.

Sucharita started as if someone had struck her. She grew
desperate to somehow push away, remove, suppress or utterly
erase the fact of Panubabu's arrival. Imagining that Gora had
not heard Satish's murmur, she quickly got to her feet.
Rushing downstairs, she confronted Panubabu.

'Please forgive me, but it will not be convenient for me
to speak to you today,' she told him directly.

'Why not?'

'If you come to Baba's place tomorrow, you may see me
there,' said Sucharita, without answering his question.

'Do you have visitors today, then?' Haranbabu inquired.

'Today I shall not have the time,' repeated Sucharita,
evading this query as well. 'Please excuse me.'

'But I heard Gourmohanbabu's voice from the street,'
persisted Haranbabu. 'He is here I suppose?'

Sucharita could not suppress this question. 'Yes he is,' she answered, blushing.

'All the better,' said Haranbabu. 'I needed to talk to him as well. If you are busy with something special, I can chat with Gourmohanbabu in the meantime.'

So saying, without awaiting Sucharita's consent, he began to climb the stairs. Ignoring Haranbabu's presence beside her, Sucharita entered the room and announced to Gora:

'Mashi has gone to prepare some refreshments for you. I'll just go to her.' She rushed from the scene.

Haranbabu solemnly took a chair. 'You seem to have lost some weight,' he observed.

'Yes sir, for some time now I was under treatment to make me lose some weight,' Gora replied.

'Indeed,' remarked Haranbabu, feigning concern. 'You suffered a lot.'

'No more than what's expected.'

'There is something I must discuss with you concerning Binoybabu. Perhaps you have heard that he is preparing to join the Brahmo Samaj next Sunday.'

'No, I had not heard.'

'Do you consent to it?'

'Binoy did not seek my consent after all.'

'Do you think Binoy is willing to receive this initiation out of genuine conviction?'

'Since he has agreed to receive initiation, your question is utterly redundant.'

'When our instincts grow powerful, we have no time to think about our convictions. You know what human nature is like.'

'No,' Gora declared. 'I don't engage in needless discussions on human nature.'

'We don't share the same opinions, or the same community, but I have a high regard for you. I know for sure that whatever you believe in, whether true or false, no temptation can divert you from your convictions. Yet . . .'

'What is the value of that little shred of respect you have retained for me,' interrupted Gora, 'that it would be such a great loss for Binoy to be deprived of it! Indeed there are good and bad things in this world, but while you may evaluate them if you wish according to your respect or disrespect for them, you can't tell the rest of the world to accept your judgement.'

'Very well, we need not resolve this matter immediately. But I ask you—won't you oppose Binoy's attempts to marry into Poreshbabu's family?'

'Haranbabu,' protested Gora, flushing, 'how can I discuss such things about Binoy with you? Given your constant awareness of human nature, you should also have realized that Binoy is my friend, not yours.'

'I brought up the subject because it concerns the Brahmo Samaj, or else . . .'

'But I have nothing to do with the Brahmo Samaj, so what do I care about your anxieties!'

At this moment, Sucharita entered the room.

'Sucharita,' said Haranbabu, 'I have something special to discuss with you.'

Not that he needed to say this. It was only to show Gora his special intimacy with Sucharita that Haranbabu pointedly made this remark. Sucharita made no reply. Gora remained unmoved, showing no signs of getting up to give Haranbabu a chance for private talk.

'Sucharita, come into the next room for a moment,' urged Haranbabu. 'Let me just tell you something.'

'I hope your mother is well?' Sucharita asked Gora, without answering Haranbabu.

'I have never seen Ma unwell,' Gora responded.

'I've seen how easily she finds the strength to remain

well,' Sucharita observed. She remembered having met Anandamoyi while Gora was in jail.

At this point, Haranbabu suddenly picked up a book from the table, and opening it, he first glanced at the author's name before turning pages at random and running his eyes over them. Sucharita flushed. Knowing what book it was, Gora smiled faintly to himself.

'Gourmohanbabu,' asked Haranbabu, 'are these your childhood writings?'

'That childhood is not yet over,' smiled Gora. 'For some living beings, infancy is short-lived, but for others it lasts rather long.'

'Gourmohanbabu,' declared Sucharita, 'Your refreshments should be ready by now. Let's go into the other room then. Mashi will not emerge before Panubabu. Maybe she's waiting for you.' This last statement was deliberately directed against Haranbabu. She had borne a lot on this occasion, and could not help retaliating in some measure.

Gora rose to his feet.

'I'll wait, then,' declared Haranbabu, undaunted.

'Why wait in vain?' Sucharita objected. 'After this I won't have the time.'

Still Haranbabu did not arise. Sucharita and Gora left the room. Seeing Gora in this house, and observing Sucharita's behaviour towards him, Haranbabu's heart was up in arms. Would Sucharita lose her footing in the Brahmo Samaj in this fashion! Was there nobody to protect her! This must be prevented, at any cost. Snatching a piece of paper, Haranbabu began composing a letter to Sucharita. He had a few fixed notions, one being that when he reprimanded people in the name of truth, his fiery words could not fail to have effect. He did not even consider that apart from words alone, there was also something called the human heart.

After a long chat with Harimohini at the end of his meal,

when Gora entered Sucharita's room to collect his walking stick, it was almost dark. A lamp had been lit on Sucharita's desk. Haranbabu had departed. A letter addressed to Sucharita lay upon the table, prominently visible immediately upon entering the room. The sight of that letter instantly hardened Gora's heart. It was undoubtedly written by Haranbabu. Gora knew Haranbabu had a special claim upon Sucharita; he was unaware that this claim had been eroded in any way. Today, when Satish whispered to Sucharita about Haranbabu's arrival, and the startled Sucharita rushed downstairs to reappear shortly with Haranbabu in tow, Gora's heart had been struck by a very discordant note. Subsequently, when Sucharita left Haranbabu alone in the room and took Gora downstairs for refreshments, her behaviour certainly appeared rude, but thinking that intimacy might permit such conduct, Gora had taken it for the sign of a close relationship. After that, the sight of that letter lying on the table was a heavy blow for Gora. A letter is a very mysterious thing. Because it displays only the name on the outside, concealing everything else within, it can torment a person needlessly.

'I shall come tomorrow,' Gora announced, glancing at Sucharita's face.

'Very well,' replied Sucharita, with downcast eyes.

On the point of leaving, Gora paused suddenly.

'Your place is in the solar system of Bharatvarsha,' he declared. 'You belong to my own country; we can never allow some comet to sweep you away on its tail, whirling you off into empty space! Where you truly belong, there must I place you firmly on a pedestal, only then shall I desist. These people have persuaded you that your notion of truth, your dharma, would forsake you in that place; but I tell you clearly, your notion of truth, your dharma, does not merely consist of opinions or words belonging to you or a few others. It is entangled in every direction with the strands of countless lives; one cannot uproot it from the forest and transplant it into a flowerpot at will. If you wish to keep it sparkling and alive, to bring it to complete fulfillment, then you must assume the position assigned to you long before your birth, at the heart of popular society. You cannot afford to say: "I am unfamiliar with it, unrelated to it in any way." Should you say such a thing, your idea of truth, your dharma, your power, will fade like a shadow. If your opinions drag you away from the position assigned to you by the Almighty, whatever that position may be, I can convince you for sure that your opinions will never triumph. I shall come tomorrow.'

With these words, Gora left the scene. For a long time afterward, the air inside the room seemed to resonate. Sucharita remained motionless as a statue.

~58~

'Look Ma,' Binoy told Anandamoyi, 'Truth be told, whenever I have offered pranam in obeisance to an idol, I have inwardly felt a strange sense of shame, which I have suppressed. On the contrary, I have written wonderful essays in praise of idol worship. But to tell you the truth, when I have bowed at the idol's feet, my inner heart has not acquiesced.'

'As if your heart is so simple!' declared Anandamoyi. 'You cannot take a broad view of anything. In every matter, you look for finer nuances. That is why you can never shed your fussiness.'

'True indeed. Because I have such fineness of perception, I can use hair-splitting arguments to prove even what I don't believe in. I deceive myself as well as others as it suits me. All my arguments about religion so far have been prompted not by faith but by partisanship.'

'That's what happens when one has no real attachment to

dharma,' Anandmoyi asserted. 'Then even dharma, like family, social prestige and wealth, becomes a matter of pride.'

'Yes, we no longer perceive it as dharma in general, but as our own personal dharma, fighting our battles for its sake. That's what I too have been doing all these days. Still, it's not as if I can completely deceive myself. Because I pretend faith where belief fails me, I have always felt ashamed of myself.'

'Don't I know that! From the fact that you all go to such extremes, beyond the ordinary, it is clear that you are forced to use many resources to fill the void in your hearts. Where faith comes easy, one need not go to such lengths.'

'That is why I have come to ask you whether it is good to pretend that I believe in something that does not inspire my faith,' said Binoy.

'Just listen to him! What sort of question is that?'

'Ma, I'm going to formally join the Brahmo Samaj the day after tomorrow.'

'What's this you say, Binoy!' Anandamoyi exclaimed. 'Where is the need to seek formal initiation?'

'That need is what I was trying to explain all this while, Ma!'

'Can't you remain within our community and still keep your faith in whatever you believe in?'

'To remain, I would have to resort to deceit.'

'Don't you have the courage to remain with us sans deceit? The members of our community will make you suffer, but can't you withstand that?'

'Ma, if I don't follow the dictates of the Hindu community, then . . .'

'If three hundred and thirty-three crores of opinions can prevail within the Hindu community, why should your opinions not be acceptable too?'

'But Ma, if members of our community were to say, "You are not a Hindu," can I still insist that "I am a Hindu"?'

'People in our community call me a Khristan, after all. In practice, indeed, I don't eat with them. But still, just because they call me a Khristan, I don't assume I must accept what they say. When I know something to be right, I consider it wrong to run away and hide myself on that account.'

Binoy was about to reply, but before he could say anything, Anandamoyi interrupted: 'Binoy, I shan't let you argue; this is no matter for argument. Can you conceal anything from me, after all? I can see you're trying to forcibly delude yourself on the pretext of arguing with me. But don't plan those false tactics in such a grave matter.'

'But Ma,' said Binoy, hanging his head, 'I have promised in writing that I shall accept my initiation tomorrow.'

'That cannot be allowed. If you explain to Poreshbabu, he will never urge you to proceed.'

'Poreshbabu has no enthusiasm for my initiation; he is not participating in the ritual.'

'Then you have nothing to worry about.'

'No Ma, the matter has been decided, and can't be reversed. Never.'

'Have you told Gora?'

'I haven't met Gora.'

'Why not?' asked Anandamoyi. 'Is Gora not at home now?'

'No, I hear he has gone to Sucharita's.'

'But he went there yesterday!' exclaimed Anandamoyi in surprise.

'He has gone there today as well.'

At that moment, they heard palki bearers approach the yard. Expecting the visitor to be some female relative of Anandamoyi's, Binoy went out.

Lalita came in and touched Anandamoyi's feet in a pranam. Anandamoyi had not expected her to come there that day, under any circumstances. Looking at her face in surprise, she

at once realized that Lalita had come to her because of some
problem concerning Binoy's initiation.

'Ma, I am delighted to see you here,' said Anandamoyi,
to give Lalita a chance to raise the subject. 'Binoy was here a
moment ago. Tomorrow he is to join your community. That's
what we were talking about.'

'Why must he seek initiation?' Lalita burst out. 'Is there
any need?'

'Is there no need, Ma?' asked Anandamoyi, astounded.

'I can't think of any.'

Unable to fathom Lalita's intentions, Anandamoyi stared
at her in silence.

'It is demeaning for him to suddenly seek initiation in this
way,' continued Lalita, hanging her head. 'Why is he accepting
such humiliation?'

'Why'! Didn't Lalita know why? Did she have no cause to
rejoice?

'Tomorrow is the date set for his initiation. He has given
his word,' said Anandamoyi. 'Now it is beyond his power to
change it, so Binoy told me.'

'In such matters one's word means nothing,' declared
Lalita, fixing her burning gaze on Anandamoyi's face. 'If
change is necessary, it must be allowed.'

'Ma, don't be shy with me,' Anandamoyi coaxed her.
'Let me be completely open with you. All this while I was
trying to persuade Binoy that whatever his religious beliefs, he
should not, and need not, abandon his community. I'm not
sure he himself is blind to the fact, whatever he might say. But
ma, you are not unaware of his feelings. Surely he knows that
he can't be united with you unless he leaves his own society.
Don't be shy ma, tell me honestly if that's true?'

'Ma, I shan't be shy with you at all,' said Lalita, raising
her head to look at Anandamoyi. 'I tell you I don't believe in
all these things. I have thought things over very thoroughly.
Whatever a person's religion, faith or community might be,

it can never be possible that people can only come together by erasing all those things. In that case, there can be no friendship between Hindus and Christians either. Then we might as well raise high walls and keep each community confined within its own separate fence.'

'Ah, your words make me very happy!' beamed Anandamoyi. 'That's exactly what I say. One person's appearance, talents and nature may not match another's but that doesn't prevent a union between two persons; so why should a difference of opinion stand between them? Ma, you have brought me great relief, for I was very worried about Binoy. I know he has surrendered his whole heart to you people; he could never bear it if his relationship with all of you were affected in any way. The Lord alone knows how it pained me to oppose him. But how fortunate he is! It is no trifling matter that you should so easily dispel such a grave threat to him! Let me ask you a question: have you discussed this matter with Poreshbabu at all?'

'No I haven't,' confessed Lalita, suppressing her embarrassment. 'But I know he will understand everything.'

'If he wasn't capable of that, from where would you have imbibed such intelligence and strength of mind? Ma, let me send for Binoy; you should come to a direct understanding with him. Let me take this opportunity to tell you something ma: I have seen Binoy since he was ever so small. He is the kind of boy about whom I can say emphatically if you all suffer any pain on his account, he will make that suffering entirely worthwhile. How often I have wondered, who is there so fortunate as to gain Binoy's hand! Now and then a proposal has come our way, but I have not liked anyone! But today I see that he is no less fortunate.' With these words, Anandamoyi chucked Lalita under the chin and kissed her own fingers in a gesture of affection. Then she sent for Binoy. Leaving Lachhmia in the room on some pretext, she went away to arrange some refreshments for Lalita.

Now there was no room for embarrassment between Lalita and Binoy. The demands of the difficult situation threatening their lives made them see their mutual relationship in natural and significant terms; no haze of emotion came between them like a coloured screen. Without any discussion, they unhesitatingly accepted, humbly and solemnly, that their hearts were united and that like the rivers Ganga and Yamuna the twin streams of their lives were about to merge at a holy junction. Society had not called upon them to unite; no belief had brought them together; theirs was no artificial bond. Aware of this, they perceived their union as a merging of dharmas, in a faith that was immensely simple, that did not squabble over small things, that could not be obstructed by any panchayat pundit.

'I can't bear the dishonour of your bending and belittling yourself in order to have me,' declared Lalita, her eyes and countenance aglow. 'I want you to stand firm exactly where you are.'

'You too must stand firm in the place where you belong,' Binoy responded. 'There is not the slightest need for you to displace yourself. If affection cannot admit difference, then why should difference exist at all in this world?'

That was the gist of what the two of them said to each other over nearly twenty minutes. They forgot whether they were Hindu or Brahmo. That they were human spirits, both of them, was the sole thought that blazed in their hearts like the steadfast flame of a lamp.

~59~

After his prayers Poreshbabu sat silently in the veranda in front of his room. The sun had just set. At this juncture Binoy arrived there, accompanied by Lalita. Prostrating himself, he touched Poreshbabu's feet in a pranam. Poresh was rather surprised to see the two of them arrive together.

'Come, let's go in,' he said, as there were no chairs at hand.

'No, please don't get up,' Binoy insisted. He sat down on the floor. Lalita, too, placed herself at Poresh's feet, a little way off.

'We have come to you together, the two of us, to seek your blessings,' declared Binoy. 'That will be our real initiation.'

Poreshbabu stared at them in amazement.

'I shall not take my vows in the Samaj in fixed words according to fixed rules,' Binoy continued. 'Your blessing is the initiation that will bend our lives in bondage to truth. It is at your feet that our hearts have prostrated themselves in reverence. It is through your hands that the Lord will grant whatever is best for us.'

For a while Poreshbabu remained speechless and still. Then he asked:

'You won't become a Brahmo then, Binoy?'

'No.'

'Do you want to remain within the Hindu Samaj itself?' Poreshbabu persisted.

'Yes.'

Poreshbabu looked at Lalita.

'Baba,' she said, sensing his feelings, 'I still retain my faith and always will. It may cause me inconvenience, even suffering; but I can never think that it would hinder my faith not to alienate and reject those whose beliefs and habits differ from mine.'

Poreshbabu remained silent.

'Formerly I used to think of the Brahmo Samaj as the only world that existed. Everything beyond it seemed a mere shadow,' Lalita explained. 'As if renouncing the Brahmo

Samaj amounted to renouncing all forms of truth. But of late, I have completely lost that feeling.'

Poreshbabu smiled wanly.

'Baba, I can't tell you what a great change of heart I have undergone,' she continued. 'Even if I share their faith, I am in no sense identical with the people I encounter in the Brahmo Samaj. I see no sense, now, in using the name of the Brahmo Samaj to call these people specially my own, keeping everyone else in the world at arm's length.'

'Can one make reliable judgements when one's heart is agitated for personal reasons?' asked Poreshbabu, gently patting his rebellious daughter's back. 'One needs a community to ensure the welfare of one's family line from ancestors to future progeny. That is no artificial need. Will you not think of your community, which bears responsibility for the far-reaching future of your would-be descendants?'

'But there is the Hindu community,' Binoy pointed out.

'What if the Hindu community does not take responsibility for you two, refuses to accept it?' asked Poreshbabu.

'We must take it upon ourselves to make them accept it,' declared Binoy, recalling Anandamoyi's attitude. 'All along, Hindu society has extended shelter to new communities; any religious community can belong to Hindu society.'

'In verbal argument we may represent things in a certain way, but it may not be borne out in practice,' Poreshbabu replied. 'Otherwise, could anyone willingly leave their old social world? To believe in a community that would use outward rituals to shackle people's religious thoughts to the same fixed position, we must become puppets for the rest of our lives.'

'If the Hindu community has indeed become so narrow, we must assume the responsibility of setting it free. If one can let in more light and air into the house simply by multiplying its doors and windows, nobody wants to demolish a well-built structure in a fit of rage.'

'Baba, I understand nothing of all this,' Lalita blurted out. 'I have not resolved to take responsibility for the advancement of any community. But I am so oppressed by injustice from all quarters that my heart feels suffocated. I should never tolerate all this with compliance. I don't even understand what's right or wrong, but, Baba, I can't accept this!'

'Wouldn't it be better to allow yourself more time?' suggested Poreshbabu gently. 'Your mind is restless now.'

'I don't mind taking some more time. But I know for sure that untrue rumours and unjust oppressions will keep on multiplying,' declared Lalita. 'That is why I am terrified lest, if things become intolerable, I end up doing something that might hurt you as well. Don't imagine, Baba, that I have not given the matter any thought. I have considered everything well, and concluded that given my habits and education, I may have to accept a great many constraints and sufferings once outside the Brahmo Samaj. But my heart does not shrink from that at all; rather, I feel a certain strength arise within me, a certain elation. My only anxiety, Baba, is lest some action of mine should cause you the slightest pain.' With these words Lalita began to gently stroke Poreshbabu's feet.

'Ma,' said Poreshbabu with a faint smile, 'if I depended solely upon my own intellect, I would be hurt by any action that contradicted my desires and beliefs. I can't say with conviction that the passion that possesses both of you now is entirely inauspicious. I too had once left home in revolt, with no thought for pros and cons. The attacks and counter-attacks constantly directed against our community nowadays are clear signs of the Lord's power at work. How do I know what He will create and how, through his process of breaking, making and mending things in various ways? What does the Brahmo Samaj mean to Him, or the Hindu community either? He perceives only the human element in us.' With these words, Poreshbabu closed his eyes for a moment, as if to steady himself inwardly, in the private recesses of his soul.

'Look here Binoy,' he continued after a short silence, 'In our land, society is completely entangled with religious beliefs, hence all our social practices involve religious rituals. Because outsiders to our religion cannot be allowed inside the boundaries of our society under any circumstances, there is no loophole for that purpose. I cannot think how you might circumvent this fact.'

Lalita did not understand him properly, for she had never witnessed the difference between the customs of other communities and her own. She assumed that their customs and rituals did not differ very much, on the whole. As if the relation between different communities resembled that between Binoy and her own family, where differences were not apparent. Actually she was not even aware that the Hindu marriage rites might pose any particular problem for her.

'Are you referring to the fact that our wedding ritual takes place before the holy stone, the shalgram?' Binoy inquired.

'Yes,' replied Poreshbabu, casting a glance at Lalita. 'Can Lalita accept that?'

Binoy looked at Lalita's face. He realized that her whole being was shrinking at the thought. In the heat of passion Lalita had arrived at a point that was unfamiliar and dangerous for her. This aroused extreme compassion in Binoy's heart. He must save her, bearing the whole brunt of the onslaught himself. It was intolerable to allow such a fiery spirit to turn back in defeat, and equally terrible that in her indomitable eagerness for victory she should bare her bosom to these arrows of death. She must be allowed to triumph, but must also be protected.

For a while Lalita sat with drooping head. Then, raising her face once, she looked pitifully at Binoy and asked: 'Do you really believe in the shalgram, with all your heart?'

'No I don't,' responded Binoy at once. 'For me the shalgram is not a deity, merely a social symbol.'

'But what you privately recognize as a symbol must be publicly acknowledged as a deity?' Lalita persisted.

'I shall dispense with the shalgram,' declared Binoy, glancing at Poresh.

'Binoy, you two are not considering everything clearly,' complained Poresh, rising to his feet. 'We are not speaking only of your views or someone else's. Marriage is not just a personal matter after all, it is a social act—how can we afford to forget that? Give yourselves some time to think things over. Don't make up your minds just yet.' With these words Poresh left the room and went out into the garden. He began to pace up and down there, all by himself.

Lalita paused briefly before she too left the room. Her back to Binoy, she said: 'If our desires are not wrong, and if they don't entirely coincide with the laws of a particular community, must we then hang our heads and turn back defeated? This I utterly fail to understand. Is there room for false behaviour in society, but none for conduct that is just?'

Slowly Binoy came up to Lalita. 'I am not afraid of any community,' he declared. 'If we two make truth our refuge, where can a greater community be found than the one we have created?'

Borodasundari stormed into the room. 'Binoy, you will not take initiation, I hear!' she demanded.

'I shall accept initiation from a guru worthy of the name, not from any community,' Binoy informed her.

'What is the meaning of all your conspiracies, all these deceitful acts!' cried Borodasundari, in a rage. 'Think of the mess you have created, fooling me as well as the Brahmo Samaj by pretending these last two days that you will be initiated! Did you not think even once of the disaster you will bring upon Lalita?'

'But all members of your Brahmo Samaj do not approve of Binoybabu's initiation,' protested Lalita. 'You have read the papers, haven't you? What is the need for such an initiation ceremony?'

'Without that how can the marriage take place?' Borodasundari demanded.

'Why not?' countered Lalita.

'Will it take place according to Hindu custom then?' Borodasundari asked. 'That may be possible,' said Binoy. 'I shall deal with the minor obstacles that remain.'

Borodasundari was speechless for a while. Then in a choked voice she said:

'Binoy, go away from here. Please leave. Don't come to this house again.'

~60~

Sucharita knew for sure that Gora would visit her that day. Since dawn her heart trembled inwardly. As if the joy of anticipating Gora's arrival was mixed with a certain apprehension. For at every step she was tormented by the conflict between Gora's pull in a certain direction and the direction in which her life had grown since infancy, roots, branches and all. So when Gora had bowed at the idol's feet in Mashi's room the previous day, Sucharita felt as if daggers had pierced her heart. She could by no means comfort her heart by telling herself: so what if Gora offers pranams, so what if such are indeed his beliefs? When she detected anything in Gora's behaviour that contradicted her basic religious beliefs, Sucharita's heart trembled in fear. What sort of battle had Ishwar flung her into!

To offer a good example to Sucharita, the proud novice in their faith, Harimohini led Gora into her prayer room on this occasion as well, and again Gora bent to offer pranams to the deity.

As soon as Gora came into her sitting room downstairs, Sucharita demanded: 'Do you feel any devotion for this thakur?'

'Yes I do indeed,' replied Gora with a little more emphasis than necessary. Hearing this, Sucharita hung her head in silence. Her humble, silent suffering wounded Gora to the heart. 'Look, I'll tell you the truth,' he hastened to clarify. 'I can't say for sure that I feel devoted to the deity, but I am devoted to patriotism. I believe in revering the object of the entire nation's worship through all these ages. I can never regard Him with venom like a Christian missionary.'

Sucharita fixed her gaze on Gora's face, preoccupied with her thoughts.

'I know it is very difficult for you to really understand what I'm saying,' Gora told her. 'For having grown up within a community, you people have lost the ability to view these things in a natural way. When you look at the thakur in your Mashi's room, all you see is the stone, but all I see is your Mashi's tender heart, full of devotion. Seeing that, how can I remain angry or indifferent! Do you think the deity who rules that heart is made of stone?'

'Is it enough to be devoted? Must one not consider the object of one's devotion?' Sucharita demanded.

'In other words you consider it a delusion to worship a finite object as divine! But must finitude be determined only by one's own time and place? Suppose a particular line in the scriptures arouses your devotion when you remember it; would you determine the significance of that line merely by measuring the size of the page on which it is inscribed or counting the letters of the alphabet in its words? After all infinitude of emotion is a much greater thing than infinitude of extent. That tiny little idol is more real for your Mashi than the boundless sky embellished with moon, sun and stars. It is because you quantify your idea of the infinite that you must close your eyes when you think of it; I don't know if that proves effective. But with open eyes one can find the infinitude of the heart in even the smallest things. If that were not accessible, how after losing all her happiness could your Mashi still cling to that idol? Is it possible to fill such a great void in one's heart casually, with a piece of stone! Without infinitude of emotion, one can't fill the emptiness in one's heart.'

Sucharita could not answer such fine arguments, yet nor could she accept them as true. Hence, her heart only resonated with a pain without language, without power of retaliation. Gora had never felt the slightest sympathy when arguing with his opponents. Rather, in such situations, his heart was aggressive as a beast of prey. But now Sucharita's silent defeat began to strangely affect his feelings.

'I don't want to say anything against your religious beliefs,' he assured her, softening his tone. 'All I have to say is, that the deity you attack as a mere idol cannot be known merely by seeing his image; only the person whose heart has found stability, whose soul has been satisfied, whose nature has found a refuge, would know whether this deity is clay or spirit, finite or infinite. I tell you, no devotee in our country worships the finite; the joy of their devotion lies in dispelling all constraints within the limits of the finite.'

'But everyone is not a devotee,' Sucharita pointed out.

'Who cares what someone who is not a devotee may worship!' countered Gora. 'What happens to a member of the Brahmo Samaj who is faithless? All his worship ends up in a bottomless void. No, worse than a void: partisanship is his deity, with pride itself for its priest. Have you never witnessed the worship of this blood-thirsty deity in your own community?'

'Do you speak from your own experience when you say these things about religion?' asked Sucharita, without answering his question.

'In other words,' smiled Gora, 'you want to know whether I have ever sought Ishwar. No, my mind has never been inclined that way.'

His words should not have pleased Sucharita, yet she could not help feeling relieved. She felt rather comforted that Gora had no right to speak assertively in these matters.

'I claim no right to offer religious guidance to anybody,' Gora admitted. 'But I also cannot tolerate it if all of you should mock the beliefs of my countrymen. You call out to our people: "You are foolish, you idol worshippers." But I want to call all of them to announce: "No, you are not foolish, nor idol worshippers, but wise, and devoted!" By professing my respect, I want to awaken the nation's heart to the greatness of our sacred philosophy, the profundity of our devotional tradition. I want to arouse its pride in its own riches. I shall not let the country bow its head in shame, nor make it blind to its own reality by generating self-hatred. That is my vow. That is also why I have come to you today. Ever since we met, a new idea haunts my mind, night and day. I had not thought of it before. I constantly feel that Bharatvarsha cannot be completely represented through the masculine perspective alone. Its existence will be fully realized only when manifest to the eyes of our women. I seem to be consumed by the desire that you and I should jointly keep the nation's image before us. As a man I may strive to death for my Bharatvarsha, but without you, who would ceremonially welcome the nation with a lighted lamp? If you remain distanced from it, the act of serving Bharatvarsha can never acquire beauty.'

Where was Bharatvarsha, alas! And where, far removed from it, was Sucharita! Where did he come from, this worshipper of Bharatvarsha, this delirious ascetic! Why, pushing all others away, did he take his place by her side! Why, ignoring all others, did he call out to her! Without any diffidence, brooking no opposition! Why did he say: 'We can't do without you, I have come to take you away, our yajna, this holy sacrifice, will not be complete without you'? Tears streamed from Sucharita's eyes, but she could not fathom why. Gora glanced at her face. She did not lower her tearful eyes before that glance. Like a dew-bedecked blossom, free of care, her gaze turned itself unselfconsciously upon Gora's face.

Before those unconstrained, undoubting, tear-flooded eyes, Gora's entire being seemed to tremble like a stone palace in the throes of an earthquake. With supreme effort he turned away, looking out of the window to regain self-control. It had grown dark. Where the alleyway narrowed, joining the main road, stars were visible against the stone-black darkness of the open sky. That piece of sky, those few stars, carried Gora's soul away tonight, to a place remote from all worldly demands, far, far away from the mundane routines assigned for this workaday world! Transcending the rise and fall of so many kingdoms and empires, far beyond the efforts and prayers of so many ages, that patch of sky and those few stars were waiting, in complete detachment. Yet when one heart called out to another from within the bottomless abyss, that wordless yearning from the solitary edge of the world seemed to set off a vibration in that remote sky, in those stars so far away. At this moment, the movement of traffic and pedestrians on the busy Kolkata streets appeared shadowy and immaterial to Gora's eyes. The hubbub of the city did not reach him at all. Glancing within his own heart he found that he too was silent, lonely and dark like that sky. There, it seemed, a pair of tear-filled, simple, sorrowful eyes had been gazing at him unblinkingly, from before the beginning of time, towards an eternal future.

'Baba, please taste some sweets before you leave.'

At the sound of Harimohini's voice, Gora started and

turned around. 'Not tonight I'm afraid,' he declared hastily. 'You must excuse me tonight. I'm leaving right away.' Gora rushed from the place without waiting for any more words.

Harimohini stared at Sucharita in surprise. Sucharita left the room, What was this astounding situation? Harimohini wondered to herself, shaking her head.

Not long after, Poreshbabu arrived there. Not seeing Sucharita in her room, he went to Harimohini and asked:

'Where is Radharani?'

'How would I know?' responded Harimohini, sounding annoyed. 'She was chatting with Gourmohan in the sitting room all this while. Now I suppose she's walking on the terrace by herself.'

'Walking on the terrace so late at night, in such cold weather?' asked Poresh in surprise.

'Let her cool down a little,' declared Harimohini. 'A bit of cold will not harm these girls of today.'

Because Harimohini was feeling upset that evening, she had not sent for Sucharita at mealtime. Sucharita too had lost all sense of time.

When Poreshbabu himself came up to the terrace, Sucharita felt very embarrassed. 'Come Baba, let's go downstairs,' she insisted. 'You will catch a chill.'

Back in the room, when she saw Poresh's anxious face in the lamplight, Sucharita felt deeply disturbed. Severing all her childhood ties, who was now drawing her away from the man who for so long had been both father and guru to a fatherless girl! Sucharita felt she could never forgive herself. When Poresh sank down on the chowki in fatigue, Sucharita stood behind the chowki to hide her uncontrollable tears, and began to stroke his grey hair.

'Binoy has refused to accept initiation,' Poresh informed her. Sucharita offered no reply.

'I had many doubts about Binoy's initiation,' Poresh continued. 'So I was not greatly upset. But from Lalita's tone, I can sense that she sees no obstacle to her marrying Binoy even without his initiation.'

'No Baba, that cannot happen,' Sucharíta suddenly exclaimed, very vehemently. 'Never!' She generally did not speak with such unwarranted urgency. Rather surprised at this sudden emotional force in her voice, Poresh asked:

'What cannot happen?'

'If Binoy does not become a Brahmo, what rites will be followed at the wedding ceremony?'

'Hindu rites,' Poresh declared.

'No, no,' protested Sucharita, vigorously shaking her head. 'What sort of things are we speaking of these days! One should not entertain such ideas at all. That idol worship should take place at Lalita's marriage, ultimately! I can never allow that to happen.'

It was because she felt drawn to Gora that Sucharita showed such unaccustomed agitation at the mention of a Hindu wedding. The fact of the matter, concealed within this agitation, was that she was holding Poreshbabu to a certain position as if saying: 'I shall not let you go. Even now, I shall not, by any means, allow my bonds with your community, your worldview, to be severed.'

'Binoy has agreed to dispense with the shaligram at the wedding ceremony,' Poresh informed her. From her place behind the chowki, Sucharita came forward to take a chowki facing him. 'What do you say to that?' he asked her.

'In that case, Lalita must leave our community,' she replied after a brief pause.

'I have had to think deeply about this,' Poresh told her. 'When a person comes into conflict with society, there are two things to be considered: of the two sides, who is just, and who is more powerful. Since society is undoubtedly more powerful, the rebel must suffer. Lalita assures me repeatedly that she is not only prepared for suffering, but also happy to embrace it. If that is true, how can I stop her unless I perceive something unjust in it?'

'But Baba, what sort of development will this be?'

'I know it will cause some trouble. But since there is nothing wrong in Lalita's marrying Binoy, since in fact it is justified, my heart tells me it is not our duty to accept the objections offered by the community. It can never be true that it is the human being who must always submit to social considerations. It is society that must constantly grow and extend itself for the sake of human beings. Hence I cannot bring myself to blame those who are willing to undergo suffering on this account.'

'Baba, it is you who must suffer the most on this account,' Sucharita reminded him.

'That is not a consideration at all.'

'Baba, have you given your consent?'

'No, not yet. But I must. Given the path Lalita has taken, who but I can offer her blessings and who but Ishwar can come to her aid?'

After Poreshbabu left, Sucharita remained stupefied. She knew how much Poresh privately loved Lalita. She had no illusions about the extent of his distress at the fact that Lalita was abandoning the prescribed path to enter a realm of such great uncertainty. Still, at his age, he was ready to support such a rebellion, and yet, how little bitterness he harboured! He had never displayed his own strength at all, yet how immense was the power that lay easily concealed within him!

Formerly, this aspect of Poreshbabu's nature would not have struck her as unusual, for indeed she had known him since childhood. But because Sucharita's whole inner being had endured Gora's assaults only a little while earlier that day, she could not help feeling, very clearly, the complete contrast between these two types of human nature. How tremendously Gora's own desires mattered to him! And with what overwhelming power he could impose these desires upon others! Anyone who accepted any sort of relationship with Gora must bow to his will. Sucharita had submitted that day, and even derived pleasure from it, feeling she had gained something significant from her self-surrender. But still, when Poresh, his head bent with worry, emerged slowly from the lamplight in her chamber into the darkness outside, it was after contrasting his image with Gora's youthful radiance that Sucharita inwardly offered up her special reverence at Poresh's feet. And for a long time she sat calmly, hands folded in her lap, motionless as a picture.

~61~

That day there was a great to-do in Gora's house, starting from dawn. First Mahim appeared, puffing away at his hookah.

'So Binoy has finally flown the cage, it seems?' he asked Gora.

Gora stared at Mahim in bewilderment.

'What's the point trying to fool us any longer?' said Mahim. 'After all the news about your friend is no secret anymore—it's being drummed all over town. Look here, look at this.'

Mahim handed Gora a Bengali newspaper. It contained a pointed article about the news of Binoy's initiation into the Brahmo Samaj that very day. The writer had deployed a great deal of harsh rhetoric to elaborate upon the fact that while Gora was in jail, some eminent members of the Brahmo Samaj, burdened with marriageable daughters, had secretly tempted this weak-willed young man away from the sacred Hindu community. When Gora denied any knowledge of this news, Mahim refused to believe him at first. Then he repeatedly expressed his amazement at such profound deceit on Binoy's part. Before leaving he added that when Binoy started equivocating even after clearly agreeing to marry Shashimukhi, they should have realized he was already headed for disaster.

'Gourmohanbabu, what a terrible situation!' cried Abinash, who now arrived, breathless and panting. 'This is beyond anything we could have dreamt of! That Binoybabu should ultimately . . .' Abinash could not finish what he was saying. So delighted was he at Binoy's ignominy that it had become hard for him to feign worry or anxiety.

In no time all the prominent members of Gora's group had assembled there. Binoy became the subject of a heated discussion among them. Most of them agreed there was nothing surprising in the present development for they had always noticed signs of vacillation and weakness in Binoy's conduct. In fact, Binoy had never surrendered himself wholeheartedly to their group. Many of them declared that Binoy from the outset had tried to somehow pass himself off as Gora's equal, a tendency they could not tolerate. Where all others, out of deference, had maintained an appropriate distance from Gora, Binoy would go out of his way to show his intimacy with Gora, as if he was different from everyone else, and on an equal footing with Gora. It was because of Gora's affection for Binoy that everyone tolerated such extraordinary brazenness. This sort of unbridled arrogance always led to such deplorable results.

'We are not learned like Binoybabu,' they asserted, 'nor do we boast of great intellect. But bapu, we have always followed a principle. We don't say one thing and believe in another. Call us fools if you like, or idiots, or what you please, but we are incapable of acting one way today and another way tomorrow.'

Gora added not a word to this discussion. He sat silent

and motionless. As the day advanced, after they had all gone away, one by one, Gora saw Binoy going up the staircase at the side without entering his room.

'Binoy!' called Gora, rushing out of his room.

Binoy came down the stairs. As soon as he entered the room, Gora said: 'Binoy, have I unwittingly wronged you in some way? You seem to have abandoned me.'

Having already decided that he and Gora would quarrel today, Binoy had come there with a hardened heart. But now, seeing Gora's dejected expression and sensing an aching tenderness in his voice, his mental defences crumbled instantly.

'Bhai Gora,' he exclaimed, 'please don't misunderstand me. Life brings many changes, and one must give up many things, but why would I give up a friendship?'

'Binoy, have you been initiated into the Brahmo Samaj?' asked Gora after a short silence.

'No Gora, I have not, and I shall not, either. But I don't wish to give the matter any importance.'

'What does that mean?'

'It means I no longer feel there is any need for a great hue and cry about whether I accept the Brahmo path or not.'

'What were your feelings formerly, and what are they at present, may I ask?'

At Gora's tone Binoy again braced himself for battle. 'Formerly,' he declared, 'if I heard of anyone converting to Brahmoism, I would be enraged and wish him to be specially punished for it. But now I no longer feel that way. I feel one can counter opinion with opinion and argument with argument, but to punish an intellectual act with anger is barbaric.'

'You will no longer be enraged at seeing a Hindu become a Brahmo, but seeing a Brahmo perform penance to convert to Hinduism, you will blaze with fury,' asserted Gora. 'That's the difference between your former state and your present one.'

'You say this because you are angry with me; your words are not spoken judiciously.'

'I say this out of respect for you,' Gora insisted. 'Things should indeed have turned out this way. It would have been the same with me. If adopting or rejecting religious beliefs were a superficial matter, no different from the colour changes of a chameleon, there would be no problem at all. But because it was a matter of inner significance, I could not take it lightly. If there were no hindrances, if one did not have to pay a penalty, why would a person use all his intellectual powers when accepting or altering an attitude towards some significant issue? One must prove to people whether one is acknowledging the truth solely because it is true. One must accept the penalty for it. To claim the jewel without paying its price—trading in truth is not such an artful business.'

There was no longer any check on the argument. Words met words like a volley of arrows, clashing in a shower of sparks.

'Gora,' Binoy asserted, finally rising to his feet after a long war of words, 'there's a basic difference between your nature and mine. All this while, it had remained suppressed; whenever it threatened to rear its head, it was I who forced it to subside, aware that you don't know how to compromise where you detect any difference. You just rush on, sword in hand. So to protect our friendship, I have always repressed my own nature. Now I realize that this was not beneficial and can never be.'

'What are you intentions now?' Gora inquired. 'Please tell me frankly.'

'Now I stand alone,' Binoy declared. 'That one must somehow pacify the monster called society by daily sacrificing human beings to him, and bear the yoke of his dominance by whatever means whether it kills one or not, is something I can never accept.'

'So will you set out to kill the stork-headed demon Bakasur with a straw, like the Brahman-infant in the *Mahabharata*?' taunted Gora.

'I don't know if my straw would destroy Bakasur,' retorted Binoy, 'but I can never accept that he has the right to chew me up, not even while he is chewing me up!'

'You speak in metaphors,' complained Gora. 'All this is hard to understand.'

'It's not hard for you to understand,' countered Binoy, 'accepting it is what you find difficult. You know as well as I do, that where man is independent in nature, independent in his religious beliefs, our society imposes meaningless restrictions even upon his food, sleep and rest. But you want to use force to obey this enforcement. Today I declare that I shall not submit to force from any quarters, in such matters. I shall accept the claims of society as long as it protects my rightful demands. If society does not count me as a human being, if it tries to make me a clockwork toy, I too shall not worship it with flowers and sandalwood. I shall consider it an iron machine, nothing more.'

'So, in short, you will become a Brahmo?' Gora asked.

'No.'

'Will you marry Lalita?'

'Yes.'

'By Hindu rites?'

'Yes.'

'Does Poreshbabu approve?'

'Here is his letter.'

Gora read Poresh's letter twice over. The concluding lines read:

I shall not mention my own likes and dislikes at all. Nor do I want to discuss your convenience or inconvenience. The nature of my beliefs, and the community to which I belong, are known to both of you. Nor are you unaware of the education Lalita has received since her childhood and the traditions within which she has been brought up. Knowing all this fully well, you have chosen your path. I have nothing more to say. Do not imagine that I have given up hope without thinking about anything or because I can't find a way out. To the best of my ability I have thought about it. I have realized that there is no religious cause to oppose your union for I have full respect for you. In such a situation you are not obliged to accept any objections raised by society. I just have a small thing to say: if you wish to exceed the limits of society then you must rise above society, be greater than it. Let your love, your conjugal life, not merely signal revolt but also contain elements of creativity and stability. It is not enough to suddenly express a certain daring in this single undertaking; after this you must let the thread of heroism run through all your life's works, or you will become utterly degraded. For society will no longer support you from the outside on an equal footing with the ordinary populace. If you cannot rise above the masses on your own strength, you must descend to a level beneath them. I remain gravely concerned about your future welfare. But I have no right to hold you back because of this concern. For in this world, those who have the courage to solve ever-new problems by the example of their own lives are the ones who raise society to greater heights. Those who merely follow rules only support society, they do not help it advance. Hence I shall not block your path with my timidity and my anxieties. Follow what you have chosen to believe, in the face of all adversities, and may Ishwar support you. Ishwar does not chain Creation to a single state of being; through ever-new transformations, he awakens it to eternal renewal. As the emissaries of that renewal, you two are forging ahead on a difficult path, lighting the way with the flaming torch of your lives, guided by the One who steers the entire

*universe. I cannot impose upon you the restriction of having
always to follow my path alone. At your age, we too had
once unmoored our boat and set it afloat in the face of a
storm, brooking no prohibitions. I do not regret that to this
day. Even if there had been cause for regret, what of it?
Human beings must err, be thwarted, suffer pain, but they
cannot remain still. They must surrender their lives to what
they understand to be right. In this way, the pure stream of
this world's river will remain ever-flowing and unpolluted.
To dam the flood forever, fearing it might occasionally erode
the river banks causing temporary damage, would bring
pestilence upon us; that I know for sure. Hence I offer my
devoted pranam to the force that draws you at relentless
speed beyond the boundaries of happiness, ease and social
law, and I leave you in His hands. May He make it all
worthwhile, all the shame, humiliation and separation from
kin that you have suffered in your lives. It is He who has
summoned you to this difficult path, and it is He who will
guide you to your destination.*

After reading this letter Gora remained silent for a while.
Then Binoy urged him:

'Just as Poreshbabu has given his consent, so must you,
Gora.'

'Poreshbabu may give his consent, for it is their current
that is eroding the rivershore,' Gora countered. 'I cannot give
my consent for our stream preserves the shore. On this shore
of ours are so many monumental creations, hundreds of
thousands of years old, that we can by no means declare that
only the laws of nature should apply here. We shall pave our
shores with stone, whether you blame us or not. This is our
sacred ancient city; from our perspective, it is not desirable
that new layers of soil should be deposited upon it every year
or that droves of peasants should plough this land, whatever
we may stand to lose. This land is for habitation, not farming.

Hence we don't feel dire shame when all you people from the agriculture department condemn the hardness of our stone.'

'So, in short, you will not recognize this marriage?'

'Certainly not.'

'And . . .'

'And I shall part company with all of you.'

'What if I had been a Muslim friend of yours?'

'Then it would have been a different matter. When a branch breaks off, severing itself from the tree, the tree can never take it back as its own, as before. But it can offer shelter to a vine that approaches it from outside; in fact, if the vine is cast down in a storm, there is nothing to stop the tree from offering it support once again. When our own dear ones become alien to us we have no choice but to abandon them completely. Hence all the ritual prohibitions, all the desperate attempts to rein us in.'

'That is why the reasons for separation should not have been so flimsy, nor the rules of separation so accessible,' argued Binoy. 'True, an arm once severed cannot be joined again but that's why the arm doesn't break off easily. Its bones are very strong. Will you not consider how hard it is for people to freely pursue their lives in a society where the slightest blow is enough to cause separation and where the separation becomes an eternal fact?'

'Such considerations are not my responsibility. Society is collectively involved in thought processes so vast that I don't even become aware of them. I survive on the belief that for thousands of years it has been thinking, and protecting itself as well. I don't worry about whether the earth is following its proper orbit around the sun or not, whether it deviates from its path or not, and so far I have not been let down despite my oblivion. I feel the same way about society.'

'Bhai Gora,' laughed Binoy, 'I too have been saying just such things in this fashion, all these days. Who could have known that I too would now have to listen to such words? I realize only too well that I must now pay the penalty for all my made-up speeches. But it's no use arguing. For today I have seen something very closely, something I had not observed before. I have understood now that human life flows like a great river; by the force of its own current, in unimaginable ways, it travels in new directions which it had not taken before. That is the extraordinary quality of its movement, and its unforeseen transformations are precisely what the Maker of our destiny intends. It is not a manmade canal, we cannot keep it confined within a fixed channel. Now that I have witnessed this directly within my own self, you can't beguile me with made-up arguments anymore.'

'A moth about to fall into the flame uses the very same argument, so I too shall not try in vain to persuade you now.'

'That's a good idea,' declared Binoy, rising from his chair. 'I'll be off then. Let me go and see Ma.'

After Binoy had left, Mahim slowly entered the room. 'Didn't make much headway, did you?' he asked, chewing on his paan. 'You won't, either. I have been warning you since so long that you should be careful, that there are signs of his going astray, but you ignored my words. If we had somehow forced him into marrying Shashimukhi at that time, these problems wouldn't have arisen at all. But *ka kasya paribedana*! And who am I speaking to? No amount of head-banging would help me convince you of something you fail to understand yourself. Now, isn't it regrettable that a boy like Binoy should defect from your group?'

Gora made no reply.

'So you couldn't make Binoy change his mind?' Mahim persisted. 'Let that go, but the question of his marriage to Shashimukhi has created too many complications. Now we can't afford to delay Shashi's marriage any further. You know the attitudes of our community: if they get after a person they won't rest until they have reduced him to abject misery. So we need a groom—no, have no fear, you won't have to act as go-between. I have taken care of that myself.'

'Who is that prospective groom?'

'Your very own Abinash.'

'Has he consented?'

'As if he wouldn't! He's not like our Binoy is he? No, whatever you might say, in your group, it's that boy Abinash who has proved truly devoted to you. He virtually danced for joy upon hearing that he would acquire a family connection with you. "This is my good fortune, my glory!" he cried. I asked him about money. He at once covered his ears and said: "Forgive me, but please don't mention such things." "Very well," I said, "I shall discuss these matters with your father." I went to his father as well, and found a big difference between father and son. The father didn't block his ears at the mention of money, not at all. Rather, he started saying such things, I almost had to stop my own ears. The son, too, I found to be extremely devoted to his father in these matters— regards his father as absolute divinity—so it will be no use asking him to mediate. This time liquidating my company assets will not suffice. Anyway, you too must discuss a few things with Abinash. A word of encouragement from you . . .'

'That will not reduce the sum of money to be paid,' Gora interrupted.

'I know that. When filial devotion proves useful, it becomes hard to control.'

'Is the wedding fixed?' Gora asked.

'Yes.'

'Have the date and hour been determined?'

'Determined indeed, for the full-moon night in the month of Magh this winter. That's not far away. The father has decreed he has no use for diamonds and gemstones but the gold jewelry must be very heavy. Now I must spend some days consulting the goldsmith on ways of increasing the weight of gold without adding to its price.'

'But why such haste? There's no fear of Abinash joining the Brahmo Samaj in the near future.'

'No indeed, but you people haven't noticed that Baba's health has deteriorated a great deal recently. The more the doctors object, the more rigid he becomes about his ritual restrictions. The sanyasi who now keeps him company makes him bathe three times a day and to add to that, he has started Baba on such a course of hathayoga that his eyes, eyebrows, breath, nerves, are all precariously jumbled up. It would be convenient if Shashi's wedding took place while Baba is still alive; I wouldn't have much to worry about if we could accomplish the act before Baba's pension savings fall into the clutches of Omkarananda Swami. I had even mentioned it to Baba yesterday, but found it was no easy matter. I have decided I must ply that rascally sanyasi with ganja for a few days to bring him under control and then get him to perform the rites. Know this for sure: middle class householders, who have the greatest need for money, will never get to enjoy their father's wealth. My problem is that someone else's father pressurizes me with demands for money and my own father takes to meditation at the very mention of money. Must I now drown myself with that eleven year old girl tied to my neck as deadweight?'

~62~

'Radharani, why didn't you eat anything last night?' asked Harimohini.

'Why,' said Sucharita, surprised, 'indeed I did!'

'As if you did!' persisted Harimohini, pointing out the food that still lay covered. 'There's your food, still untouched.'

Sucharita now realized she had indeed forgotten her dinner the previous evening.

'These are not good signs,' declared Harimohini roughly. 'From what I know of your Poreshbabu, I don't think he likes such excesses. He looks so calm and reassuring. Tell me, what would he say if he got to know all about your current inclinations?'

Sucharita was left in no doubt what Harimohini wanted to imply. At first, she felt momentarily embarrassed. She had never imagined that her relationship with Gora could be equated with an utterly ordinary man-woman relationship, bringing such false social aspersions upon them. Hence she was upset at Harimohini's insinuations. But the very next moment, she sat upright, casting aside the chores at hand, and looked Harimohini in the eye. Instantly resolving not to be coy about her relationship with Gora, she asserted:

'Mashi, you know Gourmohanbabu was here last evening. Because I was preoccupied about the subject of our discussion, I had utterly forgotten my dinner. Had you been present there last night, you could have heard us talk of many things.'

The things Gora had said were not quite what Harimohini wanted to hear. She wanted only to hear about devotional matters. But Gora's words did not ring with simple and interesting feelings of devotion. It was as if he was constantly confronting an adversary, against whom he must struggle. He wanted to persuade disbelievers, but what could he preach to the converted, after all? Harimohini was utterly indifferent to the things that enthused Gora. It caused her no inner anxiety if members of the Brahmo Samaj retained their own beliefs instead of merging with the Hindu community. As long as there was no cause for separation from her own dear ones, she was quite content. Hence she had not found her discussion

with Gora interesting at all. Subsequently, once Harimohini
sensed that it was Gora who had captured Sucharita's heart,
she found his conversation seemed even more unappealing.
Sucharita was completely independent, both financially and in
her opinions, beliefs and conduct. Therefore, Harimohini had
been unable to fully control her in any respect; yet Sucharita
was Harimohini's sole support in her declining years. It was
for this reason that Harimohini felt deeply perturbed if anyone
but Poreshbabu asserted any sort of claim over Sucharita.
Harimohini was haunted by the feeling that everything about
Gora was false, from beginning to end; that his real aim was
to attract Sucharita by some ruse. In fact, she even began to
imagine that Gora was chiefly tempted by Sucharita's material
assets. Identifying him as her prime enemy, Harimohini
mentally braced herself to oppose him.

Gora was not expected at Sucharita's house that day, nor
had he any reason to visit. But he lacked diffidence by nature.
When he chose a course of action, he did not pause to think
about it, forging straight ahead like an arrow. Now, when
Gora came to Sucharita's room at dawn, Harimohini was at
her prayers. Sucharita was tidying the books, notebooks and
papers on the table in the sitting room, when Satish came in
to announce Gora's arrival. Sucharita was not particularly
surprised. It was as if she had expected Gora to visit her that
day.

'So Binoy has finally abandoned us,' observed Gora,
taking a chair.

'Why? Why would he abandon us?' Sucharita asked. 'He
hasn't joined the Brahmo Samaj after all.'

'If he had gone to the Brahmo Samaj he would have been
closer to us than he is now,' declared Gora. 'It is by clinging
to the Hindu community that he is causing it so much trouble.
Better if he had made a clean break.'

'Why do you have such extreme views about society?'

demanded Sucharita, inwardly very hurt. 'Is it natural for you to place such excessive faith in the community? Or is it self-coercion, rather?'

'But it's coercion that is natural in the present circumstances,' Gora asserted. 'When treading on shaky ground, one must step more firmly with every stride. Because we are in a hostile environment, our speech and behaviour are somewhat extreme. That is not unnatural.'

'Why do you consider the hostile environment to be entirely unjust and unnecessary? If society obstructs the progress of time, it must suffer.'

'The progress of time is like a series of waves; it keeps eroding the soil. But I don't believe it is the soil's duty to accept such erosion. Don't imagine I have no consideration for the welfare of our community. It's so easy to pass such judgements that today even a boy of sixteen presumes to be a judge. It's harder by far to see everything as whole, and to view it with respect.'

'Does respect always yield the truth? It also leads us to blindly accept falsehoods, after all. Let me ask you a question: is respect for idol worship allowed too? Do you believe such things to be true?'

'I'll try and tell you the exact truth,' answered Gora after a short silence. 'I have from the outset taken these things to be true. I did not hasten to challenge them simply because they contradict European traditions and because some lowly arguments can be deployed against them. I am not committed to any particular religious pursuit. But I cannot blindly parrot the idea that deism and idol worship are identical, or that idol worship does not represent the culmination of devotional philosophy. In art and literature, even in science and history, the human imagination has a place. I do not accept that relgion alone denies a place to the imagination. It is in religion that all human faculties find their ultimate expression. This attempt to fuse imagination with knowledge and devotion in the form of idol worship in our country—hasn't it made religion more completely real for the people of our nation, compared to other nations?'

'Idol worship was practiced in Greece and Rome as well.'

'The human imagination that produced those idols relied more on aesthetic sense than on knowledge and devotion. In our country, the imagination is closely allied with knowledge and devotion. Whether you take our Radha-Krishna or our Hara-Parvati, they are not merely historical objects of worship; they contain elements of eternal human philosophy. That's why the devotion of a Ramaprasad or a Chaitanyadev found expression through all these idols. When did the history of Greece or Rome produce forms of devotion of such a high order?'

'You do not wish to accept any change at all in religious or social practices, in tune with changing times?' Sucharita inquired.

'Why would I not!' protested Gora. 'But change should not become a form of madness. Changes in human life follow a human course: a child grows gradually into an old man, but a human being doesn't suddenly change into a dog or cat, does he? The transformation of Bharatvarsha should follow the path of Bharatvarsha itself; if we suddenly adopt the path of British history, the whole process will be ruined and rendered meaningless. The nation's power and wealth are stored within the nation itself: I have dedicated my life to the task of making all of you aware of this very fact. Do you understand my words?'

'Yes I do. But I have never heard nor thought of such things before. I am like someone who takes time to recognize even the most obvious things when she finds herself in an unfamiliar place. Perhaps because I am a woman, my comprehension is not very strong.'

'Never,' declared Gora. 'I know many men, and have long been discussing these matters with them. Doubtless they have assumed that they understand me only too well. But I tell you for certain, what you see before your mind's eye today is something not one of them has perceived at all. Within you is a depth of vision that I had sensed as soon as I saw you. That is why I have come to confide in you everything my heart has ever wanted to say, all these years. I have laid bare my entire life before you, without the slightest diffidence.'

'When you speak like that I feel very perturbed. What you expect of me, how much of it I can offer you, what tasks I must undertake, how to express the overwhelming emotions arising within me—I can't understand any of these things. I feel afraid all the time, lest your trust in me should one day prove to be utterly misplaced.'

'It is not misplaced at all,' Gora insisted, his voice deep as the rumbling of clouds. 'I shall show you how great is the power within you. Don't be anxious in the least. It is my responsibility to draw out your worth. Depend on me.'

Sucharita said nothing; but wordlessly the signal was conveyed that she was completely ready to depend on him. Gora too was silent. For a long time, there was a total hush in the room. Outside in the alleyway, a hawker selling old utensils passed by their door, his brass vessels clanging.

Having completed her prayer rituals Harimohini was on her way to the kitchen. It had not even occurred to her that there might be any other person in Sucharita's silent chamber. But glancing into the room, when she suddenly saw Sucharita and Gora lost in silent thought without any small talk, she instantly felt anger streak like lightning, to her very head. Then she controlled herself.

'Radharani!' she called from the doorway.

When Sucharita arose and came to her, Harimohini said in a low voice: 'Today is the ekadashi, the eleventh lunar day, but I don't feel well. Go and light the stove in the kitchen. Meanwhile, let me spend some time with Gourbabu.'

Agitated at her Mashi's expression, Sucharita went away to the kitchen. When Harimohini entered the room, Gora touched her feet respectfully. Without a word she took a chowki. Lips pursed, she remained silent for a while. Then she asked:

'Baba, you are not a Brahmo are you?'

'No.'

'Do you believe in our Hindu community?'

'I do indeed.'

'Then what sort of conduct is this?'

Utterly failing to comprehend Harimohini's complaint, Gora gazed at her in silence.

'Radharani has come of age, and you people are not related to her after all. What do you have to say to her at such length? She is a woman and must attend to the housework. What need has she to involve herself in such matters? It distracts her mind. You are a learned man indeed, and across the land, people are all praise for you; but when was such conduct accepted in our country and what place does it have in our scriptures?'

It was as if Gora had suddenly received a great blow. It had not even occurred to him that such comments on Sucharita could arise from any quarters.

'She is a member of the Brahmo Samaj,' he observed after a short silence, 'and I have always seen her mingle in this fashion with everybody; so I thought nothing of it.'

'Very well, so she is a member of the Brahmo Samaj, but you have never supported such conduct after all. Your words are arousing the consciousness of so many people today, but if you behave like this, why should they respect you! You just chatted with her till late evening yesterday, but still you didn't finish what you had to say, and here you are again this very morning! Since morning today, she has entered neither larder nor kitchen. It didn't even occur to her to help me today, though it is the ekadashi. What sort of education is she receiving! There are women in your own households too. Are you giving them the same education, halting all their work? Or do you approve if someone else imparts such training to them?'

Gora had no answer to all these charges. He only said: 'Because she has grown up with this sort of training, I thought nothing of the matter.'

'Whatever her training, as long as she stays with me and as long as I live, such conduct will not do. I have succeeded in turning her around, to a great extent. Even while she was at Poreshbabu's, it was rumoured she had become a Hindu after mingling with me. Later, after moving to this house, I don't know what she began discussing with this Binoy of yours, and everything turned topsy turvy again. He is now going to marry into a Brahmo family. Anyway, I got rid of Binoy with great difficulty. After that, a person called Haranbabu used to visit. Whenever he came, I would take Radharani upstairs to my room, so he didn't find it encouraging. In this way, after much hardship, she seems to have changed her attitudes again, a little. After moving to this house she had again started accepting food touched by all and sundry, but yesterday I found that she had stopped. Yesterday she fetched her own rice from the kitchen and forbade the bearer to bring her water. Now, baba, I beg you with folded hands, please don't ruin her again, all of you. Having lost all my dear ones in this world, she's the only one I have left, and she too has nobody she can exactly call her own, except for me. Please leave her alone, all of you. They have so many other grown girls in their house after all—there's that girl Labanya, and Leela; they too are intelligent, educated. If you have anything to say, go say it to them. Nobody will forbid you.'

Gora was utterly stupefied. After a short silence, Harimohini resumed:

'Think about it: she must marry, she's old enough. Do you suggest she should always remain a spinster like this? A woman needs to perform her domestic duties after all, it is her dharma.'

In a general way, Gora had no doubts about this; indeed, he was of the same opinion. But even in private, he had never tried applying his own opinion to Sucharita. He could not imagine Sucharita as a housewife, busy with domestic chores in the antahpur of some middle-class home. As if she would always remain exactly as she was now.

'Do you have any thoughts about your bonjhi's marriage?' Gora inquired.

'I must think about it indeed. Who will, if I don't?'

'Can she marry into the Hindu community?'

'One must try. If she does not create any more trouble, and conducts herself properly, I can pass her off. I have mentally planned everything, but so far her tendencies were such, I could not summon up the courage to act. Now, these last couple of days, I find her attitude softening again, so I'm hopeful.'

It was not proper to ask too many questions, thought Gora, but he could not refrain from asking:

'Have you thought of a prospective bridegroom?'

'I have. The patra is rather nice—he's my younger deor Kailash, my husband's brother. He lost his wife some time ago. It's because he couldn't find a grown girl he liked that he's waited so long, otherwise could such a boy remain single! He will suit Radharani very well.'

The sharper the sting he felt, the more inquisitively Gora asked about Kailash. Among Harimohini's deors it was Kailash who had, by his own efforts, acquired some education, but about the extent of his education, Harimohini could not say.

In the family it was he who was reputed for his learning. When lodging a complaint with the authorities against the village postmaster, it was Kailash who had composed the entire document in such extraordinary English that a senior official from the post office had come there personally to conduct the investigations. At this, all the villagers had been amazed at Kailash's skill. But despite the extent of his scholarship, Kailash's commitment to orthodox restrictions had not flagged.

When Kailash's life-history had been recounted completely, Gora rose, touched Harimohini's feet, and left the room without a word.

As he descended the stairs leading out into the courtyard, Sucharita was busy working in the kitchen across the courtyard. Hearing Gora's footsteps she came and stood near the door. Gora went straight out, without glancing in any direction. Sighing, Sucharita resumed her chores in the kitchen. At the corner of the alley, Gora bumped into Haranbabu.

'Here so early in the day!' remarked Haranbabu with a faint sneer.

Gora made no reply.

'You have been there, I suppose?' asked Haranbabu, with another sneer. 'Sucharita is home, I hope?'

'Yes,' replied Gora and quickly strode away.

Going directly into Sucharita's house, Haranbabu glimpsed her through the open kitchen door. Sucharita had no escape route, nor was her mashi nearby.

'I just met Gormohanbabu,' Haranbabu informed her. 'He was here all this while, was he?'

Without answering his question, Sucharita suddenly became very busy with her pots and pans, as if she did not have time to breathe at that moment. But this did not deter Haranbabu. Standing in the courtyard outside the kitchen, he struck up a conversation. Harimohini came to the stairs and coughed two or three times, but that too had no effect. Harimohini could have confronted Haranbabu directly, but she knew for certain that if she emerged but once before him, neither she nor Sucharita would find any refuge in this house to shield themselves from this earnest young man's irrepressible enthusiasm. Hence if she glimpsed the mere shadow of Haranbabu, she would draw her sari aanchal so low over her face that it might have seemed excessive even when she was a young bride,.

'Tell me Sucharita, tell me, what direction have you people taken?' Haranbabu accused her. 'Where will it ultimately lead you? Perhaps you have heard that Lalita and Binoybabu are to marry according to Hindu rites. Are you responsible for that?' Receiving no response from Sucharita, he lowered his voice and asserted severely: 'You are the one responsible.'

Haranbabu had imagined Sucharita would be unable to endure the blow of such a major, terrible accusation. But seeing her wordlessly go about her chores, he adopted an even more severe tone and declared, wagging his finger at her:

'Sucharita, I repeat, you are the one responsible. Can you swear with your right hand upon your heart that the Brahmo Samaj will not hold you guilty?'

Silently Sucharita placed her oil-filled karahi on the stove, and the oil began to splutter.

'It was you who invited Binoybabu and Gourmohanbabu into your household,' Haranbabu continued. 'And you have encouraged them so much that these two have become more important to you people than all your eminent Brahmo friends. Can you see what that has resulted in? Did I not warn you from the start? What has happened today? Who will dissuade Lalita now? You think she alone will bear the consequences and the problem will blow over? Not at all. I have come to caution you today. Now it will be your turn. Today you must be secretly remorseful at Lalita's mishap, but the day is not far when you will not even feel any remorse at your own downfall. But Sucharita, there is still time to turn back. Just think, how once we two had met, in a state of such great and noble optimism; how brightly our life's goal shone ahead, how expansively the future of the Brahmo Samaj stretched before us. How many resolves we made and how much support we garnered, each day! Do you think all that is ruined? Never. The ground of our optimism remains ready for us, as before. Look back but once. Come back, just for once.'

A lot of greens and vegetables were sizzling in the boiling oil, and Sucharita was stirring them with her spatulate khonta as required. When Haranbabu fell silent, waiting to observe the effect of his call, she lifted the karahi off the fire, turned around and declared firmly:

'I am a Hindu.'

'You, a Hindu!' exclaimed Haranbabu, utterly dumbfounded.

'Yes, I am a Hindu.' With these words, Sucharita replaced the karahi on the fire and began to stir violently with her khonta.

It took Haranbabu a short while to regain his balance. Then he demanded sharply: 'Is that why Gourmohanbabu was giving you initiation, night and day?'

'Yes, it is from him I have received my initiation. It is he who is my guru,' Sucharita asserted, without turning her head.

Haranbabu had once considered himself Sucharita's guru. Today, if Sucharita had told him she loved Gora, he would not have felt so hurt. But to hear from her that Gora had wrested from him the right to be her guru was like being pierced through the heart by a stave.

'However great your guru,' he said, 'do you think the Hindu community will accept you?'

'That I don't know, nor do I know the community, but I know I am a Hindu.'

'Do you know that simply for having remained unmarried for so long, you have lost your caste status in Hindu society?'

'Please don't worry about that needlessly. But I tell you I am a Hindu.'

'Will you sacrifice at your new guru's feet even the training in dharma you received from Poreshbabu?'

'As for my dharma, the omniscient One knows what it is. I don't want to discuss it with anybody. But please understand, I am a Hindu.'

'However staunch a Hindu you might be, it will bring you no rewards, I tell you,' cried Haranbabu, now completely losing his patience. 'Your Gourmohanbabu is not like Binoybabu. Even if you declare yourself "a Hindu, a Hindu," until you are hoarse, don't entertain the slightest hope that Gourbabu will accept you. Easy enough to play guru to the disciple, but don't dream that he would therefore take you into his home to set up house.'

'What's all this!' flashed Sucharita, turning around at lightning speed, cooking completely forgotten.

'I say Gourmohanbabu will never marry you.'

'Marry!' exclaimed Sucharita, eyes blazing. 'Didn't I tell you he was my guru?'

'You did indeed. But I also understand what you didn't tell me.'

'Please go away. Don't insult me. From now on, I tell you, I shall never come out in your presence.'

'How can you come out, tell me, now that you are zenana, a woman in seclusion! A Hindu woman! One so pure the sun has never witnessed her beauty! Now Poreshbabu's vessel of sin is full to the brim! At this advanced age, let him taste the fruits of all his actions. I take your leave.'

Slamming the kitchen door, Sucharita sank to the floor and stuffing the end of her aanchal into her mouth, struggled to stifle her uncontrollable sobs. Face dark as thunder, Haranbabu left the house.

Harimohini had heard the entire exchange between the two. What she had heard from Sucharita's lips today was beyond her expectations. Swelling with pride, she said:

'Wouldn't it be so! Could all my heartfelt prayers to the Lord Gopiballav prove futile!' She immediately went to her prayer chamber and prostrated herself before her deity, promising to increase the quantity of food offered in the bhog ritual, from that day. So far, her devotion had been a quiet affair, a consolation for her sorrows. But now, as soon as they took the form of self-service, her prayers became extremely aggressive, fierce and greedy.

~63~

Gora had never spoken to any other person as he had done in Sucharita's presence. All these days, for the benefit of his listeners, he had merely spouted sentences, opinions and advice. But that day, it was his own self he presented before Sucharita, projected from deep within himself. At the joy, and not just the power, of this self-expression, all his views and resolves were filled with a spirit of elation. A feeling of grace enveloped his life, as if the gods had suddenly rained heavenly nectar upon his life's pursuit.

It was in the grip of this exultation that Gora had visited Sucharita every day for a few days, without thinking anything of it. But now, Harimohini's words made him suddenly remember that he had once scolded and taunted Binoy severely for a similar infatuation. Now, realizing he had himself arrived at the same state without his own knowledge, he was startled.

Like a person suddenly jolted awake as he sleeps uncovered in an unfamiliar place, Gora summoned up all his strength to become alert. He had always preached that while many powerful races in the world had been utterly destroyed, Bharatvarsha had survived all adversities through all these centuries, only by firmly adhering to its principles. Gora would not permit any slackening of these principles anywhere. According to him, all else in Bharatvarsha was going to the dogs, but it was beyond the power of any oppressive ruler to touch the holy spirit that Bharatvarsha had sustained, permeating all these harsh restrictive practices. As long as we remain under the yoke of an alien race, we must firmly adhere to our principles. This is not the time to think about right and wrong. A person swept away by a lethal current clings to whatever support he finds, without considering whether it is beautiful or ugly. Gora had said this all along, and was expected to say the same thing on that day as well. But when Harimohini cast aspersions on Gora's own conduct, the king elephant was wounded with the proverbial goad.

When Gora reached home, Mahim was inhaling tobacco, barebodied, on a bench he had placed on the street, just in front of the entrance. His office was closed for the day. He followed Gora in.

'Just a minute Gora,' he called, 'I have something to say.'

Taking Gora to his own room, Mahim said: 'Don't be angry bhai, but let me inquire first if you have caught a touch of Binoy's illness? Your visits to that place have grown very frequent, I must say!'

'You have nothing to fear,' declared Gora, flushing.

'From the signs, it's hard to tell. You think it is a morsel to be easily swallowed, before you return home as usual. But within it the fishhook lies concealed, as you would realize from your friend's predicament. Arré, where are you going? I haven't come to the main point yet! Binoy's marriage to a

Brahmo girl is completely certain, I hear. But once that happens, we can't have any truck with him, let me inform you beforehand.'

'No indeed,' Gora assented.

'But if Ma creates problems, it won't be easy,' warned Mahim. 'We are simple householders, harried by the burden of marrying off our daughters. If on top of that you install the Brahmo Samaj in our midst, I too will have to uproot myself from this place.'

'No, that will never happen,' Gora declared.

'The marriage proposal for Shashi is taking shape. Our behai, her prospective father-in-law, will not be satisfied without extracting gold worth more than the girl he's taking into his household, for he knows that human beings are perishable goods, while gold lasts much longer. He is more interested in the chaser than in the medicine. Behai is an inadequate name for him, because he is utterly behaya, without shame. It may cost me some money, but from this man I have learnt a lot that will stand me in good stead when I get my son married. I felt very tempted to be reborn into the present age, and using my father as go-between, arrange my own marriage according to the rules, to make one hundred percent capital out of being born a male! That's what manhood is all about! To utterly ruin the bride's father. No mean achievement, is it! Anyway, I can't find the enthusiasm, bhai, to join you night and day in celebrating the Hindu community's triumph. My voice fails me. All this has left me completely exhausted. My Tinkori is only fourteen months old: having produced a daughter at the very outset, my wife has taken very long to rectify her mistake. Anyway, Gora, please keep the Hindu community alive, all of you, until my son is married. After that, whether the people of this country become Muslims or Christians, I'll have nothing to say.'

'That's why I was saying,' Mahim added, when Gora rose

to his feet, 'it won't be appropriate to invite your Binoy to
Shashi's wedding celebrations. We can't let him create a fuss
all over again, about all this. Please caution your mother
beforehand.'

Approaching his mother's room, Gora saw Anandamoyi
on the floor, with her spectacles on, making some sort of list
in an exercise book. Seeing Gora, she removed her glasses,
closed the notebook, and said:

'Come and join me.'

When he had found a place to sit, she said: 'I need to
consult you on something. You have heard about Binoy's
marriage, haven't you?'

Gora remained silent.

'Binoy's kaka, his father's younger brother, is displeased,'
Anandamoyi continued. 'None of them will attend. It is also
doubtful if this wedding can take place in Poreshbabu's house.
Binoy himself must make all the arrangements. So I suggest –
since the ground floor of our house, on the northern side, has
been rented out and the tenants on the first floor have moved
out as well—that if we arrange for the wedding ceremony on
that upper floor, it might be convenient.'

'How would it be convenient?' Gora enquired.

'Who will supervise everything if I am not present at the
wedding?' Anandamoyi pointed out. 'Binoy will be in a fix. If
the wedding takes place there, I can arrange everything from
home, without any trouble.'

'That's not possible, Ma!'

'Why not? I have persuaded the one in charge.'

'No Ma, I tell you this wedding cannot take place here.
Please believe me.'

'Why, Binoy is not marrying according to their customs
after all!'

'Those are mere arguments. You can't use legal arguments
with the communnity. Binoy may do as he pleases, but we

cannot accept this marriage. There is no dearth of houses in Kolkata. He owns a house himself, after all.'

Houses were there aplenty, as Anandamoyi was aware. But it rankled in her heart that Binoy, abandoned by relatives, friends and everybody else, should somehow undergo the wedding ritual in his own home, like some godforsaken wretch. Therefore she had privately decided to organize the wedding ceremony in the part of their house set aside for renting out. Thus, without opposing their community, she could have enjoyed the satisfaction of arranging the auspicious ritual in their own home.

Seeing that Gora was firmly against the idea, she remarked: 'If all of you are so averse to this suggestion, we must rent other premises. It will put a great strain upon me, though. But never mind, if this option is impossible, what use dwelling upon it!'

'Ma, you ought not to participate in this ceremony,' Gora objected.

'What's this Gora, how can you say such a thing! If I don't participate in our own Binoy's wedding ceremony, then who will!'

'That is simply not possible, Ma!'

'Gora, you and Binoy may not see eye to eye on some things, but must we therefore behave like his enemies?'

'Ma, that is an unfair thing to say!' protested Gora. 'It brings me no joy that I can't join in the merriment of Binoy's wedding. How dear Binoy is to me, you know better than anyone else. But Ma, this is not a question of love; it has nothing to do with friendship or enmity. Binoy has chosen this course, knowing its consequences fully well. We have not deserted him, it is he who has deserted us. Hence the present estrangement will not hurt him beyond his expectations.'

'Gora, it's true Binoy knows he will have no connection with you where this wedding is concerned. But surely he also

knows I can never abandon him on this auspicious occasion. If
Binoy imagined I would not receive his bride with my blessings,
he could never have gone ahead with this wedding, not if it
cost him his life. Don't I know Binoy's mind!' Anandamoyi
wiped away a tear from the corner of her eye. This stirred up
the deep, painful feelings for Binoy that Gora nursed in his
heart.

'Ma, you belong to a community and you are indebted to
them,' he insisted. 'That's something you must bear in mind.'

'Gora, I have told you repeatedly that my links with the
community have long been severed. That is why the community
disdains me, and I too keep my distance.'

'Ma, these words of yours wound me most deeply.'

'Bachha, Ishwar knows it is beyond my powers to protect
you from the pain of this blow,' replied Anandamoyi, her
tender, tearful gaze seeming to caress every part of Gora's
body.

'Then let me tell you what I must do,' declared Gora,
rising to his feet. 'I shall go to Binoy and tell him not to widen
the gulf between you and the community by involving you in
his wedding plans. For that would be extremely unfair and
selfish on his part.'

'Very well, do what you can,' smiled Anandamoyi. 'Go
tell him, and I'll handle what follows.'

After Gora had left, Anandamoyi thought for a long time.
Then she slowly arose and went to her husband's quarters.
Tonight being ekadashi, there were no arrangements for
Krishnadayal to cook for himself. He had found a new Bengali
translation of *Gherandasamhita*, which he was reading, seated
on a deerskin. Seeing Anandamoyi, he grew agitated. Keeping
a suitable distance from him she knelt on the threshold.

'Look, this is very unfair,' she declared.

Krishnadayal was beyond worldly things like fairness or
unfairness. So it was with indifference that he asked:

'What is so unfair?'

'We ought not to keep Gora deluded for a single day longer. Things are getting out of hand.'

This had occurred to Krishnadayal the day Gora had spoken of penance. Subsequently, busy with sundry yogic practices, he had not found the time to think about it.

'There is talk of getting Shashimukhi married,' Anandamoyi told him. 'Perhaps it will happen soon, this coming month of Phalgun. Previously, whenever any community ritual has taken place in our house, I have always taken Gora elsewhere on some pretext or other. So far, no major ritual has taken place either. But now that Shashi's wedding is due, tell me what I should do with Gora. The wrong we have done him becomes more serious with each passing day. Every day, morning and evening, I beg the Almighty's forgiveness with folded hands. Let me bear any punishment He wishes to inflict, but I am constantly afraid that we can't hold out any longer, that there will be trouble with Gora. Please give me permission now, let me frankly disclose the whole truth to him, whatever misfortune it may bring upon me.'

What sort of hurdle had Indra, king of gods, cast in Krishnadayal's way, just to disrupt his holy pursuits! These pursuits, too, had grown very intense of late. He was accomplishing impossible feats with his breathing, and his diet had also gradually dwindled to such frugal proportions, it would not be long before he achieved his resolve to flatten his abdomen until his stomach touched his back. What a nuisance all this was, at such a juncture!

'Are you mad?' Krishnadayal demanded. 'If these facts become public now, I shall have to offer all sorts of explanations. My pension will be stopped for sure, and maybe even the police will be after me. Let bygones be bygones. Try to manage as best you can. If you can't, even that won't be too bad.'

Let things take their own course after his death, Krishnadayal had decided. Meanwhile he would remain detached. Then, one could somehow manage by turning a blind eye to what others were doing without his knowledge.

Unable to decide what was to be done, Anandamoyi arose dejectedly and stood in silence for a while. Then she said:

'Can't you see what's happening to your body?'

'My body!' Krishnadayal gave an abrupt guffaw at her stupidity. Their discussion on this subject did not lead to any satisfactory conclusion. Krishnadayal once again immersed himself in the *Gherandasamhita.*

Meanwhile, Mahim was in the outer chamber, discussing lofty spiritual truths with Krishnadayal's sanyasi. Having anxiously inquired, with extreme humility, whether mukti or spiritual liberation was possible for householders, he folded his hands and awaited the reply so attentively, with such excessive devotion and eagerness, it seemed that he had pledged all he possessed to attain mukti. The sanyasi was trying to console Mahim somehow, assuring him that heaven, though not mukti, was available to householders. But Mahim refused to be consoled. His heart was set on mukti, heaven was of no use to him. If he could somehow marry off his daughter, he could devote himself to the pursuit of mukti by serving the sanyasi. Who could deter him? But marrying off a daughter was indeed no easy matter. Not unless the sanyasi baba took pity on him.

~64~

Remembering that he had lately forgotten himself somewhat, Gora became even more rigid than before. He had decided it was due to slackness in his observance of restrictions that he had been overwhelmed by a powerful enchantment, forgetting his own community.

Completing his sandhya rituals in the morning, Gora entered the room and found Poreshbabu there. Lightning seemed to streak through his heart. Even his nerves and blood vessels could not deny Poresh's deep, intimate connection with his own life. Gora found himself bowing to touch Poresh's feet in a pranam.

'You must have heard of Binoy's marriage plans?' Poresh asked him.

'Yes.'

'He is not willing to be married by Brahmo rites.'

'Then this wedding should not take place at all.'

Poresh smiled faintly, without arguing about it. 'No one in our community will participate in this wedding ceremony,' he told Gora. 'Even Binoy's own relatives will not attend, I hear. I am there to represent my daughter's side; on Binoy's side there is perhaps nobody but you. That is why I have come to consult you.'

'What use consulting me on this? I have nothing to do with it.'

Poreshbabu stared at Gora in surprise. 'You have nothing to do with it?' he repeated, after a while.

For a moment, Gora felt a little awkward at Poresh's astonishment. But the very next moment, because he felt this awkwardness, he declared with redoubled firmness: 'How can I be involved in this!'

'I know you are his friend,' persisted Poreshbabu. 'At such a time, doesn't he need his friends most of all?'

'I am his friend, but that's not my only tie in the world, or the most important one.'

'Gour, do you find anything wrong or irreligious in Binoy's conduct?'

'But there are two aspects to dharma,' Gora insisted. 'The eternal aspect, and the everyday one. Where dharma takes the form of social laws it cannot be ignored, for then the world would be devastated.'

'But there are countless laws. Must we take every law for an expression of dharma?'

Poreshbabu had touched the very area of Gora's consciousness that was already in turmoil, where Gora had already drawn a certain conclusion from the churning of his thoughts. So, even before Poreshbabu, he had no reservations in pouring out the words accumulated within. The gist of what he had to say was this: unless we defer completely to society by following its rules, we obstruct its innermost, profoundest purpose; for this purpose lies deep, and every man does not have the capacity to perceive it clearly. Therefore we must have the strength to obey society even by suspending our judgement.

Poreshbabu calmly heard Gora out. When he stopped, rather embarrassed at his own garrulity, Poresh remarked: 'I accept your premise. It is true that the Maker of our destiny has a certain purpose in creating each community. Nor is that purpose clearly evident to everyone. But it is human duty to try and perceive it clearly. There is no fulfillment in following rules blindly, like members of the plant kingdom.'

'What I'm saying is, that only if we first follow our society's dictates in every respect, can we attain a pure awareness of our society's true purpose,' Gora persisted. 'To oppose society is not only to hinder its progress but also to misinterpret it.'

'Without opposition and obstacles, the truth can never be tested,' Poreshbabu countered. 'Not that the truth is tested once by a group of wise men in some ancient age, after which the matter is permanently settled. The truth must be discovered afresh by the people of every era, through obstacles and conflict. Anyway, I don't wish to argue about all this. I believe in the personal freedom of human beings. It is only by attacking the truth with this personal freedom that we can discover what is permanent and what is passing fancy. Upon that knowledge and the pursuit of that knowledge depends the welfare of society.'

With these words Poresh rose to his feet, and Gora, too, arose from his chair. 'I had thought I would have to remain somewhat aloof from this wedding, at the request of the Brahmo Samaj, and that you, as Binoy's friend, would see the whole thing through. That is a friend's advantage over a relative, for he does not have to endure the onslaughts of society. But since you have deemed it your duty to abandon Binoy, the entire responsibility now rests with me. I must accomplish this task alone.'

How alone Poreshbabu felt, Gora did not realize at the time. Borodasundari opposed Poreshbabu, the daughters of the house were not pleased, and fearing Harimohini's objections, Poresh had not even consulted Sucharita about wedding preparations. Meanwhile, everyone in the Brahmo Samaj had taken up cudgels against him, and the couple of letters he had received from Binoy's khudo, his paternal uncle, abused him as an evil, scheming kidnapper.

As soon as Poresh left, Abinash and some other members of Gora's group came in, ready to make fun of Poreshbabu. But Gora objected:

'If you are incapable of respecting someone worthy of it, at least spare yourselves the pettiness of mocking him.'

Once again Gora had to immerse himself in his customary activities involving his group. But how distasteful everything seemed! It was all worthless. This could not be described as work at all. There was no soul in it. Until now, it had never struck Gora so forcibly that merely by saying things on paper, or giving speeches, or forming groups, nothing real was being accomplished; rather, a vast amount of useless effort was being accumulated. Broadened by his newfound powers, his life-stream now demanded a true channel where its current could flow in full force. His present activities no longer pleased him.

Meanwhile, arrangements were under way for the ceremonial penance. Gora had been particularly enthusiastic about these preparations. This penance was not only for the impurity of life in prison, it seemed a way for him to purify himself in every respect, to be reborn into his field of work with a new body. They had obtained instructions about the rites of penance, the date and venue had also been fixed, and invitations were ready for distribution to famous teachers and scholars of East and West Bengal. The affluent among Gora's group had also raised the funds. All members of the group had assumed that the country had at last undertaken a worthwhile task. Abinash had secretly conspired with his group that on this occasion, all the learned men present at the gathering would confer upon Gora the title of 'Hindupradeep,' Light of the Hindu World, along with flowers, sandalwood paste, rice grains, holy durba grass, and sundry other religious offerings. Gora would be gifted a sandalwood box containing some Sanskrit shlokas inscribed in gold and signed by all the learned Brahmans present. Alongside, a volume of Max Mueller's edition of the Rig Veda, bound in priceless Morocco leather, would be presented to him by the seniormost and most eminent professor, as a token of blessing from Bharatvarsha. This would beautifully express the feeling that in the modern era of depravity, it was Gora who was the true guardian of the sacred Vedic faith.

So, unbeknownst to Gora, members of his group conspired daily to make the event extremely appealing and productive.

~65~

Harimohini received a letter from her dear Kailash. He wrote:

> By the grace of the revered One, all is well here. Please relieve us of our anxiety by informing us of your well-being.

Needless to say, ever since Harimohini had left their home, they had been burdened with this anxiety, but had made no effort to address the lack of information about her well-being. After exhausting all the news about Khudi, Potol, Bhajahari and everyone else, Kailash wrote in conclusion:

> Please send us proper details about the paatri, the prospective bride. You inform us she would be about twelve or thirteen years old, but she is a growing girl and looks a little mature—no harm in that. From what you indicate about her claims to property, if you let us know after proper verification whether her ownership is valid for life or permanently, I shall consult our elders about it. I think they would not object. I am relieved to hear that the paatri is committed to the Hindu faith, but we must try to suppress the fact that she was reared in a Brahmo household all this while. Hence you must not divulge this to anyone else. The lunar eclipse on the next full moon is auspicious for a bath in the Ganga. If possible, I shall visit you then to see the girl.

She had somehow remained in Kolkata all these days, but at the faint hope of returning to her in-laws' home, Harimohini lost all patience. Each day of exile now seemed intolerable. 'Let me talk to Sucharita at once and fix a day to complete the task,' she began to wish. But she did not dare make haste. The more closely she observed Sucharita, the more clearly she realized she had not understood her. Harimohini waited for an opportunity, and became even more vigilant about Sucharita's conduct. Now she tended to spend less time at her prayers than before, no longer willing to let Sucharita out of her sight. Sucharita noticed Gora's visits had ceased abruptly. She realized Harimohini must have said something to him.

'Very well,' she resolved, 'let him not come, but it is he who is my guru, my own guru.' An absent guru exerts a much greater influence than one present in the flesh. For then the heart compensates from within for that absence. Where Sucharita would have argued with Gora if he were present, she now read his works and accepted his statements unresistingly. If she did not understand them, she told herself he would surely have explained if he had been there.

But it was not easy, indeed, to quench her hunger for the sight of Gora's radiant image, and to listen to his words, charged with lightning like thunderclouds. Her insatiable inner yearning seemed constantly to erode her physical being. From time to time Sucharita would think, achingly, of the many people who had ready access to Gora, night and day, though they could not understand the value of such a sight.

One afternoon, Lalita came to Sucharita and embraced her.

'Bhai Suchididi!'

'What is it, bhai Lalita?'

'It's all arranged.'

'What date has been fixed?'

'Monday.'

'Where?'

'I don't know about all that. Baba knows.'

'Are you happy, bhai?' asked Sucharita, putting her arm round Lalita's waist.

'Why would I not be happy!'

'Now you've got everything you desired, you have no reason to quarrel with anyone about anything. That makes me fear you might lose your enthusiasm.'

'Why? Why should I lack people to quarrel with? Now I need not look beyond the home.'

'Is that so!' cried Sucharita, rapping Lalita on the cheek. 'Are you plotting such things already! I shall warn Binoy. The poor fellow still has time to put himself on guard.'

'Your poor fellow has no time left to put himself on

guard, my dear,' Lalita retorted. 'There is no saving him now. What was destined for him has come true, now he can only smite his forehead in despair, and weep.'

'How can I tell you how pleased I am, Lalita!' said Sucharita gravely. 'I pray that you should prove yourself worthy of a husband like Binoy.'

'Indeed! Is that so! And must nobody prove themselves worthy of me! Just try discussing it with him once. If you hear his opinion once, even you will regret that you failed to appreciate such a wonderful person, all these days. How blind you were!'

'Never mind,' Sucharita responded, 'at last we have found an expert on jewels. No point crying over the price he offers, for now you will no longer need appreciation from ignorant people like us.'

'Shan't I, indeed! Of course I shall,' Lalita insisted. She pinched Sucharita's cheek so hard, she cried out in pain. 'I want your appreciation always. You can't evade that and offer it to someone else.'

'I shall not offer it to anyone else, anyone at all,' Sucharita assured her, placing her cheek against Lalita's.

'Anyone?' Lalita persisted. 'Not to anyone at all?'

Sucharita only shook her head.

'Look bhai Suchididi,' said Lalita, moving away a little. 'You know bhai that I could never tolerate it if you cared for anyone else. I didn't tell you all these days, but I tell you now, when Gourmohanbabu used to visit . . . No, Didi, you can't do that, today I must speak my mind—I've never concealed anything from you, but that's one thing I could never bring myself to tell you, I don't know why, and that has troubled me all along. I can't bid you farewell until I have told you about it. When Gourmohanbabu visited us I used to feel very angry. What made me angry? Did you think I didn't understand anything? I noticed you wouldn't even mention his

name to me, and that would infuriate me even more. I found
it intolerable that you should love him more than you loved
me. No, bhai Didi, you must let me speak—how can I tell
you what I suffered on that account? Even now, you
won't discuss that subject with me, I know. But even if you
don't, I'm not angry anymore. I would be so delighted, bhai,
if your . . .'

'I beg you, bhai Lalita, don't utter those words!' pleaded
Sucharita, quickly placing her hand on Lalita's mouth. 'I want
to sink into the ground when I hear that suggestion.'

'Why, bhai, is he . . .'

'No, no, no!' cried Sucharita in great agitation. 'Stop
saying such crazy things! One must not utter the unthinkable.'

'But this is too much, bhai,' protested Lalita, annoyed at
Sucharita's embarrassment. 'I have been watching very closely,
and I can tell you for sure . . .'

Breaking free of Lalita's grasp, Sucharita rushed from the
room. Lalita ran after her and dragged her back

'Achchha, achchha, I won't mention it again,' she swore.
'Never again!'

'I can't make such a big promise,' Lalita responded. 'I'll
mention it if I turn out to be right, not otherwise. That much
I promise.'

These few days, Harimohini had hovered close to Sucharita,
keeping a strict watch on her. Sucharita had realized it, and
Harimohini's wary vigilance weighed heavily upon her mind.
Though inwardly desperate, she could not say a word. Now,
after Lalita had left, Sucharita wept in exhaustion, head
between her hands, elbows on the table. When the attendant
came to light the lamp, she forbade him. That was the hour
for Harimohini's evening prayers. From the upper floor,
having seen Lalita depart, untimely she came downstairs and
entered Sucharita's room.

'Radharani!' she called.

Secretly wiping away her tears, Sucharita quickly rose to her feet.

'What's going on?' Harimohini demanded.

Sucharita offered no reply.

'I fail to understand what's going on here!' declared Harimohini harshly.

'Mashi, why do you watch me like this, day and night?' Sucharita demanded.

'Don't you understand why? All this fasting, all these tears, what do these things mean? Am I a child, not to understand something so simple?'

'I tell you Mashi, you have not understood anything at all. You have misunderstood things so terribly, I'm finding it harder to endure, every moment.'

'So if I have misunderstood, why don't you explain things to me properly?'

'Achchha, let me explain then,' said Sucharita, determinedly subduing all her diffidence. 'From my guru I have learnt something new, something it takes a lot of strength to accept. It is that strength I seem to lack now. I can't cope with the constant need to fight you. But Mashi, you have a distorted view of my relationship with him. You have insulted him and sent him away. Whatever you said to him was wrong, and your view of me is false! You have wronged us! It is beyond your power to degrade a man like him. But why did you torment me so? What have I done to you?' As she spoke, Sucharita's voice became choked. She left the room.

Harimohini was stupefied. 'Never in my whole life have I heard such words!' she said to herself. Allowing Sucharita some time to compose herself, she called her to dinner. Then she said:

'Look Radharani, I am not so young, after all. Since

childhood I have followed what the Hindu religion says, and heard a lot about it as well. You know nothing about such things, that is why Gourmohan can beguile you, posing as your guru. I have heard some of the things he says; there is nothing genuinely traditional in his words, those scriptural truths are of his own making. We can detect such things because we have been trained by gurus. I tell you Radharani, you need not follow any of those injunctions. When the time comes, my Guru, who is not so false, will himself offer you the mantra of initiation. Have no fear, I shall get you into the Hindu community. Never mind that you were part of a Brahmo family. Who would ever know? You are indeed a little too mature, but there are so many girls like you, older than required. Who will check your birthchart after all? And since there is money, there will be no hurdles, everything will be accepted. I have myself seen a low-caste kaibarta pass off for a higher-caste kayastha. I shall marry you into such a good Brahman family in the Hindu community that nobody will dare gossip, for the family would themselves be the leaders of the community. For that, you won't have to suffer, worshipping a guru and shedding so many tears.'

While Harimohini was waxing eloquent, Sucharita discovered she had lost her appetite, and her food seemed hard to swallow. But she silently forced herself to eat. For she knew that even her lack of appetite would invite the sort of comment she would not find at all palatable.

Finding Sucharita unresponsive, Harimohini said to herself: 'One must hand it to them! Shedding all these tears in the name of Hinduism, and then ignoring such a great opportunity! No need for penance, no excuses required, just spending a little money here and there to gain easy entry into the community—if even that fails to enthuse her, can she call herself a Hindu!' Harimohini was left in no doubt about the extent of Gora's duplicity. But trying to determine the motive

behind such deception, she felt it was Sucharita's wealth that
was at the root of all this mischief—that, and Sucharita's
youthful beauty. The sooner she could rescue this girl, company
documents and all, and confine her in the fortress of her
marital home, the better. But without softening her mind a
little more, the plan would not work. In the hope of softening
Sucharita's mind, she began to constantly sing the praises of
her own in-laws' family, for Sucharita's benefit. Using diverse
examples, she extolled their extraordinary influence, their
impossible achievements in community affairs. How even
blameless persons suffered social opprobrium for trying to
oppose this family, and how many people supported by this
family managed to survive comfortably within the Hindu way
of life even after consuming chicken cooked by Muslims—
Harimohini authenticated all these anecdotes with names,
addresses and detailed descriptions.

Borodasundari made no secret of the fact that she did not
want Sucharita to frequent their house, for she prided herself
on her bluntness. She often announced this virtue when being
unabashedly harsh to others. Hence Sucharita had plainly
received the message that she should not expect any warmth
in Borodasundari's household. Sucharita also knew that Poresh
would have to face tremendous domestic discord if she visited
their house regularly, so she did not go there unless strictly
necessary. Hence Poresh would drop by at Sucharita's house
to see her, once or twice a day.

    Poreshbabu had been unable to visit Sucharita for a few
days, preoccupied with various concerns and responsibilities.
Sucharita had eagerly awaited his arrival, yet privately she too
had felt rather uneasy and hurt. She knew for sure that her
deepest ties of harmony with Poresh could never be severed,
but was tormented by the painful awareness that some major
outer strands were threatening to snap. Meanwhile Harimohini

had made her life more intolerable by the hour. Hence, braving even Borodasundari's displeasure, Sucharita now arrived at Poresh's house. At that hour, the late afternoon sun had slanted to the back of the three-storied building on the western side, casting a giant shadow. And beneath that shadow, head bowed, Poresh was walking slowly on the garden path, all by himself. Sucharita joined him.

'Baba, how are you?' she asked.

Poreshbabu's trend of thought was suddenly broken. 'I am fine Radhé,' he replied after a brief pause, gazing at her face. The two of them strolled along together.

'Lalita is getting married on Monday,' said Poreshbabu.

Sucharita thought of asking why her advice or assistance had not been sought in organizing this wedding. But she too felt hindered now by a certain constraint. Formerly, indeed, she would not have waited to be asked for help.

Then Poresh raised the very subject that was on her mind. 'I couldn't send for you this time, Radhé,' he said.

'Why Baba?'

Poresh looked at her without offering any reply. Sucharita could bear it no longer.

'You thought I had undergone a change of heart,' she said, lowering her face.

'Yes, that is why I thought I would avoid embarrassing you with any request.'

'Baba, I had planned to tell you everything but I didn't get to see you at all. That is why I have come here today. I don't have the ability to properly communicate my innermost feelings to you. I am afraid I might not manage to convey the exact truth.'

'I know such things are not easy to communicate clearly,' Poreshbabu assured her. 'There is something you have discovered in your heart, through your emotions alone; you feel it, but its nature is not yet known to you.'

'Yes, exactly!' said Sucharita, relieved. 'But my feelings are so strong, how can I describe them to you? As if I have found a new life, a new awareness. I have never viewed myself from such a perspective. All these days, I felt no connection with my nation's past or future, but so powerfully has my heart now recognized the great reality of that connection, I simply cannot drive it from my mind. Look, Baba, to tell you the truth, I could never have declared earlier that I am a Hindu. But now my heart vehemently and unabashedly proclaims: "I am a Hindu." That brings me great joy.'

'Have you considered all aspects, all angles of this matter?'

'Have I the capacity to consider everything as a whole? But I have read a lot on the subject, and discussed it extensively too. Before I learnt to take a large view of the matter, I used to magnify the petty details of what it means to be a Hindu. That made me very contemptuous of the whole business.'

Poreshbabu was surprised at her words. He clearly realized that Sucharita had developed a certain awareness, that she undoubtedly felt she had attained something real. She was not merely adrift on a vague tide of emotion like one entranced, uncomprehending.

'Baba,' persisted Sucharita, 'why should I say I am an insignificant person, divorced from my country and my community? Why can't I say "I am a Hindu"?'

'In other words Ma,' laughed Poreshbabu, 'it is me you are asking, why I don't call myself a Hindu. When one thinks about it, there seems to be no major reason why. One reason is that the Hindus don't acknowledge me as a Hindu, and another is that the people who share my views on religion don't identify themselves as Hindus.'

Sucharita was silent, lost in thought.

'I have already told you,' Poresh continued, 'that these are not major reasons, merely outward ones. One can ignore such obstacles. But there is also an internal, deeper reason. There can be no entry into Hindu society. Or at least, there is no front gate, even if a backdoor exists. This community is not for the whole of humanity, it is only for those who happen to be born as Hindus.'

'But that is true of every community,' Sucharita protested.

'No,' insisted Poreshbabu, 'it is not so with any major community. The gates of the Muslim community are open to the whole of humanity, and the Christian community also welcomes everyone. The same law applies to all communities belonging to the Christian world. If I want to become an Englishman, it would not be entirely impossible: by living in England and obeying their laws, I can gain entry into their society; I need not even become a Christian. Abhimanyu knew how to enter the battletrap but he did not know the way out. With Hindus it is the exact opposite. The way into their community is completely shut, but there are a hundred thousand ways out of it.'

'All the same, Baba, the Hindu community has not declined to this day. It still survives.'

'It takes time to sense the decline of a community,' explained Poresh. 'Before this, the backdoor to Hindu society was open. Non-Aryan people then felt a certain glory in entering the Hindu world. Later, during the days of Muslim rule, the Hindu kings and zamindars exerted considerable influence almost everywhere in the country, hence there was no limit to rules and restrictions against leaving the community easily. Now British rule offers everyone protection under the law, so it is no longer so easy to use such artificial means to guard the doors leading out of the community. That is why for some time we have seen a constant decline in the number of Hindus in Bharatvarsha, while the Muslim population increases. If this continues, the country will gradually develop a Muslim majority. Then it will be unjust to even call it Hindustan.'

'Baba, shouldn't we try to prevent it, all of us?' cried Sucharita in distress. 'Shall we too abandon the Hindu world and aggravate its decline? This is indeed the moment for us to cling to it with all our might.'

'Can we keep someone alive at will, by clinging to him?' said Poreshbabu, affectionately stroking Sucharita's back. 'To gain protection, there is a worldly law to be followed. One who rejects that natural law is naturally rejected in turn by everyone else. Hindu society insults people, excludes people, hence in today's world it is becoming daily more difficult for it to protect itself. For it can no longer remain in seclusion, now that all roads to the world are open, and people from everywhere are coming into contact with the community. Now it cannot dam or fortify itself with the shastra-samhitas, to somehow shield itself from contact with everyone else. If the Hindu community does not foster within itself, even now, the power of conservation rather than the disease of decay, then this unchecked encounter with people from outside will become a lethal blow to its survival.'

'I understand nothing of all this,' declared Sucharita, in agony. 'But if this is indeed true, I cannot bring myself to reject the community today when all of you are ready to abandon it. As its children born in times of need, we must now attend upon its sickbed.'

'Ma, I shall say nothing to contradict the feelings that have arisen in your heart,' Poreshbabu assured her. 'Steady your mind with prayer, and judge everything by the truth, the ideal of greatness, that you carry within. Gradually everything will become clear to you. Don't regard the greatest One as inferior to the nation or to any human being. That will not be beneficial for you or your nation. With this in view, I wish to surrender myself wholeheartedly to Him. Then I can easily remain true to the nation and to every human being.'

At this juncture, someone delivered Poreshbabu a letter.

'I don't have my glasses, and the light has waned,' said Poreshbabu. 'Please see what the letter says.'

Sucharita read the letter to him. It was addressed to him by a Brahmo Samaj committee, bearing the signatures of several Brahmos. In sum, the letter declared that since Poresh had consented to non-Brahmo rites at his daughter's marriage and was prepared to participate in the ceremonies himself, the Brahmo Samaj in such circumstances could by no means count him among the civilized. If he had anything to say in his own defence, the committee must receive a letter to that effect before the coming Sunday. That day the matter would be discussed and resolved according to the views of the majority. Poresh took the letter and put it in his pocket. Gently clasping his right hand, Sucharita silently walked beside him. Gradually, dusk descended and the darkness deepened. In the alley to the south of the garden, a light came on.

'Baba, it is time for your prayers,' said Sucharita softly. 'I want to pray with you this evening.' So saying, Sucharita led him by the hand to the secluded prayer chamber. There, the mat had been spread and a candle lit, as usual. That evening, Poresh meditated silently for a long time. Ultimately after uttering a small prayer, he arose and came away.

As soon as he emerged he saw Lalita and Binoy waiting quietly outside the door. Seeing him, the two of them bent to touch his feet in a pranam. Placing his hands on their heads, he blessed them in his mind.

'Ma,' he said to Sucharita, 'I shall visit your house tomorrow. Let me complete my work tonight.' With these words he went into his room.

Tears were streaming from Sucharita's eyes. Motionless as a statue, she stood silently in the darkness of the verandah. For a long time, Lalita and Binoy also did not utter a word. When Sucharita prepared to leave, Binoy came before her.

'Didi, will you not bless us?' he asked in a low voice.

He and Lalita bowed together at Sucharita's feet. What Sucharita said in a tear-choked voice was audible only to the One who resides in our hearts.

Back in his room, Poreshbabu wrote a letter to the Brahmo Samaj committee:

> *I must take charge of Lalita's wedding. If you abandon me for that reason, it will not be unjust of you. At this moment I only pray to Ishwar that he remove me from all social shelter and grant me a place at his own feet.*

~66~

Sucharita became desperate to tell Gora what Poresh had said to her. Had Gora not realized that the very Bharatvarsha for whose sake he had expanded his outlook and drawn his heart to a powerful love, was now affected by Time and on the path to decline! Because Bharatvarsha had survived on the strength of its internal organization all these years, its people had not needed to be vigilant. But was there any time left now for such a complacent existence? Could we afford to stay indoors, clinging to old systems as before?

'I too have a duty to perform here,' Sucharita began to think. 'What might it be?' At this point, Gora should have come before her to offer instructions and show her the way. Sucharita said to herself: 'If he could have rescued me from all my constraints and ignorance, and positioned me in my proper place, would the significance of that not have overridden all petty questions of social propriety and malicious gossip?' She was infused with a sense of her own superiority. She asked herself why Gora had not put her to the test, why he did not ask her to accomplish the impossible. Was there a single man in Gora's group, capable like Sucharita of effortlessly surrendering all they possessed? Did Gora see no need for such voluntary self-sacrifice and such strength? Would it not harm the nation at all if this urge was rendered ineffective by the shackles of propriety? Refusing to acknowledge such indifference, Sucharita dismissed it from her thoughts. 'He could never possibly reject me in this fashion. He must come to me, seek me out, giving up all constraints and hesitations. However powerful a man he is, he needs me: he told me so himself, once. How could he forget that now simply due to some meaningless speculations!'

'Didi!' cried Satish, rushing up to stand close to Sucharita's lap.

'So, bhai bakhtiar!' she responded, hugging him.

'Lalitadidi's wedding is on Monday. I stay with Binoybabu for the next few days. He has sent for me.'

'Have you told Mashi?'

'I told her. She got angry and said: "I don't know about that, speak to your didi, she'll decide what's best." Didi, please don't forbid me. My studies will not suffer at all there, I'll study every day. Binoybabu will guide me.'

'You will cause disturbance in a house where everyone will be busy,' Sucharita told him.

'No Didi, I shan't disturb anything,' Satish promised anxiously.

'Will you take your little puppy along, then?'

'Yes, I must take him. Binoybabu has specially asked me to. There was a separate invitation for him printed on red paper. It says he must attend and savour the refreshments, along with his family.'

'And who might his family be?'

'Why, Binoybabu says it's me,' Satish hastened to assure her. 'He has also asked us to bring along that organ, Didi. Please let me have it. I won't break it.'

'But I would be relieved if it were to break. So now it's quite clear—it is to play the organ at his wedding that your friend has invited you? Does he intend to avoid the professional musicians of the rowshan-chowki altogether?'

'No, never!' cried Satish, greatly agitated. 'Binoybabu says he will make me his mitbar, the groom's young double. What is the mitbar's role, Didi?'

'He must fast all day,' Sucharita informed him. Satish was utterly incredulous. Now Sucharita drew him firmly to her lap and asked: 'Tell me bhai bakhtiar, what will you become when you grow up?'

Satish was mentally prepared with his answer. It was his class teacher who stood for his ideal of indomitable power and extraordinary learning. He had already decided to become a mastermoshai, a schoolteacher, when he grew up.

'There's a lot to be done, bhai!' Sucharita told him. 'Brother and sister, we two must perform our duties together. What do you say Satish? We must give our lives to enlarge our nation's stature. Indeed, what is there to enlarge! Is there anything as great as our nation! It is our spirit we must enlarge. Do you know that? Do you understand?'

Satish was not one to readily acknowledge that he had not understood.

'Yes,' he affirmed emphatically.

'You know how immense is our country, our population,' Sucharita declared. 'How would I explain it to you? What an extraordinary nation this is! How many thousands of years the Maker of our destiny has spent, preparing to place this nation on the world's pinnacle; how many people from diverse lands have come here to join in the preparations, how many great men have been born here, how many great wars fought, how many great utterances pronounced, how many great tasks accomplished, how diversely religion has been viewed in this country and how many varied solutions have been found here for life's problems! Such is this Bharatvarsha of ours. Know its greatness bhai, don't ever disdain it even by mistake. What I tell you now you must one day understand. Not that I imagine you have understood nothing of it even today. Bear this in mind—you have been born into a very vast country; you must revere this immense nation with all your heart, and lay down your life in its service.'

'Didi, what will you do?' asked Satish after a short silence.

'I shall do the same,' Sucharita assured him. 'You'll help me, won't you?'

'Yes I shall,' declared Satish, immediately swelling with pride.

There was no one at home to whom Sucharita could confide the thoughts that swelled in her heart. Hence all her emotions overflowed when she found this younger brother close at hand. What she said, and the words in which she said it, were not meant for a young boy's ears, but that did not deter her. She had sensed that only if she gave a complete account of the insight she had gained in her present excitable state, would everyone, young or old, somehow interpret it according to their own levels of comprehension. But if she held things back, trying to explain them in other people's terms, the truth would inevitably become distorted.

Satish's imagination was aroused. 'When I grow up, when I have a lot of money . . .' he began.

'No, no, no!' objected Sucharita. 'Don't talk of money. We two have no need for money, bakhtiar. For our undertaking we need devotion, the commitment of the heart.'

At this moment Anandamoyi entered the room. The blood raced in Sucharita's heart. She bent to touch Anandamoyi's feet. Pranams did not come easy to Satish. Awkwardly, he somehow performed the gesture. Drawing Satish to her lap, Anandamoyi kissed the top of his head and said to Sucharita:

'I came for a bit of consultation with you, ma. I don't see anyone else after all. Binoy was saying, "The wedding will take place at my own house." "That cannot happen under any circumstances," I objected. "As if you are a great nawab, that a daughter of ours should come to your own home for the wedding ceremony!" That can't be allowed. I have located a place, not far from yours. I have just come from there. Please speak to Poreshbabu and convince him.'

'Baba will agree.'

'And then ma, you too must go there. The wedding is on this very Monday. In these few days we must stay there and make all the arrangements. Indeed, we don't have much time. I can handle everything alone, but if you are not involved Binoy will feel very hurt. He can't bring himself to request you directly, in fact he did not mention you even to me, but from that itself I can sense that for him it is a very sensitive issue. You can't afford to remain detached any longer, ma. Lalita too would be deeply hurt.'

'Ma, can you participate in this wedding?' asked Sucharita, rather surprised.

'How can you say that, Sucharita! Participate! Am I an outsider, to merely participate! This is Binoy's wedding after all! It is I who must handle the whole affair. But I have told Binoy, "As far as this wedding is concerned, I'm no relation of yours. I represent the bride's party." He is coming to my house to marry Lalita.'

Anandamoyi's heart was heavy with the sorrow of knowing that despite having a mother, Lalita had been abandoned by her at this auspicious moment. For that very reason, she was trying single-mindedly to ensure that the wedding ceremony did not smack of neglect or disrespect. Taking her mother's place, she would personally adorn Lalita for the ceremony, organize the ceremonial reception of the bridegroom, ensure that there was not the slightest lapse in hospitality if a few invitees should turn up. And she would decorate this new dwelling in such a way that Lalita would regard it as a home. Such was her resolve.

'Will this not create problems for you?' Sucharita asked her.

'Indeed it might, but so what?' responded Anandamoyi, recalling the upheaval Mahim had caused at home. 'There are always some problems, but if we bear them quietly, in time they too disappear.'

Sucharita knew Gora had not participated in the wedding preparations. She was curious to know whether he had made any attempt to dissuade Anandamoyi from participating. But she could not broach the matter directly, and Anandamoyi did not even mention Gora's name.

Harimohini had heard of the developments. Having completed the chores at hand in a leisurely way, she entered the room and asked:

'Didi, I hope you are doing well? We don't see you, nor do you enquire after us.'

'I have come to fetch your bonjhi,' responded Anandamoyi, without answering her complaint. She then proceeded to explain her purpose. Displeased, Harimohini remained silent for a while. Then she said:

'I can't attend, in the middle of all this.'

'No bon, my sister, I don't ask you to attend,' Anandamoyi assured her. 'Don't worry about Sucharita. I shall be with her, after all.'

'Let me tell you, then,' declared Harimohini. 'Radharani has been telling people she is a Hindu. Now she feels inclined towards Hinduism. So if she wants to follow the Hindu ways, she must be careful. As it is it will cause a lot of gossip, but I can counter that. But from now on, she should mind her ways for a while. The first thing people ask is why she isn't married, at such an advanced age. That can somehow be suppressed. Not that one couldn't find a good match for her, if one tried. But if she again takes to her recent ways, how many fronts can I manage, tell me? Daughter of a Hindu family, you understand everything; so how can you say such things either? If you had a daughter of your own, could you have sent her to attend this marriage? You would be compelled to worry about getting your daughter married!'

Anandamoyi glanced in amazement at Sucharita, whose face flamed blood-red.

'I don't want to exert any force,' she explained. 'If Sucharita objects, I . . .'

'I can't fathom what you have in mind, the two of you!' protested Harimohini. 'It is your son who has accepted her according to Hindu tradition, so how can you appear so surprised?'

Where was the Harimohini who in Poreshbabu's house was always afraid of making a mistake, clinging avidly to anyone who showed the slightest signs of being favourably inclined! Now she was poised like a tigress to defend her rights, always on edge, suspicious that adverse forces were at work everywhere, to wrest her very own Sucharita from her possession. Unable to surmise who was her friend, and who her enemy, her mind could not remain at ease. Her spirit could not find equilibrium even in worshipping the deity in whom she had previously sought refuge in desperation, finding the whole world hollow. She was extremely worldly, once; when extreme grief made her indifferent to material things, she could never have imagined that she might some day regain the slightest attachment to money, property or family relationships. But now, as soon as her heart had recovered somewhat from its wounds, the world was again present before her, tugging at her emotions. Once again, all her hopes and desires had reared their heads, fed by her long-time hunger. So strong was the urge to resume what she had renounced, she had not experienced such restlessness even when she had formerly belonged to the everyday world. Anandamoyi was astonished at the unimaginable transformation that had taken place in just a few days, its signs evident in Harimohini's facial expressions, body language and social conversation. Anandamoyi began to feel very sorry for Sucharita in her tender heart. Had she sensed such imminent danger, she would never have come to call Sucharita. Now she found it a problem to protect Sucharita from pain.

When Harimohini made pointed remarks about Gora, Sucharita hung her head and silently walked out of the room.

'Have no fear, bon!' Anandamoyi assured her. 'I was not aware of this. Well, I shall not trouble her with any more requests. Please don't say anything to her either. She has previously been brought up in a certain way. If you suddenly pressurize her too much, she cannot endure it!'

'As if I don't realize that, considering my advanced age!' retorted Harimohini. 'Let her declare in your presence then, if I have ever caused her any pain. She does whatever she pleases, I never say a word. I pray the Lord should protect her, that is all I ask. Such is my misfortune, I can't sleep for fear of what may happen someday.'

When Anandamoyi was on her way out, Sucharita emerged from her room and touched her feet.

'I shall come ma, and bring you all the news,' promised Anandamoyi, patting her tenderly. 'Nothing will hinder you. With Ishwar's blessings, the auspicious event will materialize.'

Sucharita did not say a word.

Early next morning, when Anandamoyi, along with Lachhmia, had unleashed a torrential flood to wash away the long-accumulated dust in their building, Sucharita arrived on the scene. Quickly dropping her broom, Anandamoyi drew her to her bosom. Now there was a great to-do, washing and mopping, moving things about and decorating the place. Poreshbabu had given Sucharita a suitable amount of money for their expenses. With that capital in hand, the two of them made countless lists, and then proceeded to amend them.

Not long after, Poresh himself arrived there with Lalita. Her own home had now become intolerable for Lalita. Nobody dared say anything to her, yet their silence had begun to assault her at every step. Ultimately when Borodasundari's friends began to visit their home in groups, to express their sympathy with her, Poresh judged it better to take Lalita away from this household. When it was time to depart, Lalita went to offer her pranams to Borodasundari. But the latter kept her face averted and started weeping after Lalita had left. Labanya and Leela were quite curious about Lalita's wedding; if they could somehow gain permission, they would not have wasted a moment in rushing to the wedding celebrations. But when Lalita took her leave, they maintained an extremely grave exterior, bearing in mind the harsh requirements of the Brahmo community. At the door, Lalita came face to face with Sudhir for a split second. But as some elderly members of their community were just behind him, she could not speak to him. Mounting her carriage, Lalita spotted a paper-wrapped package tucked into a corner of her seat. Opening it she found a German silver flower vase. Inscribed on it in English were the words: 'May Ishwar bless the happy couple.' Accompanying it was a card bearing only Sudhir's initials. Hardening her heart, Lalita had determined not to shed any tears that day. But as she clasped this sole token of love from their childhood friend at the moment of departure from her paternal home, tears streamed from her eyes. Poreshbabu sat motionless, his eyes closed.

'Come, come, ma, come,' Anandamoyi welcomed her, taking both Lalita's hands and drawing her inside, as if she had been expecting her just then.

Poreshababu sent for Sucharita. 'Lalita has left our house for good,' he told her in a trembling voice.

'She will not lack for care and affection here, Baba,' Sucharita assured him, clasping his hand.

When Poresh was about to leave, Anandamoyi appeared before him, head covered, and greeted him with a namaskar. Flustered, Poresh returned her greeting.

'Please have no worries about Lalita,' said Anandamoyi. 'She will never suffer any pain at the hands of the one to whose care you have surrendered her. And after all this time, the Almighty has filled a gap in my life. I had no daughter, but now I have acquired one. For a long time, I had been waiting in the hope that Binoy's bride would compensate for my lack of a daughter. Well, just as Ishwar has granted my wish at last, He has also brought me unimaginable good fortune in gifting me such a daughter and in such a wonderful way.'

For the first time since the upheaval about Lalita's marriage had begun, Poreshbabu's heart found a glimmer of hope in this world, and felt genuinely comforted.

~67~

After his release from prison so many visitors thronged Gora's house all day, it became impossible for him to remain at home amidst the suffocating verbosity of their prayers and homage, arguments and discussions. So he resumed his travels across the countryside.

He would leave home in the morning after a light repast, and return only at night. Travelling by train, he would alight at some station near Kolkata and enter the village. There, he would seek hospitality from localities where oil-men, blacksmiths, fishermen and others lived. Why this fair-skinned, towering Brahman should wander among their dwellings asking after their wellbeing, the people could not comprehend at all. In fact, all sorts of suspicions arose in their minds. But dismissing all their diffidence and wariness, Gora roamed in their midst. At times he faced hostile comments, but even that did not deter him.

The deeper he penetrated into their world, the more a certain thought began to trouble his mind. He observed that in these rural areas, social restrictions were far more powerful than in educated, cultured society. In every household, food, sleep, rest, work, everything was conducted, day and night, under the unblinking gaze of society. Each individual had a very simple faith in popular traditions, never questioning such things. Yet social restrictions and adherence to custom did not empower them at all in their fields of activity. It was doubtful whether such timid, helpless beings, so incapable of judging what was good for themselves, existed anywhere else in the world. Beyond adherence to tradition, there was no other good that they wholeheartedly acknowledged, or were willing to understand. It was prohibition, enforced through punishment or partisanship, that they regarded as supreme. The awareness of what must not be done entrapped their nature in a net from head to toe at every step, through various forms of discipline. But this was the net of indebtedness, the moneylender's bond, not the bondage imposed by a king. There was no broad unity within them that could draw them all together in good times or bad.

Gora could not help noticing that humans were using these practices as weapons to suck the blood of other human beings, brutally robbing them of their selfhood. How often he had observed that in performing social rituals, nobody showed the slightest compassion for anybody else! One man's father had been ailing for a long time. The poor man had spent all he had on his father's treatment and medication, with no help from any quarters. On the contrary, the people of his village insisted his father do penance for the unknown sin that caused his permanent ill-health. No one was unaware of that unfortunate man's poverty and lack of resources, but there was no forgiveness. It was the same with every ritual. Just as a police investigation was a worse calamity for the village than a robbery, so also was the parents' funeral a greater source of affliction for their offspring than even their parents' death. No one would accept low income or lack of strength as an excuse; the heartless demands of social custom must somehow be fulfilled to the letter. When arranging a marriage, the bridegroom's party would adopt every strategy to make the burden intolerable for the bride's father, without the slightest pity for the wretched man. Gora observed that this society did not help a man in times of need, nor supported him in times of trouble; it only used discipline as a threat to subdue him.

In educated society, Gora had forgotten this, for in that world, the power to unite for the general good operated from the outside. Various attempts at achieving unity had begun to manifest themselves in that social realm. The only cause for anxiety there was lest these collective efforts, being imitations of other societies, should prove fruitless.

But in the total passivity prevalent in the villages, where external pressures did not work in the same way, Gora saw his nation's profoundest weakness completely exposed. The dharma that gave everyone strength, energy and wellbeing in the form of service, love, compassion and self-sacrifice, was nowhere in evidence. The practices that only drew boundaries, divided people and tormented them, that would even deny the intellect and keep love at arm's length, were the ones that constantly hindered everyone in every respect, in every movement and activity. In the rural areas, the harmful effects of this foolish compliance drew Gora's attention so clearly and in so many forms, and he saw it attacking people's health, knowledge, religious sense and activities from so many angles, in so many ways, that it became impossible for him to continue deluding himself with the illusion of abstract thought.

The first thing Gora observed was that, among the lower castes in the villages, either because of a low female population or for some other reason, a large sum was required for obtaining a bride. Many men had to remain bachelors all their lives or until an advanced age. But widow remarriage was strictly forbidden. Owing to this, in every household, the atmosphere had become polluted and every member of society experienced the damaging effects and inconvenience that resulted. Everyone was obliged to tolerate this evil, yet it was not in anyone's power to oppose it. The same Gora who was reluctant to relax any restrictions in educated society, now attacked the restrictions prevalent in this place. He succeeded in influencing their priests, but failed to win the consent of community members. Incensed at Gora, they declared: 'Very well, when the Brahmans allow their widows to marry, so shall we.' Their main cause of anger was that they imagined Gora regarded them with contempt as a lowly community. They felt Gora had come there to preach that it was appropriate for people like themselves to adopt the meanest of customs.

Roaming in the villages, Gora had also observed that the Muslims possessed the unifying element that could draw them together. He had noticed that in times of trouble or difficulty in the village, the Hindus would not close their ranks to stand by each other like the Muslims. Gora had repeatedly wondered why such a vast gap should exist between these two communities, the closest of neighbours. He did not want to accept the answer that came to mind. It pained his entire being to acknowledge that Muslims were united by their dharma, not merely by their practices. Just as the bonds of tradition had not needlessly restrained all their activities, so also were their bonds of religion extremely close. Together, they had all accepted something that was not merely a 'no' but a 'yes', not impoverishing but enriching, for which human beings could, at a single call and in a single instant, stand together and readily surrender their lives.

In educated society, when Gora wrote, argued or delivered speeches, to persuade others and make them toe his line he had naturally coloured his ideas with the attractive hues of fancy, embellished the concrete with abstract analysis, presented even redundant ruins as enchanting images illumined by the moonlight of emotion. Because a section of his own countrymen were hostile to the country, because they viewed all aspects of their country in a negative light, a strong sense of patriotism had prompted Gora to protect his land from the humiliation of this self-detached view by trying day and night to cover his country's entire image with a dazzling emotional aura. That had become his habit. All was praiseworthy, even what others called a fault was somehow a virtue. Not that Gora tried to prove this like a lawyer; rather, he believed it with all his heart. Even in the most impossible situations he had flaunted this belief boldly like a victory flag, grasping it firmly and holding it aloft as he stood alone, confronting all his jeering adversaries. He had just one thing to say: he must first renew his countrymen's respect for their own land, before he took on any other task.

But when he entered the village, there was no audience to face, no need to prove anything, no longer any need to arouse all his confrontational instincts to subdue the contempt or jealousy of others. Here, therefore, he did not view the truth through any sort of veil or screen. It was the force of his patriotism that added extraordinary sharpness to his vision of the truth.

~68~

Dressed in a tussar jacket with a Chinese collar, chador wrapped around his waist, canvas bag in hand, Kailash came in person to Harimohini and greeted her with a pranam. He was close to thirty-five, of short, compact, sturdy build, his shaven moustache and beard sprouting like fresh grass after a few days minus the shaving blade. Seeing a relative from her husband's side of the family after so long, Harimohini exclaimed:

'What's this, it's Thakurpo is it not! Come, come, sit down!' She hastened to lay out a mat.

'Will you wash your hands and feet?' she asked.

'No, there is no need,' Kailash replied. 'Well, you seem to be in good health.'

'I'm hardly keeping well,' responded Harimohini, sensing that it was culpable to be in good shape. She proceeded to offer a catalogue of her various ailments and added: 'Well, I would be relieved to lay down my wretched body, but death doesn't favour me.'

Kailash objected to this indifferent attitude to life, and to prove that they derived great comfort from Harimohini's being alive even after dada, their elder brother, was no more, he declared:

'Don't you see, it's because you are there that one had reason to visit Kolkata, and found a place to stay, at least.'

After exhaustively recounting all the news about relatives and fellow-villagers, Kailash suddenly enquired, looking all around: 'Does this house belong to him, then?'

'Yes,' replied Harimohini.

'A brick-and-mortar house, I see.'

'Indeed it is,' affirmed Harimohini, fanning his enthusiasm. 'All of it.'

He also noted that the building's beams were made of sturdy sal and that the doors and windows were not built of mango wood. Nor did he fail to observe whether the walls of the house were a brick-and-a-half in thickness, or two. He also found out through interrogation the number of rooms, upstairs and down. Altogether, the whole affair struck him as rather satisfactory. It was hard for him to gauge what the cost of constructing this house might have been, for he did not know the exact price of all these building materials. Thinking it over, jiggling his crossed ankles, he told himself: 'It would have cost ten to fifteen thousand rupees at least.' Verbally reducing his estimate, he asked: 'What do you say Bouthakrun, it might have cost seven or eight thousand, maybe?'

'What's this you say Thakurpo, what is seven or eight thousand?' exclaimed Harimohini, expressing surprise at Kalilash's provincial ignorance. 'It wouldn't have cost a paisa less than twenty thousand rupees.'

With great attention, Kailash began to silently inspect everything around him. He derived a tremendous satisfaction from the thought that at this very moment, at a single nod of the head, he could become the sole master of this brick-built house, complete with sal beams and segun doors and windows.

'This is all very well, but where is the girl?' he asked.

'She has been invited away to her pishi's house,' Harimohini hastily replied. 'She may take three or four days longer.'

'Then how is one to see her?' Kailash said. 'I have another legal case coming up, and must leave by tomorrow.'

'Forget your legal case for the moment,' Harimohini urged him. 'You can't leave until the business here is settled.'

'Well, maybe the court case will be stalled, decreed one-sided. So let it be,' Kailash decided after some thought. After inspecting his surroundings once more, he judged that there were provisions here to compensate him. Suddenly he noticed some water that had collected in a corner of Harimohini's puja room. The room had no drainage, yet Harimohini constantly washed and cleaned it with water. Hence some water always remained in a corner.

'Bouthakrun, that's not good,' Kailash exclaimed in agitation.

'Why, what is the matter?'

'That water collecting there, it won't do at all.'

'How can I prevent it Thakurpo?'

'No no, that can't be allowed. The roof will be completely damaged. Let me tell you Bouthakrun, we can't let you pour water around in this room.'

Harimohini was forced to remain silent. Kailash then expressed curiosity about the beauty of the prospective bride.

'That you will notice as soon as you see her,' Harimohini assured him. 'I can venture to say that your household has not received such a bride.'

'What! Our Mejobou . . .'

'There's no comparison! As if your Mejobou can match her!' Harimohini was none too pleased that it was Mejobou he named as the ideal of beauty in their family. 'Whatever you may say bapu, I like our No'bou much better than Mejobou!'

Kailash was not enthused at all by this comparison of Mejobou's beauty with No'bou's. In his imagination, he had added elongated eyes and a banshee-like nose to some previously unseen image, unleashing his fancy amidst a mass of ankle-length tresses. Harimohini realized that this matrimonial prospect was full of hope. In fact, she felt that even the bride's significant social shortcomings may not count as insurmountable obstacles in this case.

~69~

Knowing that Gora set out at dawn these days, Binoy arrived early at Gora's house on Monday, while it was still dark. He went straight upstairs to Gora's bedchamber. Not finding him there, he asked a servant and was informed that Gora was in the puja room. He was privately rather surprised. Going to the door of the thakurghor, he found Gora in an attitude of prayer, dressed in a raw-silk dhoti, a raw-silk wrap around his shoulders, but with the greater part of his massive white body uncovered. Seeing Gora at his prayers, Binoy was even more astonished. Hearing his footsteps, Gora turned around and seeing Binoy, he rose to his feet.

'Don't enter this room,' he cried in agitation.

'Don't worry, I won't,' Binoy assured him. 'It was you I had come to see.'

Gora emerged, changed his clothes, and led Binoy to the room on the second floor.

'Bhai Gora, it's Monday,' Binoy reminded him.

'It must be Monday,' Gora responded. 'The almanac might be wrong, but you cannot be mistaken about today's date. At least it's not Tuesday, that's for sure.'

'You may not attend, I know, but on this day, I cannot proceed with this undertaking without asking you once. That is why I have come to you first thing in the morning, immediately upon awakening.' Gora remained motionless, saying nothing. 'So it is decided that you will not be able to attend my wedding celebrations?'

'No Binoy, I can't attend.'

Binoy remained silent.

'So what if I don't attend?' smiled Gora, completely suppressing his inner anguish. 'The victory is yours. You have managed to drag Ma away after all. I tried so hard, but I could not hold her back by any means. Ultimately, even with my own mother, I had to lose to you! Binoy, will you take away everything from me then, one by one—*sab lal ho jayega*? Will I alone be left on the map that I have drawn?'

'Bhai, please don't blame me. I had told her very emphatically: "Ma, you can't attend my wedding under any circumstances." Ma said, "Look here Binu, those who will not attend your wedding would boycott it even if you invited them, and those who will attend it would do so even if you forbade them. Hence I advise you to remain silent: neither invite nor prohibit anyone." Gora, is it to me that you have lost? Your defeat is at your mother's hands, a thousand times over. Can there be another mother like her?'

Although Gora had tried with all his might to restrain Anandamoyi, in his heart of hearts he had not felt hurt that she had gone away to attend Binoy's marriage, disregarding all his restrictions, ignoring his anger and pain. Rather, he had felt a sense of joy. Now he knew for certain that, however wide the gulf between him and Binoy, he could never succeed in depriving Binoy of his share of that deep nectar of affection, that portion of his mother's boundless love to which Binoy had acquired a claim. The knowledge seemed to console and pacify Gora's heart. In all other respects he might drift far apart from Binoy, but at a very profound level, this bond of invincible maternal love would forever bind these two eternal friends in the closest of relationships.

'Bhai, I'll take your leave now,' said Binoy. 'Don't attend if it is utterly impossible for you, but don't harbour displeasure in your heart, Gora! If you can feel within you the tremendous fulfillment my life has attained through this union, you will never be able to banish this marriage of ours from its place in your heart—this I declare with conviction.' Binoy rose to his feet.

'Wait, Binoy! The hour for your wedding ceremony is late at night. What's the hurry so early in the day?'

At Gora's unexpected, affectionate request, Binoy's heart melted and he at once resumed his place. Now after a long time, at this early hour, the two of them engaged in intimate conversation as in old times. Gora struck the very note to which Binoy's heart was tuned these days. Binoy's words did not seem to end. The histories of so many trivial events, which if written in black and white would seem insignificant if not ridiculous, rose to his lips like the taan of a classical song, repeated like a refrain with effusions of new sweetness. In his skilful language, Binoy began to describe, in very fine yet deeply moving terms, the exquisite range of emotions evoked by the wonderful drama currently being played out on the stage of his heart. What an unprecedented experience his life had offered him! Surely the indescribable substance that had filled Binoy's heart was not for everyone! Not everyone had the power to accept it, did they? In the union between men and women generally seen in this world, one rarely heard this supreme harmony. Binoy repeatedly urged Gora not to compare the two of them with all the rest. He doubted that such a thing had ever happened before. If it were so common, society would be surging with the spirit of restless energy, just as a single touch of the spring breeze inspires a rapturous blossoming of new leaves and flowers in every forest and grove. Then people could not have spent their days eating, drinking, sleeping and relaxing in indolent ease. Then all the beauty or power that each person possessed would have blossomed everywhere in different ways, in different forms. This was a magic wand indeed—who could remain inert, ignoring its touch? It transformed even ordinary people into extraordinary individuals. If a human being savoured that extraordinariness even once, he understood what life was really about!

'Gora, I assure you, love is a way to instantly awaken the whole of human nature,' Binoy marveled. 'For some reason love manifests itself very faintly in our lives, so each of us is deprived of complete understanding, remaining ignorant of what we possess, unable to express what is concealed, and not empowered to expend what we have accumulated. That is why there is such joylessness everywhere, such utter joylessness. That is why only a few persons like you recognize that there is any greatness within us. There is no general awareness of it at all, in people's minds.'

When Mahim arose from bed with a noisy yawn and went to wash his face, the sound of his footsteps halted the flood of Binoy's enthusiasm. He took his leave of Gora and went on his way. From the terrace, gazing at the blood-red eastern sky, Gora sighed. For a long time he roamed the terrace. He did not make it to the village that day.

Gora found himself unable to compensate by any means, through any activity, for the longing, the lack he now felt within his heart. Not just his self, but all his endeavours, seemed to reach upward with arms outstretched, begging: 'I need a light—a bright, beautiful light.' As if all the ingredients were ready, as if diamonds, gems, gold and silver were not priceless, and iron, thunder, armour and leather were not scarce, but only the soft, beautiful light, aglow with hope and solace, suffused with the rosy hue of the sun, was missing. It required no effort to augment what was already there, it was only waiting to be rendered more bright, more lovely and more clearly visible.

When Binoy declared that an indescribable wonder arises from the love between man and woman at certain auspicious inaugural moments, Gora could not dismiss the matter as a joke, like before. He privately acknowledged that this was no ordinary union, but complete fulfillment. Everything gained value from contact with it. It gave body to imagination and infused the body with energy. It not only redoubled the soul's vitality and the mind's capacity for reflection, but also crowned them with a new rasa, a new flavour.

On this day of their social separation, before he departed, Binoy's heart played a complete, singular melody upon Gora's. Binoy went away, the morning advanced, but that music refused to fade. Like the merging of two oceanbound rivers, the stream of Binoy's love encountered Gora's and the waves began to resonate as they met. What Gora had been trying to conceal from himself by somehow obstructing, suppressing or enfeebling it, now broke its banks and manifested itself in a clear, forceful form. Gora no longer retained the strength to denounce it as illicit, or dismiss it as negligible. The entire day passed in this fashion. Ultimately, as afternoon was fading into dusk, Gora picked up a wrap, flung it over his shoulder and stepped out into the street.

'I shall claim the one who belongs to me,' he declared. 'Otherwise I shall remain unfulfilled on earth, my life will be futile.' Gora remained in no doubt that in the whole world, Sucharita was awaiting his call alone. This very day, this very evening, he must answer this expectation. He rushed through the crowded Kolkata streets. Nobody and nothing seemed to touch him. His mind seemed to outrun his body, advancing single-mindedly, far ahead.

Arriving before Sucharita's house, Gora seemed to suddenly come to his senses. He paused. All these days, he had never found her door closed whenever he came, but today he discovered that it was not open. He pushed, and found it locked on the inside. After pausing briefly to think, he banged on the door a few times. The bearer opened the door and came out. Seeing Gora in the indistinct twilight, he declared, without waiting for any questions: 'Didithakrun is not home.'

'Where is she?'

'She has been busy elsewhere these last few days, organizing Lalitadidi's wedding.'

For a second Gora considered going to Binoy's wedding celebration itself. At this moment, an unknown gentleman emerged from within the house and asked:

'Yes mahashai, what do you want?'

'No, I don't want anything,' replied Gora, inspecting him from head to toe.

'Please come in for a while,' Kailash invited. 'Perhaps you might fancy some tobacco.'

Kailash was at his wits' end for lack of company. If he could only drag someone, anyone, into his room for a chat, he would feel relieved. During the day, he somehow passed his time standing at the corner of the alley, hookah in hand, observing the passers by. But in the evening, confined indoors, he grew desperate. All that he had to discuss with Harimohini had been completely exhausted. Harimohini's capacity for discussion was also extremely limited. Hence Kailash had ensconced himself with his hookah on a wooden divan in a small room next to the outer door on the ground floor, and would occasionally send for the bearer to pass the time chatting with him.

'No,' said Gora, 'I can't stay now.' In the blink of an eye, even as Kailash began to repeat his request, he had already crossed the alley.

Gora had developed the fixed notion that most events in his life were not arbitrary, nor prompted by his personal wishes alone. He had been born to fulfill some purpose of the Maker of his nation's destiny. Hence he tried to attach some special meaning even to the minor events of his life. Today, driven by such a powerful desire, when he suddenly arrived at Sucharita's door and found it locked, and upon the door being opened, discovered that she was not home, he took it to be a significant event manifesting some purpose. The One who guided Gora had chosen this way to forbid him. In this life, Sucharita's door was closed to him, she was not meant

for him. A person like Gora could not afford to be obsessed
with his own desires, for his own joys and sorrows did not
count. He was a Brahman who belonged to Bharatvarsha, he
must worship the deity on Bharatvarsha's behalf, his duty it
was to meditate upon Bharatvarsha. Attachment and love
were not for him. Gora told himself:

'The Maker has clearly shown me what attachment is like.
He has demonstrated that it is not fair, not peaceful, but red
like wine, and pungent like wine. It does not allow the
intellect to remain steady, it presents things in a false light. I
am a sanyasi, and in my holy endeavour such an emotion has
no place.'

~70~

After many days of torment, the comfort Sucharita enjoyed
with Anandamoyi was beyond anything she had experienced
before. Anadamoyi had drawn her so close so easily, it was
impossible for Sucharita to imagine she had ever been unfamiliar
or remote. She seemed somehow to have understood
Sucharita's heart completely and seemed to offer her a deep
solace even without words. Never before had Sucharita uttered
the word 'Ma' with all her heart. Even without any need, she
would invent various pretexts for addressing Anandamoyi as
Ma, and call her by that name. When arrangements for
Lalita's wedding were complete, lying tiredly in bed, she was
haunted by the thought: how could she now leave Anandamoyi!
'Ma, Ma, Ma!' she repeated, involuntarily. As she spoke, her
heart swelled and tears streamed from her eyes. Then she
suddenly saw Anandamoyi raise her mosquito net to enter her
bed.

'Were you calling me?' asked Anandamoyi, patting
Sucharita. Now Sucharita realized she had been calling for

'Ma'. Unable to reply, she hid her face in Anandamoyi's lap and wept. Without a word, Anandamoyi slowly stroked her body. That night she slept by Sucharita's side.

Anandamoyi could not depart as soon as Binoy's wedding was over.

'They are novices, both of them,' she declared. 'How can I go away without organizing their household a little bit?'

'Then I too shall stay here with you these few days, Ma,' Sucharita decided.

Hearing this proposal, Satish rushed up to embrace Sucharita. 'Yes Didi, I'll stay with you all too,' he cried, bouncing up and down.

'But you have your studies, bakhtiar!' Sucharita pointed out.

'Binoybabu will tutor me.'

'Binoybabu can't tutor you now,' said Sucharita.

'I certainly can,' Binoy called from the adjacent room. 'I fail to see how I could have become so infirm in a single day. Nor do I feel a single night has made me forget all I had learned from many nights of study.'

'Will your mashi agree?' Anandamoyi asked Sucharita.

'I'll write to her,' Sucharita proposed.

'Not you,' Anandamoyi said. 'I shall write to her myself.'

Anandamoyi knew Harimohini would feel offended if Sucharita wished to stay there. But if Anandamoyi requested her, she would become the target of any rancour Harimohini might feel, and there was no harm in that. In her letter, Anandamoyi intimated that she must spend some time in Binoy's house, to set up Lalita's new household. She would find it a great help if Sucharita were also permitted to remain with her these few days. Harimohini was not only incensed at Anandamoyi's letter, she also developed a certain suspicion. She thought, since she had forbidden the son to visit the house, the mother was now casting her web of deceit upon

Sucharita. She clearly detected a conspiracy between mother and son, also recalling that Anandamoyi's attitude had displeased her from the beginning. She would be relieved to ensure Sucharita's safety by making her a member of the famous Ray family at the earliest, without further delay. How long could Kailash be kept waiting like this, either? The poor fellow was close to blackening the walls of their house from puffing on tobacco day and night.

The very morning after receiving this letter, Harimohini traveled in her palki to Binoy's house in person, accompanied by her bearer. Sucharita, Lalita and Anandamoyi were busy with cooking preparations in the room downstairs. From upstairs, Satish's voice had roused the entire neighbourhood in his attempts to memorize the spellings of English words and their Bengali equivalents. At home, one could scarcely sense his vocal powers, but here he must expend much unnecessary energy on the sound of his voice, to prove beyond doubt that he was not neglecting his studies at all. Anandamoyi welcomed Harimohini with special warmth.

'I have come to fetch Radharani,' Harimohini announced bluntly, ignoring such civilities.

'Very well, so you shall. Please spend a little time with us.'

'No, all my prayers and rituals are unfinished, I haven't even completed my ahnik. I can't linger here now.'

Sucharita was quiet, busy chopping a pumpkin.

'Do you hear me?' Harimohini called to her. 'It's getting late.'

Lalita and Anandamoyi remained silent. Sucharita completed her task and rose to her feet. 'Come, Mashi, let's go,' she said. As Harimohini went towards the palki, Sucharita grasped her hand and said: 'Come, please come inside this room just for a moment.' Leading her into the room, Sucharita firmly declared: 'Since you have come to fetch me, I shall not turn you away immediately in front of everyone. I shall accompany you indeed. But I shall come back here this very afternoon.'

'What a suggestion!' spluttered Harimohini. 'You may as well announce that you will remain here forever!'

'Indeed I can't remain here forever. That is why, as long as I can remain with her, I shall not leave her.'

Harimohini fumed at her words, but did not deem it wise to say anything now.

'Ma, I'll go visit my home once,' smiled Sucharita, going up to Anandamoyi.

'Very well ma, we shall see you again,' Anandamoyi responded, asking no questions.

'I'll be back this afternoon,' Sucharita whispered to Lalita. 'Satish?' she called, waiting near the palki.

'Let Satish stay here,' said Harimohini. Thinking that Satish might prove a hindrance if he went home, she considered it prudent to let him remain away. When the two of them had mounted the palki, Harimohini tried to broach the subject.

'So Lalita is married now,' she began. 'That's a good thing. Poreshbabu can be relieved about one daughter at least.' She then proceeded to explain how great a burden an unwed daughter was upon her family, a cause of such unbearable anxiety. 'What can I tell you, I have no other anxieties. When I chant the Almighty's name, I'm haunted only by that one worry. Truth be told, I can no longer concentrate on my Thakur's service as before. Gopiballav, I pray, after snatching away all I possessed, what is this new trap you have devised for me!'

This was not merely a worldly concern for Harimohini: it was blocking her path to spiritual liberation. But still, even after being told of such a major threat, Sucharita remained silent. Harimohini could not fathom her exact state of mind. She felt it suited her purpose to accept the common saying, silence means consent. She thought Sucharita's heart had softened a little. Harimohini hinted that she had made it extremely easy for a woman like Sucharita to accomplish the immensely difficult feat of joining the Hindu community. She was about to receive such an opportunity, that even at feasts hosted by the most eminent of kulin households, nobody would dare say anything against her dining in their company.

When the preamble had reached this point, the palki reached their house. As they mounted the stairs after alighting at the door and entering the house, Sucharita glimpsed, in the room beside the entrance, a strange man receiving an oil massage from the bearer, to the accompaniment of loud thumps. Seeing her, the man showed no embarrassment. He stared at her with special curiosity.

Once upstairs, Harimohini informed Sucharita of her deor's arrival. Tallying this with Harimohini's preamble, Sucharita correctly surmised the significance of this event. Harimohini tried to reason with her, saying there was a visitor in the house, and it would not be civil of Sucharita to abandon him and depart that very afternoon.

'No Mashi, I must go,' Sucharita insisted, shaking her head vehemently.

'Very well, stay tonight and go tomorrow,' her aunt proposed.

'I shall bathe now, and immediately go to Baba's place for lunch. From there, I'll move to Lalita's house,' Sucharita asserted.

'But he has come to see you,' Harimohini now declared bluntly.

'What is the use?' demanded Sucharita, flushing.

'Just listen to this! Can such events take place without viewing the bride, nowadays? It was the custom, rather, in earlier times. Your mesho had not seen me before the shubhodrishti.' Having uttered these words, Harimohini quickly added a few more remarks to mask the explicitness of her suggestion. She recounted how, when it was time to see the bride before fixing the match, an old family retainer called Anathbandhu and an elderly maidservant named Thakurdasi had been sent by the eminent Ray family, how the two had arrived with a pair of staff-bearing turbaned guards to view the girl in her parental home, how nervous her guardians had become on that occasion, and how their household had been thrown into a frenzy of activity to please these representatives with food and hospitality. Sighing, Harimohini observed that times were different now.

'It'll be no trouble, he'll just see you once for five minutes,' she told Sucharita.

'No,' said Sucharita. So emphatic and clear was her 'no,' that Harimohini had to retreat a little.

'Achchha, let it be. He need not see you after all. But still, Kailash is a modern, educated young man, and like the rest of you he doesn't observe any rules. "I'll see the paatri for myself," he insists. So, since you girls come out in public, I told him, "Seeing her is no problem. I'll arrange a meeting with her some day." But if you feel shy, let the meeting not take place.'

She now waxed eloquent about Kailash's extraordinary learning, how with a single stroke of his pen he had overwhelmed the village postmaster, how no-one from the surrounding villages could afford to take a single step without consulting Kailash about handling court cases or writing applications. And as for his moral character, it was needless to elaborate. After his wife's death he had not wanted to remarry under any circumstances; when greatly pressured by his relatives, he had simply bowed to his elders' command. Hadn't Harimohini herself found it so hard to make him agree to the present proposal? As if he was willing to listen! They were of such eminent descent after all. They enjoyed such immense social prestige!

Sucharita utterly refused to damage that prestige. Not under any circumstances. She expressed total disregard for her own honour or self-interest. In fact, she indicated she would remain quite unperturbed even if she were refused a place in Hindu society. The foolish girl failed to realize that Kailash's hard-won consent to this marriage was no mean honour for her. Instead, she found it humiliating. Harimohini was completely stupefied at these perverse attitudes of the modern age. Now she vented her inner rage through repeated insinuations about Gora.

'However much Gora may boast of his Hindu identity, what is his place within the community? Who takes him seriously? If he is tempted into marrying some rich girl from a Brahmo family, by what means will he earn a reprieve from the disciplinary processes of society? He will have to burn up all his money just to stop tongues wagging.' And so on, in the same vein.

'Mashi, why do you say such things?' Sucharita protested. 'You know such remarks are baseless.'

Harimohini retorted that at her age, no-one could deceive her with words. She kept her eyes and ears open. She could see, hear and understand everything, but was speechless with surprise. She expressed her firm conviction that Gora was conspiring with his mother to seek Sucharita's hand in marriage, that the deeper motive behind this was not a noble one, and that unless she managed to protect Sucharita with the Ray family's help, matters would indeed take this course.

Though patient by nature, Sucharita found this too much to bear. 'I respect the persons you mention,' she objected. 'Since you will never truly understand the nature of my relationship with them, I have no other option but to leave this place at once. When you calm down, when it becomes possible for me to come and live in this house with you alone, I shall return.'

'If you are not partial to Gourmohan, if it is certain that you will never marry him, then what's wrong with this present suitor?' demanded Harimohini. 'You wouldn't remain a spinster, after all.'

'Why not? I shall never marry!'

'Until you are old . . .' spluttered Harimohini, wide-eyed and incredulous.

'Yes, until I die.'

~71~

This blow brought about a change of heart in Gora. He tried to determine why his heart had become vulnerable to Sucharita. He had mingled with these people, and at some stage, unbeknownst to himself, had become involved with them. Where lines of prohibition were drawn, Gora had arrogantly overstepped those limits. This was not the way of our nation. Unless each person safeguards his own boundaries, he not only harms himself intentionally or unintentionally, but also loses the unsullied power to do good to others. Through commingling, various strong urges are aroused, polluting one's knowledge, commitment and strength.

Not that he had discovered this truth solely through his interaction with the women of a Brahmo family. When Gora had tried to mingle with the common folk, there too he seemed to have been sucked into a whirlpool, almost losing touch with himself. For at every step he felt pity, and overwhelmed by this emotion, he constantly told himself: that is evil, that is unjust, that must be removed. But did this pity itself not distort one's judgement concerning right and wrong? The stronger our urge to show pity, the more we lose our ability to view the truth objectively. Darkened by pity's smoky vision, what is utterly pale appears to us in very intense hues.

That is why, Gora argued, it has always been customary in our land for the person responsible for the general good to remain unattached. It is baseless to claim that only by closely mingling with his subjects can a ruler look after his people. The kind of knowledge about his subjects that a ruler requires grows tainted through commingling. Therefore the subjects themselves have deliberately kept their king confined to a certain distance. If the ruler becomes their companion, there would no longer be any need for him to rule. A Brahman, too, was similarly remote, similarly unattached. A Brahman must do a lot of good, hence he must be denied close association with many others.

'I am that Brahman of Bharatvarsha,' Gora declared. He did not count among the nation's living substance those Brahmans who were dying of suffocation, having tied the noose of lowcaste Shudra tendencies around their own necks by getting entangled with all and sundry, wallowing the mire of trade, and succumbing to the lure of wealth. Gora considered them inferior to the Shudras, for the Shudra remained alive by virtue of his designated Shudra ways, whereas these Brahmans were virtually dead from having lost their Brahman qualities, and therefore impure. It was because of them that Bharatvarsha today was undergoing such a degraded phase of grieving without purity.

Gora now prepared his mind to practice within himself the Brahman's revival mantra. 'I must be extremely pure and clean,' he resolved. 'I do not occupy the same ground as everyone else. Friendship is not necessary for me. I do not belong to that ordinary category of people who delight in the company of women. And I must completely reject close intimacy with the base commoners of this land. They look up to Brahmans as the earth gazes at the sky in hope of rain. If I come too close, who will save them then?'

Up until now, Gora had never concentrated on idol

worship. But ever since his heart had been thrown into turmoil, ever since he became unable to restrain himself, ever since his work began to seem hollow and meaningless and life seemed to be broken in two, crying out in anguish—ever since then, Gora had been trying to concentrate on his prayers. Seated motionless before the idol, he tried to completely immerse his mind in that image. But he could not arouse his own devotion by any means. He would analyze the deity with his intellect, unable to accept divinity in any but a symbolic form. But one cannot offer devotion to a symbol. One cannot worship a metaphysical explanation. Rather, instead of trying to pray in a temple, when he stayed home and allowed his mind and speech to float away on a tide of emotion while arguing with himself or someone else, he felt the stirrings of bliss and devotion within his heart.

Still Gora did not give up. He sat down to pray regularly, everyday, accepting it as a discipline. He persuaded himself that where one could not unite with everyone on an emotional basis, it was the law that preserved such unity everywhere. Whenever Gora had visited a village, he had entered the local temple and after deep meditation had told himself: 'This indeed is my special place. Deity on one side, devotees on the other, and between them the Brahman, a bridge to shore up the union between them.'

Gradually Gora felt that a Brahman had no need for devotion. Devotion was a special commodity meant for the common people. It was knowledge that formed the bridge between devotee and object of devotion. This bridge upheld the union of the two, but also protected the boundaries of both. Without pure knowledge to distance devotee from deity, everything became distorted. Hence, overwhelming devotion was not for the Brahman's consumption. Seated upon the pinnacle of knowledge, the Brahman meditates in order to keep this stream of devotion pure for the general public to consume. Just as the Brahman has no comforts to enjoy in his worldly life, so also he has no devotion to relish in his life of prayer. That is the Brahman's glory. For the Brahman, worldly life offers discipline and control, and the pursuit of prayer offers knowledge.

His heart had overpowered him. For this crime, Gora condemned his heart to exile. But who was there to lead it into exile! Where was the army to perform that task!

~72~

Preparations were under way for the ritual penance at the garden estate on the Ganga shore. Abinash felt rather regretful that this ceremony would not draw much public attention because it was taking place outside Kolkata. He knew Gora had no need to perform penance for himself: it was for the sake of his countrymen. For moral effect. Hence this ritual ought to be performed before a crowd.

But Gora would not agree. The interior of Kolkata was not suitable for the massive sacrificial hom fire and the chanting of Veda mantras that were part of his plans for this ceremony. One required a forest grove for meditation. On the secluded Ganga shore, resonant with the chanting of mantras and illuminated by the hom fire, Gora would summon the ancient Bharatvarsha that was the entire world's guru, and having bathed to purify himself, he would accept His initiation into a new life. Gora was not concerned about moral effect.

Abinash now had no other recourse but the newspapers. Without informing Gora, he announced the penance ceremony in all the papers. Not only that, he wrote lengthy pieces in the editorial columns, insisting that no blame could attach to a strong, pure Brahman like Gora, who had nevertheless undertaken this penance on the entire nation's behalf, shouldering all the sins of the depraved Bharatvarsha of today. 'As our nation now frets in the prison of foreign rule owing to its own misdeeds, so too has Gora, in his personal life, accepted the pain of living in that prison,' he wrote. 'Just as he has personally borne his nation's sorrows, so also is he prepared to do penance for the nation's wrongdoings, at this personal ceremony. Hence, bhai Bengalis, you beloved, suffering, hundred thousand children of Bharat, you . . .' and so on.

Reading these pieces, Gora was beside himself with fury. But there was no curbing Abinash. Even if Gora swore at him, he did not mind. Rather, it pleased him. 'My guru inhabits the realm of lofty ideas, he understands nothing of such worldly matters. He is like Narada on the mountain Baikuntha, who created the river Ganga by melting Vishnu's heart with the music of his veena. But bringing that river down to this earth to revive Sagara's offspring from their ashes is a task for the Bhagiraths of this world, not for those who inhabit the heavenly sphere. These two activities are completely separate.' So, when his activities enraged Gora, Abinash was secretly amused, and his devotion to Gora increased. 'Our guru resembles Shiva in appearance,' he told himself, 'and his moods too are similar. He comprehends nothing, has no practical sense, loses his temper at the slightest provocation, but doesn't take long to cool down either.'

Abinash's efforts caused a general sensation about Gora's penance. An even larger number thronged Gora's house to see him and talk to him. So many letters started pouring in everyday from everywhere, he stopped reading his mail. He began to feel this countrywide discussion had eroded the dispassionate purity of his penance, making it a worldly, passion-based affair. The times they lived in were to blame.

Nowadays Krishnadayal did not touch newspapers, but public rumours penetrated even into his prayer-sanctum.

With special pride, Krishnadayal's beneficiaries communicated to him the news that his worthy son Gora was readying himself for penance with great pomp and ceremony, and the hope that following in his father's sacred footsteps he would one day become an enlightened man just like him.

It was hard to say how long it had been since Krishnadayal had last set foot in Gora's chamber. Shedding his silk attire for cotton, he went directly into Gora's room. He did not see Gora there. Upon asking the attendant, he was told that Gora was in the puja room. What! What business had he in the puja room? He was praying there. Rushing in agitation to the puja room, Krishnadayal found that Gora was indeed at his prayers.

'Gora!' he called from outside.

Surprised at his father's arrival, Gora rose to his feet. Krishnadayal had specially installed his own tutelary deity in his prayer-sanctum. Theirs was a Vaishnava family, but having accepted the shakti mantra, Krishnadayal had not had direct contact with their household deity for a long time.

'Come, come,' he called to Gora. 'Come out.' Gora emerged from the room. 'This is outrageous!' spluttered Krishnadayal. 'What are you doing here?' Gora offered no reply. 'There is a Brahman priest to perform the daily puja on the entire household's behalf,' Krishnadayal insisted. 'Why must you come into this!'

'There is nothing wrong in that.'

'Nothing wrong! How can you say that! It's very wrong indeed. What is the need for someone to attempt what he doesn't have the right to do? That is sinful. Not only for you, but for all of us in this house.'

'In terms of inner faith, very few people have the right to sit before the deity, indeed. But are you saying I don't even possess the same rights as that Ramahari Thakur of ours, who is entitled to pray here?'

Krishnadayal was suddenly at a loss for a reply. 'Look

here,' he said after a short pause, 'performing puja rituals is
Ramahari's family trade. Occupational sins don't matter to
the deity. Looking for lapses here would put a stop to the
trade itself, making it impossible for society to function. But
in your case, that excuse doesn't apply. What is the need for
you to enter this room?'

It did not seem totally incongruous for a man like
Krishnadayal to declare it a sin even for a disciplined,
committed Brahman like Gora to enter the prayer chamber.
So Gora bore his remarks in silence.

'There's something else I hear, Gora!' Krishnadayal
continued. 'You have invited all the pundits to perform a
ritual penance, I believe?'

'Yes.'

'I shall never allow it, as long as I live!' cried Krishnadayal
in great agitation.

'Why not?' Gora demanded, beginning to feel rebellious.

'Why not indeed! I had told you once before that the
penance cannot take place.'

'Indeed you had, but you had not offered any reason.'

'I see no need to offer reasons. We are your elders after
all, you owe us respect. There is no law that permits you to
perform such religious rituals without our consent. The ritual
involves praying for your ancestors' souls, do you know that?'

'Why is that forbidden?' asked Gora in astonishment.

'It is utterly forbidden,' insisted Krisnadayal, in a fury. 'I
cannot allow it.'

'Look, sir, this is my personal business,' said Gora,
wounded to the quick. 'I have planned this for my own
purification. Why torment yourself with futile argument?'

'Look Gora, don't try to argue about everything. These
are not matters for argument. There are many such things that
remain beyond your comprehension. I tell you again—you
imagine you have entered the Hindu faith, but that is a

completely mistaken assumption. It is not within your power to do so. Every drop of your blood, from head to toe, is against it. You cannot suddenly become a Hindu, even if you want to! You need the accumulated virtue of many births.'

Gora's face grew flushed. 'I don't know about past births,' he asserted, 'but may I not claim even the right that flows in your ancestral blood?'

'Again you argue! Aren't you ashamed to answer me back! And you call yourself a Hindu! Where will your British arrogance hide itself, after all! Listen to what I say. Stop all those preparations.'

Hanging his head, Gora stood silent. 'Unless I perform the penance, I'm afraid I can't join everybody at Shashimukhi's wedding feast,' he said after a while.

'That is fine,' Krishnadayal responded enthusiastically. 'What's wrong with that? They'll arrange for you to sit separately, then.'

'So I shall have to remain separate within the community.'

'All the better.' Observing Gora's surprise his enthusiasm, Krishnadayal added, 'Take me for instance. I don't dine with anybody, even when invited. What contact do I have with society? Considering the pure, disinterested life you wish to lead, you too should adopt such a path. This will be most beneficial for you, I can see.'

At noon, Krishnadayal sent for Abinash. 'So all of you together have incited Gora, am I right?'

'How can you say that! It is your Gora who incites all of us. In fact he himself is less easily swayed.'

'But I tell you, baba, all your penance and suchlike cannot be permitted. I don't approve of it at all. Stop it at once.'

What sort of obdurate whim had this old fellow developed! Abinash wondered. History offers many instances of famous men's fathers who failed to recognize their sons' greatness.

Krishnadayal was a father of that category. If he could have taken a few lessons from his son instead of spending his days and nights in the company of some useless sanyasis, he would have benefited greatly. Abinash was a crafty man, not one to waste words where argument was futile and even moral effect a remote possibility.

'Very well sir,' he said. 'If you don't approve, it will not take place. But now, with all arrangements complete, invitations issued and no time for delay, there's one thing we can still do: let Gora be, it is we who will perform penance on that day. There is no dearth of sins committed by our countrymen, after all.' At Abinash's assurance, Krishnadayal felt relieved.

Gora never had much respect for anything Krishnadayal said. On this occasion, too, he did not privately accept the idea of obeying his orders. In the realm beyond worldly life, Gora did not feel obliged to follow the prohibitions imposed by his parents. But still, a terrible pain now tormented him all day. In his heart arose the indistinct suspicion that some truth lay concealed in all that Krishnadayal had said. He seemed to be haunted by a vague nightmare, which he could not dispel by any means. He felt as if someone was assaulting him from every direction, trying to push him away. Today his own loneliness manifested itself to him in a gigantic form. The field of work before him was vast, and his task was enormous, but no one stood by his side.

~73~

The penance ritual was scheduled for the following day, but Gora was supposed to move into the garden estate the night before. As he was preparing to set out, Harimohini arrived on the scene. Gora was not pleased to see her.

'You have come, but I must leave immediately,' he said. 'Ma has not been home these last few days either. If you need to see her . . .'

'No baba, it is you I have come to see,' Harimohini insisted. 'You must wait a little, but not for long.'

Gora waited. Harimohini broached the subject of Sucharita. She observed that Sucharita had benefited greatly from Gora's tutelage. In fact, nowadays she did not accept water from anyone and everyone, and had become more sensible in every way.

'Baba, how worried I was about her! I can't begin to tell you what a great service you have done me by bringing her on to the right track. May the Almighty make you king of kings. Marry a nice girl from a good family, worthy of your eminent lineage; may she light up your home, and may goddess Lakshmi bless you with wealth and male offspring.'

She then observed that Sucharita was of age, and must marry immediately without an instant's delay. Had she belonged to a Hindu family, her lap would have been teeming with infants by now. Gora must surely agree that delaying her marriage had been a grave lapse. After a long period of intolerable anxiety about the problem of Sucharita's marriage, Harimohini, with much pleading and cajoling, had ultimately persuaded her deor Kailash to come to Kolkata. All the major hindrances she had feared had been removed, by Ishwar's grace. Everything had been decided, the groom's party would not take a paisa as pledge money, nor raise any objections about Sucharita's past history—Harimohini had adopted special strategies to solve these problems—but at this juncture, surprisingly, Sucahrita had dug her heels in. What she had in mind, Harimohini did not know. Whether someone had put ideas into her head, whether she was partial to someone else, who could say! . . .

'But bapu, let me say openly that this girl is not worthy

of you. If she marries into a provincial family, nobody will get to know the truth about her, and things will somehow be managed. But you people live in the city; if you marry her, you will not be able to show your face to the people here.'

'What are you talking about! Who has told you that I have gone to her with a marriage proposal?'

'How would I know baba! It's out in the papers. I'm dying of shame after hearing of it.'

Gora realized that either Haranbabu or someone of his party had publicized this affair in the papers. 'These are bare lies!' he proclaimed, clenching his fists.

'So I believe too,' said Harimohini, startled by his thunderous tone. 'Now you must keep one request of mine. Just come with me to Radharani.'

'Why?'

'You must explain to her once.'

Gora's heart was instantly ready to approach Sucharita on this pretext. 'Come, let us go and meet her today, one last time,' his heart counseled him. 'Tomorrow is your penance, and after that, you will be a hermit. There is just this one night, and just a small part of it. There is no sin in that. Even if there is, it will be reduced to ashes tomorrow.'

'Please tell me what I must explain to her,' Gora asked, after a short silence.

'Nothing, just that according to Hindu principles, it is the duty of a mature woman like Sucharita to marry without delay and that in the Hindu community, it is an unthinkable blessing for a girl in Sucharita's circumstances to acquire a worthy groom like Kailash.'

Gora was pierced to the heart. Remembering the man he had met at Sucharita's door, he was stung, as if by a scorpion. Gora could not bear to even imagine that this man would possess Sucharita.

'No, this can never be!' his heart thundered in protest.

It was impossible that Sucharita's should unite with anyone else. Her deep, silent heart, full of profound intelligence and emotion, had never revealed itself to any second person but Gora, and could never reveal itself thus to anyone else. How extraordinary that revelation had been! How exquisite! What an indescribable reality had manifested itself, in the innermost chamber of mystery's abode! How often could one behold a human being in this way! The man who by divine grace had seen Sucharita in a dimension so profoundly true, and experienced the vision with his whole being, was the very one to possess her. How could anyone else ever possess her!

'Will Radharani always remain a spinster like this?' demanded Harimohini. 'Can that be possible?'

True, indeed. After all, Gora was about to do penance tomorrow. Then he would be completely purified, a true Brahman. Must Sucharita remain unmarried forever, in that case! Who had the right to impose this lifelong burden upon her! What heavier burden could a woman bear!

Harimohini prattled on. Her words did not reach Gora's ears. He began to think:

'When Baba forbade my penance so strongly, did his admonition have no value? The way I construe my life might be merely a figment of my imagination, not congenial to my nature. That artificial burden would cripple me. Under that relentless weight, I would be unable to accomplish any task with ease. For instance, I find desire permeating my heart. Where shall I move this boulder? Somehow Baba realizes that in my heart of hearts I am not a Brahman, nor an ascetic. That is why he forbade me so strongly.'

'Let me go to him,' Gora thought. 'Now, at once, this very evening, I shall ask him forcibly to disclose what he had seen in me. Why did he say even the path of penance is closed to me? If he can explain, I shall be relieved on that score. So relieved!'

'Please wait a little,' Gora requested Harimohini, 'I'll be right back.' He rushed to his father's quarters. He felt Krishnadayal knew something that could offer him an instant reprieve. The door to the prayer sanctum was closed. He banged on it a couple of times. It did not open, nor did anyone respond. From within, the scent of incense wafted out. Tonight, behind closed doors, Krishnadayal, along with the sanyasi, was practicing an extremely esoteric and difficult mode of yoga. Nobody would be allowed in that night.

~74~

'No,' said Gora, 'my penance is not tomorrow. It has begun this very day. The fire ignited today is far greater than the one to be lit tomorrow. It is because a tremendous sacrificial offering is required of me at the start of my new life that the Almighty has aroused such a powerful desire in my heart. Or else why would such a strange thing happen! Where was I located before this! There was no earthly likelihood of my encountering these people. Nor does such a contrary union generally take place in this world. Nor could anyone have imagined that this union would arouse such a great, invincible desire even in the heart of a detached person like me. This very day, I needed such a desire. So far, whatever I have given my country has been easy to part with, no donation ever caused me pain. I could not fathom why people should be at all miserly about sacrificing anything for the nation. But a major yajna does not require such easy donations. It is pain that this sacrificial ceremony requires. The umbilical cord must be cut for my new life to be born. Tomorrow, at daybreak, I shall perform my earthly penance before the general public. On the very eve of that occasion, Destiny has knocked on my door. Unless I perform the profoundest penance within my heart, how can I achieve purification tomorrow! Only after completely surrendering to my deity the offering that is hardest for me to yield, can I become utterly, purely dispossessed. Only then shall I become a Brahman.'

'Baba, please come with me once,' exclaimed Harimohini as soon as Gora appeared before her. 'If you come, just a word from you would take care of everything.'

'Why should I go?' Gora protested. 'What have I to do with her? Nothing whatever!'

'But she reveres you like a god, and calls you her guru.'

Like a bolt of lightning, a red-hot pain pierced Gora's heart. 'I see no need to go,' he declared. 'There is no possibility of my ever meeting her again.'

'True indeed,' agreed Harimohini, delighted. 'It is indeed not a good idea to mingle with a girl so mature. But baba, you can't get away without doing me this favour today. After that, see if I ever call upon you again.'

Gora repeatedly shook his head in refusal. No more, never. It was over. He had surrendered to Destiny. He could not allow any blot upon his purity at this stage. He would not go to see her. Realizing from his expression that it would be impossible to budge him, Harimohini said:

'If you truly cannot go there, then please do me this one favour, baba. Write her a letter.' Gora shook his head. There was no question. No letters. 'Very well,' persisted Harimohini, 'write a couple of lines addressed to me. You know all the shastras. I have come to you for a clarification.'

'What clarification?'

'Whether or not it is the greatest duty of a girl from a Hindu family to marry at an appropriate age and obey the laws of domestic life.'

'Look, please don't entangle me in such affairs,' said Gora after a short silence. 'I am not a pundit to offer such clarifications.'

'Then why don't you tell me frankly what you really want?' demanded Harimohini rather sharply. 'It was you who first knotted the noose, and now it's time to undo it, you say, "don't entangle me"! What is that supposed to mean? The fact is, you don't want her mind to be cleared of all doubt.'

At any other time, Gora would have flared up in fury. He could not have tolerated even such an accurate charge. But now his penance had begun, he did not lose his temper. Probing his heart, he found Harimohini was indeed right. He had become ruthless in order to break his major bond with Sucharita, but he still wanted to preserve a fine thread, pretending not to have seen it at all. He had not yet managed to accept giving up his relationship with Sucharita completely. But he must vanquish this miserliness. It would not do to give away with one hand while holding on with the other. Immediately drawing out a sheet of paper, he firmly inscribed, in large letters:

Marriage is a woman's path to religious pursuits, domesticity her main dharma. Such a marriage is not for wish-fulfillment, but for the benefit of all. Whether the home is a happy one or not, to welcome that home, to remain virtuous, devoted and pure, to preserve the image of dharma within the house—that is the holy pledge of womanhood.

'In a similar vein you could make some small mention of our Kailash, baba!' urged Harimohini.

'No, I don't know him. I can't write about him.'

Having lovingly folded the piece of paper and knotted it into her sari aanchal, Harimohini returned home. Sucharita was still with Anandamoyi at Lalita's house. Fearing it might be difficult to discuss things there and that contrary remarks from Lalita and Anandamoyi might arouse doubts in Sucharita's mind, Harimohini sent word to Sucharita, inviting her to lunch the following day. There were urgent matters to discuss. She could go back the same afternoon.

The next day, Sucharita arrived at noon, having steeled herself for resistance, aware that her mashi would again bring up the same marriage proposal, in some other way. She had resolved to end the matter once and for all with a very strong reply.

'I went to see your guru last evening,' Harimohini remarked, after Sucharita had eaten.

Sucharita's was inwardly distressed. Had Mashi insulted him by bringing up her name!

'Don't worry, Radharani,' Harimohini assured her, 'I did not go there to quarrel with him. I was alone, and thought I would go across to hear a few words of wisdom from him. In the course of our conversation, your name came up. Well, I found he was of the same view. Indeed, he doesn't approve of a woman remaining unmarried for long. He says, according to the shastras, it goes against one's dharma. Such things may prevail in sahebi families, but not in Hindu homes. I have also told him frankly about our Kailash. The man was indeed learned, I realized.'

Sucharita cringed in shame and misery.

'You consider him your guru after all,' Harimohini continued. 'You must obey him, mustn't you?' Sucharita remained silent. 'I told him,' Harimohini pursued, '"Baba, please come and explain to her yourself, she doesn't listen to us." He said, "No, it will not be right for me to see her again, it goes against our Hindu social custom." "Then what's the solution?" I asked. Then he wrote down these words for me in his very own hand. Here: why not have a look?'

With these words, Harimohini extracted the piece of paper from her aanchal, unfolded it and held it open. Sucharita read it. Her breath seemed to choke. She sat stiff as a wooden puppet. The words contained nothing that was new or improper. Nor did Sucharita's views differ from the ideas expressed in those words. But the implications of his specially sending her this written missive through Harimohini wounded Sucharita in many ways. Why such a decree from Gora today? Certainly, Sucharita's time would come, and she too would have to marry some day; but what had caused Gora to make such haste on that account? Was Gora completely finished with her? Had she done him any harm? Had she posed an obstacle in his life? Was there nothing left for her to offer Gora or to expect from him? But she had not felt that, she had still been waiting for him. Sucharita struggled against this intolerable pain within herself, but could find no consolation in her heart.

Harimohini gave Sucharita a lot of time to think. She even took her usual daily nap. Upon awakening, she came to Sucharita's room to find her sitting quietly, just as before.

'Tell me Radhu, why do you think so much? What's so worrisome about this matter? Why, has Gourmohanbabu written something wrong?'

'No, what he writes is true indeed,' replied Sucharita quietly.

'Then why delay any more bachha?' cried Harimohini, highly reassured.

'No I don't want to delay things. I'll go across once to Baba's place.'

'Look Radhu, your Baba will never want you to marry into the Hindu community. But the one who is your guru has . . .'

'Mashi, why do you say the same thing again and again?' protested Sucharita impatiently. 'I am not going to Baba to discuss marriage, not at all. I'll go to him once, just like that.'

Poresh's company was indeed Sucharita's source of solace. Going to his house, she found him busy packing his clothes into a wooden trunk.

'Baba, what is this?'

'Ma, I am going for a vacation to the Shimla hills,' Poresh smiled. 'I shall depart by the morning train tomorrow.'

That Poresh's smile encompassed the history of a major rebellion, Sucharita did not fail to realize. His wife and daughters at home and his friends outside were leaving him no room for peace. If he did not go away to some far-off place for a few days at least, he would remain in the eye of a storm at home. He had resolved the day before to travel elsewhere, yet none of his own people came forward to pack his clothes today. He had to perform this task himself, and observing this scene, Sucharita suffered a powerful blow. Forcing Poreshbabu to desist, she first completely emptied his trunk. Then folding the clothes with special care, she began to rearrange them in the trunk, placing his favourite books so even movement would not damage them. While packing the box, she gently inquired:

'Baba, are you going alone?'

'That is no problem for me, Radhé!' replied Poresh, sensing a hint of pain in Sucharita's question.

'No Baba, I shall go with you.' Poresh stared at her. 'Baba, I shan't trouble you at all,' she assured him.

'Why do you say that? Have you ever troubled me Ma?'

'Unless I stay close to you it will not be good for me Baba! There are many things I don't understand. If you don't explain them to me, I shall not find my feet. Baba, you tell me to rely on my wits, but I don't have the intelligence, nor the necessary strength in my heart. Please take me with you Baba!'

She turned away from Poresh and bent low over the clothes in the trunk. Large tear-drops fell from her eyes.

~75~

When Gora handed that piece of writing to Harimohini, he
felt he had signed away his relationship with Sucharita. But
work does not cease as soon as one signs a document. His
heart utterly ignored that document. The document had been
signed with a firm hand by Gora's willpower alone, but it did
not bear his heart's signature. So his heart remained
disobedient. So extreme was this disobedience, it almost sent
Gora rushing to Sucharita's house that very night! But at that
very moment, the church clock struck ten and Gora came to
his senses, realizing that this was no time to visit anyone.
Subsequently he heard the church clock strike virtually every
hour. For he did not go to the garden estate at Bali that night.
He had sent word that he would go there early the next
morning.

At dawn he duly went to the estate, but where was the
pure, strong frame of mind in which he had resolved to
receive his penance?

Many scholars and pundits had arrived there. Many others
were expected. Gora asked after everyone and greeted them
with civility. They showered praise on Gora for his unwavering
commitment to the ascetic dharma. The garden gradually
filled with the hubbub of human voices. Gora went about
supervising the arrangements. But amidst all the hustle and
bustle, a single thought haunted the deepest recesses of his
mind. 'You have done something wrong! Something wrong!'
someone seemed to accuse him. There was no time to clearly
determine what wrong he had committed, but he was unable
to silence his innermost heart. Amidst all the elaborate
arrangements for the penance ceremony, some internal enemy
within his heart was testifying against him: 'The wrong you
have done still remains.' That wrong was not a breach of rules

or an error in mantra-chanting, or a violation of the shastras. That wrong had occurred within his nature. Therefore, Gora's whole inner being had become averse to the preparations for this ceremony.

The time drew near. Outside, a marquee had been raised on bamboo frames to create a pavilion. After his bath in the Ganga, Gora was changing his attire when he sensed a stir in the crowd. Some agitation seemed to be gradually spreading in all directions.

'They have sent word from your house that Krishnadayalbabu is bleeding at the mouth,' Abinash finally informed him dejectedly. 'He has sent someone with a carriage to fetch you quickly.'

Gora rushed away. Abinash wanted to accompany him. 'No, please remain here to receive everybody,' Gora insisted. 'You can't afford to leave the venue.'

Entering Krishnadayal's chamber, Gora saw him lying in bed, with Anandamoyi gently stroking his feet. Gora anxiously searched their faces. Krishnadayal signaled to him to take the chowki beside the bed. Gora obeyed.

'How is he now?' he asked his mother.

'A little better now. They have gone to fetch the saheb-doctor.'

Shashimukhi and an attendant were present in the room. Krishnadayal waved them away. After ascertaining that everyone had left, he silently glanced at Anandamoyi, then addressed Gora in a low voice:

'My time has come. Unless I disclose what was concealed from you all along, my soul will not be free.'

Gora's face grew ashen. He remained motionless. For a long time, nobody said a word.

'Gora,' said Krishnadayal, 'I did not believe in anything then, that was why I made such a great mistake. After that,

I had no means of correcting my error.' He again fell silent. Gora also remained motionless, asking no questions. 'I had thought it would never become necessary to tell you, that things would go on as before,' Krishanadayal continued. 'But now I realize that is not possible. After my death, how will you perform my sraddha?' Krishnadayal seemed to tremble at the very prospect of such a calamity. Gora became impatient to know the real truth. He glanced at Anandamoyi.

'Ma, you tell me what that means,' he urged. 'Have I no right to perform the sraddha?'

All this time Anandamoyi had been silent, with downcast face. At Gora's question, she raised her head. 'No baba, you don't,' she declared, looking him steadily in the eye.

'Am I not his son?' Gora demanded, startled.

'No,' she replied.

'Ma, are you not my mother?' The words burst from Gora's mouth like flames from a volcano.

Anandamoyi's heart broke. Her voice choked with unshed tears, she said: 'Baba, to me you are the son granted to a childless woman, dearer by far than a child of one's womb, baba!'

'Where did you find me then?' Gora now asked, looking at Krishnadayal.

'During the Mutiny,' Krishnadayal answered. 'We were at Etowah. Your mother had sought refuge in our home one night, fleeing in fear of the sepoys. Your father had died in battle the previous day. His name was . . .'

'No need to name him!' roared Gora. 'I don't want to know his name.'

Krishnadayal stopped abruptly, amazed at Gora's agitation. Then he continued: 'He was an Irishman. That very night, your mother died after giving birth to you. You have been brought up in our own house ever since.'

In a single instant, Gora's felt his entire life become like an extraordinary dream. The foundation of his life, developed over all these years since his very infancy, was utterly destroyed. What he was, where he was, he did not seem to understand. As if behind him there was nothing called a past, and before him, the future, so purposeful and clearly determined for such a long time, had completely vanished. As if he was simply floating like a momentary dewdrop on a lotus leaf. He had no mother, no father, no country, no caste, no name, no family gotra, no deity. All he had was a 'No.' What would he cling to, what would he do, from what point would he begin again, where refix his goals, and from where would he slowly gather, day by day, all the necessary resources for his work! In this strange, directionless void Gora remained transfixed, utterly speechless. Seeing his face, no one dared say another word.

Just then the saheb-doctor arrived, accompanied by their Bengali family physician. While observing the patient, the doctor could not refrain from glancing at Gora as well. 'Who is this?' he wondered. Gora's forehead still bore its tilak of Ganga earth and he had come there still wearing the raw silk fabric he had donned after his bath. He wore no upper garment; through the gaps in his wrap, his massive body could be seen.

Earlier, the very sight of a British doctor would have instinctively aroused Gora's hostility. But now, as the doctor examined his patient, Gora looked at him with special curiosity. 'Is this man my closest relative here?' he began to ask himself, again and again.

'Why, I see no special cause for anxiety,' pronounced the doctor, having completed his examination and asked some questions. 'His pulse is not alarming, nor are his organs malfunctioning. As for the symptoms, if one is careful they can be prevented.'

After the doctor had departed, Gora wordlessly tried to

rise from the chowki. Anandamoyi had gone into the adjacent room when the doctor came. She now rushed in and clasped Gora's hand.

'Baba Gora, please don't be angry with me,' she pleaded. 'Otherwise I shall die!'

'Why didn't you tell me, all these days!' Gora demanded. 'It would not have done you any harm.'

Anandamoyi took all the blame upon herself. 'Baap, it was from fear of losing you that I committed such a great sin. If that is what ultimately happens, if you abandon me today, I cannot blame anyone. But it will be a death sentence for me, baap!'

'Ma!' was all Gora could say. Hearing him address her thus, Anandamoyi's suppressed tears burst forth at last.

'Ma, I'll go to Poreshbabu's now,' Gora declared.

A load was lifted from Anandamoyi's heart. 'Go ahead, baba!' she said.

There was no fear of his dying soon, yet the truth had been revealed to Gora! Krishnadayal became extremely alarmed.

'Look here Gora, I see no reason to disclose all this to anyone,' he urged. 'Just act prudently and with caution, and things will continue as before. Nobody will suspect a thing.' Gora walked out without giving an answer. He felt comforted to remember that he was no relation of Krishnadayal's.

Mahim could not suddenly stay away from work. After sending for the doctor and making all the necessary arrangements, he had gone to the office, just to ask the saheb for leave of absence. Just as Gora was emerging from the house, Mahim arrived on the scene. 'Gora, where are you going?' he demanded.

'Good news,' said Gora. 'The doctor was here. He said there's no cause for worry.'

'Thank heavens,' said Mahim, greatly relieved. 'The day

after tomorrow is an auspicious date. I shall get Shashimukhi married that very day. Gora, you will have to be a little enterprising, I tell you. And please warn Binoy in advance, not to come there that day. Abinash is a Hindu fanatic: he has specially decreed that such people must not be allowed at his wedding ceremony. Let me tell you something else bhai: I shall invite the big sahebs of my office on that day, but you must not attack them. If you just say "Good evening sir" with a slight nod of the head, no more, it won't pollute your Hindu shastras. Better that you seek the pundits' advice. Do you understand bhai? They are of kingly caste: you won't be demeaned if you curb your arrogance a little in their company.'

Without offering any reply, Gora walked away.

~76~

As Sucharita bent over the trunk, busily arranging clothes in order to hide her tears, they received word that Gourmohanbabu had arrived. Hastily wiping her eyes, Sucharita abandoned her task and rose to her feet. And just then Gora entered the room. He was not even aware that the tilak still marked his forehead. The silk fabric still swathed his body. No one usually came visiting in such attire. Sucharita was reminded of that day when she had first encountered Gora. She knew he had come armed for battle on that occasion; was he in battle-gear today as well?

As soon as he entered, Gora prostrated himself at Poresh's feet in a pranam. Agitated, Poresh drew him up, saying,

'Come, come, baba, join us.'

'Poreshbabu, I have no ties,' Gora blurted out.

'What ties?' asked Poreshbabu in surprise.

'I am not a Hindu.'

'Not a Hindu!'

'No, I am not a Hindu. I was informed today that I am a
foundling from the days of the Mutiny. My father is an
Irishman. From north to south across the whole of Bharatvarsha,
all temple doors are now closed to me. Today, in this whole
country, there is no place for me, at any level, to sit down to
a meal with others.'

Poresh and Sucharita were dumbfounded. Poresh could
not think of what to say to him.

'Today I am free Poreshbabu!' Gora declared. 'I am no
longer afraid of becoming a fallen person, or losing my caste
status. I need no longer watch the ground at every step for
fear of losing my purity.'

Sucharita gazed transfixed at Gora's radiant countenance.

'Poreshbabu,' Gora continued, 'all these days I strove
wholeheartedly to realize the idea of Bharatvarsha, and always
came up against some obstacle or other. All my life, day and
night, I have constantly struggled for a compromise between
all those obstacles and my sense of respect. In my effort to
strengthen the basis of that respect, I was unable to accomplish
any other task; that was my sole endeavour. That is why,
when I tried to serve Bharatvarsha while viewing it in the light
of truth, I repeatedly turned back in fear. Creating an
untroubled, unblemished abstract image of Bharatvarsha, how
I battled on all fronts to keep my devotion safe within that
impenetrable fortress! Today in a single instant my imaginary
fortress has evaporated like a dream. Set completely free, I
have suddenly arrived at the heart of a great reality! All
Bharatvarsha's virtues and flaws, joys and sorrows, knowledge
and ignorance, have come directly close to my heart. Today
I have gained the right to true service. The real field of action
now lies before me. It is not the arena within my heart, but
the actual site for promoting the welfare of those hundred
crore people in the world outside.'

Poresh too felt stirred by the force of Gora's tremendous

enthusiasm about this newfound insight. Unable to contain himself, he arose from his chowki.

'Do you comprehend my words?' Gora inquired. 'Today I have become what I earlier strove day and night to become, but without success. Today I have become an Indian— Bharatvarshia. In me there is no hostility towards any community, Hindu, Muslim or Christian. Today, I belong to every community of this Bharatvarsha, I accept everyone's food as mine. Look, I traveled to many districts of Bengal, accepting the hospitality of even very lowly localities—please do not imagine that I only lectured at city assemblies—but I could never bring myself to sit in the company of all and sundry. All these days, I went about carrying with me an invisible gap, which I could never bridge. Hence there was a great void within my heart. I constantly tried to disown that emptiness by various means; with sundry outward embellishments, I tried to specially beautify this void itself. For Bharatvarsha was dearer to me than my own heart: I could not tolerate the slightest reason to criticize any feature of the partial aspect of Bharatvarsha visible to me. Now, freed of such futile attempts at embellishment, I am relieved, Poreshbabu!'

'When we attain the truth, it satisfies our soul even with all its lack and incompleteness,' assented Poreshbabu. 'One feels no desire to decorate it with false ingredients.'

'Look Poreshbabu, last night I beseeched the Almighty to grant me a new life this morning, a new birth after completely destroying all the falsehoods and impurities that had enveloped me since infancy. Ishwar paid no heed to the imaginary reward I was praying for. Instead, He startled me by delivering His own truth directly into my hands. I did not dream that he would remove my impurity so radically. Today I have become so pure that even in a lowcaste chandal's home I will no longer be afraid of sullying myself. Poreshbabu, at dawn today, with my naked soul, I was born directly into Bharatvarsha's lap. At last I have fully understood what a mother's lap signifies.'

'Gour,' responded Poreshbabu, 'Please lead us also into the mother's lap, to which you have gained the right of entry.'

'Do you know why I have come to you first of all upon attaining my freedom today?' Gora asked him.

'Why?'

'You are the one with the mantra for this freedom. That is why, in our present times, you could not find a place within any community. Make me your disciple. Initiate me today into the mantra of that deity who belongs to everyone, Hindu, Muslim, Christian or Brahmo, whose temple doors are never closed to any community or any individual, who is not merely a deity for Hindus but the deity of Bharatvarsha!'

The profound sweetness of devotion passed its gentle shadow across Poreshbabu's face. He stood in silence, with lowered gaze.

At last, Gora turned to Sucharita. She remained motionless on her chowki. 'Sucharita, I am no longer your guru,' Gora smiled. 'This is my prayer to you: please take my hand and lead me there, to your guru.' With these words Gora advanced towards her, stretching out his right hand. Arising from the chowki, Sucharita placed her hand in his. Taking her with him, Gora bent to offer his pranams at Poresh's feet.

EPILOGUE

When he came home after dusk, Gora found Anandamoyi waiting silently in the veranda outside her room. He knelt at her feet and drawing them close, bowed his head upon them. With both hands, she raised his head and kissed it.

'Ma, you are my real mother! The mother I sought everywhere was waiting in my own home. You have no caste, no discrimination, no contempt for anyone. You are the very image of goodness! It is you who is my Bharatvarsha! . . .

'Ma, please send for your Lachhmia now. Ask her to fetch me some water.'

In a low, tearful voice, Anandamoyi whispered, close to Gora's ear: 'Gora, let me send for Binoy now.'

NOTES AND GLOSSARY

Abhimanyu: heroic son of Arjuna in the *Mahabharata*, killed on the battlefield by his Kaurava uncles who trapped him in a circular battle formation

Agrahayan: eighth month of the Bengali calendar, mid-November to mid-December

ahnik: a daily Hindu prayer ritual

alna: traditional clothes rack

Annapurna: goddess of bounty; another name for Shiva's consort Parvati, who went from door to door seeking rice to appease the hunger of Shiva when he came to her as a mendicant

antahpur: inner part of the house, where women stay in seclusion

asana: prayer mat

Ashwin: sixth month of Bengali calendar, mid-September to mid-October

Baikuntha: celestial abode of Vishnu

Bakasur: crane-headed demon destroyed by Bhima in the *Mahabharata*

Bakhtiar Khilji: Aide of Qutbuddin Aibaq, he conquered Bihar and Bengal in the early thirteenth century; 'bakhtiar' means 'talkative'

bala: armlet

Bangadarshan: a monthly magazine (1872–1876), founded and edited by Bankimchandra Chatterjee

baul: unorthodox religious mendicants, nomads who sing mystical devotional songs

behai: father-in-law of a son or daughter

beyan: mother-in-law of a son or daughter

Bhadra: fifth month of the Bengali calendar, mid-August to mid-September

bhadra: belonging to the respectable class

bhadralok: member of respectable Bengali society

Bhagavad Gita: verses Krishna is said to have uttered as Arjuna's charioteer in the *Mahabharata*, advocating the path of duty that forms one aspect of Hindu philosophy

Bhagirath: King Sagara's great-grandson, he brought the river Ganga down from Heaven to the earth and to the nether regions, to purify the ashes of his 60,000 ancestors

bhakti: the path of devotion in Hindu philosophy

Bhatpara: village near Kolkata, a centre of orthodox Brahmanical learning

bhog: food offered to a deity

Bhrigu: a sage who kicked Vishnu (Krishna) to awaken him from his pre-creation sleep. Vishnu responded so gently that Bhrigu declared him the only god worthy of worship

bon: sister

bonjhi: sister's daughter

boro: paddy crop harvested in April

Brahman: member of the priestly caste

Brahmo Samaj: a monotheistic religious community founded by Raja Rammohun Roy; they advocated social reform

Brahmosangeet: Brahmo hymns

Brindavan: holy place for Hindus, associated with Krishna

Chaitanyadev: religious reformer and founder of Vaishnavism in medieval Bengal

champa: variety of magnolia

chapkaan: knee-length upper garment

chor: strip of sandy land arising out of a river-bed

churning the ocean: amrita, heavenly nectar, was cast up when deities and demons churned the ocean

crore: ten million

dada: elder brother

deor: husband's younger brother

devi: female deity

didi: elder sister

Dosad: a low caste

ekadashi: eleventh day of the lunar fortnight; widows would fast on this day

Gherandasamhita: ancient Sanskrit text dealing with the tantrik practices of Shakti devotees

Ghor Babu: a dandy

ghoti: small round water pot

Goldighi: another name for College Square in Kolkata

Gopiballav: another name for the deity Krishna

Hara-Parvati: the deity Shiva and his consort

Harish Mukhujje the second: Harishchandra Mukherjee (1824–61), Brahmo leader and editor of the *Hindu Patriot*

hathayoga: form of abstract meditation involving harsh self-discipline

Hemanta: late autumn to early winter; the months Kartik and Agrahayana of the Bengali calendar

Indra: king of the gods

Ishwar: the Creator, Lord of the universe

Jagaddhatri: mother goddess who upholds the universe

jamai: son-in-law

Jamaisashthi: annual ritual performed by parents-in-law to bless the son-in-law

jamun: blackberry

Janak: Sita's father in the *Ramayana*

jatra: a form of indigenous theatre in Bengal

jatragaan: open air performance of jatra

kaibarta: a fisherman by caste

kaka: father's younger brother

Kalisingha: Kaliprasanna Sinha (1840/1841–1870), who translated the *Mahabharata* into Bengali

Kaliyug: fourth or last age of creation according to the Hindu Purana; the age of sin

kamandulu: an ascetic's water-pot, made of wood or metal

kantha: embroidered coverlet made of layered soft fabric.

karabi: oleander

karahi: narrow-bottomed cooking utensil

karma: the path of duty or action in Hindu philosophy; the law of karma decrees that one must be rewarded or punished according to one's past deeds.

Kartika: god of war, son of deities Shiva and Parvati. Also the seventh month of the Bengali calendar, mid-October to mid-November

Kashi: Varanasi, sacred to the Hindus

Kaurava: the Kuru side in the *Mahabharata*

kazi: a dispenser of justice under the Muslim law

kayastha: a Hindu caste

Keshabbabu: Keshub Chunder Sen (1838–84), who succeeded Debendranath Tagore, Rabindranath's father, as leader of the Brahmo Samaj

kharam: wooden sandal

khansama: an orderly

khatanchikhana: ledger room, where accounts are kept

kheer: milk condensed by boiling, used to prepare sweets

khonta: a flat cooking spoon

khunche: a small tray

khuro: father's younger brother

khurima: wife of father's younger brother

kirtan: a form of devotional music in praise of Radha-Krishna or Kali

krishnachura: gulmohur, a tree with red and yellow flowers

Krittivasa: a poet and scholar of Bengal, who wrote the first Bengali *Ramayana*, probably in the fifteenth century.

krosh: a measure of distance, a little over two miles

Kuber: god of the dead and of wealth

kulin: born of a Brahman family of unblemished caste status; men of such families enjoyed and often misused the privilege of polygamy

Lakshmi: goddess of fortune

Lanka: the capital of demon king Ravana in the *Ramayana*

Lakshyabheda: a feat of marksmanship performed by Arjuna to win Draupadi's hand in the *Mahabharata*

madur: mat

Magh: tenth month of the Bengali calendar, from mid-January to mid-February

mahaveena: a string instrument

Manu: father of the human race; the law-code of the *Manusmriti* is ascribed to him

mashi: mother's sister

mesho: mother's sister's husband

maya: in Hindu philosophy, the illusory material world

mela: fair; exhibition

mitbar: a young boy accompanying the bridegroom as his supposed substitute or double

mora: low stool made of cane and bamboo

Mutiny: the uprising of 1857, termed the 'Sepoy Mutiny' and 'Sipahi Revolt' by British and Indian historians respectively.

nabina: young woman who follows modern ways

namavali: a wrap with the deity's name inscribed on it

Nandokumar: Raja Nando Kumar, faujdar of Hooghli during the Palashi battle and diwan of Mir Jafar, was hanged for forgery in 1775 at the instigation of Warren Hastings

Narada: a sage who fomented discord among gods and men

Narayan: another name for Vishnu, or Krishna

Narayani Sena: when Krishna (Narayan) asked the Kauravas in the *Mahabharata* to choose either him or his troops, the Narayani Sena, they chose the troops

ojha: exorcist; one who cures snake bites and other fatal wounds by ritual means

palki: palanquin

panchayat: village council with five or more members

Pandavas: the descendants of kind Pandu in the *Mahabharata*

Parashar: ancient law-giver in the Hindu tradition

pathshala: primary school

patra: prospective bridegroom

Phalgun: eleventh month of the Bengali calendar, from mid-February to mid-March

pinri: low wooden seat

pishi: father's sister

poite: sacred thread; ritual of wearing the sacred thread for the first time

prachina: woman who follows traditional, old-fashioned modes

Prajapati: god of marriage

Prakriti: Nature; the female principle

prasad: food blessed by a deity or spiritual guide

puja: worship; prayer

punya: the virtue that accrues from meritorious deeds

Radha-Krishna: Krishna and his consort Radha are the subject of much romantic lore

ragini: a musical mode in the Indian classical tradition

Rahu: a demon beheaded for trying to drink nectar with the gods, believed to cause eclipses when he attempts to devour the sun and moon; considered a malign planet

Rama: son of Dasharatha, hero of the *Ramayana*

Ramaprasad: Ram Prasad Sen (1720–71), who composed devotional songs in praise of goddess Kali and other forms of Shakti

Rig Veda: the first of the four Vedas, the ancient spiritual hymns that created the first stage of Hindu mythology

rowshan-chowki: orchestra of shehnai and other instruments

sab lal ho jayega: Hindi phrase meaning 'everything will turn red'. Gora is alluding to British rule in India, for British troops wore red uniforms and the territories under their direct control were coloured red in contemporary maps of India

Sagara: The 60,000 sons of King Sagara were cursed by sage Kapila, and saved only when Bhagirath brought the river Ganga down from Vishnu's feet onto this earth

saji: round, high-rimmed wicker-basket

sal: tree valued for its timber

samhita: ancient Hindu law-book

sandesh: sweet made of cottage cheese

sanyasi: ascetic

segun: teak

sej: oil lamp with a glass shade

shakti mantra: the occult worship of goddesses Kali-Durga-Shakti as embodiments of divine energy

shalgram: sacred stone supposed to represent Vishnu, worshipped by the Vaishnavas

sharat: early autumn, the months Bhadra and Ashwin in the Bengali calendar

shastra: Hindu scriptures

Shiva: third god of the Hindu triad

shivalinga: phallic image worshipped as Shiva

shubhodrishti: wedding ritual where bride and bridegroom first look at each other

Shudra: fourth or lowest of the Hindu castes

Sirajuddaula: Nawab of Bengal, defeated by the British at the Battle of Palashi in 1757

Sita: daughter of Janak and wife of Rama in the *Ramayana*

Sravan: fourth month of the Bengali calendar, mid-July to mid-August

stotra: hymn of praise

supari: betel nut

swadesh: one's own land

swadeshi: of one's own country; phase of Indian National Movement favouring indigeneous elements and boycott of foreign goods

taan: combination of notes in a classical melody

taktaposh: a plain rectangular bedstead

tandava: a frenzied dance of destruction

tehsildar: officer in charge of revenue collection in a demarcated area called a tehsil

Tantrik: follower of the doctrine of the Tantras of Shaktas

thakur: a Hindu deity; an idol; a Brahman; a Brahman cook

thala: a metal dish

tilak: a Hindu sectarian mark on the forehead, usually of sandal paste or sacred clay

togor: a small white flower

tol: village school for teaching Sanskrit

Triveni: sacred confluence of rivers Ganga, Yamuna and Saraswati at Allahabad

tussar: coarse silk made from silkworm cocoons

vaishnava: follower of Sri Chaitanya; member of a modern Hindu sect devoted to the deity Vishnu

Vedanta: monistic school of Hindu philosophy that became popular after the Vedic period; their teachings are summarized in the treatise called the first *Brahmasutra*

veena: musical instrument, usually with seven strings

yajna: sacrificial rite